WITCHDEMON

Jessy Karma

authorHOUSE

AuthorHouse™
1663 Liberty Drive
Bloomington, IN 47403
www.authorhouse.com
Phone: 833-262-8899

Published by AuthorHouse 04/14/2021

ISBN: 978-1-6655-2280-9 (sc)
ISBN: 978-1-6655-2279-3 (e)

Library of Congress Control Number: 2021907656

Print information available on the last page.

Any people depicted in stock imagery provided by Getty Images are models, and such images are being used for illustrative purposes only. Certain stock imagery © Getty Images.

This book is printed on acid-free paper.

Dedicated to:

My son. My best friend. My hero.

Introduction

I could tell you that your world is safe and that everyone is equal and loved by God or whoever it is that you pray to. But that would be a lie. I for one, am living proof of that. I don't remember much of my youth; I just remember being about ten years old and it was my birthday. I was sore and bleeding and I first noticed the rain on the pavement in front of the church I was left at. St James Anglican church to be exact, in downtown Vancouver. It was Father Douglas who found me. Normal people would have called an ambulance, but I started healing right in front of him. Or that's what he told me when this subject came up. Anyways, he took me inside and carried me to the thing where people light a prayer candle. Five minutes later, I was all healed up.

Like I said, I had no memory of myself, just that it was my birthday. My teeth remained dramatically uneven but no one really got grossed out because I wasn't one to really smile growing up. Father Douglas home schooled me, obtained false identification for me; which is actually pretty easy if you know the right people. At sixteen I got my provincial I.D, legally but obviously under false pretenses. Finally, at seventeen, I went to the local high school to get my grade twelve equivalency and actually scored third in my class.

I'm not telling you this for an ego boost, I'm just doing the intro thing. Oh! My name is Gabby or Gabriel, you know after that angel? My 'father' named me that. I heard Gabriel was the one that fell in love too easily and one of his 'loves' caused him horrible grief and he went insane or something. I don't know. I was raised by the church but I'll be damned if I actually remember any of it. I just smiled and nodded and then did whatever I wanted. I can be quite promiscuous, got some pretty decent tattoos, but I cover myself when I'm around 'father'. Not to mention, *if* he knew I was no longer a virgin he'd probably suffer a stroke.

I didn't go to College right away because he was acting really weird. He got crazy obsessed with the supernatural. I didn't pay attention too much to his rants about Angels and Demons until he started getting really sick looking. His temperature was high and he was really scaring me. I thought he was going to die. He was having this dream recall about some ultimate heavenly being that saves the world but is half angel and half demon. Let me explain; you know how vinegar makes French fries taste good and baking soda is great for getting rid of those odours and together they explode? Well um....it's kind of like that. The angelic powers get rid of some demons and then the demon powers get rid of the stronger ones, kind of like fighting fire with fire, and then there are these ultra-demons that can only be destroyed when the being turns into a combination of both bloods. Creating a being that isn't even in the record books. Making something that isn't even labelled. Well, my 'father' calls it, The Witchdemon.

It's a pretty fucked up story, or so I thought. Oh, and apparently Vampires and Werewolves have souls. If they don't kill of course; if they do, their souls' shrink until their humanity is gone and they become soulless monsters or whatever. 'Father' says they were created in the original attempt to save humanity from Hell's hordes. Only God gave them free will too and some of them became corrupted. Then there's something about the three Obedients who help the Witchdemon, I don't know much about that, but the Witchdemon has free will and can't be corrupted. I think that probably has something to do with the angel blood.

Anyways, I didn't believe any of this till my twenty third birthday.

CHAPTER ONE

You ever get the feeling you're going to instantly regret waking up? I didn't know it yet but I was half way there. I was just having the best sex dream. It was about these three guys, at separate times of course! But I didn't want to wake up. 'Lust' is a horrible sin, or that's what my father always tells me, but I just can't help it. Men just seem to be drawn to me. I'm not drop dead gorgeous or anything, I'm seriously average and have savagely crooked teeth but in the moment that doesn't seem to bother them. Which leads me to believe all they want is sex, which is fine with me. Baby you sexy! Come over here and be next on my list!

So obviously I've never had a really serious relationship or even felt remotely in love before. Sometimes I prefer the lonely days with a good book or video game, but when I get antsy I can party harder than anyone I know. So yea, I've fantasized about having that one and only.....but let's get serious, me? In love? I've been accused of having a personality disorder, I also contradict a lot but mean everything I say, or maybe that's just because of my religious upbringing?

I'm getting sidetracked. The dream felt so real and I swear I 'loved' these guys. Weird. Worse, I didn't want to wake up. Weirder, it was for the emotional feelings instead of the physical.

Okay so today is my first day at college, nearly six years late but my father simmered down and then pressured me into going. I worked for a bit here and there so I was able to save enough to take one course at Douglas College in New Westminster. I'm going to be taking psychology. I wanted psychiatry but I think you need to go to Med-School for that and I simply don't have the money or the motivation to research whether or not that's true. I mean obviously because you have to be able to prescribe meds and

1

whatever...Beautiful British Columbia, that's where I lived, in the lower mainland accumulated of four major cities around a transit system. And then the East, West, North, and South versions of those cities and a few scattered others. But basically just Vancouver, New Westminster, Burnaby, and Surrey.

I opened my eyes slightly taking in the blurred ceiling. I stayed over at my best friend's house for my first day. I met Stacey at 'Bible Study' for the pre-teens at my church. We weren't friends at first but after her parents died, my father took her in until her Aunt and Uncle came from Ontario to take care of her. She stayed for two weeks and then after that we were inseparable. She's in her last year at Douglas College. Stacey moved out of her Aunt and Uncle's place at sixteen and got job after job to pay for her business course. She's actually engaged now to her on and off boyfriend of three years, Stan Holder.

Jeez, Stacey Holder sounds stupid. Mine is Gabby Douglas so I guess it isn't any better.

"Get up!"

A pillow smacked me in the face.

"Ugh! I'm up!" I said slightly annoyed. Stacey giggled, she was already showered and dressed. Her make-up was perfect and her hair was blow dried into perfect waves around her face. I felt a little envious for a second, then, I took in her joyous mood.

"What's with the shit eating grin?" I asked.

"There's going to be a new psychology teacher this year. Remember I told you about him? He's probably going to teach *your* course! He's older but sooo fuckable!"

This is why Stacey and I get along, our brains and hormones are on the same page. She's just in better control over hers.

"Yes well, that may be true but you're taken." I teased.

Stacey rolled her eyes and again, hit me in the face with the pillow.

* * *

After a shower, and God knows I needed one, I got dressed in a dark low V-neck t-shirt and white cut-off jean shorts. I put my hair in a simple pony tail. One of the perks about summer I'm going to miss is my tan. I don't have to wear cover up if my face is evenly tanned, and I'm not going to pay for a stupid tanning bed. I don't actually have skin problems, maybe the random zit, but overall pretty good. Stacey is a pale red head who astonishingly had no damn freckles on her face but she burned to a crisp in the sun. This I noticed as we walked down the street.

Last week we got our hair done; she went blonde while I went from auburn to black. We had headed out at seven thirty in the morning, down to Columbia Street to our favourite coffee shop.

"Oh my God Gabby, look at the new clerk, he's super fucking cute!" Stacey whispered as soon as we walked in. She always swore when she saw someone she thought was attractive or if she was super serious. I was day dreaming about something when I looked up. When I laid eyes on the guy she pointed to my mind and body froze for a second. I couldn't even fucking breathe. Oh, F.Y.I. I swear all the time.

His hair was a light brown with subtle blonde highlights cropped short. His eyes were blue and he had the perfect amount of facial hair around his mouth. Just a little bit more than a five O'clock shadow. He wore a grey t-shirt under his apron, but what made me tingle inside was the fact that those tattooed muscles of his arms were wrapped around me in my dream last night.

In my fucking dream!

As soon as I made that realization he looked up at me. Yup, same guy. My heart felt like it was on speed. I glanced at Stacey and she was smiling and waving at him. He waved back and smiled himself. The room started to spin. I grabbed onto Stacey. Startled, she looked at me, grabbed my arm and then hissed in my ear.

"Fucking breathe! Jeez Gabby don't faint! He's just another hot guy. What's gotten into, oh great now he's coming over to us."

I looked up. He wasn't smiling as he made his way over to us.

Oh God does he recognize me? From the dream? Gabby don't be stupid.....or try not to.

"Um, are you okay?" He tried to ask discreetly.

The combination of his eyes and his voice was too much. My brain only stopped for a second before, now it was completely useless. I think something gurgled in my throat and I ended up making a weird noise, all the while staring blankly in response. I probably looked like I took too much medication. To my surprise he laughed. The moment of surprise snapped me out of it and I shook my head.

Now I felt really, really stupid.

"Oh, um, I'm sorry. I'm really tired and in need of a coffee." I said lamely.

"Make that two please." Stacey chimed in, giving me a look with her eyes that asked if I *did* take someone's medication.

"Well you've come to the right place." He turned around and went back behind the counter. Stacey followed and tried to get me to come too. I shook my head.

"Are you insane?" She whispered, "Get his number! Not cringing after that scene makes him a keeper!"

"Number?! Scene?" I shook my head again, "I don't even know his name!" I whispered back. Then I thought; or do I?

"Here's two black coffees." He came back to the register with the two cups and handed one to Stacey and one to me. The one to me had a piece of paper with it. I opened it and saw a phone number, I gaped at him.

"My name's Joseph, call me sometime." He winked, 'cause he just fucking heard everything. Stacey grabbed the paper and then tried turning me around towards the coffee fixings.

"She sure will." She told him and then pulled me across the coffee shop. I couldn't speak and if my heart doesn't stop thundering in my chest I was going to end up in the hospital. We walked outside and I couldn't help but stare at Joseph through the window as we walked past.

"Not a bad start to the day eh?" Stacey smiled.

"Don't say that."

"Say what?"

"The word 'eh' is so stereo typically Canadian."

She rolled her eyes.

* * *

I felt so stupid for my brain failure in the coffee shop that I forgot about my class in psychology. When I remembered, Stacey was handing me a map of the College and raced away to her business course. When I got to my classroom I had only five minutes to spare. I opened the door and without looking at the teacher's desk I walked across the room and sat down by the window. There weren't many students in this class. I counted with my eyes; there were twelve of us. The teacher's desk was empty. I subtly adjusted my t-shirt and was glad I had put on some perfume at the last minute. My morning encounter in the twilight zone left me a little sweaty. I looked down at my fiddling hands.

"Good morning class." The voice sent pleasant shivers down my spine. Trying to compose myself, I looked up and watched as the teacher wrote his name on the blackboard. I leaned my chair back out of habit.

"I am Dr. Ramsey; I will be your new psychology teacher as well as the College psychologist if you need to talk." He turned around to face us and I nearly fell out of my fucking chair. There was no way this was happening. The chair snapped me forward with a loud bang. His eyes met mine instantly. My dream flashed in my mind and I knew how soft his lips were; my heart flew again and my eyes tried to bug out but I blinked repeatedly to keep them in.

"Are you okay?" he asked.

I simply nodded and looked away out the window to my left.

Holy shit. What the fuck was going on here? The emotions nearly surfaced that time.

"Err, so as I was saying, if you need some help I'll be glad to listen. And please, call me Peter." He continued.

Peter; save that in the memory banks. As class went on, I continued to stare the other way out the window while I listened to his voice. My heart didn't want to burst out of my chest when I wasn't looking at him. But his voice still had an effect on it, I just couldn't understand how. I should be taking notes but everything he said just blurred together because as I was listening to his voice, I was imagining him saying other things........

Then class ended. I slowly got up and gathered my things.

"Um, Miss Douglas?"

I froze; I swear my heart turned into a helicopter and the whole damn world could hear it. I tried to compose myself again. I turned and looked at him. I think I startled him for a second or I was just imagining things, I don't know, my mind was more focused on trying *not* to go into dream recall mode. He had dark hair with some grey at the sides, his face was aged but still youthful like he laughed a lot but because he was drunk a lot. The thought made me smirk. He had brown eyes, like Doe eyes. Can guys

5

get Doe eyes? 'Deer' eyes sounds stupid. 'Stag' eyes didn't sound so bad. Anyways, he definitely was fuckable. He saw my smirk and smiled back.

"Can I talk to you for a second?"

I nodded, I wasn't as 'insta' brain-dead this time but I was thinking very inappropriate thoughts. My dreamed poked in to remind me, out of the three men, he was the one I actually went all the way with. I noted he was well dressed while shutting the door on the other thought. I took a few steps over to him as he moved from behind his desk and stood facing me with the friendly smile on his face. Did he look nervous? His eyes seemed to flicker.

"Yes Dr. Ramsey?" I said smoothly.

"Peter, please." He smiled but this time his eyes didn't shift from mine. I was trapped.

"Peter." I whispered. Okay now I was getting brain dead. AH! Focus! What was that smell? It smelled so good. Was that him? This isn't fair! It's driving me nuts, and with him so close all I have to do is step forward, grab his face and game over.

But like I said his eyes had me, I was trapped.

"Did you come from a private school?"

I blinked.

"Um, no. I was home schooled at my Father's church. I would have come to College sooner, but he needed me." I was beginning to feel a little uncomfortable. I'm not one to spill private things to a stranger. But he didn't feel like a stranger......

"When was this?" he looked sincerely curious.

"When I was seventeen, almost six years ago."

"Almost?"

"Yea, I'll be twenty three this Saturday, September eleventh."

Was it me or did something just twinkle in his eye?

"Interesting." He put his hand to his mouth and stared past me at the floor. What was he thinking about?

"What do you mean?" I was confused. He smiled, looked at me, and then took a smooth step forward towards me.

"We seem to share the same birthday." He said in a low voice. At this tone something seemed to take over. Like I got my game back or something.

"Oh? And how old will you be?" as soon as the words left my mouth, I had the sneaking suspicion he wasn't going to tell me. So I quickly added without thinking, "Maybe we could celebrate together."

He took another step forward and cocked his head to the side as he smiled. "Wouldn't we look odd together? You looking so young, and me so old?"

It was my turn to smile without showing my teeth and I stepped forward, "Age never bothered me," I said softly, "You can keep it to yourself if you want but there's a saying that states 'you only as old as you feel." I subtly bit my bottom lip as I looked him in the eye and placed my hand on his shoulder. All this to emphasize the full effect of my sentence. We didn't speak for a few seconds and I swear I saw him swallow. But then, if it was possible, he stepped even closer where our lips were merely centimeters apart.

"You're good. Have you been using that technique for a while?" his smirk vanished as he moved to whisper in my ear, "I may be older than you but trust me when I say, I can definitely keep up." He put his hand around mine and trapped me with his eyes again. My bravado was gone as soon as he went to my ear. The fucker mind reversed me! I fucking wanted him right then and there. And he fucking knew it too. He smiled, winked, and then let go to turn around towards the doorway.

Right before he opened them, he spoke aloud, "I'll see you tomorrow Miss Douglas."

He left.

* * *

"Mother fucker! Are you serious?" Stacey was looking at me with shock as I just finished telling her about Peter.

I nodded. "Yea, it was seriously intense."

My brain was in overdrive. Now I was expecting guy number three to come out of anywhere like a bad talk show. I was almost jumpy at the sight of every guy that walked in through the doors of the cafeteria.

"It's the end of the day for me though." As I only had funds for one course.

"Okay well, I'll meet you at the station tomorrow around seven thirty?"

"Yea I'll be there." I turned towards the exit and noticed in the corner of the room that Peter was staring at me. I stuck my tongue out at him and left. I swear I heard him laugh. Fucker.

*   *   *

It was time for my self defense class. Well...Some Kung Fu crap my father made me take for my mood swings. To center myself so to speak. Teaching a person who is quick to anger how to fight doesn't seem like the brightest idea, but whatever I'm not really one who fights a lot. I'm all about the psychological warfare, and Peter's days are numbered. I was still fuming about him when I walked into my class. My 'Sensei' called out and waited for us to gather before we went to change. It seems he had an announcement.

"Gather round, gather round." Today is my last day with you for three months. In my absence, my colleague will be teaching. I believe you all have progressed well in hand to hand combat. He will be teaching 'weapons training'."

Everyone clapped as someone came out of the back room. I couldn't see because Charlie the fucking Amazon was in my way. The newcomer had his back to the class when I finally caught sight of him. Everyone sat down; he was facing my sensei in a stance everyone here knew well. Obviously they were going to show a demonstration. The 'colleague' had two fork-like swords. I instantly thought he robbed a ninja turtle. Shaking my head I watched as my sensei grabbed a sword from his bag. His sword was the only real sword in the place. Strictly speaking he wasn't allowed to condone or teach the ways of the sword to us. I don't know why, don't really care actually. They circled each other and then I saw his face.

I fucking knew it was going to happen but it still left me gasping for breath as my heart hammered in my chest like I was a giant humming bird. I watched with partial amazement as they fought. When I couldn't see his face my mind wasn't as fuzzy, but when I did my dream came back to me. He looked a bit younger then Peter but older then Joseph. Light brown hair that fell in his eyes, blue eyes and a perfectly pointed nose. He was firmly built but not ripped.

Well I didn't actually know that for sure, technically his shirt was still on but I wasn't going to doubt my dream recall right now. Especially when it's given me a complex three times today. Just go with the flow Gabby,

I told myself. The demo ended, everyone clapped and then he stepped forward.

"Hello, my name is James and I will be teaching the weapons training portion of this year's class." His eyes scanned the faces of his future students till he stopped at mine. I could have sworn my heart would stop forever. He only looked at me for a second and then looked away. My heart started again, only a little bit painfully. We didn't actually use any weapons, we ended up being put into pairs to demonstrate to James what we had learned.

Not to toot my own horn but I'm actually pretty good. I'm not much of an attacker but not one person in my class has been able to get me. I'm pretty quick. In the end they get sloppy and leave themselves open for me to strike. Except my sensei. He's so fast. Kicks my ass every damn time. So, as you can guess, I was severely disappointed when he placed himself as my opponent which made James look at me again. I tried not to look at him, which didn't help because no matter how hard I tried to concentrate on my sensei, that damn dream popped into my head.

We were both naked, his one arm around my waist as I bent backwards, his mouth on my chest as my hands were in his hair. I snapped out of it just in time to see my sensei's fist flying at my face. I jumped back, lost my footing and landed on my ass.

* * *

I walked out of the change room after class and noticed James putting some mats away. Where did everyone go? He looked at me and smiled.

"Interesting day today." He commented. I shrugged. It was alright except for the constant embarrassing moments or your naked body against mine and me fighting with the fact that reality is just not my friend today. But of course I kept that in my head.

"I noticed you're pretty quick and alert when it comes to the other students. But you're slightly distracted when it comes to your sensei."

Was he implying something? Okay I confess, I slept with my sensei a long time ago. It was very disappointing and I never want to talk about it again. But I wasn't going to tell him that or mention that I was distracted because I was remembering almost fucking *him* in my dream last night.

"Uh, yea. I had something on my mind." I stated dumbly.

He stood up, "I'm curious though, just how skilled you really are. May I have a demonstration?" He took his shirt off and went into the stance. Looks like my dream was correct again, firm but not ripped. Alright Gabby, concentrate. I dropped my bag and stepped forward. We began to circle one another.

He had me pinned after fifteen minutes. I would have been proud of myself if my heart wasn't totally freaking out. I was pinned under him in quite the position. His eyes stared into mine.

"Not bad." He said slightly out of breath. We stared a little longer than necessary.

Oh my God, just fucking kiss me!

He smiled and got up. Dammit.

"Okay well, I'll see you tomorrow." He turned and went into the office. I sat there and stared after him until he shut the door. Then I finally stood and left with my bag over my shoulder. I was in my jogging pants and baggy sweater. Gloves on and started down the street. The studio was only a few blocks from my church.

Yes I actually lived at the church, the attic actually. My father was in his office when I walked by.

"Gabriel."

I stopped and turned around.

"Yes?" I said as I walked in.

"It is almost your twenty third birthday and I was wondering what your plans were."

"Uh, hanging out with Stacey I guess." He has something up his sleeve, I can feel it.

"Are you going to go drinking and have sex with strangers?"

W-what? My eyes bugged out. Shit I'm done for. He fucking knew.

"Um..." my brain stuttered. What do I say? *Yes?*

He sighed, "I've become aware that you are no longer a virgin and haven't been for quite some time."

"How?" I stammered.

"That doesn't matter. I understand the world isn't what it used to be and the sanctity of marriage doesn't necessarily apply to most anymore. But after your twenty third birthday, I want you to be careful. Use..... Protective measures."

I froze a second to comprehend what I was hearing. Okay, I hit bizzaro world. And I really shouldn't be surprised given the day I've been having, but my father giving me the 'safe sex' talk? Wait....... What did he say?

"My twenty third birthday? I've always used protection first of all," this is so weird! "But what does that have to do with my birthday?"

He looked down at his fingers and I noticed they were trembling. This is when he told me I was 'adopted' *illegally*. Hell I knew I was adopted but this is when the real story came out. How he found me, why he kept me......

"I believe it is you who are the Witchdemon my dear Gabby. Gabriel is a very fitting name for you. I noticed your pull of those around you. They listen. You're always too kind to those who don't deserve it and the way you looked when I found you. Then to be perfectly fine within minutes."

I shook my head, he's lost it. Or he's drunk and he's the master at hiding the bottle and smell. I've never known him to drink but that only adds to the proof. I shook my head but something he said still stuck.

"I still don't get it. What if I don't use protection after I turn twenty three?" Of course I would ask the sex question.

"If he doesn't truly love you? He dies."

My eyes popped open wide as they could go.

Shove over AIDS, there's a newer and more potent killer in town.

"Instantly at his climax." He added.

Okay this was getting more than a little fucked up.

"And if they do love me?" I whispered.

"They become half angel and half demon as well." I shook my head. I was almost sucked in. This was too much. I subtly checked his desk for a crack pipe now. Nothing. Maybe he is just simply losing it. That made me sad, and then really pissed off.

"Go to bed father, I think you need some rest." I don't know why but the thought of me being this so called Witchdemon really irritated me. Give me a fucking break, that shit isn't real.

"You'll see when the time comes." He sighed as I turned around. I closed the door behind me and went to my room.

Chapter Two

The next day I was full blown irritated. I dreamt of Peter and was rudely awoken in the middle of the night by sirens outside my window. I couldn't get back to sleep and now I was groggy. In the dream we were at a park sitting on a tire swing just laughing. It was sweet. It made my chest feel heavy and it made me feel sad at the same time. I felt irritated because logically I knew what that meant but I wasn't going to pay attention to it.

I met Stacey at the station at seven thirty as promised and walked with her to the coffee shop. Joseph wasn't there today so that made me feel worse. Usually a hot guy would take my mind off things and the major bonus that he was obviously into me for some fucked up reason. Then I was even more irritated that I suddenly felt guilty about thinking that way about Joseph because of Peter. Acting like I was with him or something. So I dwelled in my disappointment and irritation while Stacey prattled on about wedding plans or whatever.

"Okay what the fuck is up with you Gabby? I can handle your mood swings but your silence is like finding a bag of money. It *never* happens. What's wrong with you?"

Hmmmm. I didn't think she was paying attention. Should have known better. I wasn't going to tell her though, so I shrugged. She looked at me for a second and then stopped walking.

"You know, I was curious about your father. Is he doing any better?"

I stopped too. I looked around and noticed we were already at the front steps of the College.

"Yea he's good." Maybe smoking crack, but overall he's good.

"Okay." She said with a smile. She reached out and squeezed my arm. "I'll see you at lunch."

I nodded. We started to part ways when she caught my attention again.

"Gabby I almost forgot. Every year the College has a mixer slash fundraiser for the homeless shelter. This year's theme is a masquerade ball. Like eighteenth century stuff I think. Its tomorrow night. They announced it through e-mail a couple weeks ago but since you don't have a computer, I guess you didn't get the memo." She smiled a mischievous smile.

Oh fuck off.....

"I guess you're dragging me there?" I asked.

"Of course I am. I already got your dress." She beamed with a full flash of her teeth. She waved and then half ran to class. It was as if just by her mentioning it, now everyone was talking about it. I could hear people talking about dresses or pranks nearly everywhere I went. I ended up getting to my class just in time to see everyone leaving. My heart sank. I went up to one of the girls before she got away.

"What's going on? Isn't there class today?"

She shook her head. "No, Dr. Ramsey said for us to enjoy the day because he has an appointment this morning." The girl hurried off immediately after speaking and left almost rudely like I was a plague or something.

Bitch.

I walked into the classroom anyways, and saw Peter closing his bag. My heart started pounding again. He spotted me and smiled.

"Ah, Miss Douglas."

"Gabby." I corrected.

"Is that short for something?"

"Gabriel." I looked down; I could feel my face heat up.

"Gabriel," he whispered, "how fitting."

A knock sounded at the door making us both look in that direction. But before either of us could respond, the door opened and a woman poked just her head through.

"Oh I'm sorry Dr. Ramsey, but your morning appointment just cancelled and gives their deepest apologies."

"Well then I guess I'm free for the morning." He looked at me and added, "Would you like to go for a walk with me?"

I blinked and looked at the woman but she was already gone.

"Sure......" Now my face was seriously heating up. I could feel that heavy feeling in my chest again. He motioned towards the door and we both left the classroom. We made it through the building mostly in silence.

"So how are you feeling?" he asked in the elevator.

"You're not going to do some psycho analysis on me are you?" I looked at him with a questioning look. He was amused by the question. He turned towards me and stepped closer to me.

"Did you want me to?"

I licked my lips at the question as I stared at his, but once I glanced up at his eyes I quickly answered, "No." and moved towards the doors, waiting for them to open. They opened but I didn't run away, we continued to move through the College side by side. Finally, after weaving through the cafeteria he spoke,

"Are you afraid to reveal too much to me?"

I didn't answer; I just stopped and looked around. We had gone through the cafeteria and were outside. The wind blew my hair around my face. He stopped too and I could tell from my peripheral vision that he was analysing my face. I looked down at our feet and he stepped closer to me. My heart thudded in my chest. If I look him in the eyes he'll know everything. He put his hand to my chin and lifted my face to look me in the eyes.

"Are you going to answer me?" he said softly, his face oh so close to mine. But I still didn't answer; I kept glancing from his lips to his dark brown eyes. He sighed, "What am I going to do with you?" His hand moved from my chin and stroked my left cheek. I closed my eyes at the touch. When I opened them, I blurted out the first thing in my head.

"Are you going to the ball tomorrow?"

This caught him by surprise, to my disappointment he dropped his hand but smiled.

"Do you want me to?"

I nodded. He brought his face closer.

"Then I'll be there."

He went to walk away but I grabbed his arm. He looked at me and smiled again as he put a hand over mine. I don't know what I wanted to say but I think he knew by the look on my face that I didn't want him to go just yet. Gently, he loosened my grip and winked at me.

"I'll see you tomorrow Gabriel."

I suddenly wanted to cry as I watched him walk to his car, get in, and drive away. I didn't want to be parted from him. Before any tears could drop, I quickly reminded myself that I would see him tomorrow in class and now, at the Ball. I sucked in a deep breath and went inside.

I waited patiently for Stacy but she had to stay to talk about some assignment so she couldn't join me for lunch. I gave a quick goodbye and left the college. My 'Kung Fu' class was a little bit entertaining as Charlie the Amazon practically chased some poor girl with a stick. My head was so full of Peter that I didn't even notice James at all. Afterwards, I went home right away but couldn't even eat. Finally I snapped out of it when the phone rang. It was Stacey.

"So tomorrow, I want you to meet me at ten in the morning at New West Station." She ordered.

"I can't, I have class." I stuttered.

"There's no classes tomorrow Gabby, because of the Ball. It's also a fundraiser for the homeless shelters." Stacey said impatiently. Yea I got that the first time you told me. "They throw one every year and the funds buy clothes and food and stuff for them. So everyone who shows up must bring a donation and tickets are like ten bucks."

Holy fuck.

"Don't worry, I got you covered."

It's like she read my mind.

"Peter is coming." I blurted.

"Who?" this stopped her.

"Dr. Ramsey." I said patiently, "He said that if I wanted him to come then he would show up."

"Oh my God!" she practically yelled, "Why didn't you tell me?!" Now she yelled. I quickly gave her the play by play of what happened, leaving out my heart and emotional behavior and she squealed.

"This is great! Okay so meet me at ten and I have everything planned. Hair, nails, makeup, everything! Girl, I'm going to hook you up!" Stacey squealed again and we both laughed. We always acted like this when we were trying to hook in a new guy. She's been off the playing field but the enthusiasm is still there as she lives vicariously through me. But for me, this time was a little bit different. I wanted to keep him. I was surprised not just by the feeling, but how intense it was. Stacey and I said our goodnights and I went to bed.

* * *

I was flying, well, spinning through the air in his arms. I felt so blissfully free. And happy. I was truly, madly, deeply, happy.

* * *

"Jeezus Gabby, you look like shit!" Stacey stated oh so subtly. I stuck my tongue out and did a raspberry at her. We met at New West Station as planned.

"I just had some interesting dreams last night." I admitted.

She looked at me with a mischievous smirk, "I'm sure you did."

I rolled my eyes.

"Well, let's go get dolled up." She grabbed my hand and led me back to the trains. We got on the train and headed for Metro-town Station, which held one of the biggest malls in the lower mainland. There was an entrance to the mall as soon as we got off the train.

"Let's get our hair done first." I heard Stacey mutter as we entered the mall. She dragged me through the maze of shoppers. I never bothered to memorize where the stores were anymore. Every time I thought I had it, a week later the damn place switched around on me. I wasted years of memorizing and rememorizing to the point where I said 'fuck it' about five years ago. Stacey never quit though; this place was her second home. And for once, I thanked God for that.

I hated the idea of being in a mall all day; the quicker we get to where we need to go, the quicker we can get the fuck out of here. We got to the hair salon and I went with big curls and thick red hair extensions. Blood red. A little punkie but with the curls it looked great. Stacey agreed enthusiastically and revealed that my dress was pretty much the same colour. After an hour and a half we were done. Stacey had gotten some platinum highlights to go with the blonde she already had. She had waves parted down the middle while my hair was parted from one side.

Next, we went to the make-up store where we got some fake eyelashes and obviously our make-up done. We bought some kits for any touch ups that might be required throughout the day. Finally, we went and got our nails done. We both went for acrylic French manicures, nothing glittery. So after four hours and just over six hundred dollars later, we left the mall and went right to Stacey's house.

Stacey explained to me that the 'ball' would start at seven and go on till eleven. We had two hours left when we decided to put on our dresses. I gasped at the dress she got me. Since the theme was supposed to be in the eighteenth century, she went to 'The Past' and got me a dress. 'The Past' is an old vintage clothing and furniture store slash costume shop full of antiques and old clothes from supposedly way back when. But this dress was straight out of a book. There was a corset like waist with red ribbon and rose patterned lace outlined in black. It was beautiful. Open neck and open shoulders. There were straps that held on the arm under the shoulder. I knew I was going to have some killer cleavage. After an hour of simply adoring all the details, I put it on and looked in the mirror of the bathroom.

Holy shit! I looked fucking awesome. I giggled to myself; Peter was going to shit when he saw me. My make-up was bang on and the dress was fantastic. I made a mental note not to smile too much; my teeth might ruin the whole effect. I adjusted a breast and then stepped out of the bathroom.

Stacey had a silk baby blue dress on. It was in the same time frame as mine, I assumed, for it had the same corset like waist. We looked at each other and squealed. She was wearing a white mask and white gloves that went up to the elbow. She handed me a black mask and black gloves. Then the doorbell rang.

"Who's that?" I asked Stacey just smiled at me and left to answer the door.

What a dumb question, obviously it was Stan. But then I heard *three* people laugh, two men and Stacey.

"She's in the living room." I heard Stacey say.

"Is she ready?" My heart stopped for a second, then surprisingly thundered rapidly at his voice. What was Joseph doing here? Footsteps made their way to the living room. I turned away from the window just as he was walking in the room. He was wearing a dark blue suit from the same time frame as my dress. His eyes appraised my face and dress.

"You look amazing." He said in his rough, yet very sexy voice.

"So do you." I meant it too, he looked down right delicious. He stepped closer to me and took my hand. He lifted it to his mouth and kissed my knuckles.

Fucking cornball. I smiled.

"Let's go shall we?" his blue eyes twinkled with amusement.

Stacey and Stan were outside talking. She turned to face me and Joseph with a camera in her hand.

"Okay, embrace for a photo!" She shouted.

Joseph put his arms around me and I put my head on his chest as we both looked at the camera.

"That's so hot." Stacey beamed. I rolled my eyes and the four of us got into Stan's black Jetta. It was ten to seven when we got to the 'Ballroom'. The College had rented out the Sapperton Hall. It used to be way smaller but it was destroyed by a freak fire and so were many of the buildings around it. They were mostly abandoned by then anyways. So the city cleaned the area and rebuilt it bigger and better, and now all kinds of events are held here. It's in the main part of New Westminster, so the Hall is used for many fundraisers like the College's and even political meetings have been held here.

According to Stacey; because of the popularity of the fundraiser, the College had to do little convincing in order to obtain permission to use the Hall annually. The Hall was decorated with elaborate imitation wall fixtures giving the illusion of the eighteenth century. It was like a movie set; the four of us slipped on our masks.

"Oh Stacey? Can I ask you something privately?" I whispered. She nodded and told the guys we were off to get drinks. Joseph winked at me as we walked away.

"What's up Gabby?"

"Why is Joseph with us?" I whispered almost hysterically. She looked at me confused. With the excitement of playing matchmaker she obviously forgot the game plan we had yesterday.

"Why not? I thought you liked him? I saw him this morning and told him to come with. I gave him Stan's number to pick him up. Is there a problem?"

I stared at her for a second unsure if I should tell her why I was freaking out about Joseph, but instead I cocked my head to the side. I silently tried *not* to scream profanities as I prayed real hard for her to remember. Then I swear I heard her brain click.

"Oh shit! Gabby I'm sorry! Of course you wanted to be with Dr. Ramsey tonight!" She whispered back. She looked at the guys across the room as I looked at her impatiently for a solution. "Okay I got it. Stan wasn't thrilled to be here anyways, so how about this; I'll convince him to take Joseph to the liquor store and have a few beers at the docks and wait for us to join. I'll say we have to stay for a bit because it's our College and officially we're on the actual guest list to represent the College. Eventually I'll have to tell him the truth and explain it as a front because of Joseph but he'll understand, but you might totally owe him one."

I sighed with relief, "No problem. Oh my God Stacey, *thank you*."

She smiled at me. But I froze as I glanced across the room.

"Okay I'll go tell him now before Dr. Ramsey gets here. Gabby? Hello?" She turned around and followed my eyes. "Shit there he is!"

She spun around to face me as I watched him enter the room. Scratch the Joseph-being-delicious part; Peter looked so fucking good, I almost felt my heart clot. I looked back at Stacey but she was already across the room to my right calling for Stan's attention. Joseph and Stan walked up to her. I looked back at Peter; he didn't seem to know which girl was me because he kept scanning the room. His eyes lingered on me for a second then one of the other teachers asked him something. I looked back at Stacey and saw that she was alone; she gave me the thumbs-up.

In my peripheral, I caught sight of the guys headed for the doorway. As they were leaving, Peter caught Joseph's eye and they stared at each other for an awkward looking second and then Joseph and Stan left. The teacher left Peter as well. I walked towards Peter. The butterflies were back as soon as I noticed *him* noticing my approach. I smiled without showing my teeth and took off my mask. He looked mildly surprised at first but his eyes trapped me where I stood directly in front of him. I had a feeling he wanted to kiss me which was ridiculous, but it made me feel slightly light headed like a high of giddiness. He was dressed like a prince, all in black.

"You look like a goddess." He whispered as he stroked my cheek. I reacted again by closing my eyes at his touch. When I opened them he was frowning slightly, deep in thought.

"What?" I asked.

"Ever since I noticed you, I haven't been able to think of anyone or anything else." He stared into my eyes with a longing I wasn't imagining. At his words I felt myself blush. I nearly fell to the floor when I first saw him, in real life that is, but I felt the same way. The music finally started the same moment I took a step forward.

"Dance with me Peter." I said to him.

I put my left hand on his shoulder and he put his right on my waist as our other hands entwined. We moved gracefully in a square formation while turning at the same time. I didn't know what kind of dance we were doing, but if felt as if we've done this for years. Natural, without a stutter or hesitation.

This is so fucking intense! I loved it.

We danced for three songs and then there was a slow song. He wrapped both arms around me and I put my head on his shoulder. His smell filled my lungs. If he wasn't holding me up, I'd probably fall to the floor. I was so happy in this moment. Is this what love felt like? So soon? I lifted up my head when the song ended and stared up at him.

"Peter I-" I started but he moved so fast. His lips were on mine, soft and powerfully addictive.

My heart soared with emotions of joy and bliss. I didn't want it to end. And it didn't till I literally had to gasp for breath. I looked at him and suddenly remembered we weren't wearing our masks. I looked around and saw that everyone was watching. He put both hands on either side of my face and made me look at him.

"No one will recognise you if that's what you're worried about."

I shook my head, "No. I don't care if the whole world knows. I just don't know what's going to happen next."

"What do you mean?"

I hesitated for a second. "I want to be yours." I whispered. I wasn't prepared for the emotions that engulfed me from my confession. My eyes started to tear up.

"Then you shall be mine, and I shall be yours. Is that what you want?"

"Yes."

He kissed me again, only briefly, and then led me to the doors.

"Gabby!" A squeal shouted from the other side of the room. I turned and saw Stacey jumping on the spot with excitement; her eyes were all bugged out and it was pretty comical.

"Have fun! I'm going to the docks. I'll say you got sick or something okay?"

I gave her a thumbs-up and left with Peter at my side. Once outside, he grabbed my hand and led me to his car.

"Do you want to go home or do you want to come to my place?" he asked.

Like he really needed to ask.

"Your place please." I smiled. I got into the car and waited for him to do the same. Soon we were crossing the bridge to Surrey. I started fidgeting with my fingers; I was so fucking nervous. He grabbed my hand and set it on his lap as he drove, his fingers interlinked with mine.

*　*　*

We stopped in front of a house on a block where every house looked almost exactly like this house. The differences were very slight. I got out and waited for him to lead me to whichever one was his. The house he led me to had three levels. Main floor, second floor, and attic. Once inside, I couldn't help but look around in wonder and amazement. It felt so cultured, yet modern. I felt so out of place either way. I took off my shoes out of respect for the beautiful wooden flooring. He stood in front of me and held out his hand. I took it and followed him up the stairs.

In the stairway, there were pictures on the walls. One caught my eye and instantly raised a lump in my throat. It was of Peter and another woman who was obviously older and in her arms was a baby.

"Is that your family?" I felt alarmed and slightly hurt. He looked at me and assessed the expression on my face.

"That's my ex-wife and my daughter. She four now." He said simply.

Ex-wife? I felt slightly better. We walked into a bedroom that was obviously the master bedroom. It even had its own bathroom. I walked up to the bed and gently stroked the silky white sheets. There was no quilt. My hands were shaking. He came up behind me, moved my hair to expose my neck and placed his lips upon my shoulder. Then my neck, and then just under my jaw bone. Peter pulled at the red ribbon that tied the back

21

of the corset like dress. I slipped out of the arm straps and the dress fell to the floor.

"Interesting." He whispered. I knew at once he was noticing the large tattoo on my back. I knew he noticed it on my shoulders a bit, but now he saw the full thing. Black angel wings flowed from my shoulder blades, up a little past my shoulders, and down my back to the bottom of my spine. Some feathers spread across each rib cage as well. He turned me around to face him. My black, strapless, lace bra hugged my breasts perfectly. My black lace booty-short-underwear laid low on my hips.

Peter took off his coat and then his shirt. He may have been older but he was still fit and very sexy. I touched his chest, tracing the contours of his muscles. My fingers lingered on his belt, then suddenly his hands were there to undo it. His pants fell and his lips were on mine.

CHAPTER THREE

I woke up without opening my eyes. I was unusually warm. Then that warmth moved and held me tighter. I opened my eyes and looked down at my hand. There was another hand underneath mine with soft skin. I stroked the veins and traced the knuckles to the fingertips. I bit my lip at the memory of what those fingertips did to my skin. The smell of him was soaked through the sheets and even the pillow I was laying on. It was intoxicating. I turned my head into the pillow and inhaled deeply. I couldn't help but moan.

"I don't think I'll ever get used to hearing you do that." He said softly in my ear before he kissed my cheek. I turned around, still in his arms, and kissed his soft lips. I wanted to do more but the doorbell rang. We both looked at the doorway.

"Shit." He whispered, "Stay here." He said to me. He got up and put on a robe before he left the room. I got up and got something on just in case I needed to make an escape. I had no intention of actually leaving, but I guess old habits die hard. I slowly crept out of the room and stopped just at the corner of the wall just before the top of the steps. I was careful not to be seen as he made a lot of racket. The doorbell rang again; this time he opened the door.

"Daddy!" a little girl squealed.

"Hey honey bee." His voice sounded surprised but he recovered well. I glanced down to see him hugging an adorable little girl. Standing in the doorway was the woman from the picture.

Oh fuck!

I hid myself again as he spoke, "What are you doing here Linda?"

"Not happy to see your daughter?" Linda had a menacing edge to her voice. Instantly I hated her.

"Of course I am, it's *you* I'm not happy to see." His voice sounded strained.

"I doubt it. It's been three years and you're still pathetically alone. I at least, had some sense to remarry." She said, mockingly smug.

Heat rose to my face. I looked at my reflection through one of the pictures on the wall. I knew I was going to have to go down there and give her a piece of my mind if she didn't cut the crap. And I sure as hell wanted to look as attractive as possible doing it. Amazingly enough, my make-up survived the night. Not as dark but my eyes still had that smoked look from the slightly smudged eyeliner.

"Yes that's right. How is Howard doing these days?" Peter asked sarcastically.

I quickly went back into the room to where my dress lay on the floor. My lip gloss was stuffed in the left breast cup. A convenient hole hid it there. I was wearing his black dress shirt from last night. I quickly applied the gloss and tossed my hair, then bee-lined it back to the steps to listen some more.

"Better than you. You're barely a Doctor anymore; having to teach at a College." She scoffed, "They say, 'those who can't do, teach'."

That's it you bitch! I started down the stairs.

"And those who can't do anything, suck the life out of those who can. I always found jealousy to be a teenage immaturity. Trust me honey, green really isn't your colour." It was the best I could think of without being vulgar in front of his daughter. But as I put my arm around Peter's waist, I saw my words had the effect I was looking for anyways. Linda's face looked like she smelled something sour as she looked at me. Peter and I shared a smile as we looked at one another and then back at Linda.

"How dare you," she said to me, "Peter, I'm not going to have my daughter around you if you're going to sleep around with prostitutes and have then disrespect me in front of her." Linda glared at me.

What a weak comeback. I glared back, but only for a second. Keeping the daughter in mind to put my language in check I responded with a short chuckle.

"First of all, I'm not a prostitute. But I'm assuming anyone who looks better than you must be right? Or are you simply afraid that Peter's finally gotten over you after all? I would ask you not to belittle him or disrespect him anymore because I'm not going to stand here and witness it. He is her father and I'd hate for her to grow up and treat people the way you do."

She looked as if she wanted to hit me but was interrupted by her daughter tugging on her pants.

"Mommy, I want to be with daddy. You promised!" The little girl stuck out her bottom lip. Linda looked at Peter with more than enough frustration to make me smile.

"Unfortunately for you, I have other arrangements for this weekend. That's why she's here now instead of your birthday. We're going to the States for a few months." Linda spoke with a stiff jaw.

"I thought that trip wasn't until next week?" Peter picked up his daughter and she planted a wet kiss on his nose. Linda scowled with annoyance.

"Things came up." She turned to pick up a small black bag from behind her. "I'll be back tomorrow night to pick her up. These are her things." And with that she stiffly kissed her daughter's forehead and left. Peter closed the door as soon as she stepped off the porch.

"Who are you?" Peter's daughter asked me. I smiled.

"My name is Gabriel. But you can call me Gabby. And your name is?"

"My name is Mary." She said proudly. She had his big, beautiful brown eyes. Peter kissed her cheek and she squealed again.

"I love my daddy. Do you love my daddy too?" Mary asked me. My brain stuttered at the question. The both of us looked at Peter.

"Hey honey bee, let's go put your things in your room okay?"

"Okay daddy." Said Mary excitedly; instantly forgetting her question.

I looked down at the floor. My heart was pounding, the butterflies were back. I watched them go up the stairs but I didn't follow. I didn't want to say it because I didn't know if he felt the same way. Wasn't it a little soon? It hasn't even been a week!

Sure, he did say that I would be his and he would be mine, but that could have meant anything, like, 'hey let's have sex'. And I didn't want to pressure him into saying it back to me either. What the hell did I know? I've never felt like this before. No matter how I looked at it now, there was officially a giant elephant in the room.

"Gabby! Come see my room!" Mary demanded from the top of the stairs. I looked up to see her jumping up and down at the top of the steps. I took the steps two at a time and she grabbed my hand once I got to the landing, and then pulled me to the room right across the hall from Peter's. It was pink beyond pink. Frills and every Fairy tale princess on the walls mixed with various angel posters. She pulled me to the angel that I thought looked the most beautiful.

"That's Gabriel." Mary pointed. She looked up at me with a very serious look on her face.

"Make sure my daddy isn't sad anymore okay Gabriel?" she spoke in a whisper. I almost started to tear up. I crouched down so I was face to face with her.

"I promise." I whispered. She smiled and gave me a big hug. I looked up towards the doorway and saw Peter; he looked overjoyed. He looked from me to his daughter and came towards us. I stood up with Mary in my arms and he hugged us both.

*   *   *

"I think she adores you." Peter whispered. He had sat in the corner of the room while I read Mary a bedtime story at her request which took him by surprise. I guess that was normally his job, but little Mary had been obsessed with me all day, so it didn't surprise me in the slightest. I loved it actually, she was a little addicting. We shut the door after she fell asleep and made our way to his room. We sat on the bed and faced each other. A smirk touched my lips.

"What is it?" he asked. I raised an eyebrow at him.

"Okay, tell me something."

"Shoot."

"How old are you turning on Saturday?"

He smiled.

"Well?" I pressed.

"I'll be fifty." He looked at me kind of sheepishly.

"Hmmm." I looked away, "well that's interesting." A smile spread across my face. I was glad for his honesty I looked back at him.

"Are you not repulsed?" he asked me.

"No, why should I be? You certainly don't look fifty, I mean, that could be thanks to 'just for men' but I definitely think you're sexy." I made my fingers walk up his arm, "and you can definitely keep up."

He laughed. I loved his laugh. I loved him and nearly choked at the realization but controlled it before he noticed. I wanted to tell him but I just didn't know how to say it.

"Mary is right you know." I started.

"Right about what?"

I wimped out and looked away, "Nothing, never mind." I sighed. He grabbed my chin and turned my face to look at his.

"Do you love me Gabby?" the intensity of his eyes bore into mine. I gulped and nodded.

"Say it." He pressed.

"I-I love you." I whispered, and then, again, his lips were on mine.

*   *   *

The next day, Friday morning, I woke up and had to go to the bathroom. I stood up from the bed to make my way to the bathroom door when I nearly slipped on my ass.

What the fuck?

I looked down at my foot to see what I just stepped on. It was the condom from last night.

Oh what the fuck?!

"Ugh! Are you fucking kidding me?" I looked back at Peter and apparently he was watching as I had pretty much peeled it off my foot. The look on my face sent him howling with laughter.

"Dude that is so gross! You couldn't've aimed for the garbage can?" I went into the bathroom and threw it away. I decided to shower. As soon as I turned on the water, Mary bolted into the room. I quickly shut the door because I was stark naked.

"Daddy! Good morning! I want pancakes!" I heard her giggle.

"Just a second honey bee. Go to your room for a second please so I can get dressed. Then we'll go downstairs okay?"

Little footsteps ran out of the room. A light knock sounded at the bathroom door just as I was about to step into the shower.

"Yes?" I called. He opened the door just enough to poke his head in.

"There are some clothes in my closet. Linda didn't take everything

when she left. If you can find anything, she's about the same size as you."
Then he left.

I stood there for a second. Wow, he must have loved her a lot. He still
had her clothes because it must have been hard for him to let her go. Her
snide remarks were an even deeper wound than I thought. Stupid bitch
broke his heart. No wonder it took so long for him to get over her...

The shower was so nice and warm. Peter had quite the variety of hair
products. I had picked up two baby blue bottles but they were in a different
language.

"Which one is which?" I whispered to myself. I couldn't tell which
one was the shampoo, and which one was the conditioner. I shrugged and
chose a different bottle all together. It was a body wash but whatever, it
was in English.

When I finished, I wrapped myself in a towel and headed for the closet.
Jeez, these clothes were definitely not in my fashion taste. Super formal
and business like. I picked out black dress pants and a sleeveless, dark red
blouse. I had no make-up except my gloss but I didn't look too bad. I went
downstairs just in time to see Mary slap a syrupy pancake against the side
of Peter's face.

"You really shouldn't waste food kiddo." I teased. She still had the
pancake in her hand.

"Gabriel!" she reached out both arms to me and I bit the pancake, "I
need to be washed please!" I looked at Peter; he had syrup dripping down
his cheek.

"So do I." he smiled. I smiled back as I picked up Mary and carried her
to the kitchen sink. I washed her hands and face, dried her up and then
took her to the front room where I turned on the television so she could
watch some cartoons. Peter went upstairs, I assumed, to shower.

"Gabriel, are you an angel?" The question threw me off, I looked at her
as she continued. "I can feel something from you. I think my daddy loves
you. I've never seen him smile at anyone other than me before."

How old did he say his daughter was? She certainly didn't sound like
a four year old. I kissed her forehead.

"So are you an angel?" she asked me again while scrunching up her
nose.

"Only if you want me to be."

She smiled wide, showing me all her little white teeth.

"I do." She nuzzled her face into my arm. I was touched.

"Okay honey bee, I'll be your angel." I kissed the top of her head.

*   *   *

It was eight o'clock at night when Linda showed up to pick up Mary.

"Happy birthday daddy." Mary hugged and kissed Peter, then turned to me. I crouched down and looked at Linda as Mary hugged and kissed me on the cheek.

"Happy birthday Gabriel."

"Birthday?" Linda asked, looking at Peter.

"Uh yes, Gabby and I share the same birthday."

Was it me, or did he look a little uncomfortable?

"I see." Linda now looked at me, "And how old are you going to be?"

"That's really none of your business." Peter said quickly.

"I'll be twenty three." At my words Linda looked as if she were going to shit herself right there on the porch.

"Good bye Linda." Peter said grimly.

"Come on mommy!" Mary was tugging on Linda's hand but Linda was too shocked to move. Finally, she turned and left the patio towards her car. Peter closed the door and sighed. My heart had a sinking feeling.

"Was.... that bad?" I half whispered. But he didn't answer, he just stood there with his eyes closed. Was he ashamed of the age difference? I almost started to tear up but my mood swung hard. I glared at his back and then bolted up the stairs to get my dress. He didn't love me, he didn't even say it back last night. I should have known better; I was a fool. I stomped down the stairs and went straight for the living room to where the landline was. I picked it up and dialled Stacey's number.

"Hello?" she picked up after the first ring.

"Stacey, it's me, I need you to pick me up right away. Can you use Stan's car and get me? I'm in Surrey." My voice was firm. She noticed.

"Gabby what's wrong? Never mind, where exactly are you? I'll come get you right now."

"Just meet me at Surrey Central Mall."

"Okay, I'll be there in fifteen minutes."

I hung up the phone a little harder than I meant to and went to the front door to get my shoes. They weren't there. Intuition clicked in. He fucking hid them yesterday, that's what the racket was before he answered the door. He was trying to hide the fact he was with me. I was even more angry now, my hands started to shake.

Mother fucker!

I turned around and my shoes were in his hands. I looked him in the face as I snatched them from him. He looked sad but I was too pissed off to care. I put them on and opened the front door. As I stepped out he spoke,

"Can I take you home?" he almost whimpered. I spun on him.

"Why?! You're obviously ashamed of me! I'll *walk* to the damn mall and *Stacey* can take me home. Here I thought you cared but you're just like everyone else!" I glared at him and then stalked off across the road without looking back.

Fucking asshole.

I was crying by the time I turned the corner. I glanced back at his house just in time to see him closing the door.

I let out a heavy sigh and continued on. The walk wasn't bad. I had no fear in this part of Surrey for some reason, even though I probably should. It was known as Whalley and supposedly the most 'rank' part of Surrey. But hooker alley was empty and the mall was only five long-ish blocks away. I was so mad. I trusted that he felt the same way. I tried not to remember all the things he said.

When I finally got to the mall, Stacey was already in the parking lot waiting for me. I quickly wiped away my tears.

"So, are you going to tell me what happened?" she asked as I stepped into the car.

"No, just take me home Stace, I don't want to talk about it right now."

We drove in silence all the way to my place, my church, in East Vancouver. St James Anglican Church. I should invest in getting my own place. I looked at the dashboard; the clock read nine thirty by the time she stopped out front. I got out.

"I'll talk to you tomorrow Stacey." I closed the door and went right to the front doors of the church. Before I put the key in the hole, I looked back at her. She was on her phone and straining her neck to look at the address of the church. Weird. I waved but she didn't see.

Fuck it.

I went inside. The pews and altar were empty. To the right was the area for the prayer candles. They were all out. I wonder if that makes your prayer mute after it's blown out. I walked towards the altar with a heavy heart. My chest hurt and fresh tears made their way down my cheeks. I fell to my knees right there in the middle of the pews. My memories of the past couple days flooded my mind.

"Not like you to pray Gabby."

I turned to see Thomas, one of my father's 'priests in training'. Training he's been in since I was younger. He was about twenty or thirty years younger than my father. He was in and out of the church my whole life, or the life I remember. He was kind of like my nanny if you got real technical.

"Where's my father?" I asked through blurred eyes.

"He had some preparations to deal with." He assessed my face, the realization that I of all people was crying, something I never do in front of people, must have terrified him. His face went a little pale as he asked, "What's wrong girl?"

I looked down at my knees and kept my gaze lowered as I stood up.

"I fell in love, but I don't think he loves me back!" I wailed.

Thomas took me in his arms and patted my head as I cried, "Love is a fickle thing my dear Gabby." He sighed, "Tell me exactly what happened."

So I told him everything, the dreams, the heavy heart, everything. He wasn't very impressed with the age difference though. We sat in the back pews facing each other.

"Gabby, did you ever think you might be overreacting? He could indeed love you but is just as unprepared as you are?"

I looked up at him from my fidgeting fingers. I sniffed. "I don't know Thomas."

He looked at his watch and smiled, "Happy birthday Gabby."

My eyes widened a bit. Its midnight already? A knock echoed through the church from the front doors.

"I wonder who that could be?" We both got up and Thomas went to the door. He opened it and I could hear the rain outside.

"Hello?"

"Is Gabriel here?" The voice sent adrenaline through my veins. I was tired from crying but now I was wide awake. How did he know where I lived? Intuition clicked again; he must have called Stacey because that was the last number his phone dialed. That's why she was looking at the church address. I stepped out from the pew as Thomas stepped aside to look at me. Peter looked in. As soon as he saw me, he walked right past Thomas straight towards me. He stopped in front of me and dropped to his knees.

"Gabby please forgive me. I was foolish. I'm not ashamed of you, please don't ever think that. I never want you to feel that way ever again. I love you Gabby." He grabbed my hands and kissed them. My anger melted away as I saw the sincerity on his face. I cupped his face and bent over to kiss his lips.

"I love you too." Tears fell as I smiled. Peter stood and wiped them away.

"Happy birthday Gabby." He whispered.

"Happy birthday Peter." I whispered back. I looked over Peter's shoulder and spoke to Thomas, "When will my father be back?"

"Around the witching hour."

"Good." I grabbed Peter's arm and led him up the path to the altar, took a right, and went up the stairs to my room. My adrenaline was getting more intense, I could see clear as day in the windowless darkness. When we entered my room I turned around, closed and locked the door. I pulled Peter to me.

"I want to be yours now and always."

"O-Okay." He stuttered surprised. I took off the blouse and pants in five seconds and kicked off my heels. He looked at me for a second and then followed suit. I undid my bra and slid down my panties. I looked at him and almost laughed. He was definitely not as practiced as I was. It was almost comical the way he hopped out of his pants and boxers.

Once we were both naked, we stepped towards each other and pressed our bodies together, just holding one another for a moment. My senses were spiked. I could hear the blood flow through his veins. I could smell his body wash and natural scent. I felt so high. I kissed his chest as he ran his fingertips down my back, making my whole body tingle. I rubbed my cheek against his unshaven face. He kissed my neck, making a trail to my lips. As soon as our lips touched, my high intensified. We made our way to the bed and he gently laid me down on my back and positioned himself between my legs.

"Gabby we don't have-" he gasped through our lips but I stopped him.

"Shh. Do you love me?" I looked him hard in the eyes. He nodded. "Yes."

"Then it's okay, it's okay Peter, just love me." We stared into each other's eyes for another second and then our lips were connected once more. This time wasn't like before, it wasn't like anything I've ever experienced and I think he noticed as well. He entered me slowly, making me raise my hips with impatience. Everything was sensitive to the point of instant orgasm once he was completely within me. He kissed me with more passion. He kissed me with a desperation, possession, a claim. Again my high intensified. Every slight movement increased the sensitivity. My world was him as we moved in rhythm to each breath we took.

He grabbed my hip with one hand to pull me closer, pushing himself deeper and grinding my inner thighs with his hips. I cried out in pure pleasure. He moved his lips to kiss down my neck and chest as I arched my back. I opened my eyes to the ceiling and that's when I noticed the light, well, glow is more like it. My body was glowing. I looked around with my eyes and saw we were surrounded by golden sparkles that weaved between and around our bodies. The sparkles touched his body and looked as if they were being absorbed by him. As he continued to moved, his body slowly started to glow but he was completely oblivious to it.

Suddenly it hit me. I knew what was happening. I didn't want to believe it and I couldn't speculate on it because I was feeling incredibly happy and enjoying the continuous thrusting happening between my legs by the man I loved. For a moment I remembered a horrible detail. Peter's heartbeat increased, as did his movements. All thought left my mind as I held him in my arms. Warmth exploded through me, in complete euphoria. I looked at his face and knew when he climaxed.

He opened his eyes and to my surprise they were no longer brown. They were a crystal white with a large black pupil. The white seemed to brighten with the intensity of his climax. As I watched, they dimmed as he calmed down and then they faded back to brown. He blinked and smiled with his eyes looking dazed.

"Wow." He pulled my face to his and kissed me gently. I was thrilled with a super big grin on my face.

He didn't die! He didn't die!

But I was only joyous for a moment. His eyes became refocused as he looked at me. Suddenly he jumped off me and sat with his back to the wall pointing at me.

"Your eyes!" he looked freaked.

"Shh Peter, it's okay." I tried to calm him. I closed my eyes and tried to calm myself. I literally felt my eyes change. I opened them again and knew they were back to normal.

"What are you?" Peter asked in a trembling whisper as he tried to compose himself.

"No, it's what *we* are now." I said calmly.

"What?"

I was still happy he didn't die that I wasn't really paying attention to his confusion.

"Don't you feel it? The power? The high? Your eyes went the same colour a moment ago. I'm so glad you didn't die."

I saw his body go rigid at the last sentence.

"What are you-?" he was interrupted by a loud banging on my bedroom door.

"Gabby! Open this door!"

I turned on the spot, "Shit! It's my father."

Forgetting everything, Peter grabbed me close to him and pulled the blanket over us just in time because the door burst open and in walked my father.

"Gabby, did you-?" he froze when he saw us, his question obviously answered.

"He loves me father. I didn't believe you at first about my birthday and me being who I am, but I witnessed it and he didn't die." I blurted out as fast as I could. My father's eyes went wide, he looked furious.

"Father, its okay. I love him." I tried to assure him.

"What's going on Gabby?" Peter whispered.

I turned to him, "I'm not human Peter. I'm a Witchdemon." Peter gave me a look like I just told him I was the Easter bunny and I swear he was considering committing me. Even after the fact he just asked a moment ago 'what' was I.

"If you did not love her, truly love her, then you would have died when you had unprotected sex." My father said stiffly. Peter looked at him and silently deliberated for a moment.

"But I didn't so what does that mean?"

"It means you now possess the same powers as she does. You are half angel and half demon now."

At these words, Peter laughed a little nervously and looked at me, then my father, then back at me. I looked at him with pleading eyes. I didn't understand it myself but I needed him to believe this. Peter looked at my father's serious face and then I saw the click. He quick glanced at me and then back at my father.

"I COULD HAVE DIED?!" he practically shrieked. I almost laughed; it seemed he was accepting it on a certain level.

"This is new for Gabby too. She has just awoken at midnight."

"So what does this mean father?" I asked.

"It means an ancient war is upon us. Demons everywhere would have felt the energy of your awakening. Both of you. But the legends never mentioned the possibility of an actual mate. Are you sure you love him?"

I nearly glared at my father, "Yes, of course I do." Then I remembered something, "What were those preparations you were doing?"

My father sighed, "Both leaders, from the Vampires and the Werewolves, have requested a meeting with you once you've awakened. They have put their differences aside to come together to meet with you."

"Vampires and Werewolves?" sputtered Peter.

My father looked at him, "Yes, and they will be very surprised to see you of course."

"But aren't they evil?" Peter asked. He was so just playing along. Like he had a choice.

"No, not all. Long ago they were the first protectors of the human race. They were demons with souls. They fed upon demonic blood and their teeth held venom that turned the demon to dust once they were finished feeding. Unfortunately, they had free will and were easily corrupted by Satan. The protectors began feeding on humans and the corrupted souls were ripped to pieces. Shrinking slowly with every kill and their humanity dissolved till they were but empty monsters. Till they became the very demons they fed upon before."

My father paused for a moment, "God then punished both species to darkness. Both unable to go out into the sunlight, the uncorrupted that were left blamed one another and fought an endless battle to keep the world safe but kept their distance from each other. The feud between Vampire and Werewolf has been going on for thousands of years. Only coming together every five thousand years for the wars when the energies of Hell over flow to earth's surface. The corrupted still roam the earth and when the uncorrupted are not bickering at one another, they destroy the soulless. Their common goal to this day, is the safety of the human race."

I tried to let that sink in. I also tried not to be uncomfortable with the fact that I was butt naked during this explanation.

"I thought if you get bit by one of them, you turn into one of them." Peter commented.

"No. They mate. The humans they fed on became dust." My father said solemnly.

"So when are we going to meet with them?" I asked.

"Right now actually. They are downstairs waiting."

"Downstairs?" I said with wide eyes, "But this is a church, wouldn't they-?" I started.

"They have souls." Peter whispered to me with the side of his mouth still looking at my father. Okay so he was the expert now? My father took one last look at us and then left the room. Peter looked at me.

"Is this real? I mean, you're right, I feel high as a kite. I feel like I can do anything right now."

"Um, we probably can do anything, but we can discover that together." The thought made me smile. I stroked the side of his face and looked at his hair.

"Huh."

"What?" he looked at me.

"Your grey hair is gone."

CHAPTER FOUR

I could smell them before we even reached the bottom of the steps. Peter's hand was in mine as my father led the way. He had patiently waited outside my bedroom door while Peter and I got dressed. Two, err, men were sitting in the middle of both sets of pews. The one on the left side smelled of earth and fresh plants. It was like walking into a green house. My sense of smell was amazing. The one sitting in the right set of pews smelled like the beach. Like salty sea water, crisp but not overbearing. Both scents had a purity type of quality to them.

They stood up as we approached. The earth smelling one had dark hair and some stubble on his face. He was thickly built, slightly taller than Peter with piercing blue eyes. The other was tall and blonde, clean shaven, a little leaner but also with the same piercing blue eyes. Both were dressed quite impressively.

"This is Luke, leader of the uncorrupted Vampires." My father pointed to the blonde, "And this is Matthew, Alpha of the uncorrupted Werewolves." Pointing to the other.

Matthew nodded and spoke, "I can feel your energy my queen. It is a lot stronger than I have experienced before."

Queen? Experienced before? I looked at my father.

"I told you it's been five thousand years since Vampire and Wolf have come together. This threat of Hell's armies has happened before and will again. Twice before, there was the Witchdemon. There are also her Obedients who lead the three heavenly armies of good to conquer evil. Once each war was over, each Witchdemon and her Obedients gave their magic back to God and lived as humans. The souls and powers were then reincarnated five thousand years later when the time came that they were needed once again. And here you are."

I blinked. "Okay, but he said *queen*."

This time Luke spoke, "Yes, you shall discover your powers which are endless. Nothing can destroy you and you are unable to be corrupted. You are God's ultimate weapon. But I too feel your power is quite stronger than before. Since you've just awoken, the intensity should not be this developed. It is as if there were two of you."

I stared at the blonde Vampire for a second, glanced at Peter, then back at Luke. Luke looked at Peter then back at me. He walked up to Peter and sniffed; his eyes went wide.

"How can this be?" he whispered.

"What do you mean?" asked Matthew.

"They have mated. She has given him her power. He is not one of the Obedients; this is impossible." That last part, Luke stated more to himself than to anyone else.

"He loves me and I love him." I said simply as I looked adoringly at Peter. He smiled at me. I looked at my father who looked noticeably uncomfortable.

"I've never heard of the Witchdemon having an actual mate. This changes everything. We must go and consult the Oracle at once." Matthew hissed.

Oracle? Was I suddenly in the Matrix?

"Calm down gentlemen. I'm sure we can discuss this at another time." My father said nervously.

"There is no time. She must master herself as soon as possible. And him as well." Luke added reluctantly.

"What do you mean?" Peter finally spoke up.

Luke sighed, "Imagine every power possible. Telekinesis, telepathy, basically being able to manipulate anything and everything made of atoms and molecules. To be able to give energy to anything, creating life at its core. Then killing and destroying anything in your path. But of course, there are rules. In your case," He gestured to Peter, "you must only kill demons or evil humans who have no conscience or souls. Even humans can lose their humanity and their souls tear away piece by piece every time they kill or deceive, making them empty monsters and easy targets for demon possession."

Matthew nodded in agreement then took his turn to speak, "You can't go around killing innocent people. Even a murderer can be innocent, given the right knowledge and gifts. But you'll be able to know which have truly repented their sins."

Matthew then pointed to me, "She can't die unless she chooses. But you can, if she chooses. Now that you have the same powers as her from becoming her mate, she is the only person who can kill you. And I think the only way your soul was able to withstand the supernatural energy is because she loves you."

My father interrupted with his own words, "This was never mentioned as a possibility. This war has been fought over and over. We cannot kill Satan but we can banish and weaken him. But the last two wars, since the Witchdemon was created, the armies of Hell were led by his son, Damien. But this, this is unusual."

Luke and Matthew both nodded at my father's words. My father looked at the Vampire and Werewolf, "You must go. The sun will be up soon. Consult the Oracle and we will meet again in seven days' time."

Again they nodded, then turned and left at alarming speed. If I had blinked, I would have missed it.

"This indeed changes everything. The both of you have a lot of work to do."

"What do you mean father? So there's a war coming?"

"Yes, but you will be fine. Along with those gifts mentioned, you also now possess the same strength and speed as the Vampires and Werewolves, which will increase with time. You also feed on demons now. But unlike the Vampires and Wolves, you are able to go out into the sunlight. Unfortunately, there are some demons that can as well. Those humans possessed by the dark forces, infected by evil. I suggest the both of you do some hunting sometime soon. But for now, discover and practice your gifts. We have no time to waste. I will tell you one thing though. You don't have every power imaginable. You cannot shape shift but you are able to change your form."

I was instantly confused. My father smiled at my expression.

"You can change into your angel form, your demon form, and your warrior form which is a complete mix of angelic and demonic powers. Master yourself before you attempt to change your form. Sometimes it is difficult to change back because they require deep emotion. So be aware of yourself. You'll notice you will have to be partially demonized in order to feed. Good luck to you both." He turned to leave but I stopped him before he got to the doors.

"Father, where are you going? And how do you know so much?"

"People need to be aware that you have awakened and updated on the rather new circumstances. As for my knowledge, the legend has been passed down secretly in the church for centuries." He turned and left. I assumed he didn't mean specifically St James Anglican church. I wondered for a moment if every religion secretly knew what happened tonight.

I looked at Peter, "Well, what do you want to try first?"

Peter seemed to be in deep thought, "I've never been a religious person, that was more Linda's department, but I've never even heard of anything even remotely close to a Witchdemon. The ultimate heavenly warrior for humanity that couldn't altogether save the world, but keep it safe enough."

Must be his inner psychologist talking. Mr. Analytical.

"Inner psychologist?" he looked at me.

My eyes bugged out, "Gah! Don't do that!" I giggled.

"You know what I want to do?" He grabbed my waist. A flash of my bedroom appeared in my head.

"No fair! Your practicing gifts without me." I pouted.

"Close your eyes and concentrate on your room. I think we can get there without walking or running like a Vampire." There was excitement in his eyes.

"Okay." I closed my eyes and pictured my room. The memory became so vivid. Suddenly my body felt tingly. It felt as if my bones burst into nothingness, then my muscles followed suit, and then finally my skin. I opened my eyes and looked at my hands. It was as if sand was being lifted off my skin. My skin was the sand, I was watching myself turn into glittering sand. I could still see without the need to blink but I couldn't feel anything.

I could taste the air this way. I floated up the stairs effortlessly to my room, slipping under the door, towards my bed where I reassembled myself. First I felt my skin, then my muscles, and then my bones. All my feeling came back. I finally blinked and watched Peter materialize from a cloud of sand. We were in my room and his eyes went wide.

"I knew it! Ha!" Peter started jumping around the room like a football player that just scored a touchdown. I started laughing hysterically. He spun around looking half crazed. "Do you know what this means? We are the masters of the supernatural elements. We- we-"

"We are basically the king and queen of earth." I interrupted. "But we have to stay a secret, no showing off. We have to be responsible."

For a second he looked like I burst his bubble but then he came over to me and embraced me in him arms. "Of course." He said before he kissed me.

* * *

I awoke over twelve hours later. It was evening again but still my birthday, well, *our* birthday and I was starved.

"Peter?" I turned over to look at him.

"Hm?" He opened one eye to look at me.

"I'm hungry. Should we go out and see what we can find?" His stomach growled at my request.

"That doesn't sound like a bad idea."

We got up and I stood there thoughtfully for a moment.

"What is it?" Peter asked me.

"I wonder...." I mumbled. I picked up the clothes I wore from his house, the Linda clothes, and threw them up in the air. With a flick of my wrist, they froze in mid-air. I concentrated on what I wanted and they began to dissolve into a colourful cloud of sand. The cloud flowed towards me and took shape on my skin as a completely different outfit.

I was now wearing a white spaghetti strap top with a very supportive bra underneath and a black leather jacket. The pants were black jeans with a white fade, and black leather high heeled boots that came up to my knees. I looked at Peter and posed. He raised an eyebrow at me and then grabbed his clothes to do the same. His clothes turned into the colourful sand and reformed on his body as a dark blue dress shirt, black slacks, shiny black leather shoes and a long black coat that looked pretty damned expensive. He looked like he would fit right in with Luke or Matthew.

"Is this too much?" he looked down at himself.

"Nope." I said trying not to look at him. I was seriously rethinking the leaving part and just removing his clothes.

"I heard that." He smiled.

Fuck you, I thought.

Later, he thought back.

Let's talk like this while we're out. I have a feeling we may be watched. I said to him in my head.

Good idea.

We left the church arm in arm. I was disoriented at first. There were so many unexpected thoughts and scents. I had to focus before the thoughts shut off.

Holy fuck, Peter's voice echoed in my mind.

Just focus and tune them out so you can only hear if you want to.

I saw his mind and knew when it worked for him. He kissed me on the forehead.

Okay let's go. I pulled him forward.

There are so many different branches of scents but one lingering common factor that makes the 'human' scent. This is so fascinating. I don't even know how I know that but I do. Peter analyzed.

We walked four blocks when I smelled it. It was a sour, decaying kind of smell and it made my mouth water. Instantly I felt my eyes change. Peter smelled it too; I looked at him and his eyes glowed in the darkness. He nodded in the direction of the smell.

We should repress our energy so they don't run, I cautioned.

Why? They are soulless, they won't get away. We can probably make them do whatever we want.

Peter thought. I knew he was right.

Isn't it rude to play with your food? I teased. *What if there are humans around?*

I don't smell any, do you?

I sniffed, no humans. I shrugged as we stopped in front of an abandoned house. Or so it seemed to be. The scent was overpowering but I knew it would just get worse inside. I was practically drooling.

Do you hear that? Peter's voice inside my head asked.

Hear what?

Listen.

I focused my ears to every sound around me, blocking out Peter's thoughts just for a second before I got the hang of it. Peter squeezed my hand as he felt what I was doing.

Oh wow, there's a bunch of them in there. Now I was seriously starving. *Let's go.*

We both raised our hands and the front door disappeared to sand as we approached and walked through. They were all in the front room sitting around a large polished mahogany table. There were six of them. I noted they were all wearing suits and the inside of the house looked almost elegant if it weren't housing a bunch of demons. I raised my hand and all six shocked faces became panicked as they rose in the sir. They appeared human but one by one their eyes went pitch black.

One spoke to me, "So you're the Witchdemon."

"Yes." I said with a smile, "And I'm very hungry." I felt my eyes change again.

It seems we have to be partly demonized to consume them like your father said. Peter noted in my head.

Very well, I thought to him. I looked at him and I'm sure I looked the same. His eyes were black like the demons in front of us, but as I watched his face change, I felt mine change as well. Veins swam their way from my neck up to the edges of my chin and jaw line. I moved two demons towards us. One of them was the demon who spoke earlier.

"It seems you found one of your Obedients already. All our minds are linked, they all know now. Humans will be slaughtered in the thousands." He said smugly. I cocked my head to the side.

"If that's true, then there's one thing to say. He's not an Obedient, he's my mate."

The demon sputtered as his friends hardly supressed their surprise.

Eat him darling. I thought. Peter opened his mouth in a gruesome like smile, revealing long sharp teeth. He grabbed the demon and bit his neck, ripping the head right off after he gulped down a couple mouthfuls of blood. The demon turned to dust. Peter wiped his mouth and the leftover blood turned to dust as well.

Well that was messy. I thought. Peter simply shrugged.

I have a better idea. I twisted my wrist and the remaining five demons screamed in pain. They spread out their arms and arched their backs as black sand flowed from their bodies. I was pulling the blood right out of them. The blood sand flooded together into a stream which stopped at my other hand that I had raised. The blood pooled into a sphere like shape. The demons burst to dust, untouched by venom but literally bled dry. The orb was about the size of a beach ball. Peter looked impressed.

"Let's drink shall we?" I said aloud.

We both sucked in and the blood flowed into two separate streams to our mouths. The orb slowly shrank till there was nothing left. I felt so energized. There was something salty in the air after we were done which made me turn around to the entrance of the house.

"That was quite the racket." Luke stated as he leaned in the doorway.

"Sorry." I said a little sheepishly.

"Creative technique. I do have to say I've never seen that one before. I didn't know they would turn to dust without the venom. I'm not sure it was smart telling them about your mate though." Luke eyed Peter cautiously. I cracked my neck and felt the veins and teeth disappear. I even felt my eyes go back to their normal brown. Looking in Peter's head without looking away from Luke, I saw his were back to normal too.

"I think we'll be fine." I said completely filled with a cocky attitude.

"Yes but he has family does he not?" Luke pointed at Peter. Peter and I both froze. My smile vanished faster than a cockroach when the light turns on. Mary was with Linda God knows where.

In the States for a few months. She'll be safe. Peter thought to me.

Are you sure about that? I tested a theory; I used my memory of Mary and Linda and projected it to Luke and told them where they were from Peter's memory. *Keep an eye on them please.* I added. I felt Peter relax a bit.

Luke simply nodded. "Well then, happy birthday to you both." And with that, he left.

An idea came to mind. A memory of a dream. Peter saw the memory and turned me towards him. His kissed me while wrapping his arms around my shoulders. My eyes were closed, as were his, but I saw in his mind what he was doing. As we slowly rose into the air, a hole appeared in the ceiling, through to the next level and then the roof. This way we were able to pass through without interruption. We were soaring and spinning in the night's sky with the stars shining just a bit brighter than usual.

And just as before in my dream.

I was truly, madly, deeply happy.

CHAPTER FIVE

It had been three weeks since our awakening and I've never been so connected to someone before. I couldn't believe I lived twenty three years without him. Peter was the blood that flowed through my veins, the air that I breathed. He was my one and only true love. Our minds were one and the purity of our love was indestructible. That may be laying it on thick but in this moment I felt it was an understatement of words that barely described how I felt about him. He had grown some facial hair that made him look so delicious to me, he knew, and he smugly strutted around with me at his side.

Tonight we decided to go to the Rocky Mountains. We wanted to watch the sun set together. Of course we flew there. Peter was wearing all white, making him look exactly what he now half was. I was also wearing white, a dress I saw in a magazine. We were sitting in a small patch of grass at the base of the mountain. The air was cool but temperature didn't bother us anymore.

"I miss Mary." I stated quietly.

"Me too. But for now she's safe until we master our gifts. We have enough time." He tried to reassure me. To which he meant, we have enough time to master our gifts till she comes back from the trip Linda took her on. We were doing amazingly well as far as I was concerned.

"I know." I looked at the Valley below and smiled. "I remember when you went for a shower and she asked me if I was an angel. I guess she has a good intuition." The memories flashed across our minds. Peter smiled too.

"She's going to be thrilled." He whispered.

I felt his mind shut off from mine which made me give him a questioning look. I didn't like that. He put up a finger to make we wait a second as he grabbed a dandelion. He balled it up in his fist for a second before opening his hand to me. In his hand was a beautiful diamond ring. My eyes widened, I heard his heart thunder in his chest.

"Gabriel, will you be mine forever and always? Will you be my wife?"

My whole mind and body were in shock. When the reality of his question hit me, tears came to my eyes. I looked at him.

"Yes, of course I will." I covered my mouth and the tears fell.

"I just wanted to make it official." His mind flashed to my church's altar with us holding hands and staring into each other's eyes. I blushed at the thought. True it never came up in my thoughts because there was no going back right? This was forever, but to actually go through the ceremony and everything, isn't that what every woman dreams about?

Peter grabbed my hand and slid the ring onto the ring finger of my left hand. It had two pink diamonds on either side of a huge blue sapphire that occupied the middle.

"This is our lucky gem. Because we're both Virgo. I used to skim through a bunch of astrology books, even our element is earth. And apparently we like to think we know everything, completely self-conscious and all that." I smiled. The sunset made our white outfits glow.

"How accurate for us." He nuzzled the side of my face, but I froze a couple seconds later. An earthy smell filled my nose as if someone just put a potted plant in front of my face. It was strong but far away, making me think there was more than one Werewolf around. The scent was uncorrupted. Therefore, not food. I listened for a location as it seemed they were getting closer. We both stood for the encounter. One of them I recognized as Matthew, the others had a slightly different version of the Werewolf scent which identified them individually. There were five on the way that included Matthew.

It was hard trying to look in their minds, easy if they were human but I haven't gotten the hang of the supernatural minds just yet. From what I could gather, there was a message from my father. The Wolves took all day to track us. (Which is really saying something since going into the actual sunlight will burn them to a crisp.) Like the demons that Peter and I hunt for food, The Wolves, as well as the Vampires, can link their minds. But only the uncorrupted among the uncorrupted.

They appeared as if out of thin air but with my new eyes I saw everything. Matthew stopped closest to us and bowed low to me.

"My queen, you must come back to your father, he has news to which he has not yet shared, but stressed that your presence in important." He stood up and was flanked by two Wolves on each side. Each one bent down to one knee.

"Allow me to introduce my Guard. From my furthest left to my furthest right. Mark."

Mark stood up when his name was called. Mark was blonde and very pale, he almost looked like Luke's twin, except not as tall and more baby faced. And the fact he was a Werewolf and not a Vampire. All the Wolves had piercing blue eyes by the way. Mark bowed and then stepped back.

"Joan." Matthew's voice was deep and commanding. Joan stood and bowed. She was a beautiful redhead with thick curls that framed her face. She was very well built and her scent was more floral than the others, perhaps because she was female. She stepped back and Matthew continued.

"John."

I was surprised to see this one. John was very dark skinned; the contrast with his eyes was intimidating and beautifully exotic. It made me curious as to where he was from. I probed his mind as he stood and bowed. It seems there were clans all over the world and Matthew was not the oldest, but the strongest. Out of all the clans he picked these four who were the strongest enough to be worthy to be his personal Guard. Not that he needed them but if the numbers were against him they were there for the battle. John was from Egypt, Joan was from France, and Mark was from Scotland. And the last?

"Nicolas." Nicolas stood and bowed. He was from Germany. They all knew English, and as a matter of fact, with all their minds being able to connect to one another, speaking multiple languages is acquired nearly at birth. Suddenly I realized I could easily acquire that knowledge.

"Good evening. You are all just in time. Peter and I have just agreed to tie ourselves together in holy matrimony." I announced.

They all looked uncomfortably surprised for a moment. This irritated me. Peter felt my irritation and became irritated himself.

"Do you not approve of our engagement?" he asked them, "I see it in your mind. You fear this love we share because it is unknown. Even the Oracle could not give you her sure sight as to the outcome of our future."

Matthew sighed, "Yes it concerns everyone deeply."

I stepped in, "I don't care what your prejudices are. If you are to call me your queen, then Peter will be your king. I will not tolerate any mistreatment towards him." I felt my eyes turn crystal white as did Peter's. It was as if to show we meant business if they fucked around. The effect worked perfectly as all five sets of eyes went wide. The Wolves bowed.

"Yes my queen, we will respect him as our king." Said Matthew, "But please, the matter of your father. We ask you to join us on the journey back."

I shook my head, "Peter and I travel much faster alone."

"Very well." Again they all bowed and left at lightning speed. Peter turned me to him, our eyes changing back.

"Shall we?" he asked. I nodded. We closed our eyes and became sand. Shooting to the sky, we travelled the distance in less than ten minutes. We rematerialized in my bedroom.

"Do you smell that?" I asked instantly. It was a demon, slightly sea shore smelling. Must be a corrupted Vampire. Peter and I headed down the stairs and came out from the left side of the altar. My father, Thomas and Luke were in the center aisle of the back pews surrounding the corrupted Vampire who was screaming in agony.

"You have a minute to live before you turn to dust from being in this church. Repeat your message to the priest and I will let you go." Shouted Luke.

"No need. I already know what it is." Peter announced. I looked at him and then heard it myself. Peter was really good at looking into the supernatural mind. Maybe that was a psychologist thing; being all obsessed or fascinated by the mind and just amplified now that he's no longer human. Just left a kid in the candy store, a psychologist that can read minds... I stopped my analysis when Peter looked at me with an eyebrow raised. I smirked and looked at the three men who were now looking at Peter. The forgotten corrupted Vampire gave one last shriek and then burst into a dust cloud.

"Well, what is it?" My father asked Peter.

"Satan's first move is to gather all of the corrupted. Vampire, Werewolf, and even the unsettled spirits."

There was a question that popped into my head that Peter answered instantly.

"Unsettled spirits are imitations of souls. It's the personality imprint of someone, known to most as the 'spirit'. The unsettled are the ones who don't want to or simply can't move on. They become basically like a demon with no shell. It's a corruption that can possess people into doing horrible things. They can only 'pass on' or be destroyed by the light."

"So heavenly powers would work on them." I assumed.

"Yes."

"I still have more questions." I said as I tried to pry. Peter was getting the information from Luke and my father. Peter's words sparked their memories, making it easy to get the information.

"Not many have the answers, the afterlife is very complicated. But as the years go by, the spirits become demon like and their 'personality' disappears. Then they usually require an exorcism. This can also happen if they are too preoccupied by how they died, or with strong emotions such as anger, misery, or sadness. Depending on how they die, the usual outcome is a spirit consumed by sorrow or vengeance."

"Did you see when he'll strike?" My father asked.

"No, or at least the Vampire didn't know that information. It's interesting Luke; I did not know that even though they are pretty much a demon with no soul, you cannot feed on a corrupted."

I looked at Luke curiously, I could have answered my question from Peter's head but I wanted to actually hear it from Luke.

"It is true. Although they are corrupted and demonized, we can't feed on our fellow brothers and sisters. But they can die in other ways. Beheading by a special blade, sunlight, and Holy fire." Luke answered. I saw blue flames in Luke's mind.

"And to kill you?" I asked.

"Pretty much the same except with Hell fire instead of Holy fire."

Red flames. Not the regular orangey red, *blood* red.

"So then a war is coming." I sighed to myself. Duh.

"Yes, and the faster we find the Obedients, the better."

Peter hissed angrily and it took not even a second for me to figure out why. For the Obedients to get their powers, there was only one person who could give it to them in only one way. I was the one to give them their powers, only it had to be the same way I gave them to Peter.

"No. We can do this without them. You are a competent leader are you not? It's been thousands of years." I said.

"Only the specific Obedient can give us back our ability to be out in the sun. Give us back our gifts of flight and Holy fire. Without them, we are not evenly matched. Stronger demons are to surface with your awakening. You leave us to be slaughtered." He said this with no emotion whatsoever.

"But the corrupted can't mate. Haven't you accumulated the numbers?" I asked.

"The more that are born, the more that can be corrupted. Like your humans getting addicted to illicit drugs, the number grows." Luke answered. It was a good answer. Fuck. I felt the urgency but I still shook my head.

"There has to be another way. We will fight them ourselves if we have to but there is no way I am going to sleep with another man and hurt my husband."

They were expecting me to say 'mate'. The word 'husband' startled them slightly like it did the Wolves. Marriage was seriously sacred to these people. The Vampires and Wolves mate for life and my father being a priest; obviously I knew his view on it. Luke controlled himself first.

"When?"

"As soon as possible." I stated as I looked at my father. He sighed in defeat. Peter's thoughts swam through my head. *How fitting, there will be more than enough monsters.* I thought to him. "How about on Halloween?" I suggested with a smile. I projected my little joke to Luke and he smiled as well.

"Interesting. I assume both species are invited?" The smile and lame pun made me see without probing that he was at least considering an alternative to the inevitable battle plan. I thanked him silently and nodded. I suddenly remembered why Peter and I were there.

"Father, what's the message Matthew told us you had for me? He said it was urgent."

He rubbed the space between his eyes before he looked at me seriously, "The Oracle has requested a meeting with you, and your uh, mate."

"Husband." I corrected.

"Not yet," he pointed at me, "She wants to see you both as soon as possible. I also wouldn't try to read her mind, she has mastered her wall; you'll have to be patient." He said this last part more to Peter than to me.

"Alright, when and where?" But Peter knew as soon as the words were out of my mouth. Luke stepped forward.

"I will take you. The location changes every time but I'm sure through my memories you can quickly learn how to find her."

I tried to look as Luke opened his mind for me. It seemed psychic aura had a scent as well. It was a little faded in his memory but I knew I'd be able to recognize a fresh trail. Even psychic auras had slight differences per person and some not as distinct as others. This only happens with humans because some are not altogether aware of their gifts. Normally psychic abilities lie with supernatural creatures and can be identified immediately. With humans though, it was kind of herbal like.

"Let's get going." Luke pointed towards the door.

"Oh! We haven't tried running yet!" I said excitedly. Luke smiled and Peter rolled his eyes.

* * *

We ran at incredible speed to where the Oracle was last seen by my father. When we got there, the scent was a bit faded but stronger than Luke's memory. We were in North Burnaby, in a twisted maze of co-op after co-op. It was like a mini city known to the residents as 'Forest Grove'.

Peter sniffed, "Lucky, it seems she just moved co-ops. Since she's expecting us, why don't we just pop in?" I don't know why Peter felt childishly rude for no reason but I suspected it was the annoyance at dealing with everyone's disapproval of our relationship. Now that I thought about it, I certainly didn't give a fuck if I was being rude either. Luke raised an eyebrow but I knew we'd be able to follow the scent when we were sand. I remember being able to taste the air when I first did it. So rematerializing in front of the Oracle, popping in, was exactly what we did.

* * *

The room was dusty with thick incense in the air. The herbal scent was so strong, I felt as though I snorted a line of chamomile tea. My body automatically felt relaxed when we became whole again.

"Welcome." Said a voice. I was reminded of the octopus witch from The Little Mermaid. She walked into the room with authority and grace. She appraised Peter with curiosity and then looked at me.

"So this is the man that has captured your heart?" It was half statement, half question. She was an elderly African woman who still had great beauty. She had her hair braided down to her waist. She stepped closer to Peter with a look of great concentration on her face.

"I don't see any deception in your love for each other. This situation is so unusual. You have an ancient soul." She said to him, "I wonder who you're supposed to be? I've never been unsure before. But I have a theory. There is the Wicca believe of old. The original story of the Goddess and her Horned God. It is said they existed a millennia ago in actual physical form. The Horned God is committed to the Goddess and to the earth that is her responsibility. But he has descended to the realm of death and darkness. I hope for all our sakes that history doesn't repeat itself if this story is true." She looked genuinely frustrated with this possibility.

I have never heard of this, but then again, the closest I got to mythology was astrology. And yet, I felt she was leaving something out. I haven't mastered reading supernatural minds so even trying to read hers, especially after my father's warnings, would have been futile. For now I had to go with it.

"We need to ask you if there is a way to fight this inevitable war without the Obedients." I asked.

The Oracle looked at me thoughtfully, "Well, technically you could kill the whole army with a blink of an eye. But there is more than one army to fight and many may slip past you. Your actual opponent is Damien, the son of Satan. He is the one who has led the armies before and will want revenge. The dark prince does not travel the surface of this earth unless absolutely necessary and *only* after he is strong enough. The last two wars prevented that, thanks to the previous Witchdemons. And they had *years* of training before the actual wars took place. But in a case like this, I'm afraid that just might happen."

She didn't really answer my question but I heard the warning, which I tried not to take as an insult.

"Okay, but what about the Obedients?"

"They will surface when the time is right. They always do."

Peter spoke next, "What about Damien, can he be destroyed or just weakened like his father?"

"No, he can't be destroyed." She turned to the hallway as we were joined by Luke.

"The Wolves are here but I thought I should consult with you before letting them in. I was expected but I don't think they were." I felt Luke's tension towards the Wolves which I felt was a little out of place since he was okay a few moments ago about their invitation to the wedding, but I guess old habits die hard. I sensed Matthew's mind after that thought, he wanted the Oracle to stop the wedding. He was practically shouting it with his mind, that's how I was able to read it so easily from so far. Peter and I both tensed up.

"Let in Matthew, the rest can wait outside."

They heard her from outside, Matthew was in front of us within the second.

"You must stop this! He should not exist! We need the Obedients! The fate of the world is at stake!" He had no intention of respecting Peter.

Fucking asshole!

I was pissed. I stared at Matthew; my eyes turned crystal white, I pictured his blood on fire. Suddenly he screamed and fell to the floor.

"Gabby stop!" Peter shouted. Matthew continued to scream as his whole body turned red. Blood flowed from his eyes as if he were crying bloody tears. Peter grabbed me by the shoulders and spun me towards him, locking his lips with mine. I forgot everything and felt my eyes change back to normal. Matthew stopped screaming and just lay there on the floor, alive, but unconscious.

Peter released me, leaving me gasping for breath. It was as if he sucked all the anger out of me. I looked at Matthew's body on the floor and felt bad for my behavior. I looked at the Oracle but she was looking at Peter as if nothing had happened to Matthew just seconds ago.

"Interesting. Dangerous, but interesting." She whispered.

"What do you mean?" I was really irritated with myself.

"He has such an influence on you."

Again I felt as if she were giving me a warning. I was starting to lose it again and Peter felt it.

"Maybe we should go. I think there's been enough excitement for one night." Peter suggested.

"Yes I suppose." Said the Oracle, still completely unconcerned that the Alpha of the uncorrupted Werewolves lay unconscious on her floor, "Until next time. The wedding I assume is on Halloween?"

I froze; I didn't feel her inside my head or Peter's. And the fact she even had that ability wasn't brought up.

"How did you...."

"I saw it when he kissed you dear. Sometimes the future flashes before my eyes."

"Oh." I said stiffly. No shit. Oracles generally know the future. I'm stupid because I'm angry. I didn't hesitate any longer. I pushed past Luke to the front door, angry and embarrassed, and left the house. Peter was behind me. The Wolves looked angry and scared but I didn't care.

I want to go somewhere away from here. I thought to Peter.

Where do you want to go? His voice asked in my head. I pictured a beach that was secluded. White Pine. We exploded into colourful sand.

* * *

"I can't believe I did that!" I shouted as soon as I materialized.

"It's okay, you just have to control your emotions a little better Gabby." He didn't like it when I felt this way. Guilty, filled with anguish and sorrow. Feeling ashamed of myself was one of the things he never wanted me to feel. All because he loved me so much. I turned to face him.

"How am I supposed to save the world? I thought I couldn't be corrupted? I almost killed him!" I felt so horrible. Warm tears fell from my eyes. I fell to my knees and Peter fell with me, holding me in his arms as I cried.

"Shhh, it's okay Gabby. I know why you did it Gabby but like I said, we just have to control ourselves. No one expects you to master yourself overnight." He kissed the top of my head and I clung to him. My sobs slowed to sniffles. I rubbed my eyes and pulled away from him. There was a new determination in my thoughts.

"*We* have to do this. We have to show them we can do this together. Just us. No Obedients; No Vampires or Werewolves either if they're too afraid."

I faced the water and raised my arms. With a flick of my wrists, the water rose high into the air, splitting down the middle only a few hundred yards. The water beyond that laid untouched and still touching the sand. But stayed as if an invisible wall kept it in place. I overlapped my arms and the left side rose higher and moved to the right as the right moved under it to the left. After both small bodies of water switched sides, they both landed back on the sand in an explosion of glittering orbs of water, reflecting the moonlight as they fell. A barrier kept Peter and I dry even though the water fell all around us.

"Feel better?" he asked kissing the side of my face.

"Not really, but I think we need to start practicing everything as soon as possible. I remember someone saying we could create life from forming energy. We need to master our transformations of angel and demon in order to use those powers against the armies."

But something was bothering me.

"What is it?" Peter probed.

"The Oracle said we'd most likely deal with Satan himself because of how unusual the circumstances are. In the past two wars, the Witchdemon fought his son, Damien, who apparently wants revenge. Even the corrupted Vampire mentioned it was Satan himself who was gathering the corrupted. I'm just wondering what Damien is up to and why he hasn't made his appearance yet."

"Let's not worry about that right now. We have other things we need to do."

"Like what?"

"We kind of fell off the face of the earth. Maybe we should go back and do some research. Don't you miss Stacey?" he smiled as he kissed me again.

Oh yea, I guess I should give her some sort of explanation for my sudden disappearance.

"Come on, let's go home." He put an arm around me and hugged me tight. Those five words gave me the most comfort because they came from him in a way that stated us as a whole. Home with him is all I'll ever need. Peter wrapped his arms around me and we burst into sand.

CHAPTER SIX

Stacey wasn't too impressed at first by my explanation. I told her the truth of course. It took a couple tries but when I turned into sand and reappeared in front of her in a blink of any eye, stopping her from walking away from me, she forgave me. Well, after her heart restarted. I gave her all the details and even projected some stuff into her head. She adjusted quite well but got a little pissy when I showed her Luke and Matthew.

"What? I can't become a Werewolf or a Vampire? That fucking sucks!" I could hear her mind just drooling over them. "So I guess you're not going to college anymore. You don't really need to take psychology when your mind linked to it. I guess the college will have to find a new teacher."

"No, he still needs to make an income. Even if it is just for show. Since he could just make the money out of thin air but he doesn't need that kind of attention. I can do whatever I want because technically I don't exist. But my father wants me to continue the 'kung fu' shit he says it may help with my concentration. I go back on Monday."

It was Saturday evening and I was spending the weekend over at Stacey's house. Although I was madly in love with Peter, I felt a lot less stressed out when I was with Stacey. We were sitting in the backyard.

"Oh I know! Turn this buttercup into a butterfly. You can channel energy to create life right? Well? Practice! Come on Gabby!"

I knew the idea hit her because she was obsessed with butterflies. They reminded her of her mom.

"Okay let's see." I picked up the buttercup she pointed at and held it in my palm. I concentrated as hard as I could. My eyes changed and I heard Stacey gasp when she noticed. My hand started to tingle as my energy lifted the buttercup up a few centimetres. It started to glow to a bright white, then golden glitter burst from it revealing a white butterfly. Stacey put her hands to her mouth to stifle a sob. I looked at her and saw there were tears in her eyes. I raised my hand and we both watched the butterfly fly away.

"Oh my God Gabby, that was beautiful." I saw Stacey's memory of her mom inside her head and felt the wave of sadness that came over her. Not a depressed sad but a happy kind of sad.

"Oh Stacey," I gave her a hug.

"I'm okay. Seriously, I swear. I just can't believe this is all real. It's so amazing. Can you do it again?"

I pulled away as I smiled and picked up another buttercup.

* * *

So where are you right now? I thought out to him. It was two in the morning and I couldn't sleep. Stacey was passed out cold. I could hear her heavy breathing from the back yard where I stood looking up at the sky. I also heard him chuckle back inside my head.

Can't sleep? He asked.

Not without you, I smiled to the stars, Peter had taken a trip with Luke to Europe where the Oracle claims to have heard about the Wicca story of the Horned God. Luke had been the most supportive of my decision to fight without the Obedients. He wasn't in complete agreement but he didn't argue. He was a good little Vampire. The Wolves however, have kept their distance the last couple days since the incident with Matthew. It was amazing how connected Peter and I was. I was able to hear his thoughts across the world as if he were right beside me.

How's Stacey? He asked.

She's doing okay.

That's good. I'm glad you have her right now. I hate being so far from you. I heard his mind sigh.

You'll be back tomorrow. But I couldn't help but sigh too. I mean, I could easily see inside his head to see where he was and just bam! End up there within minutes. But I noticed it takes a lot of energy to use so much magic and with the constant practicing, I was feeling drained.

Maybe you should go hunt. He suggested at my thoughts.

Good idea. I thought smiling even wider at the sky. *I'll see you tomorrow.*

I turned and jumped high, landing lightly on the roof of Stacey's house. My eyes changed to crystal white and my clothes turned to colourful sand. The sand reformed into a full black leather one piece. Covering me from neck to toe and lifted with high heels. I projected the image to Peter and I heard him groan.

That's not fair. Do you have to look so sexy while you hunt?

Why not? I have a reputation to hold up. Why not look sexy as well as dangerous? I smiled.

Just wait till I get back. He let the threat trail to a very inappropriate image. I could see in his head that he was running through a field. Apparently he was hunting as well.

I'll be waiting patiently. Just do what you're doing and I'll do what I'm doing over here. A memory of us kissing went through my head as I said goodbye and then his mind left mine. I jumped from Stacey's rooftop to the next and so on at such speed no one from below would be able to see me.

In no time I was by the sixth and sixth cross section of New Westminster on the roof of the cinema. Across the street but down the block was the liquor store. A homeless man was sitting outside of it with a cardboard box folded like a blanket over him. It made me sad to see but then a woman came running from around the corner.

"Get away from me!" She screamed. Two men dressed in dark baggy clothing were chasing after her. Their smell hit me full force. They weren't demons yet but their humanity was pretty much shot. In their minds they were planning different ways to rape and then murder this woman. The woman tripped and fell in the middle of the deserted road right in front of the liquor store where the homeless man was. The two men had the sour smell; like a demons but not the decay part. Theirs was more like rotten fruit. The homeless man watched as the two empty men stopped and pulled the woman to her feet. She screamed and struggled. The homeless man got up and ran towards them. I took a step forward to watch. I could have easily done something but I was curious.

"Hey, leave her alone!" He swung at one of the men, hitting empty man #1 square in the mouth busting open his lip. Empty man #1 let go of the woman and swung back at the homeless guy but missed. Empty man #2 also let go of the woman and she took off without a glance back. I looked into her mind and saw she was a prostitute and she had just stolen empty man #2's wallet and didn't want to be caught. The two empty men advanced on the homeless guy. They were going to kill *him* now. This wouldn't be their first kill sadly enough. The smell of their blood became more appetizing.

I jumped high and far off the roof. Halfway down I spun like an ice skater, then did a couple forward flips before I landed in a crouch directly behind them. I would have been proud if anyone was watching, I was kind of showing off a bit but I'll show Peter that memory later. Right now I was hungry. They stopped and looked back at me when I landed.

"Hello boys." I said almost seductively. My eyes went black and my teeth went sharp. I didn't have to be demonized to consume them; they were evil but not demons. I grabbed one man by the throat and bit down on his neck, sucking furiously before my venom could turn him to dust. I pulled back, blood dripping down my chin, and then his body crumpled to the floor becoming a dust pile. The other man tried to run for it and got about half a block before I bolted in front of him, blocking his way.

Before he could even blink, I was on his throat sucking him dry within seconds. He too fell as a pile of dust. I wiped my mouth and looked at the homeless guy. He was frozen in fear at what he just witnessed. I walked towards him and he started to tremble.

"Don't hurt me please!" he fell to his knees. My eyes and teeth went back to normal. Well, my eyes went back to crystal white. I looked in his mind. He was a petty thief and a drug addict but he was good. He didn't even have the slightest sour smell. His thievery was for survival without harming anyone. I gently touched his forehead and he flinched, squeezing his eyes shut in fear of pain.

"Forget." I whispered.

He crumpled to the ground asleep. I felt bad for him. I made him float back to his make shift bed and turned his cardboard blanket into a real one. I also reached out to the street sign, making it detach from the pole, turn into sand, and reform into a bundle of twenty and fifty dollar bills. They floated into his pocket. I sighed. Evil humans weren't as filling as demons. I had more energy though. I turned and jumped back onto the cinema rooftop.

* * *

"Okay so what do you want to do today?" Stacey asked as she cooked herself an omelette. I wrinkled my nose. Human food did not smell as appetizing as it used to. As a matter of fact, the egg smell was kind of turning my stomach. I opened the kitchen window.

"I don't know." I replied, "I was kind of thinking about wedding stuff."

"Oh! I got a couple of wedding magazines we could look at." She offered. When I told Stacey about me getting married to Peter, she begged me verbally and mentally to be 'Maid of Honour'. Like who the fuck else would it be? But for her it was half for title and to be supportive, the other half was to meet the Vamps and Wolves. She was in on everything anyways.

"You know, I think you and Stan should marry A.S.A.P. too. A war is coming remember? And with me as your friend you won't have to pay for anything." I turned to look at her shocked face.

"You mean you would-?"

"Of course I would!" I cut her off. We both started squealing and giggling on the spot. Then she was serious.

"You got to be careful not to let Peter see your dress in your head or it'll ruin everything. Not to mention its bad luck."

I rolled my eyes.

"I'm serious Gabby. Shutting people out might not be a bad skill to master."

Something told me she was right. I felt a little uneasy with that realization but I didn't let it show. I smiled instead. After she ate her disgusting food we flipped through the magazines.

"Oh look at this one!" I glanced up as she pointed to a strapless white gown. There was a lace boarder at the top and two long disconnected lace sleeves that came over the hands like gloves but with no fingertips. The body had a solid slip underneath but it was sort of backless. There was lace edges on the sides that stopped along the ribs.

Here there were holes for a thick white ribbon that connected the sides to the back in a corset like look. The dress stopped just under the shoulder blades, so just under the pits of the model. The ribbon continued on its own to the back of the neck where it was tied in a bow. The bow tied a lace choker around the models neck where a heart shaped pendant hung in the front with a blue sapphire in the middle. It was perfect. I looked at the front and back photos and then closed my eyes to concentrate. My clothes did the sand thing and within seconds I was wearing the dress. The gown was silk. I even added the white heels which also held a lace design like pattern around the foot. Stacey jumped up and flapped her hands in excitement.

"Oh my God! Do this one next!" she picked up the magazine and flipped through it expertly till she got to the bridesmaid section. "I want to wear this!" she practically shoved it at me. I laughed. It was dark blue with one sleeve that only covered the shoulder. On the same side as the sleeve there was a slit in the gown that went all the way up to the hip. The dress was tight fitting around the breasts and waist but the gown flowed a foot behind the model.

I focused on Stacey's clothes and raised my hand. Stacey gasped as her clothes turned to sand and formed the dark blue dress to her body. When it was finished, she squealed. "Gabby, I love it! Thank you!" She spun on the spot. But then she started to frown.

"What?" but I already knew.

"I'm going to be the only human there. Well, besides your father and Thomas. I wish *I* was something."

I thought about something like that when I first smelled Stacey with my new nose. "Speaking of that, I think there may be something in you."

Her eyes widened, "Really? Don't fuck around Gabby. Like what?" I heard her heart beat a little faster. I explained to her the difference in scents; human, Vampire, Werewolf and the psychic aura energy with its own scent in humans.

"I smell something herbal off you but it's mostly like a spice. Also, you have that same pull, or rather, influence over people like I do. Remember our man hunter nights?"

She rolled her eyes and smiled.

"Anyways," I continued, "I noticed you kind of smell like cinnamon and sage."

She looked at me skeptically and then comically smelled her armpit. "No I don't."

I laughed. "Trust me, you do. I can't give you powers but if you already have gifts that you're not completely aware of, I might be able to give you some energy to enhance them."

"Are you serious?" her eyes went wide again.

I nodded, I was quite serious. She held her hand out to me and I grasped it in mine. The first thing I did was focus in on the flow of her blood. "Open your mind and let me see everything okay?"

She didn't answer, she just obeyed. All of her memories flooded into my head. Every thought, secret, and emotion transferred to my mind. It was weird that there were times where she was envious of me back when I was under the impression I was human. I usually envied her. Then I saw it. The pattern of coincidences in her life when life altering things happened. She had slight premonitions before those thing occurred. I saw her hug her mom for the last time and felt her say goodbye with her heart rather than just her mind.

She knew her parents were going to die. Premonitions were part of her gift.

I felt my energy flow through the cells of my skin to go through hers. In her mind I felt her hand grow tingly till it spread across her whole body The significant herbal scent became more prominent and her cinnamon and sage smell filled the air. I let go of her hand. Once the tingling in her body faded, I knew what she could do before she did.

I knew if she wanted to she could shut her mind off from me. Her premonitions happened through touch and she could force her will onto others. Her influence on others got enhanced. I projected my knowledge of her skills to her.

Wow, she thought.

She didn't have telepathy but since I could import and export thoughts from her head, communication became easy like that, and she got the hang of it. Unless she cut me out of course. She touched my hand but nothing happened.

"Um…. I got nothing." She said aloud.

"That's probably because it's me. You probably can't do it to Peter either but we can practice with other people."

"Oh! Let's go out! I want to try!" she looked at me with pleading eyes.

"Okay, okay." I gave in quickly.

"Oh, but first let's put on these!" she showed me more outfits, this time from a fashion magazine.

* * *

We were at Moody Park, also known as Murder Park for some very unfortunate reasons. But right now though, the weather was nice and there were children playing at the playground. Behind the playground was a basketball court. We sat at the bleachers to the other side of the court. Actually playing basketball were five middle aged looking men. Not one of them was in a relationship, of course I only checked initially because that was the first thought in Stacey's head, and then I became curious too. Old habits die hard. That and two of the guys were pretty hot.

"They're all single." I said to her.

"Yea but we're not." She pouted.

"But we can still have some fun." I actually wanted to see her skills in action. One of the men, the hot ones, noticed us. He was easily the hotter of the two now that we saw his face dead on. He had brown hair and brown eyes, a bit of a hairy chest-topless in October- he seemed to play a really hard game and was getting a good sweat going. His mind was a little interesting, very motivated and positive. A bit of a perfectionist. He smiled, we waved.

He was in his mid-forties and his name was Michael. All of a sudden he looked seriously confused as he stiffly made his way towards us. It was Stacey. She was willing him to come over. Interesting. She can force her will to make anyone do anything yet they were completely aware of themselves with their mind in-tact. Technically, God gave everyone free will to think, not to move. I saw in his mind he was confused because he had no intention of coming over himself. His body just had a mind of its own; Stacey's. He was only confused for a second, then he just went with it as if the decision were his own. He started to smile again with a little more confidence.

"Uh, hi." He had a deeply seductive voice. Stacy's belly squirmed. Her thoughts went seriously inappropriate. He looked like he was going to move forward but stopped.

Careful Stacey! I warned in her head. *He might actually do what you're thinking!*

This, was basically; fucking the shit out of her right here and now. She giggled.

"Hi." She said innocently to him. I could see in his head his body urging to do it but Stacey was just toying with him.

That's not nice Stacey, you're going to give him a complex, I thought to her. She giggled again. I heard him mentally question what the joke was once his body relaxed. But right away he felt nervous. And a bit like a pervert. (With the body urging on its own, the lower parts were at full attention during the episode. Now it was gone.)

"My name is Stacey, and this is Gabby." She pointed to me when she said my name. He looked at me and I heard his heart accelerate. He swallowed.

"Um, I'm Michael." He said stupidly. I was flattered by his attraction to me and back in the day I would have hooked him in, then kicked him to the curb hours later. But given my current situation and love life, I was just not interested.

"Nice to meet you." I said politely.

"You know what? I'm thirsty, are you thirsty Gabby?" Stacey interrupted. I thought about it for a second, I don't think he would like it very much if *I* was thirsty. But then I took in her tone. I knew right away she was irritated at Michael for showing obvious interest in me instead of her so I nodded.

"Go to the store and buy us both an energy drink okay Michael?" Stacey told him.

"What?"

"Now!" She demanded.

Like a puppet, he stiffly walked across the street to the store, thank God there was no traffic, and came back to us with two energy drinks in his hands. He looked seriously freaked. I sighed, stood up as he handed me mine and wiped his forehead.

"Forget." I said.

He didn't pass out like the homeless guy. His eyes went out of focus and then came back. He turned and went back to his friends who asked him what happened. He looked back at me and Stacey.

"I don't know." I heard him say. I looked at Stacey with an eyebrow raised.

"What?" she shrugged.

I rolled my eyes.

* * *

He was getting closer. It was one thirty in the morning. Stacey was dreaming about butterflies. I didn't want to intrude but I wanted to make sure she was sleeping. I wanted to change my form tonight. I had a pretty good feeling the emotion I needed to channel was 'Love'. For the angelic form anyways. I could feel his mind for a second then I disconnected again. My other senses heightened. We always had a slight connection, but since my discussion with Stacey and the wedding stuff, I had cut it off completely. There was a trace of his scent in the air. I could even feel his energy grow nearer.

"Gabby?" He spoke from behind me. I turned to him smiling. He looked unsure. I could see it bothered him being unconnected. I put up a finger to stop him from walking towards me. He went from unsure to concern. I raised my hands outwards slowly from my sides to the space above me. An invisible barrier only Peter and I could see surrounded the house and backyard. Making us invisible to anyone who looked our way.

"I want to change into my angel form." I announced.

"Are you sure?" He still looked hurt.

"Oh. I cut you off so you can't see the wedding plans." I smiled.

He let that sink in and then closed his eyes and smiled to himself. He opened them and looked at me.

"Um....okay."

"It was Stacey's idea." Just throw her under the bus, I said to myself with a smirk,

"Okay so what brought on the need to change your form?"

"I just want to try okay? I think the deep emotion I need is 'Love' and with you here....." I trailed off, "With you here it may be easier, just let me show you how much I love you." I batted my eyes at the last part, making him smile and roll his eyes. I walked over to him now. I put my finger to my lips to silence him because he was about to speak.

"Let me concentrate."

He nodded.

I spread out my arms towards the ground, focusing on the buttercups that littered the lawn. I focused on the life inside them. I was trying to get into the transformation zone before changing myself; get the magic flowing first. Or that was the theory anyways. My eyes changed to crystal white. The buttercups glowed then sparkled. I flicked my wrists upwards and they burst into white roses. Their vines grew and conquered the lawn in seconds. Hundreds of white roses popped out of the ground I raised my arms and just the heads of the roses flew up and surrounded us.

I made fists and then thrust my fingers out, making the rose heads explode into petals. I made swirling motions with my arms in the air and the petals surrounding us began to move clockwise around us as if we were in a giant snow globe. I reopened my mind to Peter. My skin started to glow as I remembered the first kiss I had with Peter and the confession I made to him. I felt energy pulse through every cell in my body. My clothes glittered to sand and became a white dress that was backless, but came up around my neck in the front to it wouldn't fall off.

The gown part floated around me and looked as if it was just a mist. It clung closely to my curves, but it looked as though wisps of fog surrounded me. I remembered our birthday when we awakened together and the gentle touch of his fingers on my skin. My heart suddenly felt as though it were pumping thick liquid.

Then I felt the pain.

I crumpled forward as I felt it pierce two places on my back. It felt like I got stabbed in each shoulder blade. A warmth came from these spots and slowly fell down my back.

"Gabby!" Peter stepped forward but I raised my hand to stop him.

"No, stay back for a minute. I'm okay." I closed my eyes and continued the memory of Peter in my arms. The pain shot down my back as if two claws were ripping my back to shreds.

I knew the warm liquid was my blood. It didn't stain the dress that floated around me, which is a bit of a fucked up thought to think at a moment like this. I looked inside Peter's head and saw for myself what was happening. I remembered the tears I almost shed when I first saw Peter walk to his car and the longing of not wanting to be parted from him. I remembered the tire swing dream and the heavy heart I felt afterwards. Then I felt my shoulder blades stretch.

In Peter's mind I saw two impossibly white bones shoot out form my back. They curved up at first then shot downwards in an arc. They were wings. They looked like growing branches; the way they suddenly split fork like, only they were growing downwards. My back tingled as it started to heal around the base of the bone. The pain was gone. One by one, little white feathers appeared at the base of the bone. They spread and got bigger as they went along the bones. Till finally, I stood up and the transformation was complete.

My wings were huge, like, fifteen feet each. My body was in a permanent glow the entire time I was changing form. I knew I could access Peter's mind but he could no longer access mine. The rose petals still twirled around us. I opened my eyes to look at Peter. He was in awe.

"I love you." I said.

"I see that."

I raised my arms up and as I did, my wings spread high above me. I slammed my arms down through the air. My wings mimicked the motion and exploded into thousands of white butterflies, taking Peter by surprise. They flew to him and landed all over his body. The rose petals fell to the ground and disappeared with the vines. The butterflies glowed with my energy. My dress disappeared as well and my original clothes reappeared. Peter reached his hand out to me. I grasped it and he pulled me close to him. With a kiss to my lips he made the butterflies fly into the night's sky.

CHAPTER SEVEN

Today, there were three days till the wedding. The Wolves received their invitation a few weeks ago, and agreed to show, the day after I went to Matthew to apologise. I had surprised him by suppressing my energy; I've gotten really good at expanding my energy and holding it in. He didn't realize I was there until I was almost directly behind him. (Oh, I informed Peter of Stacey's gifts and he wasn't surprised either, because he too noticed her scent when he dropped me off that weekend before he went to Europe with Luke.) But yea anyways, I went to Matthew to apologise for my behaviour. When he finally noticed he was no longer alone, he spun around. When he saw me, he bowed.

"What do you want?" he asked almost rudely as he straightened up. His demeanor made me feel worse.

"I came to apologise for almost killing you a few weeks ago."

"It wasn't the most comfortable experience but it was my fault. I had promised to respect your mate, then betrayed your trust. I deserved the punishment. I let my biased opinion override my loyalties to you. So it is I who must apologise to you."

I felt his guilt. I wasn't expecting that. I stepped over to him and placed my hand on his cheek. I projected my love for Peter and Peter's love for me.

"I understand your fear and I forgive you. But please don't ever think my behavior was okay. I truly appreciate your devotion to the cause, but know that I love Peter."

Matthew nodded at my words. "Yes, I see that. I'm sorry I doubted you my queen."

I then personally invited him and his Guard, and the rest of the clan that resided in B.C. "We will howl to the moon the night of your wedding."

Howling to the moon was sacred. Songs saved for celebrations and deaths. I was touched by the offer. The Wolves were not stereo typed to change only during a full moon. They could change at will at any given night, and day when they had their gifts, except when the moon is new. Their strongest change is the solar eclipse where they can come out in the technical daytime without their gifts. Weird because the real sunlight right now would turn them to dust. Lunar eclipses were strong for them too but mainly used for mating though. I left Matthew and went back home. So yea, that was a couple weeks ago. Now it was three days till the wedding.

About a week ago, for a few days I was super popular at my 'kung fu' class. I wasn't trying to show off, it's just everything got to be too easy. Now that I'm super focused and can read people's minds, I'm sooo much better than everyone. But like I said, I wasn't trying to show off. It's just that Charlie the Amazon had put fear into everybody and she was just itching to do the same to me. On my last day there I put her in her place.

I knocked her on her ass and had my stick on her throat in ten seconds. I smirked as she glared at me. James clapped in amazement. His admiration was flattering but he was secretly suspicious of my skills. I looked at him when his thoughts hit me. I was kind of having a hard time around him those few days. Not from my dream or any attraction, it was his scent. It was a little herbal like the psychic aura but earthy like a Werewolf. But then something else, like a fresh garden with something sweet in the mix. Only a fraction of his scent had the 'human' fragrance. It confused me. If he had psychic powers, I didn't see his abilities in his head. As a matter of fact it was a little hard for me to even see in his head.

No memories or patterns of unexplained occurrences. Weird. Then it hit me. Could he be? I shook my head. No, I wasn't going to go there. Class ended and I wasn't satisfied.

Well, I don't think I really need to come back here anymore, I thought to no one but myself. I walked up to James to tell him my decision when he looked at me dead in the face. My dream of him took full force in my head. I froze. What the hell?

"Um, I think I'm going to quit class." I said quickly.

He looked disappointed, "Why?"

"I just have a lot of personal things coming up." I explained. I saw him look me up and down and heard his thoughts. I almost looked at him incredulously. The guy was checking me out and memorizing it! He was going to miss me a little more perversely than I thought. This mind reading thing was too much sometimes.

"Well, good luck to you then." He sighed.

I turned away from him and saw in his head that he was checking out my ass as I walked. I looked back just in time to see him turning away with a smile on his face.

Fucking perv! I flicked my hand in his direction and all the weapons that were hanging on the wall behind him fell to the ground.

"Ah shit." He muttered.

I felt slightly satisfied and left.

* * *

Peter had had quite the few days too. That girl I spoke to that one time had been flirting with Peter the first couple days. Peter tried to ignore her inappropriate comments in class but she wouldn't quit. Finally she gave him her number and he thoroughly embarrassed her by laughing and announced in front of the whole class what she did and that he was not interested. The poor girl quit the next day. I think he was a little harsh now but when he told me I was almost furious. Peter had taken a couple of weeks off for the wedding and well... the honeymoon.

Matthew and his Guard and what was left of the Southern B.C. clan showed up last night and I introduced them to Stacey. There were only twelve in the clan. Then I found out they were the only ones left in all of B.C. Usually there are clans in every city, and about fifty in each one. Unfortunately. B.C. seemed to be almost wiped out; most were corrupted making the clans ban together. Five of the twelve were children.

Stacey took Matthew's hand with a smile but I saw something flash in her eyes. I looked and saw his death. She looked at me with fear in her eyes. He was burning in the sunlight screaming like he did when I made him bleed from the eyes.

Just recollect yourself, I said in her head.

Matthew paused and looked from her to me.

"Is something wrong?" he asked her. She looked at him again and smiled.

"Oh no, I just remembered something." She said aloud. *Come talk to me in a bit, I'll be in your room.* She thought to me.

Matthew looked after her as she walked away.

"Is she a psychic?" he asked.

"Yes."

"What did she see?"

I sighed, "You death."

He stared at me for a second. His Guard looked uneasy. John's eyes darted around, looking at everyone suspiciously.

It was Joan who spoke up, "How?"

"The sun." I answered.

The Guard's minds were littered with many thoughts at once. Matthew wasn't paying attention to them. Their mental commotion got Peter's attention. He was conversing with my father by the altar. Matthew pondered my response more rationally.

"Does she know when?" Nicolas asked.

"No." I lied. It was going to be a week after the wedding. I saw in Nicolas's mind that he was the adopted Alpha next in line. Matthew had no children. John would fight Nicolas for it and John's mind exposed his different strategies. Even though their minds were connected, they could pick and choose which ones were transferred.

It seemed they weren't entirely loyal to their leader if they were already planning his replacement at the news of his impending demise. That's why I lied. Peter was at my side then.

"Maybe you should go talk to her." He said. *Silently, many gifted ears are around.* He said in my thoughts.

"I'll see you in a bit." I said after kissing Peter on the cheek before I left.

* * *

"Stace?" I knocked on my bedroom door before opening it and poking my head in. She was sitting at the foot of my bed in a daze. I walked over to her. Her mind was cut off from me. I waved my hand in front of her face. Nothing. She was moving her lips but no sound came out.

"Stacey?" I said again but she was seeing something else and didn't hear me.

Peter! You better come up here, it's Stacey; she shut me out. She's somewhere else in her head and she's not responding to me! I thought as loud as I could. I felt him wince. He excused himself and was at my side in a fraction of a second. He cupped his hands around her face and looked into her unblinking eyes. Then I saw it in his head. Matthew was childless but had a mate. The death of his mate will cause him to commit suicide. His mate was in Egypt trying to locate something. The information was limited.

But her death happens quickly and as soon as her mind shuts off from his, he walks outside to the very next sunrise. I put my hand to my mouth. The vision plays again and again. Peter realizes that Stacey is trying to figure something out but got mentally trapped in the vision.

Help her! I silently scream. He closes his eyes with his hands still on her face. I watch as his energy flows from his finger tips to her temples. She blinks.

"Holy shit Gabby." She whispers.

Don't speak, think. Too many ears right now. I thought to her. The minds downstairs were curious.

Get some rest Stacey. Peter thought.

She nodded and moved back on my bed to lie down.

I don't know if I'll be able to sleep. She thought to me.

Let me help. I walked over and touched her left cheek. He eyes closed and she was asleep within seconds.

* * *

Today, it was Luke's turn to meet Stacey. Well, tonight. She was nervous at first. We were all downstairs in the basement where the Wolves were staying until the wedding.

Fuck he's gorgeous. She thought to me. She was normally a sucker for blonde guys. Stan had dark hair though, I never understood that. But he had the blue eyes that made her squirm, so I guess that's all that mattered. Luke smiled as he shook her hand.

Luke, like most Vampires, was a loner. No mate. Vampires usually travelled alone or in pairs with their mate. Once in a while you'll see the odd Vampire child with them but they usually left their parents once they hit their teenage years. Vampires weren't very family oriented as Werewolves. Nor as fertile. Very rare would Vampires have more than one child. While Wolves would have, well, *packs*. Four of those five kids were from one couple.

Stacey let go of Luke's hand and went quite the shade of red. I nearly lost it. The urge to laugh was so strong, even Peter had trouble controlling himself. He had to pretend a coughing fit. Looks like Luke won't be single for long. Stacey saw him right in the middle of pretty much making a baby with a very pretty brunette. She had an exotic look from what I could see in Stacey's vision. Olive toned skin and looked as though she was enjoying herself *very* much.

Luke looked at Stacey amused. "Is there something wrong?" he asked. She shook her head. Luke squinted at her and sniffed. "You're a psychic aren't you? What did you see?"

Stacey went even redder. I couldn't hold it in, I started to giggle.

"*You* tell him!" She said embarrassed and made a bee line for the stairs. The Wolves watched her go. I looked at Luke and projected the images to his mind.

He laughed, "Ah, I see." He looked around. Across the room, in the comer, were *his* Guard. Well, members of his *Court* to be exact.

The Vampires worked more like a government. Kind of like the seating arrangement of the United Nations. The inner circle was the most elite with Luke at the core. The middle circle of fifteen and the outer circle of twenty. Then there was fifty independent leaders of smaller countries and regions who report to the 'government' every now and then. The rest just keep patrol on demons and the corrupted or just make babies. The Vampires from his Court weren't very friendly about Peter and I. But their fear of me is what kept their mouths shut. And they were all seriously old. They've all been in the same rank since they were created. Nearly twenty thousand years ago. I tried to wrap my head around that.

Obviously they were led by Luke's father at first but no one before that. The Court members and Luke's parents were the only ones that actually *looked* old. Vampires grew to the age of thirty something and then stopped aging. Their hair and nails grow and they mate but once they hit the certain age, they're frozen in time. One fact is that they're kind of like snakes. They don't shed their skin in a gross fashion but they are constantly regenerating new cells. Their minds can withstand centuries of information and their memory is photographic.

As for Wolves, they have good knowledge but have to write it all down to be passed on. Except their instincts and new fighting techniques, that gets acquired while in their Wolf form. They reach their twenties but then after about twenty three normal human years they only age one after every actual five hundred or so. Almost like the laws of our common knowledge of actual dog years, reversed and set sideways.

I was lucky enough to gather all that information in a tenth of a second, just from the minds in this room. I didn't know the mind could have so many thoughts at one time and we be only aware of a couple in the moment.

Look who's acting all psychologist now. Peter teased in my head.

Luke was looking at the members of his Court but he was still smiling.

"Well, we must be getting back to our dwelling before the sun comes up." He stated.

They were staying at the Roman Catholic Church just a few blocks away.

"See you at the wedding." He bowed and motioned to his Court. They all stood simultaneously and left. My father was originally from that Catholic Church and pulled some strings. He posted Thomas over there to keep watch. I sighed as Peter kissed my cheek.

"I have to go." He said.

"I know but I don't want you to." I moaned.

My father and Stacey had banned together and forbade Peter and me from having sex till the wedding. So Peter has been staying at the Roman Catholic Church with the Vampires and I was bunked with Stacey. I was counting down the hours. Fifty eight left to go. I was actually just being polite. If I wanted to, I could take Peter and turn to sand, end up across the world and fuck him till my hearts' content.

Peter had sided with them at first so I reluctantly agreed. But now we were cheating. 'Mind fuck' had a whole different meaning to me know. At first I was going to be sadistic to get him back for siding with my father and Stacey. The psychological warfare. I believe I mentioned his days were numbered? It would have worked if he wasn't a damned psychologist and mind reversed me a second time. I swear his memory is confused with his past porno watching days.

Because, somehow, he had me in some pretty crazy positions that I'm pretty sure we didn't do.....yet. Anyways, tonight we did our usual 'mind fuck' but something changed. Something triggered my memory of the dream I had before I physically met Peter. I tried to shut it off before he noticed.

What was that? He thought

Um....nothing. I said quickly.

Don't lie Gabby. Tell me. I won't get mad. He knew I was lying because he felt my guilt.

It's just an old dream I had before I met you.

Let me see. He pressed.

I hesitated for a second, *okay......* I took him through the whole dream. Joseph and James included. Then I took him through the whole next day.

Hmmm, he said. The rest of his mind was cut off.

What? What are you thinking? I was so nervous.

Is that why you looked like you saw a ghost when I met you? His memory of me nearly falling out of my chair went through my head.

Yes.

Hmm.

Will you stop doing that? Tell me what you're thinking!

Well, he started, *the other guys are way younger and more capable of taking care of you, yet you chose me.*

I rolled my eyes. He pondered this but he was a bit smug about it.

Of course I did. I love you Peter.

I love you too.

We continued to cheat till the sun came up.

* * *

"Oh my God! This place looks so beautiful!" Stacey exclaimed. It was the day of the wedding and the church was covered in dark blue fabric and white roses. To accent Stacey's dress and my dress. And I loved white roses, it was my favourite flower. White rose petals covered the floor. There was a dark blue carpet and the pews had dark blue cushioning. I didn't want to make it too complicated. Everything was pretty simple. Candles were lit, giving the petals a glow. There was no artificial light, in the 'electricity' sense. The glow was kind of kick started by me but no one really needs to know about that.

I made the ceiling and windows sparkling clean because no one had cleaned them in a million years it seemed. The reception was going to be in the basement. Everyone was doing some last minute hunting. It was almost midnight. I just got back an hour ago from consuming some crack head that just beat his girlfriend to her last breath. He actually believed it was her fault she was now dead. He had no remorse. So I beat him purple before I bled him dry like I did those demons the first time I fed. I put up a barrier so no one heard his screams.

His soul was still there when I drained him. It was small and fading quick. I wondered what that meant. I wondered of that would affect me. The soul floated up to the sky and disappeared. His girlfriend's death was his first kill but not his first act of abuse. I shook doubt from my mind, he deserved what he got.

I finished putting up the last of the roses and linked arms with Stacey and went up to my room to get ready. I knew when everyone returned because I could smell each and every one of them. Peter was still at the Catholic Church with Luke. Luke's Court and the Wolves sat at opposite sides. The wolves chose to sit on the groom's side, probably because Peter didn't try to kill their leader nearly a month ago, not because they supported any of this.

Luke ended up being Peter's best man which I thought was very sweet.

I went rigid as two humans walked in, that's what I thought at first. One was actually salty sweet smelling.

"Stacey?" I started.

"Yes?" she was putting her hair into a braided bun.

"Why is Stan *and* Joseph here?" I had looked into their minds for identities. She froze.

"I invited Stan because he is my fiancé. Don't worry though, he doesn't know anything." She added quickly.

"And Joseph?" I pressed.

"Um, I don't know why *he's* here."

I probed the minds downstairs. It seems Stan and Joseph have given their friendship the 'bro' status. And Stan invited Joseph so he wouldn't be alone. Also it looked like Joseph was going to be Stan's best man. From the 'friends' I've met in the past, I think he made a decent choice, and I don't even know Joseph.

"Well, it's okay I guess." I allowed. No one else downstairs seemed to notice Joseph's particular smell.....shit, don't think about it Gabby. I twirled my finger and gave her the hair she was looking for.

"Thanks." She said.

My hair was chestnut brown. I did the sand thing to our clothes and our dresses appeared perfectly molded to our skin. Our make-up was perfect. My hair was curled but pinned to my right side flowing low below my breast. I couldn't change my form but I could adjust things like length and colour. There were little plastic white butterflies decorated in my curls. My eyelashes were longer too and thick with mascara. I had to darken my eyebrows a bit but I kept the makeup simple and subtle. Nothing dramatic. Slight bronzer with the mascara and a small amount of gloss.

Now Peter walked into the church. He instantly noticed Joseph's scent, it was herbal and salty sweet and only a fraction smelled human but he didn't think what I was thinking. Which I kept from him. I was getting really good at the mind thing but it was making me nervous and a little guilty. His mind was more on the wedding.

I shut off completely as I looked in the mirror at myself. I touched the silver heart and stroked the sapphire.

"Well, we might as well start." I heard my father say to Thomas. My father was going to walk me down the aisle and Thomas was going to marry Peter and me. I peaked in Thomas's head as he went downstairs. Everyone was in place. I kind of wished Mary was here. She would have made the cutest little flower girl.

"Okay Stacey, they're waiting for us."

Joan was an excellent pianist. She took the liberty of playing a song her mother had wrote when she was young. It was beautiful. I made my way down the stairs, arm in arm with my father-who I had found right at the doorway when I opened my door- and Stacey ahead of us. There was a corridor at the bottom of the steps, there was a doorway to the altar on our left where Peter stood out of sight, but we went down the corridor which moved all the way the fuck around the pews, so I could walk down the aisle. It was covered from eyes but I'm sure everyone could hear us anyways.

The music slowed when we got to the opening just behind the pews. Stacey went out first with her mini bouquet. I waited till she was at the altar, and right on time with my footsteps, 'here comes the bride' started.

My father was holding my left hand, so when we came out at first he was blocking everyone's view of me. Then we turned to walk down the aisle and I heard every mind was impressed. Total ego boost. But my main concern was Peter's mind. His heart beat a little faster but he wasn't letting me inside his head.

My father placed my hand in Peter's and I heard his heart flutter. Thomas cleared his throat and started. Peter chose a simple white tux with a white rose in the pocket. He was sporting his facial hair along the jaw line and around his mouth in a goatee. We got to the vows part, we had written our own, and Peter started.

"Since day one, I had you on my mind. I couldn't believe the emotion and curiosity you created in my head. I was alone and broken for a very long time. I never thought I'd be able to pick up the pieces, let alone feel as whole as you make me feel today. When I first met you, everything changed and I felt like I could live again. With you by my side I promise to keep you warm in the cold, happy in the darkness, and never let you go."

His mind opened up during his vow. I was shocked at first. Not from the words coming out of his mouth, but the fact he was totally winging it. The fucker didn't write his vows last night. He smiled at me and I shook my head with a smile of my own. Then it was my turn. I at least wrote mine and memorized it.

"The feeling you bring, to the depths of my soul, is serene. And I will do anything to keep that feeling. I promise to treat you with dignity and equality. I promise to give you my complete honesty and loyalty. I'll love you for as long as I live."

And I meant it. We said our 'I do' to each other and put on the rings. Finally we kissed. I was sort of prepared for it because Peter's emotions were in total overdrive, but everyone else wasn't prepared for it at all.

The moment our lips touched, I saw in Peter's mind the searing pain in two spots shoot down his back. He knew what to expect from my experience, the pain caused him to pull me deeper into the kiss. His body glowed bright enough to light the whole room. The white bones burst from his back, ripping his tux to shreds. The bones were covered in leathers in an instant.

He was so overjoyed at our union, that I was officially his forever, that his emotions highjacked him into his angel form. I was so touched I went with it. Got totally caught up in the moment that I started glowing too. It wasn't as painful this time and it happened a lot taster. His wings were bigger than mine by five feet each wing.

Our mouths parted and we looked adoringly at each other for a few seconds with crystal white eyes.

"What *the fuck*?!" Stan yelled.

CHAPTER EIGHT

Joseph didn't look as surprised as Stan. Luke sniffed the air, he didn't notice before because his mind was preoccupied by the wedding and Stacey's vision. Now he noticed Joseph's scent and his eyes went noticeably wide. Joseph looked from him to Peter. Our wings exploded into white butterflies. Peter was mad. My suspicions were true. Joseph was an Obedient and by the smell of him through Luke's memory, he was the one to lead the Vampire army. Peter went to step towards Joseph but I stepped in front of him. No one, not even the Wolves knew what Joseph was. Not even Luke's Court members. Luke recognised the scent from long ago.

Just keep it between us. I thought to Peter and Luke. But the fact that Joseph wasn't surprised at what he just saw made me curious. It seems he was already sensitive to different energies. But just because he wasn't surprised doesn't mean he wasn't scared shitless. Stan on the other hand was petrified. I turned around to look at them. I raised my hand and they both fell asleep on their feet.

I looked at Stacey, *You should take them to your place. I think I erased their memories. Make it seem as though they got really drunk and crashed.* I thought to her. I flicked my wrist and their tux's turned into party clothes. I made them both float and Luke helped Stacey take them to the doors. Luke glanced back at me, *Take them all the way to her house and help her put them inside on the couch or something. Then both of you come straight back,* I continued.

They waved a hand before they left; tugging along the floating Stan and Joseph. Peter and I looked around the room; the Vampire Court and the Wolves eyed us suspiciously.

"The reception is in the basement." I said a bit coldly. They took the hint and left for the basement in a blink of an eye.

Calm down, I thought to Peter as I turned to face him again. He was remembering the dream I showed him. My mind flickered.

You smelled it on James too! He accused.

Yes and then I quit the class if you've forgotten! Don't act like I'm going to go fuck them because they are the Obedients. Don't fucking insult me like that! I nearly screamed in his head. I've never sworn at him before. Did he not just hear my vows a moment ago? He might as well have slapped me across the face.

I spun and stomped away from him. He realized his mistake but it was too late, I was really fucking mad. He went to grab my arm.

"Gabby wait-" He tried to voicelessly explain his insecurities but that just made it worse.

I'M NOT LINDA! I mutely screamed at him. I whipped my arm from him, burst into sand, and shut my mind off from him. I sped out the door and into the night's sky. He tried to follow me by trying to taste my energy in the air but he didn't know how good I got at repressing it. I was gone.

* * *

I rematerialized outside Stacey's front door just as they were pulling up. They looked at each other for a second then got out of the car.

"Gabby what's wrong?" Stacey asked while Luke pulled the floaters out of the car.

"I'll tell you in a minute. Get those two inside, then both of you meet me out back." I turned and jumped onto the roof. I put a barrier around the house again. Peter won't be able to access anyone's mind under this. He won't even be able to see us or the car it he flies by. Even our scent and energy would be lost. I jumped down into the backyard. Seconds later Stacey and Luke joined me.

"First of all," I started by looking at Luke, "How did you know Peter wasn't an Obedient?"

He sighed, "He didn't have blue eyes."

"But you sniffed him anyways, I remember that."

"Yes because he shared some of the same qualities in his scent as you do from your powers, I was confirming exactly how much power was transferred from you to him. Both scents were the same on that point but with him there is also something else. Something familiar that I couldn't place. Something that I still cannot even place even with my extraordinary memory." He seemed really frustrated by this, "Like graveyard soil. I told the Oracle this and that's why she theorized the Horned God possibility."

Yes that's right, that's why Peter and Luke were in Europe. Peter was curious who his soul was reincarnated after. The Oracle didn't believe it was solely my love for him that helped him survive the transformation. I thought that if he truly loved me, then it wouldn't matter. But my father missed something; only the ones with reincarnated souls of powerful beings could withstand the power given by me. But yes, they would die of they didn't truly love me, powerful soul or not.

But fate had some plans brewing.

"Gabby, why are you here? What's wrong?" Stacey asked again, interrupting my thoughts. Luke looked at me curiously too. I sighed and projected what happened into their heads. I didn't feel like explaining it out loud.

"Oh Gabby, you can't really blame them for being a little jealous. With all the commotion that links you to them and how things are 'supposed' to be." She did air quotes with her fingers. "And the fact that his ex-wife did what she did doesn't necessarily mean he's comparing you to her, he just really loves you."

I tried to think about what she said logically. Eventually I realized she was right. I felt really tired but then remembered something.

"Luke, I need you to alert the Vampires in Egypt, have them keep an eye on Matthew's mate." I projected Stacey's vision into his head. "Also, find out what she's looking for."

He looked at me blankly for a second, "Couldn't the Wolves do that?"

John was from Egypt and his ready quick planning to fight Nicolas for Alpha at the potential event of Matthew's death, made me suspicious. I projected that memory as well.

Luke nodded, "Very well, I can do that."

"What do we do now? Do you want to go back to the church?" Stacey asked me. I raised my hand and removed the barrier.

"Yea I guess so." I lied. I actually didn't want to go back just yet. Stacey looked at Luke and then touched his hand.

I think he should go to Egypt personally. I also think that's where and when he finds his lady friend. Stacey thought to me. Her hand was still touching his when she closed her eyes and nodded. *Yes it's more trusted that way for Matthew's mate to survive. I can't see everything but the other vision is getting foggy with Luke in the picture. It may also strengthen the alliance between the clans.* I projected her thoughts and vision to Luke.

He nodded, "Then I shall leave right away."

"Go now." I said to him. Then he bolted to the edge of the yard. He turned to take one final look at us, waved, and then left. His scent was gone within seconds.

"Well? So Joseph and James are the Obedients for the Vampire and the Werewolf clans, what about the third one?" Stacey questioned.

"I don't know. But just because they are who they are doesn't mean anything. I don't even think they are aware of anything. Although Joseph wasn't really surprised by what he witnessed." I shook my head, "Anyways, they have to be truly in love with me and neither of them is even close. Not to mention, I'm in love with Peter and would never do what Linda did to him. We are just going to have to figure this out. And figure it out quick because there haven't been many demons around lately. More humans are losing their faith; barely anyone comes to the churches anymore."

I furrowed my eyebrows as I spoke. I was getting irritated. I knew the angelic form would work on the unsettled spirits and most demons. But without realizing it, Luke exposed that I would need my demon form to deal with the corrupted. Sure, I just have to partly demonize myself to feed on the empty, possessed, or infected. But to take on a whole army of them? And corrupted? Demon form it is then. I also knew it would probably take deeply negative emotions to do so. It looks like I'm going to have to get severely angry. I had a theory that I just needed the deep emotion to change my form the first couple times and then after that it should be easier to summon once I'm used to it.

I'm sure the need to protect the human race will make up for that. Stacey looked nervous at my previous announcement.

"It's okay, we'll figure something out." I said but a noise caught my attention. Someone was walking around in Stacey's house. The kitchen light went on. "It's....Joseph. He's awake?" I said surprised. I was sure I knocked them both out for a good twelve hours.

83

We looked at each other for a second then hurried towards the house. He was getting a drink of water when we walked in. He turned around and at the sight of me he dropped the glass, which smashed into bits when it hit the floor. He backed up against the counter with his eyes wide.

"Stay away from me." He was terrified. He pointed his finger at me and his memory flashed in my head.

What the fuck? Stacey side glanced at me.

I swear I eased his memory, I thought to her. We both looked back at him.

"What are you talking about Joseph?" She asked him.

"She changed. She's not human. I saw at her wedding. He's not human either." He stuttered.

"Um, what? The wedding went fine, then you guys came back here and drank till you passed out. You must have been dreaming dude."

I was really irritated that I apparently failed to erase his memory and no matter how hard I tried now, I couldn't do it. My wedding memory was still intact in his head, unable to be manipulated, all the way up to me waving my hand at them and now him waking up just minutes ago.

But suddenly he seemed unsure. All I needed was a little seed of doubt. Let's go doubt! He looked down at himself and patted his chest. He was wondering how his clothes changed. He blinked stupidly a couple of times, trying to remember, but couldn't. Stacey laughed and he looked at her.

"You guys were *totally* wasted." She chuckled. Sounded pretty genuine too.

He looked at me and I smiled going along with it. He put his hand to his head, then smiled to himself.

"Yea, I guess I got a little carried away huh?" His face went a little red with embarrassment. Stacey and I just nodded at him.

Good one Stace, I thought while still looking at Joseph.

No problem. Got worried for a second there. She thought back to me.

"Well, I guess I'll go back to bed after I clean this up." He went to bend down but Stacey stopped him.

"Oh don't worry about that, I'll get it. We've been cleaning up anyways. You just get some rest you really need it."

At first he paused and I didn't think he was going to listen but he straightened back out. *Nice cover there Stace didn't think about the 'no bottles to prove party mode' part.*

You can't see it but I'm winking at you Gabby.

"Okay, um, congrats Gabby. Shame I didn't meet you sooner." The day he gave me his number went through his head with a slight longing tagged onto it.

"Goodnight Joseph."

He gave a weak wave and went back into the living room. Flicked a wrist at the broken glass and then Stacey and I went back outside to the back porch.

"Do you need me to come back with you?" She asked.

"No, stay here with them and give Stan the story when he gets up."

"Okay, good luck Gabby." She patted me on the shoulder and went inside. I sighed and ran off the porch to the edge of the lawn and then jumped onto the neighbour's roof.

*   *   *

I was in my leather one piece again. I was starting to really like the running and jumping thing. I got to Downtown Vancouver by Granville Station and stood on the roof of one of the major retail stores. It was pretty high up. Demons have been pretty scarce, but tonight I could smell a couple in the air. Technically it wasn't Halloween anymore but it was the witching hour. I haven't had an actual demon since my first feed. I supressed my energy and crouched near the edge of the roof and waited.

I could see the road perfectly in the dark. My eyes were so adjusted to even the smallest details of the street. I listened close, the streets were bare but I could hear two sets of footsteps. The demon scent was a little fresher, not as sour and not quite as decayed. These must be recently possessed or infected humans.

Once infected or possessed, the blood turns black. When a human loses their humanity, their soul shrinks and they can become an empty vessel, being susceptible for possession. Once possessed, both spirit and soul are gone. Infection was different. Not bitten or anything. If demon blood is ingested or forced within the body, the soul is erased. The personality imprint is there but demonized. Some memories remain but no real emotions are felt ever again. Thus the decay and sour smell, essentially the body is dead.

The corrupted cannot infect humans; their venom still turns them to dust. Poof. The new information I was gathering subtly by the demons below me, of demons forcefully infecting captured humans made me furious. I gathered everything from these two in less than three seconds. These two were in fact newly possessed. The decay of their hosted bodies would happen over time as the bodies slowly decomposed from the inside out. I tried to poke around to find out who was responsible for the infections, but got nothing.

I did find out that they knew the Witchdemon was around but had no knowledge of Peter. This both relieved and confused me. The little demon fucker lied. Sort of. It seemed the demons were only linked involuntarily to the ones in the same clan. 'Involuntarily'; meaning without control of what thoughts and memories are transferred, no secrets allowed. This only happened in a blood ceremony. There was a head Demon to every clan. The newcomer drank the blood of the leader to be permanently linked to one another. They could of course use telepathy to other demons not in their clan if they chose.

My point is, that's how these two knew about me. Fortunately, Peter chowed down before the demon could project anything further, besides the fact that I was around and serving him as lunch. These two newly possessed demons were going to try and join the closest clan in the city. I smiled, it looks like I hit the jackpot.

The six demons I ate were just developing, they didn't even have a demon to drink from, (which is a rule to be recognized as a clan whatsoever.) and one of these two were the only demons in range of the panicked thought waves sent by one of the demons we ate that night. (Only one was able to form words thankfully and conveniently.)

One of them had notified one of these two and I knew that because these two were thinking about it and looking around scared I might get them before they reached their destination. But I repressed my energy well. I jumped across the street to the other rooftop and walked along the edge, silently following them. The demon scent grew stronger. My eyes were white but now black veins were appearing around the edges of my face. I could hear them better now and control my powers a little more efficiently.

They turned the corner to their right and went into the underground parking of another building. I jumped off the roof and landed gracefully in front of the entrance. It was dark like a cave in a mountain side. But with my eyes I could see clear as day. I followed them inside. For a second I thought I heard something behind me. I looked back but saw nothing. I froze, listened closely, I even held my breath. Nothing. I continued down the tunnel till it opened into the parking lot. There were no cars and still no light. I looked up at the ceiling. There were various pipes everywhere. I jumped up and hung onto the pipes and moved along the ceiling out of sight.

Every now and again there was an upside down step of concrete I had to climb over to get to the next pipe line, but I did everything dead silent. The possessed were just feet in front of me. I realized I was still holding my breath but I didn't necessarily need air. My cells could breathe for themselves. It was a strange feeling and I only noticed I was still holding it because I couldn't smell or taste the air. But I could feel every ounce of energy in the air, and it was sustaining me by being absorbed through my skin. Not being able to smell or taste was probably a good thing now that I remembered the scent of just six demons made me ravenous with hunger.

I needed to be able to control myself and I could already feel that there was a hell of a lot more demons ahead. Since I was about to ambush a whole clan, I continued to hold my breath. Also, I needed to wait because I needed some answers before I ate them all. Finally, the two possessed stopped at a ring of light, the only light in the damn place at the center of the parking lot. I stayed around the edge of the darkness, about ten feet away.

"Hello?" One of the possessed asked. I'll call him possessed number one. I felt the energy of the other demons and knew the two possessed were completely surrounded. These demons could kind of see in the dark. They were sensitive to energies. I looked in their heads. They couldn't sense my energy and since I was on the ceiling, they couldn't really see me either. But I saw them long before these two possessed were within fifty feet of the single light. They were against the walls of the extremely large parking lot. With nearly the same speed as a Vampire or a Werewolf, they surrounded the two possessed within the circle in half a second.

Probably why Vampires and Werewolves were born fast. Can't really hunt something faster than you. It reminded me of the road runner and the coyote. The poor fucker never had a chance.

I watched the two possessed look around themselves. The other demons got closer, making the two in the light move right into the center of it. The demons on the edge of the circle wore white masks with black cloaks.

"We've come to join your clan." This time it was possessed number two who spoke. Both were wearing black jogging outfits with their hoods up, their backs were to me so I couldn't physically see their features. So I took a peak mentally. One was red head-possessed number two, and the other was a blonde-possessed number one. Red head guy had spoken.

"And what makes you think we want you?"

Blonde guy spoke up, "An ally has told me the Witchdemon has awoken while I was in my last host. I could help fight."

All the demons laughed. It was interesting to know that the possessed demon left its last host when he found out about me. It looks like they don't project energy or scent when bodiless. Possessive demons were extremely old unsettled spirits. Fuck there were too many different variations of possessed and of infected. Long story short, because I'm getting irritated just thinking about it, the fucker didn't want to chance me finding him and he took off. The host turned to dust instantly because it was dead and anything demon, including the blood, disappears with the possessive once he jumps ship.

Every time they do this they get stronger and stronger. It's a little complicated but possessed or infected the blood is black and demonized, no turning back. Probably why most humans who get exorcized don't survive. So if the possessive demon leaves, everything and anything goes with and nothing human remains except dust. The body is completely and irreversibly consumed. I didn't fully get it but I was slightly and curiously distracted by the demon's laughter.

"We already know the Witchdemon has awakened. Every demon on Earth felt the whole planet's energy rift. All the corrupted and unsettled are coming together. That's where you should go. You possessive demons are not *true* demons, why would we mix with the likes of you?"

Wow, I didn't know there were such politics in the demon world. But talk about double standards. Technically *they* weren't true demons either. They were kind of the same as possessive demons. Their human bodies were infected sure, but with the humanity and soul gone, they were just personality imprints themselves, just in the original packaging. But I wasn't defending the possessive or doing any demon rights movements. I just wanted to see if their leader was going to make an entrance or not.

If the possessive drink the official demon blood then they'll become mentally linked to this clan. They all knew that and I got a little impatient because I knew that they were just fucking around and were just sadistically enjoying the belittlement of the two newcomers. They needed the numbers. This clan's number was at thirty, still small compared to the clan on the West side of Vancouver that was at two hundred. I made a mental note to send some Werewolves and Vampires to that spot.

"Yes, but I know what she looks like." The blonde said. This whole situation reminded me of some bad movie's version of a gang hazing. Then a side thought shoved a memory of some dude from a party who said you couldn't really be 'Gangster' in Canada. But then again soul sucking demons didn't really care about stereo types. The other demons thought amongst themselves.

They didn't want to reveal that this impressed them. I thanked God I wasn't on society's radar and the fact that I lived in a church. Not because I was afraid, which I wasn't, but if I live a normal life *and* was on record, well, I could have made some friends who could be in a lot of danger if I was traced. But since my ID and everything was falsified, they could only really link me to Douglas College that I attended for four days. And they couldn't link me to Peter or Mary because, thank God, Peter and I were impatiently hungry and he ate the fucker before he could rat me out.

It was really Mary I was worried about, but since Peter's image was safe from the demon's mind I didn't have to worry about him being traced. Finally a masked demon stepped over to another and spoke.

"Summon her." The 'real' demon demanded. I got an image of who they were summoning. *She* was a *real* demon straight from Hell. In the actual dimension, she was from a clan devoted to one of the seven deadly sins.

Lust.

Remember the different kinds of demons I was bitching about earlier? Well there were even seven clans, each devoted to a deadly sin. And there wasn't just one set of seven clans per deadly sin either. Ugh!

But only a couple from each clan had permission, from whoever lets them out, to come to earth's surface to corrupt and manipulate humans into losing pieces of their soul. Some went for the Vampires or Werewolves. Like I said too many. To me, they are all food and let's just leave it there for now. The demons collected these pieces broken from the souls they corrupt in order to sustain themselves on earth, or to bring out a fellow clan member. But human souls were weak as pieces. Bringing souls only piece by piece is not enough to actually bring another to the surface. So the ones chosen to come to earth were usually the only ones who stayed on earth. The two possessive backed up to the edge of the light as the masked demon who was commanded to 'summon her' stepped forward into the light.

The light went out and in its place was a blood red pentagram. Odd, I thought they would be a little more creative than that. I felt like I was on set of a bad movie. Red flames shot out of the star and she slowly rose from the ground. I made sure my mind and energy was repressed. I didn't even attempt to look in her head in case she sensed me in there. Without thinking, I sniffed the air. Her scent was amazing. She didn't smell like the other demons. Nothing like them actually. No decaying smell, but an anciently powerful energy kind of smell. Like Peter's which is how he survived my powers. But then I thought, she was a demon of 'Lust' so she would probably smell like whatever entices one the most.

This was a very plausible theory but I didn't do any digging to find out since I was trying to be incognito. I pressed myself closer to the ceiling. I almost smiled when I realized I was no longer holding onto the pipes. I was totally defying gravity right now. Even my hair behaved like so. Once she had completely risen, she opened her eyes. They were completely solid red. The flames disappeared. The demons shoved the two new possessive forward and they onto their knees in front of her. I decided I wasn't going to wait for the ceremony, I didn't feel like having every demon knowing my face yet and I'm guessing her telepathy can reach everyone at the same time, no problem.

The demons all circled her closely. They were all huddled around the still glowing pentagram and the light came back on, only barely as bright. I jumped down, light as a feather, in a crouch to the ground.

"My queen, we wish to join your clan." Both the red head and blonde said at the same time. Queen? Oh *hell* no mother fucker. As much as I hate it when Matthew calls me it; *I'M* the mother fucking queen around here!

I didn't care anymore, I looked into her mind. There were three sisters of the Lust clan that all had permission to surface. The eldest was killed the last time the Witchdemon had awoken five thousand years ago. And during that time the Witchdemon was in her demon form. I knew what I had to do. But just as I thought, she noticed me in her mind. She shot her head up and looked me dead in the eyes even though I was a good fifty feet away into the darkness.

She hissed and all the demons followed her gaze. I didn't bother repressing my energy now and they went into a panic. Everything happened within a traction of a second. I didn't know if I could do it at first but I just went with my gut. I didn't want to miss anyone and I didn't want to waste time. I shot my hand out and every demon except her burst into dust, leaving their blood behind. Instead of ingesting it, I pulled the blood towards me and like the oxygen earlier I absorbed the blood through the cells of my skin. I felt the immense energy make my skin glow red. I may have had the white eyes and veins but I wasn't actually partly demonized before I absorbed the blood into my body. But once all the blood was gone, everything changed. I absorbed it in two seconds.

First, my outfit got completely destroyed. My body grew taller and my feet and hands grew talon like claws. My feet looked like dinosaur feet as my heels stretched up and my toes melted into three and out with a large talon one each 'toe'. My abs became seriously ripped, and my arms more defined. My jaw and nose became slightly more pointed. My eyes went jet black with a small white pupil. Like, solid black with a white dot. The veins went a little thicker around my face. I felt my back split open without pain to allow two giant wings that had what looked like feather but were really hard scales.

My spine rippled and spiked out down my back and I felt something shoot out of the bottom, revealing a long murderous tail. It seemed impossible that the spikes at the end spun like I was part machine. The tip was hosted by a large blue spike that glowed and shot in and out of the end of my tail. I turned my wrists and pumped my arms. Two glowing blue blades shot out two feet from the top of my wrists. I realized these blades and my spike were weapons of Holy Fire. My hair clumped together into thick alien like tentacles. Two large horns grew from the sides of my forehead, they curved the side of my head like a ram's. Finally, my teeth spiked.

I felt super charged. Her demon energy not only made me want to eat her in this form but made me want to show off a little bit. I took in air and violently exhaled blue flames from my mouth, closing the distance from me to her. The flames didn't touch her but only because I wanted to rip her apart and taste her blood. I looked at her and if she wasn't a demon, she would have been beautiful. I noticed she tried to look into my head.

I blocked her easily, thank you Stacey.

"So you're the Witchdemon." She said in a seductive voice.

"Yes, and you're dinner." I said just as seductively. I was surprised, I was sure the teeth would have given me a lisp.

"I don't think so; I don't plan on dying tonight. Not without a fight. I sense you're not as strong as the last Witchdemon." She smiled but there was no humor on her lips.

"Give it time. I'm only a couple months old."

"And I am centuries older than you. What could you possibly do to me?"

I smiled at her and then licked my lips with my long demon tongue. She glared at me and started to glow herself. Her face poked out almost beaklike and her body grew taller as well. Her curves became more pronounced and her breasts fuller. Her clothes completely disappeared. Her hair wrapped itself into braids and her skin went black and scaly. Her spine spiked and then she cracked her neck. I stood there mainly out of curiosity of her transformation and then her energy and scent got a whole lot stronger. Her mind was no longer readable. Her legs melted together to a snakelike body.

Then she glowed even brighter. I closed my eyes for a second and I felt her energy double. I opened my eyes and there was fucking *two* of her! Now I was pissed. The bitch obviously didn't fight fair. I glared at her and both of them smiled.

"I'm a twin. Didn't you see that in my head? You are a pathetic child. We can't kill you but I'm sure we can weaken you pretty badly. You don't even have half the energy of your predecessor." She laughed and her sister screeched before joining in with her own glee.

"No, but she has me." A voice from behind me said.

CHAPTER NINE

Peter walked towards us. The twins were stunned frozen and silent. He looked at me and smirked.

God you're sexy when you're angry. He thought to me.

Wow. SO not the time. I thought back. He returned his attention to the twins and they looked at him, shocked at what they saw. They're minds' were blocked form me and from what I could tell, they were blocked from Peter as well.

"I really don't appreciate you talking to my wife like that. Makes me a little angry."

Was it me or did they look sincerely terrified for a second? Were they more afraid of him than me? Nah, Peter's energy is just like yours. They would think he was too weak just like they thought about you. The only thing that would maybe make them nervous is the fact that he was a Witchdemon too, and apparently *that* has never happened before.....

He started to glow and they fearfully stood there and watched. His transformation was kind of like mine, only I didn't actually need to be angry. His skin was glowing red at first like mine did but then went scaly like theirs and his wings were like a dragon's. He ended up with the dinosaur feet and talon-like claws but his eyes went solid red with a black pupil. His horns grew out to the sides then up like a bull and they glowed blue. His tail was not as deadly looking as mine was either. Well, if he looked like me it wouldn't be very interesting huh? I smiled a little.

His body became really ripped in the muscle department. His spine went spiky and blue smoke billowed from his nose on every exhale. The twins seemed to tremble at the sight of him. This actually pissed me off for some reason I couldn't pinpoint. I assessed him again and got slightly distracted. I don't know if angry sex would be out of the question but damn, if it wasn't on my mind right now; I wouldn't be me.

We'll figure that out later, he thought and winked at me.

We advanced on them and they both raised themselves at least six feet taller on their snake bodies to try and tower over us. Peter and I pounded our wings hard and rose into the air.

Blood red fire shot from their mouths but Peter and I reacted at the same time with our own Holy fire. The collision of the flames was extraordinarily beautiful, but I had no time to admire the purple collaboration. The blue blades shot from my wrists as Peter and I chose our opponents. Peter's twin seemed more afraid of him than mine was of me. Actually it looked like both sisters were looking at him with fear *and* longing.

I don't fucking think so.

I sliced at the air in front of her while still in flight but she kept dodging me. I couldn't look in her head as to why she kept glancing at Peter. This of course made my own thoughts and suspicions even worse. Especially when Peter's opponent was fearful but barely dodging, and almost smiling when contact was made.

That's it! Fuck these bitches!

The twin I was fighting whipped her tail in my direction just before I went to lunge at her sister. I spun with my wings spread out, looking like a giant spinning blade. I cut the tip of her tail off; it fell and turned to dust. She screamed, rose herself high, then threw herself at me. I shot my tail through her stomach with every individual spike making its own individual home in her abdomen. The blue spike shot out and went through her body easily. The spikes spun, shredding a hole in the middle of her. She could barely make a sound. I pulled out my tail and smiled at her before I exhaled Holy flames. Her body turned black before she turned to dust.

"Sister!" her twin screamed. While she was distracted, Peter rammed his horns into her chest, piercing her all the way through. He pulled them out and then engulfed her in blue Holy flames. I wasn't really satisfied though; for someone with such big talk for herself she sure as fuck died easily. I had a sneaking suspicion she wouldn't have been so easy to defeat if she wasn't so distracted by her Lust for Peter. But whatever, the bitch was toast and so was her ugly sister.

I looked at Peter and posed my body with my hip sticking far out to accent my curves. *So I'm sexy when I'm angry huh?* I thought. He smiled with his sharp teeth. *Listen Peter, I'm sorry about getting upset earlier.* Out of his nose there was a small puff of blue smoke that showed every breath.

That's not your fault; I shouldn't have been so careless with my emotions. I know you love me and I love you. He walked over to me and gently stroked my demon skin with his talons. It felt incredible. My skin actually rippled with pleasure. Peter noticed. The same ripple happened to him when I touched his chest.

Interesting, he thought smiling.

Our wings extended and our long tails weaved back and forth through the air behind us. He placed his hands on my hips. I was a little taller than him. We kissed and our bodies glowed bright red. I was surprised our teeth didn't get in the way but our lips moved effortlessly.

I love what you've done to your leather outfit. He thought as he moved his lips up my jaw line. My skin was ultra-sensitive; it took a minute for me to register what he thought to me. The leather outfit had shredded, yea, but stayed in all the right places, like I got attacked by a slightly perverse lion. My breasts were barely covered and my legs were completely exposed. And there was a thread of leather, almost literally, to cover my lady parts.

And dinosaur feet didn't fit well in high heeled boots, so they were completely obliterated. His outfit was kind of the same, um....shredded I mean. Not like there was pieces of shirt just covering his nipples or whatever. No shirt actually, at all, just pants that were very loose now and had a ragged looking hole in the butt part. But from the front point of view, that I saw, he looked like a red, demonized version of a particular comic book hero.

I wasn't thinking of too many details except of the feel of his lips on my skin and knowing in his head what my talons were doing to him. We didn't actually need our wings to fly. We were so engrossed in our sexual need for each other, we didn't notice that we began to rise in the air. I wrapped my legs around him. My cry of ecstasy was animal like as he entered me. It echoed through the underground parking lot and made him hunger for more of me.

* * *

Sex as a demon was definitely addicting. The high was incredible. It was like eating a thousand demons, I think, I haven't tried that many yet but I'm pretty sure I'm close. The energy was immense. It was like, the longer we went, the higher we got but it was hard to go too long because of how sensitive everything was. We were having orgasm after orgasm quite frequently, thus the addiction. I lost count in the parking lot. We only stopped when I noticed human scents. Bursting to sand, we ended up in his house and basically continued where we left off. It was *hours* before we were able to calm down enough to change into our human forms.

Our demon skins dissolved like layers of black ashes and our shape returned till just our eyes and veins and sharp teeth remained. Finally, those turned to normal as well. Only then, did we feel exhausted.

"Holy fuck, I feel like I could sleep for a month." I said slightly out of breath as I cuddled into his naked body. We were so fucking warm; we lay on top of the sheets completely exposed. He had his right arm under my neck and his left arm wrapped around me. He lifted it to stroke my arm, then my cheek, then my hair. He sniffed my hair before he brought his nose to my ear and kissed me under my jaw bone. This sent shivers down my spine. I smiled at his thoughts.

"Aren't you tired?" I asked him.

"Are you kidding? I could go for days with you around."

I laughed, "You're so corny!" I jokingly accused. I turned while in his arms and pushed him away. I got up and went to the bathroom. I didn't actually need to go to the bathroom anymore.

Seriously. I haven't taken a shit or piss since I awakened.

Since my diet is demon blood or evil blood in general, I completely absorb everything. But I did want to shower. Peter was at my side in a blink of an eye to turn the water on as soon as I opened the shower curtains. He was on me before we even stepped in. Kissing me and touching me everywhere.

Jesus! What am I going to do with you?! I laughed in my head. He had my mouth occupied with his.

There's lots you can do, like this for example. He smoothly had his two fingers inside me and nearly lifted me where I stood; making me go fucking wild. When my feet were firmly planted again, his other hand was squeezing my ass. My arms were wrapped around his neck. The new knowledge or skill that I learned of not necessarily needing to breath, definitely came in handy. Because for one; I couldn't stop kissing him. And two; like before, my sensitivity to energy spiked, and our energy was seriously sexual right now. I honestly don't remember getting in the shower at all. I remember hearing the water going and us slowly fucking on the bathroom floor, but actually getting in the shower?

Um... no sir, that did not happen.

The sun was setting when I woke up with Peter half on top of me. We were on the hard linoleum floor of the bathroom. The sunset shone through the window. My body should have been seriously sore and uncomfortable, but I was perfectly at ease the way I was. Peter was breathing evenly and I closed my eyes again to listen to the sound of his beating heart. I felt comfortable but I also felt like we've been in the same spot for a very long time. I opened my eyes and wondered, how long have we been sleeping?

Then the fucking *doorbell* rang.

Shit!

Linda was here?!

With Mary?!

They were nearly two weeks early from the thoughts I picked from Linda's head. Which means we've been sleeping for almost sixteen days!

Holy fuck!

The doorbell rang again.

"Peter wake up!" I yelled verbally and mentally. I jumped up and practically flipped him onto his back in my hurry. Sand was already forming clothing on me as I raced out of bathroom stupidly at human speed.

"What?" he said groggily.

"Mary and Linda are here!" I hissed at him. That woke him up. I was fully clothed and then I unhuman like bolted down the stairs to the front door. I had on shorts and a tank top. All my tattoos exposed. I opened the front door as Mary rang the doorbell a third time. She smiled up at me as I looked down at her. Lind eyed me and my body art and I smiled.

"Gabby!" Mary shouted and she grabbed my leg. I noticed how little Mary smelled herbal.

"Where's Peter?" Linda asked stiffly.

"Right here." He said as he came down the steps. Linda's scent was slightly sour. She was plagued by her sinfully emotionless cheating. I saw in her mind how many times she cheated on Peter and now how many times she cheated on Howard. As a matter of fact she was on her way to see someone right now. She had to drop off Mary first for the remaining two weeks that Howard stayed in the States for business. He had caught her in the act and she left early to Canada till his business down there was finished. Looks like she was headed for another divorce.

Her love for her daughter seemed to be the only thing keeping her soul alive. She packed Mary a large suitcase.

"I have some things to take care of for the next couple of weeks. I trust you'll be fine with her?"

Oh yea? Got some dick sucking lessons to get to? I thought.

Peter was trying not to react to what he heard in her mind and seriously trying not to react to what was in mine.

"Um, yes, of course." He said as he picked up his daughter.

"Oh! Pretty big ring Gabby. Did daddy give dat to you?" Mary pointed.

I looked at my hand and so did Linda, I totally forgot it was there. It survived the demon form?

"You're getting married?" Linda glared at him; I almost threw a punch to crush her face.

"Already got married actually, sixteen days ago." We both looked at each other for the private joke then looked back at her. I loved making Linda look like she was going to literally shit her pants. She was pissed.

Mary squealed, "Yay! I have another mommy!"

Linda's eyes bugged out, (hehe) Mary's words made her furious. But she controlled herself well. I'll give her this; she was good at faking it.

She plastered a smile on her face and through a clamped jaw she said. "Congratulations. Peter, I'll see you in two weeks to pick up Mary."

"That's fine, goodbye Linda." We pretty much closed the door in her face. Peter looked at his daughter and noticed the herbal smell. He looked at me and I shrugged.

"Daddy you're different." She grabbed his face and looked right into his eyes, bringing her little nose to his. We both noticed we couldn't see inside her head. "Are you an angel now too daddy?" she asked him very seriously.

"Yes honey bee." She mesmerized him into telling the truth. He couldn't help himself.

"Show me." She demanded. His love for his daughter choked me on the spot. It made me love him even more. He looked at her and projected our angel forms into her head. She closed her eyes and smiled like this happened all the time. She opened them and kissed her daddy on the cheek. "I love you daddy." Then turning to me, "I love you too Gabriel."

She was so happy. Mary was very mature for her age. She had quite the acceptance for this; of course, most children had very good imaginations, so maybe that's why it was so easy for her. Her mood was infectious.

The next day we took her to the baseball diamond park close to Gateway Station. I watched as Peter pushed her on the swings. This is my family now, I loved them both immensely. Peter looked back at me and smiled. Mary looked at me too.

"Gabby! Let's go on the seesaw!" she kicked her legs with excitement.

"Okay honey bee, I'm coming." I crouched and stalked towards her. She squealed as I got to her and giggled when I tickled her sides.

*   *   *

The past twelve days went by so fast with Mary around. After dinner I did the butterfly thing for her like I did for Stacey. She was ecstatic. The sun was setting.

"I want a kitty!" she looked at Peter and I raised an eyebrow at him.

He shrugged. "Sure, why not?"

Mary screamed with excitement. "Yay!"

"Okay, let me concentrate honey bee." I said politely.

Creating life energy was simple with butterflies, but a kitten was a whole different story. My eyes were already crystal white and I felt the life of the grass below my hand. I raised my hand and a clump of earth floated with it. The earth took shape of a kitten, then exploded with golden glitter revealing a white kitten with blue eyes. It meowed and went right to Mary.

"Kitty!" she hugged the kitten close to her. Peter patted Mary on the head. "Thank you Gabby, I'll love him forever!" she promised. The kitten meowed again and started to purr. "I'm going to name him Jeremiah." The kitten licked Mary's face.

"That's a nice name." I made a rather lame realization that just over ninety percent of the people I knew had biblical names, including myself. Except the somewhat normal people I knew, like Stacey and Stan. Linda, and I never met him, but the unfortunate Howard. I really did do the smile and nod thing in church. I haven't even read the bible. I just know most of the main names because my father consistently repeated himself and my brain gave up and finally put them somewhere. The things we think about in a matter of seconds with no actual value at all.

I pet the kitten. "Be a good kitty and don't spray or we'll chop off your nuts." I said. Peter gaped at me.

Gabby! Did you just speak like that in front of Mary? He thought.

What? Oh she'll be fine. I thought back.

"He won't spray, he'll be a good kitty." Mary said kissing Jeremiah's head.

See? I told you. I smirked. I smelled Luke at the front door of the house. Peter's head snapped up. *We're out back*, I thought to Luke. I projected caution because of Mary. Luke appeared at the back gate at normal human speed.

"Luke, this is Mary. Mary, this is Luke." Luke noticed her scent.

Mary held out a little hand, "How do you do?"

He smiled and crouched low to shake her hand. "Very well and you?"

Mary shook his hand enthusiastically, "Very well thank you." She pulled her hand back and showed him her kitten. "I just got him, his name is Jeremiah." Jeremiah meowed.

"Very nice." Luke patted Jeremiah gently and then stood to look at Peter for a short second.

"Come on honey bee; let's go make a little house for Jeremiah." Peter said whisking Mary into the house. He was giving us a moment to converse away from Mary. She didn't know everything and she was a little too young for it.

"Matthew's mate, Hannah, is safe. She was in Egypt apparently looking for the Valley of Dry Bones. It was the home of the statues that portrayed the Goddess and her beloved Horned God."

This surprised me.

"But didn't the Oracle think the story originated in Europe?"

"Yes, but the wolves heard differently. Well, Hannah's clan from Egypt knew stories that were told when she was a little, err, girl." He was going to say 'pup'.

"So what about the statue?"

"It is said to have existed over twenty thousand years ago. But when Hannah got to the Valley where it was said to be, it was gone. I got to her just as she discovered it was missing. She was very surprised to see me. I told her of your friend's vision and she believed me. Demons were crawling all over Egypt and so are the corrupted. We got out of the country and she's with Matthew now at their mountain side. He was truly grateful. There may be a stronger alliance on the horizon."

I was relieved. So much time had passed since the wedding. (Honestly? I felt guilty too because this whole time I didn't think about Matthew's mate at all. Especially since she was meant to die a week after my wedding and I woke up sixteen days after. Oops.)

"We got back two days after I left. I was informed of your fight with the twins from Hell. Oholah and Oholibah. Their energy was felt by every uncorrupted Vampire and Werewolf in the region once they went into their true forms. They felt when their energy was destroyed and they also felt yours and Peter's demon energy afterwards...."

His thoughts implicated things that made me instantly embarrassed, but I quickly changed the conversation.

"Did you meet your lady friend?"

He smiled, "Yes actually, she helped me find Hannah. Her name is Sapphira. Her pull of me was instantaneous."

I didn't need to look into his mind to know what he'd been up to the past couple weeks with her. When a Vampire meets their mate, it's like a soul deep attraction. They mate for life as do Werewolves. Marriage wasn't really necessary but was and is often celebrated. The connection was mental, emotional, and spiritual. I could definitely relate. I looked at the house and knew Peter was smiling at my thoughts. I saw in his head Mary twirling on the spot with Jeremiah in her arms. Peter had made a giant doll house like castle for Jeremiah to live in. Complete with a couple scratching posts and a few dangling mice. And it too, was very pink.

"The child is a psychic; can you see in her head?" Luke asked me.

I shook my head. "No but we can project stuff to her. Well, she allowed us to." I was pretty sure Peter was only able to do that because she *wanted* to see it.

"Too bad you couldn't distinct his scent before he changed with you."

It sounded like he was saying this more to himself than to me. I didn't respond.

Then I thought of something. Shutting Peter out, I privately asked, *can the Lust twins smell like what attracts you?* I thought curiously to Luke. Luke looked at the house and so did I, but Peter wasn't paying attention. I heard Mary squeal again and then burst into a fit of giggles.

No, they are more on physical attraction. The oldest sister, that the previous Witchdemon had the privilege of consuming, could.

I see.

Something didn't add up, but I suppose I could figure that out later.

"So why didn't you show up earlier?" I asked aloud but then I instantly regretted the stupid question the moment I saw the answer in his head.

"Um, I have a very good sense of smell and the energy that was in the parking lot was very strong here for a while."

"Oh." It may have been dark but I'm sure he saw my face go red anyways.

"Not to mention, I also showed up a week ago and the both of you were in a deep slumber."

Mary and Peter returned to the back yard. Mary with Jeremiah in her arms.

"Stacey's on her way, I can hear her mind a few blocks away." Peter announced. I listened for her.

Gabby, I have to show you something. Stacey kept repeating this sentence in her head. I couldn't see any more than that. I was relieved that she was a psychic and could shut out Peter as well as I could whenever she wanted. I sensed Peter look into Luke's head and he saw what I had asked Luke but Peter kept his speculations to himself.

"Well, I'd better get back to Sapphira." His smile said everything.

"Okay, thanks for coming." Peter shook his hand and then Luke waved at me.

"Bye bye." Said Mary.

"Goodbye little one." Luke patted her on the head and then went to the gate at human speed, went around the corner out of sight, then took off at radical speed. Stacey's car pulled up. I suddenly wondered how she got Peter's address, oh. She was with Luke a week ago.

Gabby, can you hear me? I need you to come with me for a bit. I felt the urgency in her mind.

"Um, Stacey wants me to go with her for a bit, I'll be back okay?"

Peter looked confused but Mary pouted. "How long are you going to be?" she asked.

"Not too long honey bee. Just stay here with daddy and I'll be back in a little while." I smiled at her.

"Pinkie promise?" she walked up to me with her pinkie up in the air. I took it in mine.

"Pinkie promise." I agreed.

She smiled, "Okay hurry back mommy."

My heart thudded hard in my chest. Deep emotion flooded through me. I felt at awe at those words. I almost cried on the spot but I cleared my throat.

"I will." I choked out. I looked at Peter and he was beaming.

"Hurry back." He said. I kissed him and kissed Mary's forehead.

"Okay, see you soon." I said behind me as I headed towards the front of the house. I human ran to the front of the house and then sand bolted into the car. Unsurprised, she started the car and sped out onto the road.

What's so important? I asked in her head.

You'll see in a second, she responded.

We drove for thirty minutes till we came to Newton. She pulled into a parking lot in front of the Newton Library. Which drove *me* personally up the fucking wall! I could have been there thirty minutes *ago.* We got out of the car and went in.

What are we doing here? But she ignored my thought and went right to the librarian.

"Hi I'm Stacey, I was here earlier. Can I have that book I put on hold please?"

The librarian was an elderly woman with short grey curls and thick eye glasses. She was the pinnacle of librarians.

"Yes certainly." She went into her office and came back out with a big-but-thin looking book. 'Myths and Legends' read the title. Stacey flipped to a page where there was a small mention in the European section labelled 'The Horned God'.

"His name is Cemunnos and is a man with horns, hooves, and ears like a stag." Stacey stated as she skimmed the page.

Suddenly my thought of Peter having 'doe' eyes went through my head. I laughed.

"He was wildly worshipped in Celtic Europe as the lord of beasts." She continued, "Well that makes sense because he was supposed to have worshipped the Goddess of earth right?"

I shrugged.

She continued to look at the book. Stacey looked up at me, "It doesn't mention the Goddess though and it really doesn't say any more about him."

"That's what you wanted me for?" I asked her with a raised, and annoyed, eyebrow.

"Well you haven't really been researching anything." Her head went to my activities of the past few weeks from what she gathered from the little tidbits Luke let slip. We opened the book to the Egyptian section.

"Anything about 'The Valley of Dry Bones'? Or a statue of the Goddess and Horned God?" I asked. She shook her head. We looked at the rest of the book but found nothing remotely close to the Witchdemon as mentioned.

There were lots of warrior Goddesses who had a temper but nothing about being a supreme being and having three Obedients who lead three heavenly armies against Satan or his son, Damien, and the Hordes of Hell. And there was sweet fuck all about the Horned God except the little blurb we already read and nothing about the Goddess he was supposed to be in love with.

"Well, the Horned God is supposed to be a Wicca believe right? Maybe we need to look in a Wicca book." Stacey suggested. It was so obvious, it was embarrassing. So I played it cool and just nodded. She stood up and questioned the librarian while I just sat there and bit my nails. But we seemed to be in luck because the librarian handed her a little green book of solstices. Stacey rejoined me and flipped to the first page.

"Oh here we go! The summer solstice; The Horned God is at the height of his powers. Their child is growing in the Goddesses womb." She looked at me and I motioned with my hands for her to continue and she did, "Cybele is the name of the earth mother Goddess, she is a seductive lover. Oh! Here's a quote, it says 'There is but one God and one Goddess, but many are their powers."

Okay a small tiny part of me got excited.

Stacey continued to read, "Here's about the Horned God; he has committed himself to the Goddess and to the earth that is her responsibility and is transferring his strength to the fruits that they have created together in a willing act of self-sacrifice. But in autumn his vitality is fatally exhausted and he is descended to the realm of death and darkness ruling over his kingdom."

And his kingdom was the earth......

So the God and Goddess were spiritual metaphors for the eternal cycle of the seasons and lunar cycle.

I sighed, this felt like a waste of time. Then I thought, what the fuck do humans know of legends and myths anyway?

A smell hit me and I froze with a sick feeling dropping to the pit of my stomach.

Suddenly five corrupted Werewolves walked into the library. Holy fuck! I subtly touched Stacey, making her invisible.

Hide! I thought to her.

I stood up and turned to face them, my eyes going crystal white.

CHAPTER TEN

Luckily it was dead in the library. The library normally closed at nine in the evening on weekends. It was somewhere around six, or six thirty. I was actually kind of grateful these five showed up. I was getting kind of hungry. I smelled a corrupted Vampire before, salty with a lot of decay. These were somewhat the same, the decay part. While they were corrupted Werewolves, they smelled like spoiled spinach. Whatever, same shit. Soulless food in my belly. They noticed me right away of course. As a matter of fact, I was the reason why they were here. They felt my energy. They looked at me and without looking at her, I made the librarian pass out and fall gently to the floor behind the desk.

I had no idea where Stacey was but by her scent, I could tell she was somewhere in the same area. I cracked my neck and the veins and sharp teeth appeared. My eyes went black. They seemed to think they could take me because there were five of them and only one of me. Did they not get they were food? But they wanted something from me. Stacey. I heard in their minds that one of them had overheard Luke in Egypt about her vision. So she was the reason they were here but I was how they found us. Dammit.

These were the ones who were supposed to kill Hannah. They heard Stacey was a friend of the Witchdemon and sought out my energy to find her. They had some guts to try. Their arrogance was astonishing. I put a barrier around the building so they could not escape. This, they felt and it made a couple of them nervous. But the leader looked at me.

"Where's the psychic?" He asked.

"None of your business." I spat.

"I can smell her in here with you. Smells good." He envisioned ripping out the throat of a faceless woman. This really pissed me off.

"Do your kind get really stupid when corrupted? Do your brain cells die along with your body?"

He looked at me confused.

"Hello?!?! Witchdemon here! I literally have you guys for lunch and your threatening to kill my friend?" I smiled, this was going to be too easy.

Without waiting for a response, I flicked my wrists with my palms towards them. They all fell to their knees screaming. I wanted to punish them for acting like they were hot shit and threatening Stacey's life. In their minds they projected my image to the rest of their clan but I didn't care because as I was punishing them, they were continuing to project.

Just go ahead and show the rest of them I mean business.

I was making their blood boil like I did to Matthew, only this time there will be no guilt and no stopping until I'm satisfied. One by one their screams turned into howls as their bodies stretched and bones broke and reformed. The five of them had turned into five savage looking Wolves but they were stuck laying on their sides in pain. Their eyes, when not squeezing them shut, glowed red. They thought by transforming it would lessen the pain, but it didn't.

A couple turned back into their human forms, where their skin was turning red. The others were trapped in the Wolf form. All five started to bleed from their eyes. The blood flowed to my hand and created an orb of black corrupted blood. I bled them out painfully and one by one they turned to dust. I drank the blood till there was nothing left.

"Holy fuck." Stacey whispered.

I sniffed the air, "I think more are on their way, give me your hand." I said to her.

She was invisible but when I put my hand out she grabbed it. I burst us into sand and we took off back to my place at the church. I didn't want to risk them getting anywhere near Mary, in case they confused the herbal scents. As soon as we rematerialized at the altar, I tugged her along to my father's office. She was visible again. I stopped at the doors to his office. There were voices inside, one female and two male. My father, Thomas, and the Oracle. They stopped when I knocked.

"It's okay; it's her and her friend." Said the Oracle.

"Come in Gabby." My father invited. I walked in right away with Stacey at my side.

"Father, the corrupted Wolves are after Stacey, she needs to stay here for protection for a little while." I informed him.

"I know." He nodded.

"You know? What do you mean?"

"The Oracle has seen deception in one of the hearts within Matthew's Guard. The one named John. John overheard the Oracle tell you of the story of the Horned God. And him being from Egypt, knew from his childhood the stories of where the statue was rumored to be and so did Hannah. She is his cousin. He pretended the urgency for the statue and set for her to go there and be killed. He has been informing the corrupted of Matthew's movements, we don't know for how long. He planned for them to kill her, thus creating Matthew's suicide." My father updated me.

I closed my eyes with a hard sigh and reopened them. Right, that's why he was preoccupied with fighting strategies. If I had been paying better attention, I could have done something.

"Okay, then what happened to the statue?"

He gestured to the Oracle, "Isis. If you would be so kind as to answer her. I believe that was my question before we were interrupted."

The Oracle turned in her seat to face me, I was beside my father's desk now with Stacey behind me.

"It was destroyed about ten thousand years ago by the very first Witchdemon."

"How do you know this?" I asked her.

"Because I was there child." She smiled and then opened her mind to me. The memory was so vivid, it nearly made me stumble. I knew she was only letting me see what she wanted me to see. I also knew she was full of shit since she had no idea about the Horned God before. Did she think I was a fucking idiot? But I decided to play along to see why she was lying.

I projected the whole thing to Stacey. We both saw the statue; it was an angelic looking woman embracing a demon like man. He had the same horns as a stag. In the memory, the original Witchdemon stood before the statue. She was beautiful and a lot more Caucasian looking than I am. I think I'm mixed with something, I just don't know what.

Her eyes were crystal white. She flicked her wrist like I do and a ball of blue flames appeared. She threw the flaming ball at the statue, making it turn black and crumble. I didn't understand the so called memory. I wanted to know why she apparently did that. My father's office came back to my vision.

"But why?" Stacey whispered.

"I didn't understand who the statue represented at first," glancing at me as she said this, "but those two represented the Witchdemon's worst fears."

I tried to understand the words that came out of her mouth, okay so apparently she didn't know 'at first' who that statue was. Conveniently enough. I still didn't understand the memory though.

I smiled, "She didn't want to fall in love and have her lover imprint on her a weakness for anyone to see. The Witchdemon has a certain magic out of her control. Fate. Re-incarnations tend to repeat themselves. So, not knowing she was the first of her kind, she assumed her soul was the re-incarnation of the earth Goddess. She vowed not to let it happen to her."

I shook my head. Something was missing but this wasn't it. I've already crossed out the 'Horned God' theory.

"How old are you?" I suddenly asked.

"My soul is almost as old as yours. As a psychic I remember all my past lives, which were and is now, the seer of the Witchdemon. My soul exists only when it's time for yours to exist. Same with the Obedients, have you found them?"

"No." I lied. My gut was telling me she was only giving me half truths. Like last time, she didn't really answer my question.

"You sent Luke out to Europe to find out about the Horned God. If the statue was in Egypt and you saw it get destroyed, why send him there?"

"Because the statue may have been in Egypt but it was created in Europe."

Okay I was getting impatient, now she was blatantly lying to me.

"And how do you know that?"

"I'm the Oracle child. I just do."

Right, I'm sick of your shit. I looked inside my father's head. I wanted to know what they were talking about before I got here. It wasn't much to my utter disappointment. She apologised for not being at my wedding, thank God, and it looks like she informed him of John's deceit and betrayal weeks ago, even the Matthew incident, during his last visit which was sometime during the night after the Wolves met Stacey.

I was going to mention that the Horned God was worshipped in Celtic religions but I was too frustrated to deal with her. Isis pissed me off. I wanted her to fuck off and never come back. Something told me she was lying, about what else and why, I had no idea.

"I have to go, but Stacey needs to stay here father." I said stiffly.

"Very well."

I turned and left the office with Stacey behind me.

Mood swing? Stacey asked.

Major. I replied. Since I was projecting the whole time in the office, Stacey knew my suspicions. We got to my room upstairs and she sat on my bed as I paced. What happened to John is unknown but why didn't Luke mention any of this? Did he even know? A knock sounded at my door. It was Thomas.

"Come in." I said.

He walked in with a grave look on his face and shut the door behind him, "You seemed upset, I was concerned."

A sudden thought came to me, "Thomas, where in Egypt is the Valley of Dry Bones?"

He looked at me surprised, "You should already know of The Valley dear Gabby," he looked at Stacey, "And so should you."

Stacey and I looked at each other, what?

"The Valley of Dry Bones is mentioned in the bible. It's in the book of Ezekiel. Chapter thirty seven. Essentially Israel was in great peril. The Valley of Dry Bones was a vision to Ezekiel from God as a sign of restoration coming to the great land. It showed Israel's new life depended on God's power. The Valley was a vision that God would not only restore them physically, but spiritually as well. Alas, this has not happened yet. What a world we live in." Thomas said sadly.

"So, it's not in Egypt?"

"No, it's actually a spiritual dimension for God's guidance and encouragement. But there is a doorway in Egypt, as there are doorways all over the world. Some are called different things. It is mainly associated with the dead, where the good unsettled spirits go."

"There's good unsettled spirits? I thought the opposite of an unsettled spirit was a soul." Stacey said.

"No, they are completely different entities. Unsettled spirits are personality imprints. A soul is a literal miracle." Thomas corrected.

"Okay then what's the difference between a good unsettled spirit and a bad one?" Stacy asked. I listened to them banter while I thought about the doorway to the Valley.

"Good unsettled spirits are the ones who stay behind to help the living. Generally they have unfinished business but are unable to recognise what that is. They are usually known as spirit guides. But there are some who have no memory of their life before death and they work with the angels to become new souls. To "pass on' so to speak.

Then I interrupted, "So is there a doorway here in Canada?"

"Yes, but in order to actually get to the Valley, you must spiritually leave your body behind at the celestial location. It's a spiritual dimension, for spirits only."

"Oh!" Stacey squeaked, "The Goddess and the Horned God are spiritual beings. They must have been frozen in time, making the seasons endlessly repeat themselves!" She said this in a sappy toned voice. I guess she forgot that the God and Goddess *are* the seasons.

I looked at her skeptically. In her head she wanted the story to be true for some romantically fucked up reason. Thomas gave me a look after glancing at her. I shrugged.

"That's the story, but enough Fairy tales," Thomas said this while looking at Stacey. He seemed to have the same idea that the story was crap. "The statue wasn't where Hannah thought and when she awoke, Luke was there to whisk her away in time and," he turned to me, "Just so you know, John was exiled. He was sent back to Egypt and was disowned by his native clan."

"Wasn't he punished?" I asked.

"If he was a corrupted, treason would have been punished by death. But for Werewolves who are not corrupted, being left utterly alone is punishment enough."

I thought about it for a second. Okay well, it looked like all we had to do was figure out who was responsible for the library attack and keeping Stacey safe. Also, I needed to do some research on our so called Oracle. I didn't trust her at all, and I had to figure out who the fuck was forcefully infecting humans with demon blood.

"Alright well, I have to get back to Peter and Mary. Thomas, watch over Stacey, and Stace," I pointed at her, "Don't leave the church for any reason until I get back."

She nodded. I hugged her and then walked to my window. I turned to look at Thomas. "Watch my father too, I don't entirely trust the Oracle, but keep *that* too yourself."

He too nodded. I turned to sand and raced back to my family.

*　*　*

"So you think the memory she showed you was a lie? It doesn't make sense; why would she lie about that? I think you're just being paranoid Gabby. The Vampires and Werewolves have trusted her for years." Peter said to me.

Mary was sleeping in the other room with Jeremiah in her arms. I didn't like how unsupportive Peter was being. There was something about the Oracle that was rotten. Her scent may not have evil in it but what did I know about psychics? Maybe they had the ability to control that like they can shut me out of their minds. John didn't smell evil but he betrayed Matthew. Peter listened to my silent speculations.

"Did you want to see for yourself?" He asked. He meant going to the doorway to The Valley of Dry bones. I realized I did so I nodded.

"Then we'll do that. The night Linda picks up Mary, we'll go see Luke. I'm sure he knows where it is."

I smiled at Peter and got under the sheets with him. We wrapped our arms around each other. The top of my head was under his chin.

"I love you Peter."

He kissed my hair.

"I love you too Gabby." He whispered.

*　*　*

Linda picked up Mary just after the little munchkin had supper. She wasn't pleased about Jeremiah; she wasn't an animal lover and Jeremiah wasn't a Linda lover. He greeted her with a long hiss. Peter and I both kissed Mary goodbye and watched Linda take her to her car, strap her in her car seat, and drive away. We closed the door.

"Are you ready?" Peter asked me. We were going to see Luke, and if that failed we were off to harass Matthew. If we found the doorway, we would harass Hannah because she knew how to 'walk through'. I nodded to Peter. We closed our eyes and concentrated on Luke. His mind wasn't too hard to find since we were so attuned to him. It looked like he was already with Matthew; we could see in his head Matthew's cabin by the base of one of the mountains. Perfect.

Luke felt us in his head, "Looks like we're about to have company." Luke said to Matthew. We focused on his surroundings and sand travelled there within minutes.

*   *   *

Matthew was extremely grateful to Luke, me, and especially Stacey.

But to me he said, "The Archangel saves the day."

I read his thoughts behind the comment, "Messenger of God?" I asked.

"Yes, it is said he was the one who told the Virgin Mary about her child she was to bare.

"Yes but wasn't Gabriel the one who fell in and out of love easily?"

Matthew laughed mockingly, "Where did you hear such blasphemy?"

I froze, "But," I clenched my jaw, "why are you laughing? I swear I thought that was true. That's why my father named me that. Not the actual falling in love part, but I kinda go through a lot of... well I did... I mean. Never mind." I didn't like the feeling I was feeling and now on top was a large amount of embarrassment. I almost described my past sex life in one sentence.

"No, your father named you that because of your pull of others, how they listen to you, and how you absorb and recite information. Unfortunately you didn't set those standards for the teachings your father wanted you to learn. As we have just witnessed."

I was feeling really stubborn about this. Where did I hear that then? Didn't Peter think the same thing?

Well actually I told you I'm not religious, I got that from a T.V. show. Peter thought.

What? What kind of psychologist gets his information off a fucking T.V.

113

show? I swear I was about to have my first complex in weeks. I was doing so good too.

The broken, empty kind; who lost his wife to another man and had too much to drink every night. What's your excuse?

He stumped me, I had no idea. *Where* did I get that from?

"You look confused, but there is say that Gabriel can help you manifest your deepest desire and reminds everyone the importance of loving one another." Matthew said.

I squinted at him. He was trying to make me feel better. I did, but very little. I still felt very stupid and was considering changing my name.

"Whatever, anyways, Peter and I are here to ask if either of you knew where the doorway was, if there is one, to The Valley of Dry Bones."

Matthew and Luke looked uneasy.

"You would have to go alone first of all. Two, you don't just go there for anything. There has to be a purpose or fate has linked you there. Otherwise, you're just having a dreamless sleep. Thirdly, we cannot defend your body if we get ambushed. Your body will be completely human, because when you leave for the spiritual Valley, your soul and your powers go with you. So, it is a very good thing you have brought Peter with you. He can stay with us in case that happens." Luke warned.

I frowned because I kind of wanted Peter to come with me.

"That's fine," I decided, "Do you know where the doorway is?"

"You're already here." Matthew said.

What? Peter and I thought at the same time. Wouldn't we have felt the energy of such a doorway? Matthew and Luke turned and walked behind Matthew's cabin, into the woods. Peter and I followed. There, just a few yards in, was a stone with a pentagram on it.

"What's with all the pentagrams?"

Matthew raised an eyebrow.

"It was in the parking lot too, the other day when that demon woman came out of it. It turned into a red burning star. Like, flames shot out of it when she rose from the ground." Matthew looked at Luke then back at me.

"The pentagram is a symbol of protection; it has been used in Wicca beliefs for centuries."

It was my turn to raise an eyebrow, "What's a Wicca symbol doing on a biblical doorway to the spirit world? And what do you mean a symbol of protection? Like, as a good thing? A damn demon came to earth through that fucking thing!

Luke spoke next with patience, "Wicca is not defined by good or evil. Anyone can use a magickal symbol. It was probably used to protect her doorway as this one is used to protect this doorway."

Holy fuck. This is seriously fucked up. It's like everything had a slight truth, then a fucking twilight zone episode attached to the end of it, for good measure, to give me a God damned complex. My brain was going a mile a minute. I calmed down after a few good deep breaths. My mood was swinging; what was wrong with me?

"Okay, how do we open it?" I tried to ask calmly.

"We can't be here when you do, but you simply place your hand on the stone and use your mind and heart to open it. Then you'll be on your path to whatever it is you seek or whatever seeks you." Luke said.

That's it. If he keeps talking in riddles; I'm going to strangle him with a green, stretchy, full length jumpsuit to teach him a lesson.

I think my mood was starting to show on my face because he politely tried to remind me, "Only if fate expects you or you have a sole purpose."

"Alright." Why was I so frustrated?

The three of them left me there. Peter hung back for a second then went into the trees. I didn't know what my sole purpose was. I was filled curiosity but an actual purpose? Maybe this was a fate thing. I was actually a little bit afraid of fate now that I thought about it. But I didn't want any tiny fact to prove any tiny detail of the Oracle's words to be true. So I quickly removed that from my mind.

I closed my eyes and walked forward to the stone with my hand stretched out before me. As soon as I made contact with the stone, I opened my eyes again. When I opened them I was no longer at the base of the mountain. I was in a desert. The sand was red and the atmosphere around me was white. I felt cool. The ground was littered with bones.

"Hello?" I called.

It looked as if a breeze was blowing, even though I felt nothing, as the sand gathered together into three separate piles. The piles grew tall and the sand turned to a flesh colour until three figures stood in front of me. White wings grew from their backs. Wings as big as Peter's, about twenty feet in length. I was speechless as the figure's identities were revealed to my mind. But not by a voice, but the Valley itself.

They were the first three Archangels of God. The knowledge flooded through my mind. They had no faces though. The middle one had dirty blonde hair, with a militia looking armored uniform that looked as though it came out of a gladiator movie. It looked like it was made of gold with a red sash around the waist. This was Michael; the protector and bringer of justice. The first banisher of Satan. To his right with brown hair, was Gabriel. In Gabriel's hand was a trumpet. He wore white and blue robes. The messenger, revealer of truth and sole decision maker of which souls were born. His wings had an aura of silver around them.

And finally to Michael's left, was Raphael. With shorter brown hair, he was the one who had dominion over earth. He was the one who healed those on earth who suffered the wrath of the Fallen Angels. His robes were made of the softest golden silk. He was known as the protector of children. He had a bright light illuminating around his head.

I didn't know what to do or say. Then I heard multiple voices. I thought at first it was the Angels but the voices came from behind me. I turned and saw the bones had turned into a thousand different skeletons. The voices were coming from them. Any normal person would have freaked, but the only normal people that would come here would be already dead so.....

But I knew better, the skeletons were glowing, showing to me they were good and not evil. They resided with the Angels. I looked back at the Archangels but they were replaced by three different Angels. Well, versions of Angels.

Joseph. James, and a third man I didn't know the name to, stood in front of me now. Their wings were magnificent. Golden veins in each one of the white feathers. All three had piercing blue eyes. Not one of them was wearing a shirt and each held a blue flaming sword. They were the Obedients.

"Gabby."

The voice startled me. I looked over and saw the Oracle. "Isis?" I fully faced her confused. My three Obedients disappeared.

"I hoped I'd see you here eventually." She said kindly. There was something different, something more pure about this presence of the Oracle.

"What are you doing here?" I asked.

"I have been here for a long time."

"How long?"

"I was killed five summers ago."

Dread pounded through me. I knew there was something wrong with the so called Oracle.

"But how?"

"A shape shifter demon from Hell. It killed me and consumed a piece of my soul. Thus, being able to imitate my image, scent, energy, and even some of my gifts. Like most demons from Hell, it feeds on pieces of the human soul to sustain itself. Normal demons can only use pieces that they corrupt because then it's easy to separate it from the rest. A shape shifter demon uses fear to corrupt the part of the mind to cause doubt in that human's faith. I've been watching and screaming to you. Your vision can go beyond the physical. I will show you how."

And suddenly I had the knowledge.

"You will now be able to hear and or see the good unsettled spirits, so they may guide you." The real Oracle smiled.

Overtime, evil unsettled spirits became possessive demons. Overtime, good unsettled spirits can become literal miracles. A brand new soul and pass on under the guidance of Gabriel.

"So what did happen to the statue of the Goddess and The Horned God?" I asked.

"There is no such statue here, there never was. Maybe in the physical world, but not here. Hannah never made it out here to the Valley, she must have assumed by her lack of vision that it was missing. Her legends state that the souls of the Goddess and the Horned God were set in stone in the Valley of Dry Bones. That the stones were made up of the bones of all earth's creatures. But it is a mythical story if you can believe it. No actual existence. Just a spiritual metaphor for the seasons and lunar cycles."

Even though she was the real and the 'good' Oracle, I still felt she wasn't telling me everything or the whole truth. She nodded as if she heard me. "All in good time. You'll know what you need to know when the time comes for you to know it my child.'

I knew my vision was coming to an end so I didn't argue. I wanted to ask another question.

"Where is your body?"

"Consumed by the demon, along with part of my soul."

I tried to ask more but before I could, she disappeared.

My vision went dark. The atmosphere was red and the sand went black. The bones were gone.

Peter stood there, in his demon form, only his horns were black with red tips. His wings were black too. It looked like Peter but it wasn't him. This was someone else.

But who?

CHAPTER ELEVEN

I awoke on the ground. I heard yelling from multiple voices. The Vampire Court was here voicing their disapproval of my visit to the Valley. Leaving my body vulnerable. The fact that Peter would be left to protect them in my absence infuriated them. They despised change and Peter was the epitome of it. As I walked towards them, I noticed my back was heavy. I had unintentionally changed into my angel form. Everyone on the other side of the trees quieted as they noticed my glow. My angel form was slightly different, my wings had the golden veins I saw in my vision and with my newly acquired skill, I felt evolved. Even my dress had changed to a baby blue.

At the sight of me the Court fell to their knees. Even Luke went to one knee. In their heads, I saw that the form I took now was a step closer to the true angel form of the Witchdemon. Matthew and Hannah stood frozen behind the Vampires. I could see their supernatural auras. Each of the Court members glowed violet. Luke's glow was a royal blue and the Wolves', Matthew and Hannah's had a light green glow. I turned to see Peter standing with crystal white eyes. The Court must have pissed him off, but as we looked at each other he calmed down and they went back to brown. His aura was red.

"We must go." I said to him.

The Court and Luke stood up.

"Why, what did you see?" Peter asked.

"The Oracle isn't the Oracle. I saw her in the Valley. She was killed by a shape shifter demon five summers ago. He took a piece of her soul and used her powers to portray her. I left her at my father's church."

Peter didn't need further explanation, he walked towards me.

"We shall come with you too." Matthew and Hannah stepped forth.

"And us." Luke and his Court stepped forward. We all took hands and Peter and I turned us all to sand and raced to my father and best friend.

*   *   *

We all rematerialized in front of the altar. Decay was in the air.

"But how? This is Holy ground." Matthew questioned more to himself than anyone else.

Luke was the one to answer him, "The church has been cursed. The shape shifter used the psychic energy to manipulate the spiritual aura of the church. The demons can come and go as they please."

The Court hissed. I scanned the church mentally till I found Stacey.

"They are in the basement; I sense the Oracle and twelve demons. They have Stacey, she's still alive. They were waiting for my return."

We all made our way towards the basement. Two figures lay crumpled face down on the floor just a few dozen feet from the basement doors. I smelled death from then instantly. Peter was the first to react.

"Oh my God." Peter had turned over the first body, it was Thomas. His eyes, tongue, and ears were ripped from his head without any blood left around the wounds. Peter stepped back with a hand covering his mouth. He didn't want to touch the second body, so with a wave of his hand it flipped over. I did not have to look to know it was my father's face he saw. This one also without eyes, ears, and a tongue. The demons seemed to think this was a fitting death for a priest. Hear no evil, see no evil, and speak no evil.

I could feel Peter's anger building; his eyes had turned white as soon as we arrived. I was strangely calm. I opened the doors to the basement with a wave of my hand and stepped through with everyone else behind me. The demons were all huddled in a tight group at the back of the room. They turned to look at us and then separated with grins on their faces, revealing the Oracle with Stacey forcefully kneeling at her feet. The Oracle had Stacey by the hair and a blade at her throat. The Oracle smiled.

"Let her go!" Peter demanded. The Oracle didn't even notice him. I raised my hand and put up a barrier to protect the Vampires and Werewolves from the demons. These demons, I sensed, had drank this shape shifters blood and I sensed they could imitate the shape shifters gifts such as Hell fire. I didn't want my friends to die. So my invisible bubble kept them separated.

Darling, I thought to Peter, *eat the demons while I force the shape shifter to its original form.*

Gladly. His eyes went black and veins appeared on his face.

Peter and I both raised our hands. The blade at Stacey's throat turned to sand and the shape shifter looked as if someone was choking it. Peter made the demons rise in the air and one by one they exploded, leaving behind their black sand of blood which Peter consumed. Stacey ran to Peter and he pulled her away from me and the shape shifter. Its skin rippled as its body looked as if it was trying to turn inside out. It stretched out from every angle. It stretched tall into a treelike form. The skin of the demon turned into a black bark and the hands and face were huge compared to its stretched out body. The legs and feet were thick and its toes looked like roots.

His name was Regin, he had two brothers named Otr and Fafnir. They were known as the shape shifter demons, the original three shape shifters from the first spawn of demons thousands of years ago. I knew this without looking into his mind which I couldn't do anyways just like the 'lust' demons. But it was as if an invisible being was telling me the information like a forgotten memory. He roared at me. He didn't even ruffle one feather on my back. Pathetic. This wasn't even his true form, just one of his favourites.

It didn't really matter to me. My glow increased and I beat my wings, sending a ball of white light hurtling at the beast. But he didn't budge, in fact he laughed at me. Fucker. I realized I hadn't mastered this form and had no idea what of my skills were the strongest this way. If angelic powers were making him laugh then I would have to demonize myself. But this time I would eat him, unlike the other bitch from Hell I didn't get to taste. Before I could transform, he blasted me in the chest with Hell fire. I flew back and hit the barrier. Didn't hurt but was fucking annoying.

"Gabby!" Stacey screamed.

"Stay here." I said mostly to Peter. My voice was like a nightingale's song.

I didn't take my eyes off the demon as I made my change. My white feathers burst off my wings and were replaced with sharp scales. My robes turned to sand and then returned to my body as it stretched into the demon form. The sand became a more fitting and less revealing outfit for me. My tail twitched, ready to strike. My horns just finished curving when I let out my own roar.

The demon ran at me; I jumped on him and grabbed his face. I bit down hard on his neck with my sharp teeth. It really was bark but it oozed thick, black demon blood. The scent of the demon hit me; it was the same as the 'lust' twins, the same as Peter's. Regin screamed in pain and grabbed me around the waist with one hand and ripped me off. He threw me to the side of the room just above Peter and Stacey. The blood was delicious and it was only a vague second of what I smelled filled my head, the connection I had but didn't fit in because it was too late. I landed gracefully but before I could go back for more, Peter was already running at the demon, half in transformation to his own demon form. I let him go and just stood there with Stacey and watched.

Peter jumped and fisted the beast in the face, causing Regin to stumble back to the wall. The connection I almost made disappeared as I was distracted by the shape shifters next choice of action. Peter stood there and as his horns grew, the demon fell to its knees. Suddenly it spoke a different language. It repeated the phrase over and over. It looked like it was begging.

What the fuck?

Peter ignored the demon and rushed at him, taking a bite out of the other side of the demon's neck. It screamed again but didn't try to stop Peter like it tried to stop me. I noticed the demon's aura start to fade. I then realized the aura was red. Peter drank till the demon turned black and then pulled away as Regin crumbled to bits.

I looked at the Werewolves and Vampires to see if they were okay but they were staring at Peter with horror on their faces. I looked in their heads and then looked at Peter dumbfounded. They recognized Peter's demon form. Regin was saying 'Lord please don't punish me'. In Latin. Because Peter had the same smell and the same aura as the demons we fought.

Because Peter was the reincarnation of Damien, the son of Satan.

* * *

"How is this possible? Isn't Damien a demon? How could he have a soul?" We were back at Matthew's cabin. I questioned them as soon as I was in my human form again. Peter took off absolutely freaked. Now that I know, I'm not too surprised yet I was still fighting it. I was under the impression that Damien, being a demon and all, was just banished to Hell and just didn't take as much energy to come to the surface like his father. But I was distracted; Peter shut me out of his head, I had no idea where he went and I was breaking inside. But instead of wallowing, I was taking my frustration out on the vampire Court. The one named Nathaniel spoke to me,

"First and foremost, the Devil himself was once an angel. His son was once human but given who his father was, he too had an awakening. But he did not see things the way his father did, at first. He was corrupted by his father and was in charge of his father's armies to take over the earth. Like you've been previously informed, Satan will not surface himself for fear of Michael."

He took a pause to look up to the night's sky and then looked back at me, "he used his son, but suddenly Damien had a change of heart. He figured out how to reincarnate his soul five thousand years after the first war he led against the first Witchdemon. He is completely oblivious to everything once in a new life. He did this to try to get away from his father, it did not work and he was corrupted a second time. Obviously he went the same route a second time. Evidently, Damien is reincarnated around the same time the Witchdemon is as well. Lucifer has only acted the past couple times when the Witchdemon is around Damien. We do not know why. He does not surface but he has his ways of making his presence known. Now it seems there is some sort of connection that has been brewing since the first Witchdemon arrived."

"You mean Damien never led the armies until the Witchdemon arrived?" I interrupted.

Nathaniel stared into my eyes, "Once the Witchdemon is born then everything is set in place, it has become his favourite game. We noticed this pattern when the last two wars occurred. We think he waits for his son to become acquainted somehow with her and then an event by his creation to make his son see her as an enemy. But as I mentioned, both times Damien had a last minute change of heart."

"So you think now this is the ultimate game because Peter and I are in love?"

Nathaniel nodded.

"It won't work. Peter and I are in love. He has my powers, doesn't that make him incorruptible?" I asked.

"Satan is the master of corruption. You and your Obedients are the only ones who have proven over and over again to be immune. Peter is a liability. Your love may be pure but Satan is a master of corrupting the pure. He has corrupted and is continuing to corrupt a terribly large amount of minds and souls."

I swallowed my anger and just continued to look at him; there was something else on his mind.

He sighed and then continued, "He may even try to corrupt you, taking your love for Peter as a weakness. These are very unusual circumstances indeed."

"Then what do we do?" Stacey asked him. She knew if I spoke there would be no nice words.

He looked at her gravely, "We wait."

I didn't want to fucking wait. If Satan was going to try and corrupt Peter, I wasn't going to sit here and twiddle my fucking thumbs. I didn't care if our souls were mortal enemies. I loved him. I got up and walked into the trees, I went up a pathway to the side of the mountain. After about ten minutes of walking, I fell to my knees in a clearing.

Peter! Fucking God dammit! Get your head out of your ass and come back to me! I love you! Who you're reincarnated after doesn't mean anything! I need you! I screamed mentally to him.

Tears fell down my face in streams. Now I know why he couldn't stand me feeling ashamed of myself. I knew that's how he was feeling right now and it hurt my heart deeply. I put my face in my hands and wept.

Peter, please come back. I whimpered in my head.

"Gabby." The voice made my head shoot up. It was the voice of my father. My dead father. His body, along with Thomas's was at the foot of the mountain wrapped in fine silk waiting to be burned or cremated or whatever at sunrise. But here he stood in front of me.

"Father?"

His features were intact and he smiled at me.

"Do not worry my dear Gabby. He is in deep thought right now but he will return to you. He truly does love you."

This made more tears run down my cheeks.

"I'm sorry I couldn't protect you or Thomas." I mumbled through sobs.

"Do not cry over us, we are still here, me especially if you need. We have joined the Valley and you may visit anytime. Some casualties are needed in this war."

"I love you Father."

"I love you too Gabby. Now I must go, and so should you before the sun rises. Question a member of the Court named Zachariah. Ask him about the last Witchdemon. Not everything the imposter Oracle told you was lies."

"What do you mean?"

"In this case, history tends to repeat itself." He started to disappear.

"Wait! Father wait!" But it was too late.

I stood up and looked around me, just trees. Sadly, I made my way back down the path to the others. I walked up to the one named Zachariah.

"Tell me of the last Witchdemon." I demanded.

Everyone went quiet.

"The last Witchdemon?" he looked around nervously. "Her name was Shakara. She was born in Central Africa. Once she hit the age of six, the Shamans sensed her magic and forced her out of her tribe out of fear. She was in touch with her gifts even before she awakened. She was able to communicate with the animals and ended up being raised by lions. Her flaw, as every Witchdemon has one for a sole purpose, was her inability to feel for humans. When she awoke, the animals and earth became the primary purpose of her protection. She was discovered by two brothers a couple years later and with her gifts, she was able to see into their minds, acquiring the skills of speech and civility to which our species taught, even before the first pharaoh's first breath." He smiled at the memory.

I silently wondered what my flaw was. Was it my teeth? My anger? What would be the sole purpose of those? I shook out the distracting thoughts and listened.

"The one brother had blue eyes and the other had brown eyes. They were both in love with her. We, the Court, met with Shakara and she saw the task ahead of her within our minds. We saw the pull between her and the one brother with blue eyes and we assumed he was an Obedient. The other brother was strange. He went off one night and came back a different man."

I saw the memory in his head. The brothers were David and Daniel. David was the Obedient of the Werewolves as it turned out. Shakara had slept with him when Daniel had left. When Daniel had returned, he was overcome with jealousy and vowed revenge on them both. Daniel, obviously was the reincarnation of Damien, he had come back different because, in Zachariah's thoughts it was an assumption, he had just met his father.

"That's why Damien wants revenge?" I asked.

"Yes, after that it was easy for Satan to corrupt his heart."

"Well, envy is one of the seven deadly sins." I agreed. Lame. "But I will never let that happen. This time around we love each other equally. He is my other half."

The Court members looked at one another.

"That may be true and that's probably why Lucifer has taken it upon himself to appoint every general demon on earth to do Damien's job. Gathering the corrupted and infecting humans and accumulating an army to fight you. This brings the war sooner, leaving us not enough time for you to get stronger. He must know now from Regin's mind, that hope for his son to join him once more is lost."

"You say that but you still don't trust Peter."

"No, we do not."

"But I do." Luke stepped forward. I looked at him in thanks. "As long as I follow him; then so shall my Court." Luke said to me.

"And so shall we." Matthew and Hannah, with the Guard behind them, stepped forward as well.

My eyes almost filled with tears. Almost.

"Thank you, we will figure out this war. We will not lose." I promised but there was one opinion I really needed. I turned to her; she was sitting at the edge of the trees just staring at the wrapped bodies. The Vampires and Werewolves conversed amongst themselves as I walked over to her.

"Stace?" I whispered.

She looked up at me with tears in her eyes.

"Are you okay Stacey?"

"Am I okay? What about you Gabby? You just lost your father and the man you love is your sworn enemy. Where is he? He just took off."

I sighed, "Don't worry, I'm fine. It hurts but I have a way of coping.

And my father's not truly gone. Come on, the sun will be up soon, we must start the ceremony."

The Vampires and Werewolves believe that burning the dead at the brink of a sunrise welcomes the new spirit not only to a new day but to new strength for the after life ahead. It was sweet in a way. Vampire and Werewolf souls did not reincarnate, they were given a place in heaven as an angel. Unless they were corrupted, then they go to Hell if there's any piece of soul left. But this is how the original protectors dealt with the death of the humans. This way, they lowered the possibility of an unsettled spirit while the soul went straight to Gabriel to be reborn. The whole mess with the afterlife was a bit confusing and a little overlapping but I was used to contradictions and the seriously unusual.

We walked back to the 'gang' where two rectangular piles of cedar were ready and waiting. Two Vampires carried Thomas, and Luke and Matthew personally carried my father. Everyone stood back as the bodies were laid. They were a little edgy because the sun was coming soon. Then I had an idea.

"The sun will not harm you." I told them.

My eyes went white and I fluidly changed into my angel form. Lifting my arms to the sky, a thick, blue barrier surrounded my supernatural friends. This way they could see the sun but it had no influence over their lives. It was like looking through sunglasses for them. I looked at the bodies and said a silent 'see you later'. This was not goodbye. I flicked my wrists at the bodies and just as the sun peaked, blue flames engulfed them. The sun rose a little higher and got a little brighter. The rays hit the barrier, causing golden glitter to sparkle around the Vampires and Werewolves. They were in awe; they hadn't seen the sun in centuries. They trusted me completely. I vowed to end this war with Peter at my side. I will not let them down. My father and Thomas will not have died in vain.

The ceremony didn't last very long. When it was over, I extended the barrier to the cabin so the Vampires and Werewolves could go rest. When everything was done, I changed back to my human form and Stacey and I stood there staring at the smoking piles of ash.

* * *

I floated over the ocean with a red dress on. It billowed around me like a cloud. I was sad. I was lost.

Gabby?

I didn't respond because I thought I was imagining it. I've been trying to hear his voice for days.

Gabby can you hear me?

Tears fells from my eyes.

Don't cry Gabby, I'm sorry.

I shot towards the moon, spinning as I went a few dozen yards up. I was upset and to be honest, a little frustrated. It had been days since my father's body burned in front of me. I stopped and floated there staring at the stars.

Where are you? I asked.

I'm here, in the ocean. It's peaceful down here.

I looked down and watched as the water separated, making a hole appear. Peter rose with the water under him. The water rose with him but he was completely dry. He rose with the water till her was level with me.

"Gabby, I'm sorry I left. I was just so shocked to know that, that I'm a monster."

"You're not a monster Peter. You have a choice. You are the other half of my soul. As long as we are together, nothing can stop us." I told him with all my heart.

"Do you really believe that?"

"Yes I do."

I floated to him and put my right index finger to his forehead. I stroked across it, down his cheek, to his lips which I traced in a circle clockwise. He closed his eyes at my touch. I brought my face to his and rubbed my cheek against his on each side and then kissed his closed eyes. His eyes fluttered open and he looked at me sadly.

"I love you." I told him.

A single tear fell from his right eye.

"I love you too."

Then we kissed.

CHAPTER TWELVE

We abandoned my father's church. Too many memories and I made sure it looked like it was condemned. Peter sold his house in Surrey and we bought a place in Deep Cove, secluded and by the water. I sent the Court and Guard members, and the few Wolves that showed up for my wedding, over to West Vancouver to snuff out the two hundred demons overs there, well, realistically they couldn't but they ate their till and knocked down the numbers. Peter was on edge for the first couple weeks but once Mary started coming around, he relaxed. The three of us were on the front porch looking out at the trees and admiring the Christmas lights on neighbouring properties. Tomorrow was Christmas Eve.

"Okay honey bee, time for bed." Peter whispered in her ear. Her little eyes were drooping.

"Okay daddy." She mumbled. She turned five in twelve days: January fourth. I would have been more excited if I knew what the future had in store. I was tempted to introduce Mary to Stacey but afraid all at the same time. Or maybe nothing would happen. I didn't know how psychics reacted to one another in that sense. Stacey was going to have her wedding on Valentine's Day if, as she so beautifully put it, she survived this war or if it hasn't occurred yet. I told her that Stan might have to be informed of what's going on. And that's what we're going to do tomorrow, so I guess Mary would meet Stacey after all.

Stacey was going to bring Stan over for dinner. We weren't going to tell him everything, just enough where he wouldn't get too freaked out. Didn't want to send him to a psych ward. Stacey had to see him a couple times and both times Luke was with her for protection. Not that he could do much if there was a gang of corrupted after them, but we relied on the fact that Stacey could probably see if Luke had a battle in his future simply by touching him. Luckily there was nothing to worry about. But Stacey told me Stan was a little suspicious of Luke so we agreed to let the cat out of the bag.

Oh no honey, he's a Vampire and he's protecting me from demons. Yea, the conversation was going to go just fine. I hope.

Peter carried Mary up to her room while I sat in the living room on the couch. I looked around at the walls. I remembered the look on the previous owner's face when we presented him with the amount he wanted in cash. He totally thinks we're drug dealers, but he didn't complain. The owner was just retiring from a forty five year career in dentistry and conveniently enough, he was also selling his little spot in the one building no bigger than an apartment complex this little town calls a 'mall'. It has four other places, some sort of medical this and that. We bought that as well to be a psychologist office for Peter, mainly as a front since we would be way too busy. And obviously Peter quit his job at the college.

"Gabby?" Peter came around the couch and sat down beside me.

I looked up at him. "Hmm?"

He put his hand on my cheek, "Are you sure you're not making a mistake?"

I placed my hand around his and brought it to my lips. I kissed his knuckles one by one then looked up at him again. I could see that he loved me.

"You are worth everything to me." I told him. "Mary needs you and I need you. And the world needs us."

I combed my fingers through his hair a couple of times and then kissed him gently on the lips. We looked at each other and he smiled. I was going to smile back but I didn't want to let my teeth show, it was stupid but I suddenly felt self-conscious. He heard that thought and frowned.

"If you teeth bothered me, we wouldn't be sitting here, married and in a beautiful new house."

I also wouldn't be thinking very inappropriate thoughts about you every minute of every day. He thought to me.

Very inappropriate? I raised my eyebrow.

He smiled.

Everyday? I pressed, starting to smile myself.

He leaned forward and pressed his forehead against mine. We both had our eyes closed but our hearts sang together in our minds. It might actually kill me if he was gone, never to be seen, ever again.

*   *   *

"Okay Mary, here's the star, want to put it up on the tree?" I asked her with a big smile on my face.

"Yea!" she squealed. I handed her the star and Peter picked her up so she was tall enough to put it on the tree. I clapped when she let go.

"Merry Christmas!" she shouted. I grabbed her face and gave her an Eskimo kiss; I rubbed my nose against hers. She giggled.

The doorbell announced the arrival of Stan and Stacey. I human ran to the door.

I hope you got something good, Stacey thought before I got to the door.

"Shit." I whispered to myself. I totally forgot to plan how we were going to break it to him. He was under the impression that he got really drunk with Joseph at and after the wedding and that's why he couldn't remember shit. Joseph didn't tell him of his midnight encounter with Stacey and me so Stan had no clue or even an inkling as what actually happened.

I opened the door.

"Stan, Stacey, Merry Christmas." I welcomed them. I didn't think about what to say because I was distracted on how we were going to play up dinner without him noticing that Peter and I don't actually eat human food anymore. I didn't think telling him we feed on demon blood would help with the 'non-psych ward' plan.

Mary would take most of his attention, yes she was in on it, and when he wasn't looking we would make bite sized portions turn invisible to make it look as if we were actually eating. It took only a couple seconds to explain and thoughtfully apologise to Stacey. She looked at me as she sat down on my love seat with Stan. He brought a bottle of wine. I made introductions of Peter and Stan as I poured some for the four of us. He took a big sip while Stacey just looked at hers then set it down on the end table. Odd.

Peter and I just held ours in our hands. The both of us leaned against the fireplace. There was no real need for it since the place was well heated through the flooring system. On the dining table in the dining room was a vase filled with a huge bouquet, an empty roasting pan beside it and four empty bowls with the usual plates and dinner stuff. I wasn't worried; I could whip something up in seconds, literally. That was all in the other room of course.

"So who's this?" Stan asked pointing to Mary.

"This is our daughter Mary." Peter answered. I loved how he said 'our' daughter, it made my heart flutter. A voice in my head laughed at my corniness but whatever. Mary looked at Stan a little shyly. Stan got off the couch and crouched in front of her.

"Hi Mary, I'm Stan." He smiled at her. She smiled back but hid behind Peter's leg. We all laughed.

"Awe Mary, your so cute." I said to her as I too crouched down to her height. She ran into my arms and filled them with giggles.

"Mary, say hi to my best friend Stacey." Mary turned her head and looked to where I pointed. Stacey waved at her.

"Hi." She said, then looked at Stan and hid her face in my arms again. I laughed.

"I think she has a crush on you." I teased.

"I do not mommy!" she giggled again. Then, to prove her point she pushed me away and walked right up to Stan who was still crouched.

"Hi." She said pointedly with her nose slightly in the air. Stan smiled.

"Hi." He said to her.

"Are you guys going to be my new Aunty and Uncle?"

The question surprised all of us. Stan looked back at Stacey, then me. I shrugged. Stan looked at Peter, and Peter shrugged too.

"Um, sure kiddo. Do you want that?"

"Yes." Mary put her hands behind her back and twisted from side to side.

"Okay then." Stan didn't know what else to say

"Yay!" she surprised us further by suddenly hugging him. Then she let go with a serious look on her face. "Are you guys magical too?"

The question stumped him. Stacey, Peter and I all looked at each other.

"What do you mean?" he half whispered.

Just then, Jeremiah came into the room and went right up to Mary. She picked him up and he started to purr. Peter and I looked at each other uneasily.

"Mommy made my kitty out of earth and daddy made his house out of my old dolls and clothes."

Stan furrowed his eyebrows and tried to comprehend what Mary had said.

"What's going on here?" he looked at me and Peter when he asked this. He stood up. Uh, oh. Looks like it was time to fess up.

"Honey bee, why don't you go to your room and play with Jeremiah for a bit before dinner okay please?" Peter asked her.

"Okay daddy." She left the room and went upstairs.

"Stan-" Stacey started.

"No, no let them explain, something is up here." Stan shushed her. It was the wine talking because normally this kind of thing would just make him laugh. But for some reason his ego, and the wine, made him believe we were purposely making fun of him.

I sighed. "You're not in a world you think you're in." Peter said.

"What's that supposed to mean?" Stan jutted out his chin.

"It means there are things out there that make your worst nightmares look like pleasant dreams."

He looked at me and Peter then turned to Stacey.

"Do you hear this shit?" he asked with his arms raised.

"It's true." Stacey simply shrugged her shoulders.

"Is this a fucking joke?" he was starting to get irritated for real now.

"No its not." Peter said. Stan looked back at us and in shock, stumbled backwards till he fell on his ass into the love seat next to Stacey. Peter and I had changed our eyes to crystal white.

Fear made him unable to move so he just sat there listening. Eventually he calmed down and became genuinely curious. We told him of the Vampires and Werewolves and the Witchdemon being the protectors of the earth. We didn't mention the Obedients, he said he wouldn't tell anyone but just in case we left that part out because of Joseph. I really didn't want Joseph to know. We told him the unfortunate corruption of some of the Vampires and Werewolves, causing the uncorrupted to blame each other for God's punishment of darkness.

We told him of the demons; possessive, infected, and the Generals from Hell. Then we explained how Peter and I were the Witchdemons. Then the reason for Luke's presence around Stacey and her gifts. After we were done, Stan just sat there and we didn't interrupt as it slowly sunk in for him. I could see in his mind he was very glad he never challenged Luke to a fight.

"Wow." He finally said, "So you guys, like, fly and stuff?"

I looked at Peter and then back at Stan. We both nodded to him.

"Actually, we have a confession; you didn't get drunk at our wedding. I had to erase your memory." With a wave of my hand, I returned the memory to him. He blinked a couple times before going bug eyed.

"Holy fuck. And those people?"

"Vampires and Werewolves." Peter confirmed Stan's thoughts. I was surprised at how well Stan was taking this.

"Wow." Stan said again. He grabbed Stacey's hand and looked at her.

"So what do you see?" he said with a grin. Stacey smiled. She saw lots and lots of sex. I laughed.

"Okay, are you guy's hungry?"

Stan stood, "yea, what are we having?"

"Well, you, Mary and Stacey are having the usual turkey dinner with various side dishes." I said as Stan squinted at me.

"What are you two having?"

"We ate already, a couple days ago. We don't need to eat as often as you guys do."

Stan sniffed the air, "I don't smell anything."

"Don't worry, it's one of those gifts she has." Stacey said. Stan looked confused.

"I'll go get Mary." Peter went upstairs as the rest of us went into the dining room. I took the lid off the roasting pan. Stan furrowed his eyebrows.

"Um." He started but I put up a finger to silence him.

"Food!" Mary yelled as she ran to the table and sat down. Peter was behind her, he came up to me and wrapped his arm around my shoulders. Our eyes were still white.

"You do the turkey and I'll do the rest?" I looked at him.

"Sure." He said. Stan just looked at us. Peter and I waved our hands and the flowers turned to sand, making Stan step back out of surprise. Stacey held his hand, keeping him in the dining room. The sand separated to the roasting pan and four bowls, making the beautiful golden brown turkey and filled the bowls with mashed potatoes, carrots, stuffing, and cranberry sauce. Then an apple pie especially for Stacey. If I was still human I would have preferred pumpkin pie but Stacey hated pumpkin pie, the fuckin alien. The room filled with the scent of the food which was fucking gross but in their heads it smelled absolutely delicious. Stan's eyes bugged out again and Stacey kissed him on the cheek.

"Holy fuck." Stan whispered. Stacey slapped him hard on the chest. He looked at her and she motioned with her chin towards Mary.

"Oh, sorry." He said to me and Peter. Peter and I just smiled, our eyes going back to brown. Peter and Stacey went into the front room for the glasses of wine, Peter's glass, mine and Stacey's were untouched. Dinner went well and afterwards Stan relaxed mostly because of Mary. The two of them were playing with Jeremiah and Stacey was in her glory watching them.

He's going to be such a great father. She thought to me. I smiled and then it was my turn to go bug eyed. Only for a second though.

She just revealed that she was pregnant. She was about a month along. My hand went to my mouth and a shit eating grin went on her face.

Oh my God Stacey, I thought to her. *When are you going to tell him?*

I don't know! I just found out yesterday! Her mind giggled.

Peter noticed our exchange but couldn't read our thoughts. He came over to us and kissed my cheek.

Care to let me in on the secret? He asked.

I looked at Stacey, she nodded.

Stacey is pregnant and Stan has no idea. I revealed. My mental voice all of a conspirator.

Oh. He looked at Stan and went into his mind. *Well, he's considering the possibility thanks to Mary.* Peter informed.

Well he doesn't exactly have a choice now does he? I said with a slight warning attached as I looked at Stan myself.

I think he'll be thrilled, Peter defended.

Should I tell him? Stacey asked.

Um, we already loaded him with a bunch of information. I'm not sure if his head could handle it. Maybe wait till at least tomorrow. I suggested.

I had a thought and started to laugh. Stan and Mary looked at me and I recollected myself. They went back to their game.

What's so funny? Stacey asked.

Oh, just let me know if he's ever a dick while you're pregnant. Then when you give birth. I'll just project your pain to him and let him feel what it feels like to give birth. I thought a little sadistically. I heard Peter try to envision it with a wince in his mind.

No, no none of that. Stacey said even though she totally considered it.

A howl broke through the silence; everyone looked at the patio doors. I looked at Peter, the Wolves were calling us.

"Is that what I think it is?" Stan asked. I nodded.

"We have to step out for a minute honey bee. Stay here with Aunty and Uncle okay?" I said to Mary. She hugged Stan.

"Okay mommy."

"Be careful." Said Stacey.

"We will." Peter promised. Our eyes went white. I put a barrier around the house so if a demon or corrupted came by, they would turn to dust on contact.

"Don't leave the house, the barrier will keep you safe." I said to them.

Stan looked to Stacey then to me. "Hurry back." He said.

Peter and I nodded then went outside. As soon as our feet touched the patio we turned to sand.

* * *

Matthew, Hannah, and what remained of his Guard were in the trees across the water from Deep Cove. They stood in a half circle and Peter and I rematerialized right in the middle.

"What's going on Matthew?" Peter asked. We could have found out easily but we were starting to respect the privacy of our friend's minds.

"Otr has overrun the mountains with the corrupted. He is using a Shaman's magical gift and has turned the sacred doorway to the Valley as a doorway to the underworld." Matthew bowed his head. This was taken as a sign to look in his mind as it was a lot faster to explain. Peter now looked into Matthew's memory and saw the demon for himself. He looked like a giant ugly bird.

"We have reason to believe he's going to resurrect his brother Fafnir the dragon. He was originally banished there by a warrior long before the last war. He was used to protect treasures belonging to a being who was both cruel and evil. He corrupted Fafnir, therefore corrupting his brothers as well. Greed and vengeance brought him back to the surface to fight the last war but Fafnir had fled back to Hell before the last Witchdemon could destroy him. Otr thinks your love is a weakness that, with his brother's help, he can use against you and destroy you." Matthew informed. It looked like he had a lot of fun torturing it out of an abducted corrupted.

"That's quite the assumption." I said a little annoyed.

"When does he plan on doing this?" Peter asked.

"When the moon is next full." Was the answer.

That's Mary's birthday, I thought to Peter sadly.

Then she is going to have to spend it with her mother. He thought back to me.

"That gives us eleven days." I told the Wolves. They all nodded.

"We will fight with you." Joan announced the rest of the Guard nodded.

"But the corrupted have Hell fire, you'll die." Peter tried to object.

But she just smiled. "We have our special blades and our speed. We are slightly faster than the corrupted and our native clans will come if we call them, we'll manage, and this isn't our first war."

"Yes but you don't have an Obedient to lead you." I muttered. Joan looked from Peter to me.

"We don't need the Obedient or our Holy fire. Everything happens for a reason. We will give our lives gladly for the cause."

They were devoted. I had new respect for the Wolves. Matthew and Hannah stepped forward.

"We will deal with the cards we are dealt and respect your choices. I have no fear for the corrupted."

"I sincerely hope none of you die." I said to them, "For now, take refuge here. We will return to you in seven days' time." I was suddenly reminded of my father when I said those last words. I raised my hands to the trees, turning a dozen of them into sand to create a cabin that resembled Matthew's old one by the mountain. Matthew bowed to me.

"Thank you my queen." Then turned to Peter, "My king."

"We shall leave you then." Peter said with a short nod. He grabbed my hand and we burst to sand.

* * *

We rematerialized and Mary was asleep in Stacey's arms. Stan was in the washroom.

"Here I'll take her." I volunteered.

Stacey gently handed her to me but she seemed really distracted.

"You okay?" I asked. She gave me a look and put her hand at my back.

"I'll come up with you to put her to bed."

"Um, okay."

We made our way up the stairs as Peter put the fire out in the fire place. Stacey and Stan were going to spend the night. I already had the guest room set up.

So what's going on? I thought to her.

It's Mary, she said. She bit her lower lip. *I couldn't see her after my wedding. She's going to make the cutest flower girl by the way, but I'm worried.*

What does that mean?

I had frozen when she said she couldn't see Mary after the wedding. We were right in front of Mary's door.

I don't know what it means. I told her but dread filled my heart. *Don't tell Peter what you saw. Don't tell him you saw anything. I need him to be thinking rationally right now.* I warned her.

No problem, she agreed.

We went into the room and I gently laid Mary down on her bed and covered her up. Jeremiah trotted in and jumped up on the bed to join her.

"You watch over her now." Stacey said to him. He responded with a purr. I kissed Mary's forehead and so did Stacey. We walked to the doorway and then looked back at Mary. We looked at each other with worried faces then left the room, closing the door behind us.

CHAPTER THIRTEEN

Christmas started with Mary jumping on Peter and me at seven in the morning.

"Mommy! Daddy! Presents! Presents!" she screamed at the top of her lungs. I had put various gifts under the tree before bed last night for everyone. Peter and I sat up, both with our hair everywhere. We looked at each other.

"Nice hair mad professor." I said.

He smiled and projected what I looked like into my head.

"Oh my God." I said to myself. Mary ran out of the room into the guest bedroom.

"Aunty! Uncle! Presents!"

"No I want to sleep." Stan mumbled.

"No! Presents!" Mary screamed.

Peter and I laughed and got dressed. We went the guest room where Stacey had picked Mary up into her arms and Stan tried to stumble into a pair of pants. Thank God he was wearing boxers.

"Demanding little, err, princess isn't she?"

He was going to say 'brat'. I smiled and Mary giggled.

"Okay honey bee, let's make you some breakfast." Stacey said. The nickname was rubbing off on everyone it seemed.

"Pancakes!" Mary cheered with both arms raised.

Stacey walked past me to the stairs. Stan watched her go and I heard in his head how he liked seeing Stacey with a child in her arms. I turned around and Peter was there in the doorway. The three of us followed Mary's cheers for pancakes down the stairs to the living room.

"Do you want to help me make them?" Stacey asked Mary.

"Yea Aunty I'll help you."

Stan followed them into the kitchen while Peter and I went out on the patio. The sun was just peeking out between the clouds above the trees. Then we heard a very disgusting sound behind us.

"Aunty? Is you okay?" Mary cried.

I strode into the kitchen to see Stacey heaving over the sink. Mary was covered in flour and Stan was holding Stacey's hair back. Stacey looked up at me.

"Morning sickness?" I blurted without thinking. She nodded.

"Morning sickness?" Stan froze, his hands still holding her hair, as he whispered this to himself. Stacey's hair slipped through his fingers as Stacey went forward again to heave once more. Stan just stared at her.

"What's the matter Stan?" Peter asked amused.

Stan's mouth moved but no sound came out. Stacey slowly recovered.

"I'm sorry honey bee but Aunty needs to go lay down." She said to Mary. Mary looked at her then touched Stacey's stomach.

"You have baby?" Mary asked. Wow this kid is full of surprises; Stacey was a little surprised herself.

"Yes sweetie."

Stan nearly fainted, he stumbled on the spot. Peter went to go help him but I stopped him. Stan recovered a bit but still stared in a daze.

"Okay go to bed Aunty, mommy can make me pancakes." Mary looked at me with a big grin on her face. Stacey walked from the room. Stan watched her go, went to follow, stopped, looked at Peter then to me, then actually went and followed Stacey.

I think his brain just stuttered, did you see that? I thought to Peter.

Peter just smiled and shook his head.

"Mommy! Pancakes!" Mary demanded.

"Okay, okay!" I laughed as my eyes went crystal white and with a flick of my wrist, the pancakes made themselves.

* * *

Stan and Stacey stayed in the guest room for the duration of the day. When evening came they resurfaced. Stacey was sick, in the morning. I didn't need super hearing or mind reading to know that her vision came true. Peter and I had to concentrate a bit to shut out Stan's thoughts. He was proudly shouting in his head. We didn't tell him about the mind reading part. The doorbell rang, it was Linda. She was here to pick up Mary. I went to the door.

"Linda, welcome. Please, come in. Peter is just finishing Mary's bath, would you like something to drink?" I asked politely.

Linda walked in with a stiffness that only calculated to the hatred she felt for me.

"No thank you." She said coldly. She walked into the front room with me behind her.

"Stacey, Stan, this is Linda, Mary's mother." I said as I pointed my index and middle fingers to my temple and pretended to shoot myself. Stacey smiled and Stan went to shake Linda's hand but she just stared at it.

"Charmed." Linda said. She didn't sit, she stayed in the entrance way.

Stuck up bitch, Stacey thought as she watched Linda look around the room.

"Quite the house. Are you sure it's up to scale? Kind of smells like mould." She wrinkled up her nose. Stacey got up but I got up with her in case she had any ideas. I inched the both of us towards the dining room entrance as Linda started to walk around to analyse the room some more.

Actually, Peter and I rid the house of its mould and unwanted critters, then restored the wood to its youth. Linda was just being a petty jealous bitch.

"You got to be careful with old houses like this. I'm not sure I want Mary here. It could collapse with the slightest earth quake." Linda grimaced.

That's it, I'm going to hit her. Stacey thought.

Suddenly Linda slapped herself hard across her left cheek. Linda's face was in shock as she looked down at her hand. I ducked into the dining room with Stacey as we both tried to stifle our giggles.

"Um, is something the matter?" Stan asked Linda. He knew exactly what happened but tried to play it off like he saw nothing.

Linda thought about this question. I could hear her freaking out in her head. This made Stacey and I wanted to laugh even harder as I was projecting Linda's thoughts to her. Linda walked to the patio doors trying to avoid eye contact with Stan. Stacey and I walked back into the room a little more composed.

"Mommy!" Mary burst into the room and ran right to Linda.

Doesn't that bother you? Stacey asked. I looked at her and shrugged.

Not really, she is Mary's real mother. But I did feel like grabbing Mary and kicking Linda out of my house.

"I'll bring her back in three weeks." Linda said.

"Three weeks. What about my birthday?" Mary pouted.

How old is this kid? Stan thought but no one answered him.

"That's okay honey bee, unfortunately we won't be here that day." Peter said sadly as he crouched down to her height. She put her hands on his face and looked in his eyes.

"You and mommy have to fight bad people right?" Mary whispered.

Peter blinked, "Uh, yea honey bee."

"Be careful daddy." She kissed him on the nose.

The four of us hugged and kissed Mary on the cheek. Linda wasn't pleased about Mary's new Aunty and Uncle but whatever bitch, fuck you. We waved goodbye to them at the door.

"Feel better." Stan shouted out to Linda. She gave him a weird look and drove away. Stacey slapped him on the arm and giggled. Peter looked at her and closed the door. He saw in Stan's head what happened and when Stan was heading towards the living room Peter smirked.

"Now Stacey, that wasn't very nice." He said sarcastically.

* * *

Stacey and Stan left the next morning back to Stan's place in Coquitlam. Peter and I waved goodbye to them from the door. I sighed.

"What's wrong?"

"I was just thinking, if we were still human, how different our lives could be." I thought of us walking in a park with Mary running ahead towards the swings. A newborn in my arms. Peter saw this and put his arms around me.

"You know, we could still do that one day." He said to me. I looked up at him. "The last Witchdemon gave her powers back to God and was able to live as a human after the war remember?" he reminded me.

That's true, she did. A smile crossed my face. I put a finger to his mouth and traced his lips. He went to lean in and kiss me but I ran away up the stairs at demon speed, laughing as I went. He raced after me and made it to our bed in our room. I turned and pinned him up against the wall. Our strength was supreme but equal. He smiled mischievously. We both were suddenly on the bed with Peter on top of me, pinning my arms above my head. He kissed me and I flipped him over and pinned him instead.

I have a better idea. I thought. I envisioned the open field behind the playground that we found trail walking through the woods. We turned to sand and materialized in the same position on the grass. I stood with my eyes white and shot an arm into the air. Lighting and thunder sounded in the sky. I felt so energized out of nowhere. I made clouds come from the mountains and the night's sky soon disappeared. Snow started to fall in huge chunks. They fell slowly.

My skin started to glow. I looked at Peter and he too was glowing. We turned into our angel forms. Only this time, we were naked with wings. The snow only fell in the field we were in. The playground was untouched. As soon as our lips touched, we rose into the air slowly spinning with our wings extended back. His arms were holding me close, moving up and down my body as mine were doing the same to him. We continued to glow brightly as our bodies entwined. It was a beautiful experience.

*   *   *

I awoke in Peter's arms on our patio. I looked up at the sky and saw in my mind's eye that it was just entering into the evening. A sound made me turn my head to my left; Jeremiah was pawing at the patio doors to get out.

"Peter, babe, wake up."

We were still naked but surrounded by snow and feathers, wings gone. Peter opened an eye at me.

"Since when do you call me babe?"

And for some reason I was pissed off like you wouldn't believe. "I don't fucking know, get up!"

I stood and went to the patio doors I opened them and went inside as Jeremiah went out. Peter got up and followed me in. I felt so moody, but it didn't make any sense because I had a wonderful night last night.

"Gabby?"

"Yea?"

"What's wrong?" Peter asked.

"I don't know." I shut my mind off from his before he could rummage around. I had a feeling Stacey's vision had something to do with it. I had to tell him.

I sighed. "Peter, Stacey couldn't see Mary's future after the wedding."

He looked at me, he was wide awake now.

"Why didn't you tell me earlier!?" he demanded.

"Because I wanted you to be thinking straight."

I felt really bad but he had to understand. He sighed with frustration as he read the thoughts I was projecting to him.

"I understand Gabby, but please, never keep something that important from me. After Mary's birthday, she is not leaving our sight. I don't care what Linda says."

"Okay." I still felt terrible. I needed sometime alone.

"Where are you going to go?" Peter asked, hearing my thoughts again. And again, I cut him out of my head.

"Listen, I'm really sorry Peter but I need to think about some things. Nothing to do with you." I added.

"That's hard to believe when you just shut me out of your head. We used to be so connected. Now you're keeping things from me. I don't understand why Gabby. What have I done?"

I could see I was hurting him. "You haven't done anything Peter, just trust me. I just want some time to think about a couple things. I'll fill you in when I get back, I promise."

"When will you be back?"

He looked like he was going to cry. It was breaking my heart to see him like that. But I knew what I had to do in order to figure out the questions I had. They were frustrating me. I had to find another entrance to the Valley. And I had to figure it out alone, I didn't know why exactly, but something was just telling me that was the way I had to go. For now.

"I don't know, but before we meet with the Wolves."

My eyes went white and sand covered me with appropriate clothes for the season. Not that I needed them but I wanted to look inconspicuous.

"I love you Peter but there's something I have to do." He walked up to me and placed his hands on my shoulders. He was still naked and in any other circumstances it would have been hilarious.

"Gabby, do what you need to do, then come back to me."

He kissed me harder than usual. I think he actually thought I wasn't coming back. But I wasn't going to look, I had things to do. My eyes went back to brown.

"I will." I promised. Then I walked out the front door. The house still had the barrier around it from the other night. I left it. I walked down my woodsy trail to the road. I looked up to see twirling sand mix in with the clouds heading towards the Wolves.

What the fuck was he doing? I shook my head; I'll figure that out later. I walked by a couple people and politely smiled to them. I was walking more for the mind numbing normality. I tried to focus on Luke but then decided against it. I thought at first, that if Peter was going to see the Wolves then I could go see the vampires without interruption inside Luke's head in case Peter got curious. Then I thought, what if Luke was with the Wolves like last time. He's gotten pretty chummy with Matthew lately. Besides, didn't I just decide I wanted to do this alone?

Yea, yea. That was a better idea. I followed the road as I briefly fought with myself and when I made my decision to go alone, I noticed the beginning of the trail I wanted and went for it. It led to the playground and field I was just at last night. Walking the path I nearly tripped on a rock. I turned and pointed my middle finger at it.

"Fuck you asshole." I said to the rock. Then I continued up the path. I was moody alright. Talking to rocks that have been there for God knows how long, and I was the only one stupid enough to trip over it, but it was still the damn rock's fault. I shook my head. I arrived at the playground, it was completely deserted. I walked past it to the open field.

Okay, it was time to see just how powerful my new angel form really was. My eyes went crystal white and the first thing I did was put up a barrier around the field so that I was invisible to anything and everything; physically, and by scent and energy. My clothes turned to sand and reappeared as the silky blue robes. My wings grew from my back painlessly.

Then I concentrated. I stilled the air and silenced the wind. I focused on the energy from the trees and the earth. I could suddenly see the aura of every living thing surrounding me. The ground started to split in front of me. The split shot down to the other end of the field. The split splintered into a pentagram and blue flames rose out of it.

My heart thundered in my chest and I grew a little light headed but I took in a deep breath, exhaled and continued. The wind blew fierce; it wasn't wind but unsettled spirits flooding to the doorway to the Valley I just created. Trees grew around the pentagram. I turned and closed all trails and pathways to this field by blocking them with trees. I turned the playground to sand. I decided to keep the barrier up and anyone who looked upon it would only see trees.

I changed back to my human form right down to the clothing. I stepped into the middle of the pentagram. I laid down with my palms down on the grass and closed my eyes.

* * *

It worked. I opened my eyes and I was in the Valley.

"Father, are you here?" I called out. Many voices answered me, most sounded like children but I couldn't understand what they were saying.

"Yes Gabby." His voice was behind me. I turned around to see his skeleton being consumed by the red sand and then he was whole again.

"Father, do you know what is happening at the mountains? And Mary, Stacey can't see her future. I need your help." I blurted as fast as I could; I had no idea what the time limit was. I fell on my knees. "I keep hiding things from Peter; I never did before, why now?" I looked up at him and he simply smiled at me.

"Calm down child. First off you must know that Otr is portraying an African Shaman. Not just any African Shaman. A soul catcher from thousands of years ago. The shaman wanted immortality, and he was given his wish as long as he gave himself fully when the time came for him to be useful. During that time his powers grew. He is of an ancient Haida tribe, not to confuse with the Haida Natives of this province today."

A chair formed from the red sand and he sat down, "The ancient belief was that during a possession to communicate with unsettled spirits, the soul can escape the body by accident. And with a special device the soul can be captured and returned to the body so it doesn't die. But with this knowledge in the wrong hands, his hands, the power of the device is corrupted. It could be used to force the soul from the body. This can be very disastrous, so for now my dear Gabby, this must be the last time you come to the Valley for a while. Leaving your body unprotected your soul is in jeopardy of being trapped in such a device."

I heard his warning but intuition hit me.

"No, they want Peter's soul. If they put it in a different body or something, they may have an easier way of corrupting him. Or if they put his soul in a newborn, his memory will be erased."

My heart squeezed painfully in my chest. I couldn't let that happen.

"My dear Gabby you may be right, but to answer your last question; you're not used to being with someone who loves you so completely. It's not that you don't trust him, you just need to be more confident in yourself to accept his love. You love him and you are scared. I cannot speak for little Mary, I just hope it is not what you fear it is. I'm sorry I cannot say more. As for the mountains, it is as the Wolves say. Otr has turned the doorway to the Valley into a way into the Hell dimension. Fafnir already has permission and the ability to be on the earth's surface, he just needs a doorway. Not just any doorway, there has to be a certain moon for his arrival."

The full moon.

"Therefore, he doesn't need a collaboration of souls to bring him here. But they want revenge for being thwarted of Matthew's death."

This regained my attention before I could start obsessing over Mary. This meant Stacey was still in danger. I had to tell Peter we were going to have to kidnap her and Stan, because I was sure they were a package deal now, and make them live with us for the next little while.

"One more thing Gabby, you haven't asked but you must know about one of your gifts."

"What do you mean?"

"When you turn to sand; you're really just energy. You can possess people. Both of you will be completely aware of the other. You're not like a demon that takes control and drives the soul out, your energy becomes one with them. It may come in handy."

I was suspicious, "Why? What do you see?"

"I do not know, but everything happens for a reason Gabby. I wouldn't have the urge to tell you for no reason."

My patience was waning but I had one more question, "Father, where's Thomas?"

"He's watching over you and the ones you love. Right now he's with little Mary. Did you know she can see him? He's told her to keep it secret. Most children are gifted with psychic abilities but as they get older, society washes it out of them. Very few keep in touch with their true selves, most let the world define their beliefs and morals. How they should look or dress."

"Why is he looking after her? Don't get me wrong, I'm glad he is. Actually knowing that makes me feel a whole lot better than I did two seconds before you told me, but why? He doesn't even know her."

"Because you love her. Thomas never admitted it but he loved you very much Gabby. And as you got older, the love changed. He was worried about the morals of your age difference. And he was quite jealous when he found out about Peter and his age. But then he accepted it because he loved you and wanted your happiness."

That shocked me. I always looked at Thomas as a nanny. Two percent of me was kind of creeped out. But the rest felt really sad for him.

"I wish I could have saved the both of you."

"He knows that and I know that. But this way he can be with you forever."

"Doesn't he want to move on and be a new soul?"

"He will when you're done with this war. As will I. But now you must get back Gabby. Someone is waiting for you."

I furrowed my eyebrows, "Who? Peter?"

My father just smiled. Then he turned back into a pile of sand and bones.

*   *   *

I awoke and it was night. I sat up and the pentagram was gone but I knew if I wanted it to, it would show up again. I was just sitting there in an open space amongst the trees. The trees and barrier were still in place. I was in my human form still. I smelled someone, it was Luke. I didn't want to take down the barrier so I walked out of it to meet him. He was leaning against one of the trees that blocked the path I took to get here. He looked at me.

"There you are. Your scent ended here but was pretty strong, so I assumed you were in a barrier. I didn't feel or sense the usual energy you use when you turn to sand."

"I just created a new doorway to the Valley." I said.

His eyes went wide for a split second, "Impressive." He said with a smile.

"Why are you here Luke?"

"Peter was concerned when he came to the Wolves. I simply got curious."

I knew the fucker was with the Wolves. "Well, I got a lot of answers, some entirely unexpected."

I projected my memory to Luke and he got angry.

"We must tell everyone we can. If that device is used on an uncorrupted, we will be nothing but monsters without a soul. Forcefully damned. This threatens everyone."

I didn't think of that. Shit.

"And a Vampire or Werewolf soul is a hundred times more powerful than a human soul. Not many are needed to open a doorway for an unprivileged demon to leave Hell and walk amongst the humans."

Dread was felt first, and then anger. More Generals? Luke's take on things made me feel inadequate in the fighting department. But I got over it. Otr's death needs to be my main priority.

"We need to get that device."

Luke nodded. "Let's go see the Wolves."

Luke walked up to me as my eyes went white. I grabbed his hand and we burst to sand.

CHAPTER FOURTEEN

They all witnessed me and Luke materialize. I walked right up to Peter and projected everything from the Valley to Luke's input afterwards.

"Thank you." Peter said just before he kissed my forehead. Luke was already informing the Wolves. When they parted from their huddle, they looked at me.

"We have six more moons till the full moon; I suggest you call in reinforcements. With the two brothers, Peter and I can handle them, but I will tell you all, please be careful and be very mindful of your surroundings. I can't promise all of you will live. And it will pain me deeply if any of you die. I appreciate your devotion, just don't be foolish." I said this as I projected my feelings to each and every one of them. I truly did care for them. They all went down to one knee.

"Thank you for your affection my queen." Nicolas spoke, and then stood, "We will start training right away." And with that the Guard turned into their Wolf forms with piercing blue eyes and ran into the trees. Without trying, I could hear their thoughts calling on their native clans as they ran. We would be receiving them the night before the full moon.

Zachariah stepped towards me, "You should practice your possession skills. Maybe an animal can help you gather information from the mountains. An animal could help you practice, for their minds are a little easier to live with. I've seen it done with Shakara when she possessed the lions."

"That's a good idea." Peter said to me.

"We'll both practice." I said.

Then I realized Peter's angel form didn't have the golden veins in the feathers. Could he even do it? Can he see aura's like I can? I just acquired that skill, do I have to be mindful when I transfer it? Could I even transfer it? Wouldn't he of had it by now?

There's really only one way to be sure, he thought. His impish grin implied a very naughty thought. And I was so down for that right now.

"That's settled then," said Luke, oblivious, thank God, to our thoughts. "I'll call on the local nomads and collect my government."

The Vampire government consisted of forty five Vampires alone. Peter and I nodded.

"We'll be back tomorrow night." I promised him. Luke nodded then ran to Matthew and Hannah. I grabbed Peter's hand and we travelled back home.

*   *   *

It was just past midnight when we got back. And just after the witching hour when we were done, err, playing around.

"Okay concentrate." I didn't know how to approach it but we were using Jeremiah as a lab rat. Peter won the rock, paper, scissors game so he was going to try first. I had a theory that it was kind of like the reverse of when I absorbed those demons through my skin in the parking lot. I figured he would have to make Jeremiah absorb him. I don't know, it was fucked but we were going for it.

"How about I just go in through his mouth? That seems less complicated." Peter suggested when I told him my theory.

"Oh, yea I guess." Why didn't I think of that? Why do I have to make everything so complicated?

"Okay here we go." Peter's eyes went crystal white. He stared into Jeremiah's eyes. When Peter turned to sand this time it was finer, whiter, and glowed more. I watched as Peter's sand flowed into Jeremiah's nose.

Ewe! I thought you were going to go through the mouth? I thought to him.

Shhh. I'm concentrating. He thought back.

When Peter fully disappeared into Jeremiah, the kitten's eyes went from blue to white. I picked up Jeremiah and made him face me.

"Whoa." Jeremiah said.

I dropped him in surprise. "Gah!" I wasn't expecting his lips to move like that. I suddenly felt like I was in a cartoon. I blinked my eyeballs back into my head.

"Gabby, it's me, wow, this is so weird." His mouth was moving perfectly with the words that were coming out of his mouth.

"You're telling me." I said.

Peter made Jeremiah stand like a person and twirled his tail like a man would do with a cane.

"Peter, you're giving me a complex, act like a fucking cat please."

Peter rolled his eyes and went back on all fours.

This better? He thought to me, *of all the things to be freaked out about.*

Yea well, just give me a minute to get used to it okay? I thought a little snippy.

"Fine, then I'll continue to talk like this so you get used to it." He said using Jeremiah's mouth.

Now I rolled my eyes, okay the initial freaked out vibe was gone.

"I'm calling Stacey and telling her to pack some shit and get the fuck out here as soon as the sun rises. I'll explain the kidnapping thing we have to do and why."

"Okay." He jumped on the couch and looked at me. He made Jeremiah smile a weird and slightly freaky little smile. I looked away and made my phone fly into my hand. It was a reflex that surprised me.

"Huh."

"What's up?" Peter asked, not really paying attention because he was comically scratching at the arm of the couch.

"I'm so used to creating stuff that I didn't realize I could simply move stuff with my mind. I just made my phone come to me." I explained.

"Well technically that's not true. You've made demons do stuff like float in the air while you bled them to death against their will." Now he was pawing at the loose thread he created from scratching at the arm of the couch.

I cocked my head to the side. *I love how you say that so nonchalantly,* I smiled.

Now he was standing like a person again, leaning with his side on the arm of the couch with his arms crossed. It looked more funny than freaky; I guess I got over it. He shrugged at my thought.

"I like being a cat. Your muscles are so strong and you don't even need supernatural gifts."

"Technically, Jeremiah is supernatural, we might have to practice on a real animal." I corrected.

"Don't ruin my fun; didn't you have a phone call to make?"

I shook my head with a smile and dialled Stacey's number.

* * *

"So where's Peter?" Stacey asked. It was seven something in the morning. Stacey, Stan and I were sitting in the living room. Stacey told Stan what was going on and he insisted on coming too. I didn't give a fuck.

"He's playing in the yard." I said.

"What?" they both said at the same time.

I laughed and went to the patio. I opened the door a bit to yell outside, "Oh Peter! Time to come in now!"

The white kitten came trotting into the front room with a dead mouse in his mouth. He jumped on the couch and dropped it right on Stan's lap.

"Oh gross." Stacey grimaced.

"Get that thing away from me." Stan swatted the dead mouse off his lap and the kitten jumped down to the floor. He looked up at Stacey and Stan.

"You know, when a cat brings you and dead thing; it's an act of love." Peter said through Jeremiah's lips.

Stacey instinctively screamed and they both lifted their feet off the ground to get away from the talking kitten. I laughed and Peter stood up on Jeremiah's hind legs like a person.

"What? Was it something I said?"

Stan pointed at him, "You fucking cat is talking!"

I just kept on laughing, they looked at me. "It's just Peter."

They looked back at the kitten and Peter made the little paw fingers wave separately to say hello.

"Holy fuck." Stan said. I think he was going to end up having that as his catch phrase.

"But I thought you couldn't shape shift?" Stacey said as she stared wide eyed at Peter slash Jeremiah.

"He didn't. He possessed Jeremiah."

I explained to them how the sand we turn into is actually raw energy and the process of the possession gift. After I was done, Jeremiah closed his eyes and the fine glowing sand came out of his mouth then rematerialized as Peter seconds later. Stan was holding his chest as he watched, I really hope he doesn't have a heart attack. He was almost forty.

"That was so rad!" Peter said excitedly with a smile.

That did it; me and Stacey looked at each other and just burst with laughter.

"Okay first rule, never, say, that again." I said between breaths.

"Gnarly dude!" Stacey said in her surfer imitation.

"Like radical." I joined in.

We continued to laugh hysterically as Peter and Stan just looked at each other slightly worried for our sanity. Stacey and I were having such a fit, we didn't even notice that the guys left the room and went out onto the patio. And when we did to wipe our tears, we started laughing all over again. Finally we slowed it down.

"Oh my God Gabby, I haven't laughed like that in a long time."

"I know; everything's just been so serious. This war has been so draining and it hasn't even started yet."

Stacey looked at the guys. "What are they talking about? Look in Peter's head." She nudged me.

"No way, he'll know I'm intruding, even if I looked in Stan's head. I'll just try and hear them with my ears; the door is open a bit." I was so used to mind reading that I forgot about the super hearing.

"Project it to me?"

"Of course." I said with a smile at her.

I changed my eyes white and concentrated. Then projected it to Stacey.

*   *   *

"What's it like to be a father?" Stan asked Peter

"It's the best feeling in the world if you have the right partner." Peter answered.

"Did you love Linda?"

"Immensely, but she broke my heart when I found out she was cheating on me. I didn't even have the courage to break up with her because of Mary. I didn't want to give her a broken home. But in the end, Linda left me and took Mary with her."

"And now? Sorry if I'm intruding, it's just, I've known Gabby for a while now and I've never met an guy she's actually loved or even remotely cared about before. I never thought she would settle down and get married. So I'm very curious about you, if you don't mind." Stan said.

"No, that's alright. I was broken for a while. I even kept the few clothes Linda had left behind. It was a good couple years of binge drinking before I even thought to get my life back in order. I was drinking every night and going nowhere, but one day I said 'fuck it'. I sobered up, applied for a job at the College at the beginning of summer, and then Linda let me see Mary again. I was still broken and alone but then the first day of work, I turn around and there she is. Nearly falling on her ass at the sight of me."

I looked at Stacey as she tried to stifle a laugh, I playfully slapped her leg.

"At first I was a little wary because of the obvious age difference but she didn't seem to care and I wasn't going to argue."

I smiled at that last part.

"Age difference? How old are you?" Stan asked.

Peter laughed, "I'm fifty."

Fifty? Stacey mouthed to me.

"Holy fuck." Stan whispered. Yup, that was definitely his catch phrase.

"How old are you?" Peter asked.

"Thirty nine." Stan answered.

"Ah."

"Well, continue please." Stan urged, Peter snickered a bit.

"Well, as I said, I couldn't stop thinking about her and it was obvious she was interested. But I was sceptical. Our first night together was amazing, Mary loved her instantly, but then I pissed her off and she stormed out of my house."

Stan laughed at this part, "Yea she has a temper." He agreed.

"I noticed that as I watched her go till she turned the corner of my street. I racked my brain on what to do; I didn't want to let her go. So, I went to her place at the church and well, here we are."

I smiled and so did Stacey.

"Are you nervous?" Peter asked Stan.

"Yea a little. I'm mostly psyched though. I've got a couple names picked out. Maria, if it's a girl, after her mother and the middle name,

Theresa after my mother. Then if it's a boy, it'll be Adam, after her father and the middle name, Joshua, after my father."

"That's very nice of you, have you told her?"

"No, I was going to keep it a surprise. I kind of hope it's a girl because I know she really adores her mother, but either way I'll be happy."

I looked at Stacey, tears fell down her cheeks. I hugged her. We could only see their backs but Peter clapped Stan on the shoulder.

"You'll be alright man." He said.

"I'm just nervous because I don't know if I'll be a good dad." Stan confessed.

"Well, they write many books but no one is fully prepared for parenthood. Life isn't a bunch of textbooks. Sure there are patterns and the expected habits but everyone is different. There are too many combinations of everything to be absolutely sure. I'll say one thing though; say goodbye to sleep and hello to patience." Peter said with a sigh.

I had to admit, that was good advice.

"Really?" Stan wondered.

Peter gestured with a couple fingers, "Goodbye to sleep for the first two years and hello to the ever growing patience for the rest of their lives."

Stan thought about that for a moment, "Patience huh?"

"Yea well, you get some practice with that. Pregnant women can be very temperamental."

Fuck you. Stacey thought. I laughed.

"Hmmm." Was all Stan responded with.

Stacey and I stopped listening at this point and got up off the couch to go join them outside on the patio. I opened the patio door wide and they both turned to face us. Stacey grabbed Stan and went back inside with him. I stayed out with Peter.

I know you were listening. Peter thought.

How? I asked.

I tested the waters, and confirmed it with Stacey's profanity after my comment on pregnant women and patience.

I rolled my eyes and kissed him.

"I'm so lucky to have you." I said.

"I wish I met you sooner." He said to me. I froze and looked at him with a sarcastic grin.

"Err, no you don't. I think there's laws against stuff like that."

He blinked at me, "Wow. You sure know how to ruin a moment. Only *you* would say something like that."

I laughed, "I'm joking. I love you. We met at the perfect time, under the most fucked up circumstances, but love, *our* love, is going to save the world. How do you feel about that?"

He held me tighter and brought his face close to mine, "Much better."

*   *   *

It was time to go see the Wolves and Luke. We decided to bring Stan and Stacey with us. I was impressed, Stan handled the sand travel like a pro. My supernatural friends welcomed us with open arms like we were gone for years instead of just one day.

"Were you able to practice?" Luke asked me.

"Well, Peter was." I answered. I projected the whole experiment and he laughed.

"Well it's true; you might want to try an animal you didn't supernaturally create. Let me get a friend for you."

Luke whistled by using two fingers in his mouth. I couldn't whistle for the life of me. I was a little jealous. Just then, a huge crow came out of the trees and landed on Luke's shoulder.

"Try Vladimir, he too is a special animal, but he was born from an egg, not created from a pile of earth. All of his kind are spiritual and he has been my friend for a couple years now."

"Okay." I took his word for it.

Stan turned from talking to Stacey and watched curiously. My eyes went crystal white and I started to glow. I tried not to focus on my body but my energy as a whole. I felt myself dissolve and I watched as I entered through Vladimir's nose cavity. It was like going through tunnel after tunnel till I felt his life energy. I felt myself kind of melt and fill his body till I felt everything from his point of view.

Then the mind was with me. The sight was a little colour blind, but as it felt like my eyes 'grew' in the sockets, the vision came in full colour. That's when I knew Vladimir's eyes must have went white like Jeremiah's did with Peter. The mind wasn't actual thoughts; it was like pictures and instincts with intuition and sound memory, but no actual words that I could understand. I could but at the same time, could not feel the beak. Like, I could move and adjust it, but it wasn't like there were nerve endings to actually feel the tip like I would with actual lips.

How do birds talk with these things? I thought to Luke.

"How do you feel?" Luke asked, completely ignoring my question.

"Weird." I said in my crow voice.

"Try flying." Stan suggested.

I flapped my wings but my movements sputtered and I just fell off Luke's shoulder. He caught me just in time before I hit the ground.

"Gabby, try letting Vladimir fly. Let his instincts know what you want. Let his mind work with your mind." That suggestion obviously came from Peter.

I opened my mind to him to share the experience and he saw the difficulty I was having. I closed my eyes and let go. I felt myself go more to the core of Vladimir's body. As Vladimir took over, my vision went colour blind again. It was like wearing a giant jacket while sitting in a car. Not in control but going where you want to go, all the while in someone else's skin. I saw Peter furrow his eyebrows at my analogy. Well, it made sense to me.

Vladimir took off into the sky and I went along for the ride memorizing all the muscles used so I could do it myself next time. We flew above them, circling the trees a couple time. Okay, time to take over. My vision became colourful again. I stuttered my flight sideways at first but regained control quickly. I got the hang of it pretty easily now that I knew what to do. Starting, it was kind of like riding a bike, a little wobbly at first but once you got going, you're good. Peter heard that.

That was, err, better ... He criticized.

Hey, if you don't like the way I think, then get the fuck outta my head. I said jokingly. I headed for the ground. *Oh fuck, how do I land?* I panicked and ended up swerving back up into the air.

Let Vladimir show you. Peter reminded me.

Right. I let go again and Vladimir dived towards Luke and pulled back slightly, flapping his wings twice, before gracefully landing on his shoulder.

"Good job." Luke said. I head butted him on the temple then flew over to Peter's shoulder. I squawked loud in his ear.

Where's my congrats from you fucker?

Peter laughed. "You did good hun, but I think you should let Vladimir take control if you're going to use him to spy in the mountains. Your eyes kind of give you away when you're in control."

Everyone nodded to this.

"Alright." I squawked.

Should I go now to see what's up? I thought to Luke, the bastard better answer me this time.

Yes, that would be best. We don't have much time to train before the full moon. Luke thought back.

I head butted Peter on the side of his face and affectionately nibbled on his ear before I took off into the sky with Vladimir at the wheel.

"Where is she going?" Stan asked. Stacey eventually told him after, but at that moment everyone just looked at him like they were wondering about his I.Q. level, because the answer was obvious.

*   *   *

The air was crisp and cool as it wove between the feathers on my head. Well, Vladimir's head. It didn't take too long to get to the mountains. I saw Matthew's old cabin and I landed in the trees behind it that bordered the old Valley doorway. There were about thirty corrupted Werewolves in their Wolf forms patrolling the woods. Besides the colour blind part, crows have excellent eyesight and depth perception. Actually I think most birds do or it was just Vladimir, but I could see the fur on the Wolves, even though I was a good twenty feet up from the closest one.

I was scanning till I finally found him. There were about fifteen corrupted Vampires surrounding him but I knew it was him. He was dressed in black robes and he had African tribe looking makeup on. And well, he looked African. I'm not racist but since he was the *only* black guy here, with the fancy get up I naturally assumed. That, and the makeup was a dead giveaway. A corrupted Vampire was speaking to him. I silently glided down to a lower and closer branch so I could hear what was being said. I tried to focus without taking control over Vladimir. The corrupted Vampire stopped talking.

"Good, we will get the woman and child in time for the ceremony." Otr said with the African accent of the Shaman.

No! I thought in my head. I didn't bother to stay to hear more. I bolted right away. I flew high and didn't care about my eyes anymore, I took control and tried to fly as fast as I possibly could. I realized I could fly pretty fucking fast, like when I ran in my human form, it was like I hit nitro on this bird.

Peter! Peter! Get someone, or go yourself to Linda and Mary right now! Otr is planning to get them! I thought as loud as I could.

I heard him roar.

Chapter Fifteen

Everyone was in an uproar. I was spilling out of Vladimir's mouth before the bird even landed on Luke's shoulder. Once I was whole again, I was at Peter's side within seconds. He was furious. He had his eyes closed; he was trying to find Linda's mind but it was faint and unclear. We weren't attuned to her like we were to everyone else. Honestly, we didn't care enough about her to want to. And looking for Mary's mind would be impossible. Peter was getting frantic. Stacey was silently freaking out different sentences to me all at once. Mostly about her vision, then confusion because she still saw Mary at the wedding.

"Peter, it's okay," I said trying to calm him, "Stacey still sees her at the wedding, it's not fading like Matthew's suicide did, it's still strong. There's hope, we just have to figure out what they want."

"They want me." Stacey said.

We all looked at her.

"Well isn't it obvious? They want revenge right? They'll probably trade."

"I'm not just going to hand you over Stacey." I said a little frustrated.

"FUCK!" Peter shouted. He slammed his fist into the ground and a wave of energy blew against everyone. I was blocking Stacey so Stan was the only one who fell over. The ground was now split open where Peter stood.

Luke spoke calmly, "We could make the trade," he started. I was about to literally bite his head off when Peter stopped me, he saw the full plan in Luke's head faster than I did.

Luke eyed me carefully, "Peter can possess her when you bring her to trade. Then we could ambush them to get them back."

"Them?" I frowned.

"Uh, the woman?" Luke asked.

"Oh right, Linda." Yea, I could really care less. It was Mary I was concerned about.

"I should have looked in her head when she said she wouldn't be bring Mary back for three weeks. I thought it was strange but I just wanted Mary away from all this." Peter was beating himself up inside.

"Peter, you can't blame yourself for this." 'Cause technically this was *my* fault. If I had told Peter of Stacey's vision sooner, we could have told Linda to fuck off, or kept her in the basement.

"Why didn't you just kill them while you were there Gabby?" Stan asked.

Yea, he wasn't helping. I flicked my wrist at him and he passed out falling straight back.

"Gabby!" Stacey exclaimed. She rushed to him and checked his head.

"I like Luke's plan." I decided. I didn't like endangering my friend but I believed this would work because Stacey's vision......well, it wasn't fading.

Peter nodded. His skin was reddish and his eyes were black. He was trying so hard not to go into his demon form. I held his hand. He breathed in deeply and then exhaled.

"Okay, what do we do now?" I looked at Luke.

"We sharpen our skills first, then we fight for the princess."

At those words, the salty scent in the air grew stronger. Luke looked to the trees behind us.

"Ah, just in time, I wasn't expecting you till tomorrow night." Fifty nomads from the northern region of British Columbia, and some from the Yukon, stepped out of the trees. All of them were holding brilliantly white blades. These were the special blades made from the bones of Angels and forged in Holy Fire. There were different levels of Angels. The lowest rank being the ones who came and fought the hordes. The highest rank being the personal servants in the kingdom of heaven, tending to the needs of the messiah.

I wasn't really interested in the history at this moment. Luke just noticed my curiosity of the blades and tried to mentally explain it to me from his memory but I raised a hand and cut him off.

The nomads noticed Matthew, Hannah, and the Guard. They were not impressed with the company. The bald Vampire in front spoke to Luke.

"We have come to serve you and fight with the Witchdemon." He looked at Stacey. Stacey's eyes went wide; she shook her head and jerked her finger in my direction. He looked at me and I waved.

"Are there two of you?" he asked. I saw in his head that he sensed two Witchdemons and he saw two women. Luke mentioned to him there were unusual circumstances concerning the Witchdemon, but he didn't really explain in detail.

"Yes, but she's human, a psychic, but human. The second Witchdemon you sense is my mate, Peter." I put my arm around Peter's waist. The bald reacted as I had expected, his eyes went wide and he sniffed Peter.

"Your energy is that of a Witchdemon but you're not an Obedient. The Witchdemon has always been female! You smell of graveyard soil like the demons from Hell. Explain this to me!" He demanded from Luke. I stepped forward in front of him, the little asshole just irked me.

"Don't you dare talk to him like that! He is the leader of your government and you will accept any decision or task he gives you without question or explanation!" I yelled at him. My eyes went white and so did Peter's as we felt the rest of the Vampires go tense.

"Peace, peace everyone." Luke said calmly yet sternly. Baldy calmed down. His name was Micah, but he was pissing me off so he was Baldy.

The nomads wanted answers so I sighed and gave permission for Luke to tell them everything. Like *everything*. Even the reincarnation stuff about Peter. If they were willing to die for us, then they had the right to know what they were dying for. Even though, they really didn't have a choice. Two humans were at risk and it was their duty to protect them. Even if I didn't really care about one of them, and would probably purposely distract myself if she was carried away somewhere, or if we were too late to save her I probably wouldn't be too sad.

But it was the principal that mattered. Mary was going to be in trouble, and we had no idea where she was, but we knew where she was going to be.

Ironically, we just needed patience.

* * *

Finally the night came where the different Wolf clans showed up, as well as the forty five Vampires from Luke's government. Matthew had to do the same explaining to the Wolves as Luke had to do with the nomads. Peter became an anomaly. They were fascinated and terrified of him. We left Stan at the house with Jeremiah. I told him it was for his protection seeing as he was the only one without supernatural abilities and well, I didn't say who he needed protection from so I wasn't lying, it's just I didn't want to be tempted into mentally turning him into a pretzel the next time he had something very unhelpful to say.

We did not tell him the plan only on Stacey's request. Peter was fully and understandably *against* not telling him but I reminded him it was her choice. So he reluctantly agreed, but I swore I heard subtle planning of ratting her out before he caught me and cut me out of his head. I myself, wasn't fully comfortable with the plan. I didn't want Stacey near any of it.

One of the Vampires from the inner ten of the Court approached me. His name was Isaiah, he handed me something. I looked at the object in my hand, it was a ring.

"It is said that this is the very ring the Archangel gave to King Solomon. It may be useful to protect your friend." He said in a thick, unidentifiable accent. The gesture and intention was enough to make me want to hug him. And awkwardly enough, I did.

"Stacey!" I bolted to her side so suddenly she jumped. She was talking with Joan. I handed her the ring and she held it up to admire it. It was a gold band caked in tiny shards of diamonds. Joan gasped.

"Is that King Solomon's ring?" Joan asked amazed.

"I think so; one of the Vampire Court gave it to me to protect Stacey."

"It certainly will; that was very kind of him."

Stacey looked at it, "It looks kind of big."

"It will fit any finger that wears it." Joan informed her.

Stacey put it on and suddenly I felt her energy disappear. I was looking at her and could smell her but her energy was gone.

"What does it mean that her energy is gone?" I asked Joan.

"It's not gone, it's harnessed to her core, protected and more concentrated, making her abilities more potent. Also, because she is with child, and only because of this, the pure energy will react instinctively and protectively. Therefore, if a demon or corrupted touch her skin, even slightly, they will turn to dust instantly."

"Cool shit." I blurted out, impressed, "How do you know this?"

"I was one of King Solomon's protectors; he later gave the ring to his wife who also had a child growing but after giving birth, her skin was no longer deadly to a demon or corrupted. Unfortunately, that was found out the hard way. When her child was about seven months, she had ventured out alone without protection and was killed. We still do not understand why. We hear her scream but by the time we got to where she was, all we saw was a pile of dust."

"Why dust? Why not ashes?" Stacey asked. I shrugged.

Joan smiled, "My mother says that dust clings to the air like foam clings to the sea. It has always been, since day one. In the end even a demon becomes one with the beginning, when everything was fresh, was new, was innocent."

She left me and Stacey with completely blank stares on our faces.

"Did you get that?" I asked.

"I'm not sure, I'm not poetic but that sounded like a profound poem."

"Pfft, Whatever. What were you talking about before I came up to you guys?"

"Oh, I was wondering about the effect of possession on the baby." She said as she felt her stomach.

"And?"

"Well, she says that since its energy and not a demon, the baby will be fine. I guess if turning to sand didn't harm it then this should be fine to." She said with a weak smile, "But she told me not to worry. If it was a demon possessing me, the baby would die instantly."

Wow. And then things got morbid after that for a while. The Wolves were saying silent goodbyes to loved ones and mates with their hearts and the Vampires just had magically radical acceptance of their demise.

Peter was practicing possession skills on the few nomads who volunteered. It was a little fitting that Peter would be the one doing the possession thing. He was always mind reading every chance he got, even after we decided to allow some level of privacy for our friends. He was endlessly fascinated by the mind and everything in between. These gifts just made the icing on the cake. I watched as he possessed one of the nomads. He was in and out so fast; the nomad shivered when he got out this time. The nomad's name was Brian.

"Not a very comfortable feeling is it?" I asked assuming.

"Nah, not at all. Entering is fine, kind of warm and fuzzy. It's when he leaves that makes me uncomfortable. It's like my life is getting sucked out of me." Brian said with another twitch of a shiver.

Peter was practicing because he wanted to be able to leave Stacey's body as fast as he could, rematerialize, then attack as lethally as possible while I grabbed Mary and, err, ugh, *Linda*. I would leave with them while Peter had all the fun. It was his vendetta, I would come back for Stacey of course, but with that ring she was going to be fine. I agreed that Peter be in charge of this battle because it was so personal. He was the best daddy in the world and these fuckers are trying to mess with his little princess.

So I shrugged, nodded, and said 'have fun'. No one messes with daddy's little girl.

We agreed to have the Werewolves go in first in their Wolf forms to get the corrupted Wolves patrolling the woods. The Vampires would be in the trees, swinging above them to the cabin. A howl echoed from the water's edge on the other side of the trees to my left. I smelled decay, it was a corrupted Werewolf. Peter and I looked at each other and bolted over there; this is what we were waiting for. There, a few dozen yards away on a boat, were three corrupted Werewolves, two in their Wolf forms. The one in human form spoke as soon as he saw us.

"Witchdemon, we have your precious humans. A woman and a child. If you want them back, bring the psychic to the clearing by the mountains, this time tomorrow night. Her life is ours. If you do not obey, we will kill the child first."

Peter almost lost it but I grabbed his arm.

"Tell Otr we will be there." I shouted. I saw in his head when he transferred the message to his master. I saw they were underestimating me, they were thinking I was weak, thus the theatrics. Little did they know we were just playing along and that their deaths will be utterly painful. My eyes went white, I flicked my wrist to make the three rise into the air and float towards Peter.

Honey, do you need to let go of some steam? I thought to him.

His eyes went black and thick veins appeared around the edges of his face. His mouth opened wide, revealing long sharp teeth. Peter grabbed the face of the corrupted who spoke and bit down on the bottom of his face. From my angle it looked like he was kissing the demon, until Peter pulled away with the creature's bottom jaw still in his mouth. He completely ripped it off the demon's face.

Well that's the last message that fucker will be sending. Peter drained the other two corrupted Werewolves and they turned to dust. Jawless wonder was still whole, err sort of, on his knees. I crouched down in front of him, going a little demonized myself, the black eyes and veins around my face.

"One last thing to send to your master. I hope your ready to die."

When I was sure the message got passed along, I ripped through the demon's neck with my teeth and drained him to dust.

"I want to go now." Peter said impatiently.

"The sun is almost up; we have no idea where they are being held." I stated.

Peter looked at me, it wasn't a glare but it wasn't friendly either. I fucking glared in reaction.

"The fuck are you looking at me like that for?"

"I want my daughter back." Peter said. He walked into the trees. I stood there, staring after him, my face slowly going back to normal. His mind was closed from me. The way he said it was 'my' daughter, not 'our' daughter. It hurt deeper than a knife would have in the center of my chest. I don't know if I was overreacting or just paranoid. I felt so useless. I knew this was all my fault. Tears fell down my face. I turned around to see the sun starting to peak through the clouds.

"Gabby?" Stacey came out of the trees and stood behind me. I turned again to look at her. She looked shocked when she saw my face. Out of all the years we've known each other, since we were twelve, she's never seen me cry. I was usually high or drunk or something other than sober...I only smartened up last year when it got boring.

"Oh Gabby, what's wrong?" she came up to me and gave me a hug.

"This is all my fault, I should have told Peter right away about Mary, we could have done something."

"Shh, Gabby, you guys will get her back. She'll be at the wedding and we just won't let her out of our sights."

I knew she was right; I saw it in her head, but still.

"He's still super pissed at me though." I said as I wiped my face.

"Yea, he left as soon as he got to the clearing. I think he thought something to Luke because I saw the Vamp nod to him."

"And then everyone went inside?"

Stacey nodded, "With a wave of Peter's hand, if I blinked I would have missed it." Her face looked anxious. She wanted Stan.

"You want to go?"

Again she nodded, "Are you going to be okay?" she asked me.

I shrugged, "Yea, I'll be okay." I lied. I felt like I was dying inside. She grabbed my hand.

* * *

Stacey and Stan slept till three in the afternoon. Stan stayed up all night worried and waiting for Stacey to come back. Peter was seeing how fast he could turn into his demon form again and again in the basement. I was in our room, on our bed, staring at the ceiling. I felt horribly depressed, but I kept it all in my head and kept my head all to myself. My heart was heavy and I didn't want to move. I closed my eyes, I felt so empty. Suddenly I was falling and when I realized it, I landed hard on the basement floor. Peter stepped back in surprise. I wasn't hurt, just jolted a bit.

"Whoa, what the fuck just happened?" I asked no one in particular. I didn't feel myself turn into energy or anything. But it looked like I went through my bed, the living room ceiling, the living room floor, down to the basement. Peter just looked at me. I looked up at him and then looked away quickly. I got up and went to the stairs.

"Gabby, were you crying?" he asked.

"What do you care?" I snapped. I flew up the stairs and quickly slammed the basement door behind me. I turned and saw Stacey and Stan in the kitchen.

"Uh, hi. Are you okay?" Stan saw my face. He's never seen me cry before either. I didn't even realize I was crying until Peter asked me. Then I noticed my stuffy nose and heated cheeks.

"Yea, I'm fine." I said as I plastered a half fake smile on my face.

"Is Peter down there?" Stacey asked.

"Uh, yea."

"What happened?" Stan asked.

"Oh, I was in my room on my bed and suddenly I went through all the floors of the house and landed on the basement floor." I explained.

Stan and Stacey looked at each other.

"So. you were crying in your room?" Stan asked.

Who cares if I was crying? Did he not just hear that I went through all the levels of my house? I was getting kind of irked by how nosy he was getting about my crying. It made me a little uncomfortable. He stood up and went into the basement. I was curious at the sudden departure but didn't bother to eavesdrop this time.

I looked at Stacey, "I'm going back to my room till sunset, care to join me?"

"Sure."

*　*　*

"I just feel horrible."

"Does he know how you feel?"

"I don't think he cares anymore." More tears fell, Stacey rubbed my back. We were both sitting cross legged on the floor beside each other.

"Gabby, he's just hurt and maybe he's taking it out on you a bit, which isn't fair, but it's kind of normal. Talk to him, you might be wrong."

Nope, right now I was wallowing and being a total coward. I was picking at the threads in my carpet. Stacey just sighed and continued to rub my back. We both looked up as footsteps sounded up the stairs and stopped outside the bedroom door.

"Gabby, we need to talk." It was Peter, Stacey looked at me.

Looks like you're going to whether you like it or not. Stacey thought as she got up and left, leaving Peter standing there in the doorway. He walked in and shut the door behind him.

"Is it true you've never cried in front of them before?" he asked me. I sat there picking at the carpet thread. Couldn't he just look and see for himself? Well, he couldn't see in Stacey's head I guess. If I looked at him I was going to start crying again. He sat down beside me.

"Gabby answer me."

"I don't cry. I've never cared enough to cry about anyone or anything. I only started crying when I met you." I turned my head away from him, "I'm sorry Peter; if I had told you sooner we could have avoided this. It's all my fault that this is happening." I whispered. I brought my knees to my chin and wrapped my arms around them to hide my face. Peter wrapped an arm around my shoulders.

"But I've already forgave you for not telling me. It may have been that mistake that led to this as a whole but not entirely your fault."

Yea, that wasn't any better.

I groaned.

"I'm not mad at you Gabby." He kissed my right temple.

I whimpered.

"Gabby listen to me, we'll get through this. We have everything planned and we are going to succeed. I don't blame you."

"Fine." I resurfaced but still had a pout on my face. "What did Stan say to you?" I asked curiously.

Relieved at the change of subject. Peter smirked, "He actually threatened me to apologise for making you cry."

My eyebrows went up.

"Yea, he said that if I didn't talk to you, that he was going to go home and get his gun and see if I was bullet proof. I almost let him, I'm very curious."

"What?" I was shocked, at both pieces of information actually.

"I saw in his head that you've never cried in front of him or Stacey before. I was surprised by other things as well." He smiled full on now.

Uh oh. I looked at him cautiously.

"Like what?"

"I didn't know that you and Stan used to be a thing before he hooked up with Stacey. He still cares about you, just not romantically. You really did a number on him huh? I'm surprised he let you introduce him to her at all the way you had him hooked. And the things you've done, I never thought you were wilder than you are now. Emotionally I mean. You were all over the place. I got a lot of memories out of him as he was lecturing me."

Yea, your emotions get really fucky when your high almost 24/7. But I kept that to myself.

"He lectured you?" I asked, trying to hurry the conversation away from my past.

"Sort of, I wasn't really listening to his voice. You've really never been in love before?"

I froze. He really knew how to manipulate a conversation.

"No I haven't." I admitted to him. I looked down, my fingers started to fidget. He lifted my chin with his hand and looked me in the eyes.

"Do you love me? After all the tears?"

"I don't know, do you love me? After all the bullshit?"

"I'll adjust."

My mouth popped open and I pushed him onto his side and started batting at him playfully with my hands. We were both laughing.

"You fucker!" I half squealed at him.

I knew he was joking because when I asked him that, it was his mind that said "Always."

CHAPTER SIXTEEN

It was show time. I put Stan into a twenty four hour sleep before we left. He thinks Stacey is asleep too but obviously she won't be. Peter, Stacey and I were in the backyard. Peter was going to possess her when we got to the others. We sand traveled as soon as the sunset disappeared. Luke and Matthew stood in the opening. The Wolves were already on their way to the base of the mountain with the Vampires creeping along behind them.

"Are you ready for this?" Luke asked Stacey.

"Yes."

"Okay, do it now then." Luke said to Peter.

Peter dissolved into the glowing sand, well, more like powder. Stacey kind of breathed him in. Her eyes went white for a second then went back to green. Stacey started laughing.

She looked at me. *He misses his penis.* She thought to me. I started laughing too but after looking at Luke's and Matthew's faces, we quickly collected ourselves.

Gabby, we're going to have to talk again after this. Peter's words rang in my head.

What are you looking at in there? Stop it! I yelled at him. Stacey winced.

Luke and Matthew waited patiently, Luke coughed to catch my attention.

"Can we get on with this please?"

Stacey, slash, Peter and I nodded. "Let Peter take over for a bit Stace, just till we get there."

"Okay." Her eyes went crystal white.

"Let's go." Matthew said.

The four of us ran at demon speed. Within minutes we were in a mini clearing juts outside the trees that bordered the opening of the base of the mountain. The Werewolves and Vampires were there waiting for commands. The decay in the air was so strong. I noted the slight herbal laced with it.

"She's here." I said.

"Go." Matthew said to his Wolves. The packs bolted, snapped their jaws. I only knew how the Vampires killed each other, I had no idea how the Wolves did it if they couldn't breathe Holy fire. Did they behead each other too? I peaked in Matthew's head. They simply ripped each other apart with their teeth and claws. The venom is deadly to the corrupted. But the Wolves did not feed either; they just bit and tore off anything and everything.

Normally, they exhaled Holy fire if they were led by their Obedient, this made me feel only a tiny bit guilty. But a shudder went through me, the corrupted probably could exhale Hell fire if they consumed the demon's blood and were tied to him, and most likely that was the case. Matthew yelled and transformed, turning his yell into a howl half way through. He raced to the trees to join his pack. Luke nodded to Micah and the Vampires leapt into the trees, swing from branch to branch. Luke nodded to us before joining them himself.

Stacey and I looked at each other as her eyes went green. We walked forward into the trees. The Wolves were loud and snarling at each other. Biting and ripping, some of the corrupted were doing as I feared. Matthew's Guard stayed in their human forms, I didn't notice before. Joan had two special blades, one in each hand. They were very effective. Nicolas and Mark were side by side facing five corrupted Wolves. But their blades were huge. The corrupted Wolves snarled at them with their red eyes glowing. They lunged at Nicolas and Mark but both Guard members spun on the spot insanely fast with their blades out. The corrupted Wolves exploded into dust by the tiniest cut.

We continued to walk through the Wolves till we got to the edge of the trees. My Vampires were in the tree tops waiting. Luke was above me, and then I looked into the clearing and saw Mary.

"There she is." I walked out into the open with Stacey beside me. Instantly, we were surrounded by corrupted Vampires.

"Mommy!" Mary screamed. Otr grabbed her arm and tugged her to his side.

"Let her go!" I yelled.

"You'll have to get through us first." Said one of the corrupted Vampires.

"That can be arranged." Luke jumped from the trees as did the rest of the Vampires. The corrupted were seriously out numbered. But the corrupted still had Hell fire within their hands. I could see it in their minds, but even so, the corrupted were nervous.

"Enough. Bring me the psychic and no one shall die tonight." Otr commanded.

Just then, howls were heard from the trees behind us.

"Well, no one important anyways." Otr smiled.

"Where's the woman?" I asked.

"Right here." Linda's voice said. The air went sour as she approached. Her eyes were black, they had infected her. Well that's a shame, I thought to no one.

"Give me the psychic." Otr demanded.

I looked at Stacey.

"It's okay." She said. She stepped forward and the corrupted Vampires moved out of her way.

"Give me the child." I said. Otr held onto Mary's arm, "I said, give me the child." I repeated.

"Mommy, he's hurting my arm." Mary cried.

That did it. I heard Peter's thoughts as Stacey's eyes went white and she gave a hard punch to Otr's stomach, throwing him back twenty feet. He had let go of Mary's arm and I bolted to her. White glowing powder was flooding out of Stacey as I turned on the spot, whisking Mary away in a cloud of sand.

* * *

We arrived at the house safe and sound. My eyes white, I put a barrier around the house again.

"Mary sweetie, Uncle Stan is sleeping in the guest room. Go hide with him okay? Mommy has to go get Aunty and probably help daddy and bring him back too."

"Okay mommy."

I kissed her forehead and she ran up the stairs. I headed back to the battle.

* * *

Vampires were exploding, Werewolves were being ripped apart. I looked frantically for my best friend. Then I heard her scream. It looked like a bunch of corrupted were hiding until a battle occurred. Fuck.

Luke and Matthew were on either side of her fighting valiantly, Luke slicing the air with his blade and Matthew snapping at anything he could get his jaws on. Stacey was screaming out of fear for *their* lives; that they might get hurt. There were a couple close calls as I watched everyone move at impossible speeds. But the corrupted numbers were waning. Otr and Peter were battling in the sky above us, both of them in demon forms. Otr was quick to avoid any and all of Peter's attacks. Red and blue flames erupted here and there in the dark sky.

Then Otr let out a screech and dived behind the trees. Peter followed. I ran to them; they were at the old doorway. I arrived in time to see the red flames of the doorway and Otr disappearing through it.

I'm going after him. Peter thought as he landed. I kind of panicked; there were probably many levels in Hell like there was in Heaven, and I didn't want to risk him getting lost..... or corrupted.

No, you don't know where he is. Let's go back to Mary, please Peter! I almost begged. He turned to me and for a second I didn't think it was him. But his face softened when he thought of Mary.

"Okay, let's go." He said to me.

We returned to where the battle was almost over. Peter disappeared right away. There was one corrupted Werewolf left and it was being torn apart by two other Wolves. Once it was killed, everyone cheered. Luke walked up to me, dragging the demon Linda by the hair in his hand. Stacey was behind him.

I asked him to save her for you. She thought to me.

I smiled with long sharp teeth as my eyes went black. I jumped on the now demonized Linda, ripping her throat to shreds and drinking her dry. Of course I sadistically enjoyed it and I didn't feel bad at all.

I was half demon after all.

* * *

Peter was back to the Peter I fell in love with. He was a bit miffed that Otr got away and we had no idea where Fafnir was, or if they even had time to resurrect him before we ambushed them. None of that was on my mind right now though. I watched Peter read to Mary from the doorway. I could hear Stan snoring in the other room. I heard Stacey roll over and say *shut up* in her head. They were going to stay with us to keep an eye on Mary till after the wedding. Mary's little eyes closed before Peter turned to the last page, but he kept on reading. I turned and went into our room across the hall. And crawled into bed to wait for him.

It had been a while since we had sex. Then I had another one of my brilliant ideas. Everything turned to sand for a second except for the bed and then in the next second, the room was a jungle scene and I was in cheetah print underwear. I was going to go for sexy but I preferred *wild*.

Peter walked in, and for a second he didn't see the vines hanging from the ceiling, grass on the floor and trees in the corner. But then he froze and only his eyes moved around the room.

"Um, redecorating? I want to vote next time please." He said, I laughed at him. Okay maybe not so brilliant an idea to go 'wild'. With a flick of the wrist, the grass turned to sand, the walls no longer hosted trees and the ceiling had no vines. My underwear turned to red lace and red rose petals covered the bed.

"That's a lot better." He approved. We both smiled. He took off his shirt and threw it across the room. He turned his back to me when he went to take off his pants and I just gaped at him. On his back were giant tribal style wings.

"Did you get a fuckin tattoo? When the fuck did you do that?"

He laughed and the tattoo disappeared. It was something he manipulated the atoms to stick to his skin like a tattoo. I actually felt disappointed now they were gone. It was pretty fuckin hot.

"It's not real but I could keep it for a while if you want." He said, sensing my disappointment.

"Yes please."

The 'tattoo' reappeared.

"Oh! Can we do some role play?"

He turned and looked at me while wiggling his eyebrows up and down a couple times. "What did you have in mind?"

"I could be your little slave." I said batting my eyes at him.

"That's very tempting. But I like it more when you're more dominant than submissive."

I got up and grabbed his shoulders. I spun and pinned him on his back on the bed.

"Like this?"

He squeezed my ass. "Oh yea....." he said before he kissed me. He waved his hand and the bedroom door closed.

* * *

I woke up in the middle of the night to Mary's voice screaming for me. I bolted up and got out of my bed and ran to Mary's room. I opened the door and saw her sleeping soundly in her bed. I walked up to her to make sure. I couldn't see in her head even when she was sleeping. I shook my head and left her room. I swear I heard her scream 'mommy'. I must have been dreaming. I crawled back into bed with Peter.

* * *

February was upon us. Stacey was so nervous about the wedding and Peter was nervous about Mary. He was acting like an overprotective hen. It was admirable at first but then got seriously annoying. There was a level of understanding but he was acting like if we all breathed too much, the oxygen would disappear and then she would die. Like every little thing, he was completely over doing it. Way too paranoid.

"Fuck Peter, settle down." I finally said annoyed because he just whisked Jeremiah away from Mary for pouncing at the mouse the wrong way.

"Daddy, gimmie back my kitty!" Mary cried. Peter looked down at Jeremiah and reluctantly gave him back to Mary.

"You need to relax Peter." I said to him. He looked annoyed at me.

"Can *you* relax?" it sounded like an accusation. It irked me a bit.

"No but if you keep freaking out about ghosts, you're going to let the real thing slip by and fuck everything up." I was getting really irritated with him. He just glared at me and then stormed out of the house through the patio doors. Stacey and Stan were on the couch, Stacey walked over to me.

"That was a little harsh Gabby."

"Well, he's acting like a maniac. He won't even let her leave the house."

"Would you? If you thought she was going to die?"

"I would let her live her life to the fullest. But she's not going to die, and you're wedding hasn't happened yet."

I was getting annoyed, irked, irritated, and pissed with everyone.

"Fuck this." I muttered. I walked right up to Mary, picked her up and sanded some clothes on her that fit with the weather outside.

"Come on honey bee, it's too stuffy in here."

"Gabby, I don't think you should go, Peter might-" Stan started, but I spun on him.

"Peter will just have to get over it." I snapped.

I walked out the front door with Mary in my arms. Eventually I put her down and held her hand as we walked through the trails. I don't know where we were going but for now, we were just going wherever the trails took us.

"Mommy, are you mad at Daddy?" Mary asked me.

"No honey bee, I just don't want to keep you all cooped up. Let's just enjoy the fresh air together okay?"

"Okay mommy."

We walked on the end of the trail and started on the road. There was a mini 'main' street in town that held a sushi place, Peter's office, which wasn't opening up till summer, and various other stores were across the street but were mostly food shops. We arrived at the 'main' street and went down towards the docks. To our right was an open park and to our left was a playground, the beach, and more open park. We walked up to the playground where a couple children were playing.

"Go play honey bee, mommy needs to sit and think."

Mary ran off to the slide. I sat on a bench along the playground's edge and watched her. I suddenly felt very uncomfortable. I watched her climb the different levels of the playground and felt edgy. I had to fight the urge to jump up and help her even though she didn't need it, because? Because I was afraid she was going to get hurt. The urge tweaked at every step she made.

Holy fuck I'm turning into Peter.

I had to fight with myself in my seat. I was having consistent thoughts that she was going to fall and hurt herself. I lasted about twenty more minutes before I couldn't take it anymore. I got up and grabbed Mary and walked her to the other side of the street to the open park. There was a bus stop at the corner and a bus was pulling in as Mary and I were just getting onto the grass.

"Hey Gabby!"

His voice gave me an instant complex. The normality and memories shut my brain off for a couple seconds.

"Joseph?" I looked at him in amazement. He smiled at me.

"Hey Gabby who's this?" he asked as he walked up to me. He was looking at Mary but she was glaring back at him. Strange.

"Mary, don't be rude, this is mommy's friend Joseph."

"Mommy?" I heard Joseph whisper to himself, Mary blinked a couple times then smiled.

"Hi." She said.

"What are you doing here Joseph?"

"I'm supposed to meet Stan here in an hour."

"Oh yea? Well he never mentioned any of this to me, Peter, or Stacey."

He looked a bit uncomfortable, I looked in his head, there was more. I tried to fight my surprise and more irritation.

"He said I could stay with him till the wedding."

"He did? Um, he and Stacey have been staying with me and Peter."

He smiled. "I know, that's kind of why I said yes. But I was under the assumption that you knew I was coming. By the look on your face, you had no idea I was coming did you?"

I shook my head. Peter wasn't going to be very happy about this.

"Is there going to be a problem? I can go somewhere else." He sighed and looked around. He turned to go and then my really old dream popped in my head. I grabbed his hand.

"No, I'll talk to Peter, it's just till the wedding right?"

"Yea, I'm the best man."

I already knew that and yet I was surprised still that I'd forgotten.

"I'm sure we can set up the basement for you."

He looked surprised.

"Are you sure?"

"Yea, no problem."

Mary was really quiet. I don't think she liked Joseph. I couldn't understand why.

"Mommy, I want to go back to the playground." I looked at her and she pouted at me.

"Okay honey bee. Do you want to hang out for a bit Joseph? Since you're here and all? I'll just call Stan and let him know I met up with you, and I'll be bringing you back with me. I'll tell him to get the basement cleared for me to set things up later." I grabbed Mary's hand.

"Wow." He said as we started to move towards the playground.

I looked up at him, "What?"

"Its weird. Ever since I saw you, it's like I've known you my whole life and we have barely talked to each other." He confessed to me. He was so close to me as we walked. I could smell him and it was kinda making me dizzy.

"Maybe we knew each other in a previous life." I teased. If he only knew. He was about to say something but I put a finger up and reached into my pocket for my phone. It wasn't really there, I had to materialize it from some of the flowers we went by when he wasn't looking. I pulled it out and dialled Stacey's number.

"Hello?"

"Stacey, is Peter and Stan with you?"

"No, just Stan, Peter hasn't come back yet."

"Okay well, put me on speaker."

"Why?"

"Please Stace?"

There was a little static and then she sounded far away.

"Okay you're on speaker."

"Stan, I have Joseph with me right now."

"Oh shit." I heard Stan mutter.

"Don't worry; he's going to stay with us until the wedding. I need you to clear out the basement for me." We made it to the playground and Mary took off.

"Fuck man, Gabby I'm sorry. I was drinking that wine and forgot I invited him down here." Stan nearly whined.

"Don't worry about it. Just do that for me okay?"

"What about Peter? And what about the other things?" Stacey asked. I knew what she meant.

"Just leave that to me. I'll explain most of it to Joseph." Joseph looked at me curiously. I simply didn't want to have to sneak around. Knocking him out only worked briefly since he was an Obedient, and erasing his memory was a futile effort for the same reason.

"Are you sure?" Stan asked this time.

"Yea, I'll see you guys in a bit. If Peter comes back before me, fill him in, he won't be happy but he'll just have to deal."

Joseph smiled to himself.

"Err, okay Gabby; see you soon."

"Bye."

I hung up and looked at Joseph.

"So you have something to explain to me?" he asked.

I didn't know where to start but he cut me off before I could.

"You're wedding wasn't a drunken dream was it?"

Well, that was a good way to start. We both sat down on the bench at the edge of the playground.

"No it wasn't." I analysed him a bit as I explained everything, he actually took it quite well. I gave him the same speech I gave Stan, completely ignoring the Obedient part. And the consumption of demon blood, but I left it implied. I also told him of Stacey's vision of Mary. In case Peter gets over bearing again.

I looked at Mary; one of the other children was playing with a steering wheel that was part of the playground. What the fuck was the fucking point of that thing? They always place it in the middle of the wall so the poor kid can't even pretend to be driving. There was no way to look over the edge. Mary came up and pushed him over, making the poor little boy cry.

"Mary!" I cried out shocked. The mother of the boy came to her son and picked him up. Mary just looked at him and smiled. I walked over to Mary.

"Mary, that wasn't very nice. Why did you do that?"

"I wanted to play with it and he was taking too long."

"Yea but he was just a little guy, you could have hurt him." Joseph said to her. I didn't realize he stood up with me. Mary glared at him.

"Mary what's wrong with you? This isn't like you sweetie, are you feeling okay?"

I put my hand to her forehead but she wiped it away.

"I want my daddy. Take me home." Mary jumped down off the wooden steps of the playground and grabbed my hand. We started to walk but Mary stopped.

"I want to go home now!" Mary demanded. I knew what she wanted, I looked at Joseph.

"Does she mean like, instantly?" He was implying what I was assuming. I nodded. Yes Mary wanted to turn into sand and rematerialize at home. She was impatient. I picked her up and went behind some trees with Joseph beside me. I looked around and didn't see or smell anyone close enough to see us.

"Are you ready?" I asked him, he shrugged.

"I guess so."

"Wrap your arm around me." I said. He more than willingly did so. He put his arm around my waist with Mary between us. My eyes went white and his went wide.

"Close your eyes Joseph."

He did and we burst to sand.

CHAPTER SEVENTEEN

We rematerialized in the front room. Peter was just walking in through the patio door when we reappeared. He froze and watched. Joseph and I were looking at each other when we became whole again.

"Daddy!" Mary cried. She wiggled out of my arms and I broke eye contact with Joseph to put her down and let her run to her father.

Peter knew everything from Joseph's head within seconds. He looked at Joseph and then looked at me. He didn't look angry but he didn't look very impressed either. He took Mary's hand.

"Come honey bee, let's get you washed up for dinner." Peter eyed Joseph as he walked past. When Peter was out of sight, Joseph looked at me.

"Did he just read my mind?"

I smirked when I looked at him. I didn't tell him we could do that, I had kept it from him like I did with Stan. But he didn't say anything when I did it earlier, then again I was more subtle about it. I have a feeling Peter had emotions leading him to be not so subtle.

"Uh, yea. How did you know?"

"It felt weird, like I could feel someone else in my head. Like an actual hand poking at my brain."

"Hmmm."

* * *

It was weird having Joseph around for the first little bit. He mostly chilled with Stan and didn't really talk to anyone else except for Stacey once in a while. But just the vibe I got from him every time we were in the same room together was like electricity.

Peter knew Joseph was attracted to me and was always at my side when Joseph was around. Then, after a while I had to question Joseph's sanity; if he was suicidal or not because even though he knew how powerful Peter was, it didn't stop him from making comments that could easily be taken in more than one way. Innocently or sexually. His mind implicated at both so we weren't sure how to react. Joseph only smiled when Peter gave him a look that pretty much said 'fuck you'.

Peter was surprisingly patient. He kept all his thoughts to himself, verbally and mentally. But what really got me since Joseph arrived is that Peter wasn't sleeping in the same room as me anymore, he was sleeping in the den on the couch. The wedding was a week away. Peter's behavior was giving me the biggest complex yet. He was super possessive during the day then he totally abandons me at night. I couldn't take it anymore.

I went down the stairs at the witching hour, oh F.Y.I. I haven't slept either since he stopped sleeping in bed with me so.....feeling lonely and depressed the past four nights and five days, this is technically night five, since Joseph arrived. Sure I was a little crazed by this point but I didn't care. I walked into the den and my eyes went white. I flicked my wrist and the couch disappeared. Peter fell with a hard thud on the floor. His body jolted and he rolled over onto his knees and looked up at me.

"What the hell are you doing down here Peter? You're all over me during the day then you sleep down here at night. I don't get it. You cut me out of your head after we just had a dispute about me doing that to you. I get the privacy thing if need be but this is ridiculous! What are you doing down here?"

He looked unsure at first, then he looked ashamed. "I didn't want anyone to break into the house."

I cocked my head to the side, "Are you serious?"

This was a protective thing? I struggled with relief and annoyance. I closed my eyes and breathed in slowly then exhaled.

"You weren't avoiding me?"

"No."

"Then, can I join you?"

"You made the couch disappear."

"I can fix that. Step back."

He got up and moved while I made a king sized bed appear.

I looked at him with my hands on my hips, "You do realize that being afraid of a break in is really, well, seriously?"

An evil human would be a midnight snack and a general thief could be transported somewhere else conscious or unconscious, who's going to believe them.

"Don't give me grief about this Gabby; you don't know what it's like to have a child. You don't know how worried I am." He said as he crawled into bed.

That actually kind of stung a little. Wasn't I Mary's step mom now? I got in bed but faced away from him.

"No, but I have lost my only family because of this war, do you think I want that for you?"

"Gabby, I didn't mean it like-"

"No you're just concerned about *your* daughter." I cut him off.

I tried to make my tone imply how hurt I was by his previous comment. He heard it. Tears fell from my eyes. I sniffed.

"Gabby, I did it again didn't I?"

"Did what?"

"Made you cry."

"It's a natural phenomenon nowadays." I said sarcastically. I felt him roll over onto his side, presumably staring at me.

"Turn around Gabby. Face me."

"No." I pouted.

He grabbed my arm and turned me onto my back. I stared at the ceiling stubbornly. He sighed. "Gabby please look at me."

"Why?"

"So I can talk to you." I ignored him and continued to lay there. He sighed again and got on top of me so we were face to face. I was still trying not to look at him and be mad but he was between my legs. I think he did that on purpose.

"Look at me Gabby."

I looked at him with furrowed eyebrows and a frown.

"Gabby, I'm sorry. Mary is *our* daughter now. I just don't know what I'd do if I lost her."

My face softened, "First off, you're a dick. Second, I'm worried too, but the danger isn't until after the wedding. So please stop driving me nuts!" I whisper yelled the last word at him.

He smiled, "Okay, I'll settle down."

He moved his hips and pushed between my thighs. I smirked.

"Don't make me too loud." I warned him. He looked like he was thinking about it.

"I can't help it if I'm just that good."

I laughed and then kissed him, oh he was that good alright.

That good and more.

*   *   *

Joseph came out of the basement the next morning while I was in the kitchen doing the dishes. Sometimes I like doing the human stuff the human way. Very mind numbing. And just like clockwork, Peter was at my side. I rolled my eyes. I looked at Joseph and he looked away quickly.

"What's up Joseph?" I asked. He looked at me. "Whoa, you look like shit," I stated.

He looked at Peter and then looked at me again, "Yea well, I didn't get much sleep last night." He turned and walked into the living room. I took a peak in Joseph's head and then slapped Peter across the chest.

You knew he was awake last night? I thought to him.

Well at least now he can keep his comments to himself. Peter responded. Peter had the proudest smirk on his face. But he was right, the comments ended. Luke came to us in the night, just four moons before the wedding. He brought with him a Vampire from his middle Court of fifteen. He was a monk before he was a Vampire, back in the day when God was first creating the original protectors of the human race. Only those completely devoted to him, at an insane level, were given the privilege to hold such power. Most of the Vampire Court were men of God. This Vampire's name was Ezekiel, but he was known as 'Silence'. He hardly spoke and he was the only Vampire known to be able to hide his Supernatural energy and attack in utter, well, silence.

He was a high priest now and a protector. Luke was bringing him to marry Stan and Stacey. Although he was in the middle Court, he was high ranked and considered very deadly. The inner and middle court members were more brains than brawn yet very skilled in combat none the less. The outer twenty were the ones with high knowledge of combat, and usually chosen to protect certain individuals.

"This is Ezekiel." Luke introduced the Vampire. I remembered seeing him at a glance when we saved Mary.

"She already knows everything, let's meet the couple to be." Silence said softly.

Stan and Stacey were in the dining room with Joseph and Mary having pizza. Luke stopped for a moment and looked from Joseph to Peter and then to me.

He knows almost everything; we just left out the Obedients part. You can introduce yourself. I thought to Luke. The Vampire nodded to me.

"Hello there, I am Luke; Leader of the Vampires." He said to Joseph. Joseph had a mouthful of pizza. He choked it down and wiped his hands on his jeans before he offered one hand to Luke as he stood up.

"Hiya, I'm Joseph. Err, best man for the wedding."

Luke politely shook his hand then introduced Silence to Stan and Stacey.

"Oh wow, nice to meet you." Stacey said. Silence bowed his bald head to her.

"Ezekiel would like to speak with both of you about the wedding ceremony." Luke said to them.

"Oh of course." Stacey got up and looked at Stan.

"Uh yea, sure." He got up and stood with her and Silence.

"You guys can use the den." Peter pointed.

The bed was no longer there at the moment. Every morning I turn it into sand when Peter and I wake up, it's currently in the shape of a bear rug.

As the three of them left, Luke looked at me and Peter. I looked at Joseph and in mid bite he took the hint.

"Hey kiddo, want to watch some cartoons?" He asked Mary. Mary just looked at him, she hadn't warmed up to him at all much to Peter's amusement. She rolled her big beautiful brown eyes.

"I guess so." She mumbled. The both of them left to the front room.

Once we were alone, Luke had Peter's and my full attention. There was another reason for him bringing Silence here, to protect Mary after the wedding.

"Oh my God Luke, thank you. The more eyes the better." I said.

"He will patrol the property during the night."

Good. No more sleeping in the den, I thought just to myself. But Luke's face was still grim.

"What is it?" I asked.

"The corrupted are leaving Israel and Egypt and are planning to head this way."

I couldn't help but see the rest of it in his head. They were being led by Apep, one of the Egyptian God's of the underworld. He was a Fallen. A fallen Angel or Archangel I did not know, but a Fallen none the less. That meant that my angel form and my demon form were useless individually. Luke knew I was reading his thoughts.

"Does that mean..... I have to go into my warrior form?" I asked.

He nodded.

"But how do I do that?"

I knew I needed love the first time for my angel form and anger helped Peter but I used the absorption of a large amount of demon blood to get into my demon form. How do I change into the combination of both?

"I don't know." Luke answered.

Well, that was helpful, but why ask to begin with? He really wouldn't know.

"Do you know when they'll be here?" Peter asked.

"You have until the summer solstice."

"That's kind of far; you made it sound like it was happening sooner." I muttered.

"That is because of the grave importance. Not only is Apep an extremely high ranked demon, it's not just any group of corrupted he's gathered. They are much older, wiser, and stronger in those countries. The unsettled spirits alone are so old and strong from their many hosts, they hardly need bodies anymore. They are ancient possessive demons. They possess only to gain power, making their hosts commit suicide, one of the worst sins, by hardly entering them." Luke took a breath, trying to control his emotions about the subject. His memories flashed in my mind, they were gruesome.

"The souls become unworthy to God and the ancient ones consume them. This makes them the deadliest to the human race. With their age and power, they even become a threat to Vampires and Werewolves."

Normal possessive demons can only possess humans. Apep obviously doesn't mess around.

"This is very serious." I said as I looked at Peter.

"We have to try at our very first opportunity." Peter said to me.

"What about Mary? The wedding is only a few days away."

"I think that's why Luke brought Ezekiel." Peter spoke as he returned his gaze to Luke.

"Silence." I corrected.

"Yes Silence," Luke smiled. "He got that name years ago. He's actually quite proud of it but he'd never admit that. Pride is also considered a sin as you know." But the smiled continued as if we just shared a private joke.

"Right.... So I guess we have some work to do." I quickly looked from Luke to Peter again.

"Come, let's go to the Wolves." Luke held out his hand. Peter and I took each other's and I reached out for Luke's. We sand travelled to the Wolves. When we arrived, the Wolves were all sitting around a huge bonfire. All the clans were still here. Some were in Wolf form, others in human form. The biggest Wolf bounded over to us and transformed back into Matthew.

"Welcome, I trust you've already introduced them to Silence?" Matthew asked Luke. Luke nodded. "Good, we have a few months to get organized. From my experience, the Witchdemon's warrior form is similar to the angel form, just with a darker edge to it."

I sighed, obviously you idiot! It's a combination of good and evil! Peter sensed my unease and squeezed my hand. Luke tried not to roll his eyes. He looked at me and gave his own opinion.

"I think the warrior form requires the need to protect. Try concentrating on the different energies around you, then your deep emotion for their survival. Let that engulf you and embrace your placement in the world."

I definitely like Luke better right now. I was impatient to try as I glanced at Peter. "Okay let's try."

But Matthew stopped me, "I don't think he'll be able to. See, when you transfer your powers you transfer your angel and demon powers. The warrior powers are discovered over time by the Witchdemon, not instantly known upon awakening. Even the Obedients don't have a warrior form. The Vampire Obedient has Vampire and angel forms, and the Werewolf has the wolf and angel forms. The third Obedient is the only Obedient who remotely has a form something like the Witchdemon's warrior form. He goes into the angel form and a darker angel form. He leads the angel armies of Heaven; he is also the leader of the Obedients. His darker angel form has the scarlet wings."

"But Peter's different; maybe he will have a warrior form." I was feeling stubborn about this but Luke spoke this time.

"That may be a possibility but given who he's reincarnated from, he may go into his true form as the warrior is the Witchdemon's true form."

I was starting to get a headache. I rubbed the space between my eyes.

"So your saying he'll just turn into Damien, is that it?"

They both nodded.

"And we don't want that?"

They shook their heads.

"Isn't Peter's *demon* form Damien's form? Isn't *that* why you guys freaked out?"

"It was Damien's form yes, but not his true form." Matthew said.

I sighed again. I wonder if I just punched him for something to do, if he'll just say something helpful that doesn't irritate me.

"Okay fine, I'll do it myself."

I was getting frustrated with this because I wanted to do everything with Peter. To prove he's not a liability but a necessity. Matthew wasn't making it easy for me not to think irrationally.

"It's okay Gabby." Peter whispered in my ear. I looked at him. He kissed me then stepped away. Luke and Matthew backed up. The three of them gave me room to concentrate.

I took Luke's advice and concentrated on all the energies around me. I felt my eyes change and right away I saw everyone's aura again. I focused harder and then everything changed. Everything got darker and everyone's features disappeared. I saw everyone as a dark figure with glowing electricity flowing through them. This was their energy. I still saw the aura around the dark figures, so I knew who was who. I concentrated even harder, now on the electricity. I felt a pressure in my head and my vision changed again.

This time the energy filled the figures till everyone was just glowing white figures instead of black ones. This, I knew was their souls. Even the Wolves in Wolf form glowed white as they walked around. I knew everyone was staring at me. Then suddenly I felt my emotions build with compassion for every living thing around me. My vision cleared and everyone came back to their features but I could still see the auras.

I felt my skin go hard, like it went super strong. It was a similar feeling of having one of those face masks on but all over my body. I looked down at my arm and focused in on my skin. Instead of skin cells, it looked like tiny scales. They looked sharp but smooth, almost like shark skin. I knew they were impenetrable. I felt my wings grow from my back. They were like my angel wings only the colour of the feathers were different. The top ones were black while the long bottom ones were dark red.

I felt spikes grow out from my spine. My outfit went to my black leather one piece, only with a modification to it. There was a corset like pattern down the arms and legs and it was backless for my wings. I lifted my hands and flicked my wrists. Balls of blue Holy fire emerged at my fingertips. I smiled, just like the imposter Oracle showed me in that vision. I looked at my friends and husband and that's when I noticed the rest of them. At first I thought they were the good unsettled spirits, but then I realized they had no eyes.

I don't know how I knew but I was looking at the first dimension of the realm of purgatory. This is where the spirits of victims who are forcefully infected or possessed go to. Forced to leave their bodies, confused and made blank. No soul, no personality imprint. It was really confusing because sometimes they were still left with the last emotion they felt, which is usually anger or fear. They were stuck here, not knowing where they were. They were like, how to explain....empty souls or something. No light. Unable to go anywhere or be saved or helped, Blanked out like an etch-a-sketch. The life line cut off. Minds blank, just repeating themselves over and over again of the last second or so of their lives. But no real memory of it. It actually scared me because they were *everywhere.*

I quickly waved my arm and they vanished in wisps. Fuck they were scary. My transformation was complete. My eyes, I knew from the minds in front of me, were piercing blue like the Vampires and Werewolves. I had to check myself out, and damn did I look good. Everyone went to their knees.

Honey, you can save me any day. Peter thought to me with a big grin on his face. I smiled back.

"My queen, you look magnificent." Matthew stated.

I was tempted to fan myself with my hand and be like, 'I know, I know' but I fought the urge. Peter laughed at my temptation. Luke looked at him. Peter raised a hand and shook his head.

"Sorry." He muttered.

Everyone stood up again.

"Did you see them?" Luke asked.

"Yea, what exactly were they? I got some information; I don't know how I knew some of that but it came to me when I saw them."

"Ah, some information and knowledge come from expert intuition and passed down experience from the Witchdemon's soul. It's passed on to the next reincarnation when she discovers certain gifts and magical skills or meeting certain spirits or supernatural beings. It's similar to how the Wolves pass down their instincts and newly discovered knowledge through their Wolf forms. It just appears as needed through the spiritual experience."

Fuck that's it! I'm not going to ask any more questions. Every answer is long, tedious, and confusing. I was suspicious they were dumbing it down for me too, which made my irrationality worse. I looked to see if my silent assumption was true, but it wasn't.

Luke continued, "They surround us, not hearing or seeing. I had the privilege to see for myself through a projection from the first Witchdemon. They exist in nothingness. Literally everything stolen from them when they were forced from their bodies. It is a horrible way to die."

"Can they be helped?" Peter asked.

I projected everything to Peter, and they freaked him out too. I slowly returned to my human form.

"Only when their body finally turns to dust, from destroying the demon that possessed or infected them by force, will they stop wandering and have whatever is left of their personality imprint given back to them. But the longer they are in purgatory, the smaller those chances are." Luke answered.

"How do they sustain themselves?" I asked this time.

"They feed off of any kind of energy, good or evil. Anything that's around." Luke said.

"What happens when their personality imprint returns to them?" I couldn't help myself.

Luke sighed, not from too many questions, just the sadness of the answer. "They are a version of an unsettled spirit. Only, their memory is still gone as is their light, so becoming a new soul is lost. I suppose they could go to the Valley or continue to roam the earth lost. With them being empty, they have no remorse or vengeance from their previous life. Some have maintained their last second of life that they repeat over and over. But even if they are fortunate enough to have the imprint returned, they still repeat themselves but have no idea they are doing so. Whether or not they move on or live in peace is not known. I believe they simply exist. I've never seen one with their eyes move alongside the ones without eyes. Maybe they move to another level of the dimension."

Well, that was enough for me for the night. Luke looked at Matthew, then to Peter, and finally to me. "I'm impressed you were able to succeed in your transformation on the first try but you still have to master the skills that come with it, and the other two of your forms."

Matthew spoke up, "We can help you but even we do not know how far your powers can go. Most of it you may have to discover for yourself. We shall commence tomorrow night."

A thought passed in his head that caught me by surprise.

"I can summon my own demons?"

"Not actual demons, but supernatural creatures that are not on either side of good or evil. Not summon, but more, to communicate and encourage their assistance in fighting for this earth which is also their home as well. They will be more inclined to obey you in your warrior form." Luke informed me.

"What kinds of creatures?" Peter asked. Luke said nothing but the knowledge flowed from both Luke and Matthew's memories.

"Wow, those really exist?" I asked.

They both nodded.

Peter and I looked at each other. This was above and beyond what we thought, what the world thought. This was so big we were just scratching the surface.

CHAPTER EIGHTEEN

The next couple nights I spent in my warrior form. It was a form that seemed to be completely beyond anything I imagined. I had the skill to talk to animals and spirits. Like, tree spirits and even the weather had a voice. I made lightning and thunder happen before but to actually control it you had to do a lot of praying. Not my forte but I didn't bother questioning anything. With Luke's long memory of what he had witnessed with the other Witchdemons, I was on the path of acquiring a lot of skills. When I talked to the tree spirits, I had my voice in my mind and communicated through the way I blew the wind through the branches.

It was so fucking cool but really fucked up, I just went with it. The tree spirit I spoke to was living in the pine tree directly in front of me. I only knew this because of the supernatural aura around it. Although plants and animals had no souls, they had life energy and their auras were plain white. Supernatural auras were more colourful. This tree spirit gave off a dark green aura. The tree trembled and some needles shook loose. A face appeared within the bark. It grunted and opened its eyes.

It was Luke, Matthew, Peter and I. And this, err, tree guy. This wasn't a mind I could read so when I spoke to it, I said no idea what it said in return. Where was that reincarnated sudden knowledge I usually got at a time like this? Oh yea, no pine trees in Africa. Fuck it, I'll just speak out loud in English.

"Um, can you understand me?" I asked it.

It grunted again.

"What do you want?" Uh, *he* croaked.

Rude little fucker, I looked back at the guys.

What do I say? I asked Luke.

Ask for his help, he answered. I rolled my eyes, yea thanks captain obvious. But first I had to be more subtle than that.

"Are you familiar with the other supernatural creatures around here?" I asked, looking back at the tree.

"I am with the kinds behind you, the Vampire and the Wolf. The other and you I have not encountered before. How did you know how to speak with the wind to wake me?"

Shit that was a long story. I deliberated for a second then tried to project everything to the tree. I didn't know if it would actually work but then the tree closed its eyes and made a long, weird groaning noise. When I was done, the tree's eyes fluttered back open.

"I see. We tree spirits of the wind are all connected all over the entire earth and its dimensions. Even the animals. We hear and see all. I will help the only way I can; by sending winds to speak to the animals on the other side of your world. They will keep watch for you. That way, you may know exactly what your enemy is up to."

It was that easy?

"Thank you. Is there anything I can do for you?"

"No, we do not do favours for others for personal gain. Animals can hear the wind but they cannot send it back in return. A sprite may come visit you. But be careful, you may have gained ears and eyes but the enemy may have done so as well. Like the kind of your friends, there are good and evil of my kind as well. And few don't even choose a side, they just stir things up for fun."

He didn't talk like he was an ancient spirit.

"Okay, thank you again."

"I must go."

The tree shuddered and, as I watched, the green aura lifted from the pine tree and swirled with the wind.

"Well that was interesting. What the fuck is a sprite?"

Peter shrugged but Matthew spoke, "It's a Fairy spirit. They encourage the grass to grow, the flowers to bloom, the rain to fall, and the streams and rivers to flow. They don't care much for humans and some fairies and sprites become tricksters. They were created when the earth was created. Most of them may only help to keep the earth itself whole, not for any compassion for the human race. They find humans to be clumsy and selfishly ignorant to the importance of nature."

"Do they have souls?"

"A sprite is a type of soul but more like an afterlife for a fairy. Their free will and consciousness intact. As the Witchdemon, you are not only the sole protector of the human race but the earth as well."

Peter coughed and Matthew looked at him awkwardly, "Yes well, the both of you have a large responsibility. I think that's enough for tonight, you should get back and discuss your *other* plans." He added quickly.

Matthew was talking about the wedding. It wasn't tomorrow night, err, tonight since it was the A.M. But the next night, uh, *tomorrow* night. Yeesh. I changed back into my human form.

"Yea alright, I better get some rest before Stacey bombards me with wedding magazines."

"Very well, we will leave you then." Luke and Matthew left to the cabin on the other side of the trees. Peter was with me pondering what the tree spirit had said about the enemy also having eyes and ears. He grabbed my hands and we sand travelled back to our house in our room. I looked at the clock; it was two in the morning.

"I'm so tired." I walked to the edge of the bed and just flopped face first, not even bothering with my clothes. Good thing I didn't have to breathe because I couldn't move. I was so dead tired I fell asleep instantly.

*   *   *

"Gabby?" Stacey called.

No, go away, I'm sleeping. I thought to myself.

"It's almost midnight Gabby. Exactly twenty four hours before my wedding."

She wanted a midnight wedding like I had. Well, I just wanted one at night so the Vamps and Wolves could come. She wanted it right at midnight to be right on Valentine's Day. Some weird romantic crap she came up with. I groaned into the mattress. I slowly lifted myself off the bed and looked at her. I knew what she wanted but I had to hunt first. I was soooo drained.

"Okay let me hunt, and then we'll do the dress thing. Just pick out a bunch and I'll come back ready to zap you through your fashion show." I promised. I smelled the air, where was everyone?

"Where did everyone go?" I asked.

"Oh. Stan and Joseph went to a hotel for Stan's bachelor party, and Peter took Mary flying."

"Oh." I didn't know why but I felt panicked about that last part. Maybe I was just being paranoid.

"Yea the boys won't be back till tomorrow. I don't know when Peter and Mary will be back. Try not to be too long Gabby." She stepped out of my room and went downstairs.

Okay where should I go for a quick and easy meal? West Van? Actually West Vancouver sounded perfect. I didn't really know the area well but I was sure I'd taste them in the air if I just sanded around for a bit. I dissolved to my sandy self and floated down the stairs to the patios doors.

"Oh Gabby while you're out, can you grab me some take out?"

If I had a face I'm sure I would be giving her an incredulous look.

Are you fucking kidding me? I thought to her, she giggled.

"I'm just kidding, have fun."

I left out the doors and up into the sky. I could taste Silence's energy at the back of the house as I flew by. I got to the boarder of the city when I tasted them in the air.

Well that was easy.

I rematerialized in the air and just floated there. My eyes went black and veins appeared on my face. And of course I had my leather one piece on. I followed the scent while I was still in the sky repressing my energy. I smelled some humans in the mix. Innocent ones. The demons I smelled were fresh infected demons. In their heads I saw they were planning to forcefully infect these humans. I wasn't at the location yet but from what I gathered from their minds, is that there were six humans tied to chairs and gagged. My Vampire and Werewolf friends did do a number on this clan, but in a month their numbers doubled to just over four hundred.

There was only a hundred and forty at this location give or take a couple. They were led by someone very unusual. He wasn't a general demon, so there was no blood ceremony. But they were all still linked because of the device he used on them all. Well he was kind of a demon; he was a corrupted Vampire, a really old one. His name was Judah, an old member of the middle fifteen, and also, he was Silence's brother. I stopped just above them; they were gathered in the field of some high school, and most of them looked like they used to attend. I haven't been watching the news but I wouldn't doubt the epidemic of missing teens that's been occurring say, oh in the past few months.

I thought about the spirits in purgatory, I have to stop this.

There was a huge bonfire and the humans were in a line circulating it. Music was blaring, I was surprised none of the neighbours heard the noise or saw the fire, shouldn't the police be here? Then I actually saw Judah. He was by far, the oldest looking person in the crowd. In his hand was a red blade, this was the device he used. A memory flickered. Luke said the corrupted Vampires could be killed by being beheaded by a special blade, I've even seen it done quite effectively. Corrupted Werewolves just had to be cut by these blades to be turned to dust. I remember I asked how *he* could die and he said it was pretty much the same for him only the corrupted or demons use their own version of a special blade.

That must be the kind of blade, but how is it able to infect humans? Judah twirled it in his hand and the answer popped out of his head to me. This blade was different from the usual blade the corrupted use. An uncorrupted blade is angel bones forged in Holy fire. While the corrupted's blade was made from demon bones and forged in Hell fire, but the owner crests his blade with his or her own blood as a sign of ownership. This one however, had been dipped purposely in demon blood, which infected anything it cut. It wouldn't infect a Vampire or Werewolf, it would simply be fatal to them. A Vampire would not have to be beheaded by this blade, they would be susceptible by the slightest cut.

So Judah was going to forcefully infect these humans with this blade. That's how he accumulated the numbers so quickly. With this blade, even a cut like a paper cut would do the job. The blood is what holds the life energy which is a direct line to the soul. Blood itself is not part of the soul as some may believe, but once infected the blood creates a very big doorway, and the soul cannot stay.

I flew to the bleachers on the one side of the field unseen. Judah raised a hand and the music stopped. Everyone gathered around him and the humans. The bonfire shrank a little as one by one the infected grabbed a piece of burning wood and made a circle around the corrupted and his soon to be victims. It was sort of like a ceremony. But there was no actual ceremony for this shit; Judah was just a little theatrical.

"My children, say hello to your new brothers and sisters." Judah motioned his hand to the humans and the demons cheered. There was two girls about fifteen or sixteen and the four boys looked about eighteen. Why so young? This was going to be a tragedy if I didn't stop it now. I fluidly stepped out of the bleachers and went into my demon form. The demons looked up as I turned the bonfire into blue flames. Judah turned to look at me, oddly enough the fucker smiled. At the sight of me the humans freaked out but with a simple thought, they all passed out.

"Ah, the Witchdemon, how nice to make your acquaintance. I am Judah." His smiled got bigger.

"I already know who you are and who you used to be, I'm here to stop you."

With one thought, all the demons dropped to their knees and screamed. Black blood erupted from their skin causing them to turn to dust instantly. The blood flowed and swirled around me. I absorbed it bit by bit, not taking my eyes off the still smiling Judah. Why was he still fucking smiling? He spun the blade in the air and brought it down to the ground causing the earth to crack. A gust of wind hit me hard, making me fly back through the blue flames of the bonfire and hit the high school wall that was a good thirty feet away.

I felt me energy drain from my body, the leftover demon blood I hadn't absorbed yet disappeared. I was forced back into my human form. Wind was blowing around me.

"You are weak." A voice whispered from the wind. Images from my teenage years flashed before my eyes. People picking on me and I never did anything about it.

"You are unworthy." It whispered. My insecurities growing up flooded through me.

"Doomed to be alone." It hissed. I remembered the envy and depression I felt when Stacey first told me she was getting married.

"Ugly." The whisper echoed. I moved my tongue over my teeth, I hated them. I always noticed when guys slightly grimaced at my teeth and then acted like it didn't bother them. They just wanted to fuck.

"Join me." The whisper demanded.

Then Peter flashed in my head. I remembered what he said about my teeth when we were on the couch. The way my heart felt whenever I was with him.

No. I thought. My life wasn't like what this whisper was trying to make it seem. I wasn't alone, I had Peter. He loved me and he didn't think I was ugly and I had Mary and Stacey too. Then I thought of my supernatural friends. Hell, even Stan tried to threaten Peter even though he could die twenty times over while Peter was only halfway through blinking.

"Fool!" The voice rasped.

An image of Stacey and Peter was forced in my head. They were embraced and looking in each other's eyes. I shook my head. I took note of the scent in the air and that reincarnated knowledge kicked in.

"I know who you are Lucifer."

The wind gathered as a transparent cobra. It was a wispy image, almost as if it were made of smoke. I felt my rage accumulate to the pit of my stomach. I had so many who cared about me, who loved me, who depended on me. There was no way I was going to watch them die or be the cause of it.

"I will not join you!" I yelled. My eyes went piercing blue and I burst forth into my warrior form. My glow blew the cobra back and the image changed into a cloud of smoke as it retreated back into the crack in the ground, sealing it behind him. His smell was of sulphur and graveyard soil. Judah looked from side to side assessing for an escape, he dropped his blade and made a run for it. I swooped down, grabbed him by the shoulder with one hand, and with the other I shoved it right through his back, out of his chest with blue flames at my fingertips. His body cracked around the edges of the wound then spider webbed till the blue flames spread and turned him to dust.

I turned around and picked up the blade. I knew there were more of these but I didn't know if they were corrupted or demonized or both, or even how many were using them for battle or the same purpose as Judah. I guess I'll figure that out later. I picked it up and turned it over so I could see it from every angle. I concentrated on the energy and then I felt something weird. The blade stretched into a large thick sword, turning white as it went. Blue flames in a thin layer covered its surface. The handle went from black to white. This was the kind of sword my Obedients were holding in my vision at the Valley. The energy coming off it was immense. Then I sensed an energy I've never sensed before.

I turned around to see a little orb of light shining super bright. I flicked a wrist at the blue bonfire and it went out. The bright little orb reminded me of a star in the sky, the way it was twinkling. I knew what it was right away.

It was my little sprite that was supposed to come visit me. The sprite landed in my outstretched hand. It squeaked at me in a different language.

"I'm sorry, what?"

"The demons have returned to earth, they have a device that sucks souls but no one knows where they are. The corrupted have many spies, be careful."

And with that, the sprite flew to the sky.

*   *   *

I landed on the patio with my new sword in my hand. Lucifer's technical appearance was still a large amount of energy felt by all of my supernatural friends. Peter had Mary in his arms as he stood talking to Luke by the fireplace. Matthew and Silence were in the entranceway to the dining room. Stan and Stacey were sitting on the couch and Joseph was at the patio doors waiting for *me* apparently. When I landed they all looked at me. They were pretty big patio doors. Joseph was the first one out to greet me. Even he felt the devil's energy. He stopped a couple feet away when he noticed the sword.

"Whoa." He said.

Peter gave Mary to Stan and followed Luke, Matthew and Silence onto the patio. They all looked at the sword as I raised it to eye level. I projected everything that happened to them, even the personal stuff. Peter looked at me with his 'doe' eyes. Joseph shivered making Peter look at him.

"That felt weird, I didn't know you could put stuff in my head."

Completely ignoring him, Matthew stepped forward.

"This is the heavenly sword of justice. This is no ordinary blade. Only the Witchdemon and her Obedients can wield it."

No! No! No! Don't say that! My face said but Joseph hardly heard.

"Obedients? What are the Obedients?"

Matthew looked at him curiously, "Aren't you a psychic? You have the scent of herbs," Matthew squinted as he smelled the air, "And something else..."

Oh fuck you Matthew! The smell was obvious, the fact you haven't made that connection yet is fucking amazing, but given your past episodes I'm not surprised. I thought to myself.

"What?" Joseph said looking at me. I stopped for a second; I did think that to myself right? Matthew walked up to him and smelled deeper.

Click.

He was about to say something when Peter stepped in between him.

"Weren't we going to discuss Lucifer? He surfaced and Otr and Fafnir are back, so do we have a strategy??" Peter's question was a God send as it distracted everyone.

"Yes, we must discuss the situation at hand. Other explanations can wait." Luke said to Matthew. The Alpha Wolf nodded. Joseph still looked confused. I slowly changed back into my human form and I felt more drained then when I left. The sword started to glow. Everyone watched as the sword turned into energy and went straight into my chest, filling me to the core. Wow, I felt waaay better.

"Whoa." Joseph said again.

"Um, is it supposed to do that?" I asked Luke and Silence.

"It is yours, it becomes one with you." Silence said simply.

I looked into the front room and saw that Stacey was staring at me about to have a panic attack. Because of the wedding of course, the world's demise wasn't on the top of her list apparently.

"Okay um, Peter? Can you take our friends to the den to discuss the current events and Joseph, could you do something with Stan while Stacey, Mary and I do wedding stuff?"

"Yea I can do that." Joseph ducked inside and grabbed Stan. They went to the basement while Peter and the rest bolted into the den. I walked in and took Mary by the hand.

"Come on honey bee, time to see what we're going to wear for auntie's wedding."

"Okay mommy."

The three of us made it into the guest room where Stacey had various cut outs from a mountain of magazines that now occupied the corner of her room. We went through dress after dress. All of them fit perfectly,

(Obviously I wouldn't unfit it on purpose, but I mean as in 'suits her' kind of fit.) But Stacey was being a dress Nazi. There was something wrong with something. Mary's eyes were getting droopy, what time was it? Should she even be up right now? Why did Peter take her flying so late? We weren't even half way through Stacey's cut out pile.

"Um Stace? Let me put Mary to bed okay?"

"Sure." Stacey said as she analysed herself in the mirror.

"Come on sweetie." I picked up Mary and carried her to her bed. I laid her down and tucked her in. She was in a deep sleep by the time I kissed her forehead; I made it half way to the door when I heard it.

"Mommy, help me!" an echo of Mary's voice screamed. I turned quickly and rushed to her side.

"Mary?" I shook her and she groaned.

"Yes mummy?"

"Are you okay honey bee?"

"Yea, 'm fine mummy, let me sleep 'm tired." She mumbled.

"Okay baby."

She drifted off and I stood there staring at her. What was that? My heart was heavy. I felt really sad all of a sudden. Everything was going to be okay, I told myself. I went back to Stacey and she noticed something was up.

"Are you okay Gabby?"

"Yea I'm fine, let's just continue where we left off okay?"

"Okay let's try that one." She pointed to a strapless one that glittered a bit. I didn't like it.

"Are you sure?" I looked at it skeptically.

"Come on Gabby, the faster we get through these, the faster we can get to your dress."

I rolled my eyes. Stan came back to grab something so we moved to my room, good thing Stacey was wearing a throw away because she would have been pissed. Fifty dresses later, and I mean that literally, we finally found the one she wanted. It was the very last one on the bottom of the fucking pile. From the neck it looked like a thick choker, and then came down over the breasts with a space in the middle from the neck down to just the cleavage area between the breasts.

It was completely backless and hugged her curves amazingly. It was a bright white, not egg or crème or whatever. Fucking white. The hem came down precisely to just the bottom of her feet. The shoes she chose were two inch heeled sandals, also white. I was glad she didn't go for the stilettos; she was going to have her wedding outside. We worked it out that I would put up a barrier so she wouldn't freeze to death, Joseph and Stan I'm sure, would be warm enough in their monkey suits.

"We'll figure my dress out later Stacey, go and get some rest okay?"

She twirled one more time in the mirror then with a flick of my wrist, her pyjamas came back. She quickly snatched the cut out and waved goodbye to me. Peter was at the doorway when she left. He looked at me.

"Everyone had to go, the sun is coming up."

I nodded, then looked away. I don't know if I should tell him but I didn't want to make the same mistake twice.

"Peter, there's something I have to tell you." I said uneasily.

He came and sat down next to me on the bed, "What is it?"

I projected my 'dream' from the other night and what just happened in Mary's room.

"What do you think that means?" I asked.

He was in deep thought for a moment, "I'm not sure but we really need to be careful now. Otr knows how important she is. If he got her before he will try again. I'll show everyone what you just showed me so we're all on the same page okay?"

I nodded. It was true, the only threat we had was him. Then a question hit me, "Why were you flying with Mary so late?"

"She couldn't sleep, she was having nightmares. But then I felt that energy and brought her home right away."

"Do you think that may be the reason I keep hearing what I'm hearing?"

"It's possible he may be trying to keep you paranoid," He smiled a little, "And he may be keeping you focused on so many ghosts that the real thing comes and fucks everything up."

I gave him a small smile, my words not thrown but definitely given back to me. He was right though, I wouldn't put that kind of manipulation past the devil himself.

"Why were Stan and Joseph back so soon? I caught a glimpse of something and they were back long before you were, like nearly half an hour after I left."

Peter laughed, "The hotel they went to was a bust, literally. They were in half an hour and the whole place got raided by police. They had to leave. Joseph felt the energy too." He said almost as an afterthought. I squinted at him, he was enjoying Joseph's unease just a little too much.

"Alright well, I have a lot to do tomorrow, err, today. I need some sleep."

I got comfortable on top of the blankets, not bothering with my clothes again.

Peter sanded off our clothes and tried to go in for the kill.

"I said sleep!" I sanded a giant pillow and smacked it in his face.

"Oh come on." Peter laughed.

CHAPTER NINETEEN

I awoke to Mary's giggles. It was a great way to wake up actually. I sanded some clothes on and walked towards the giggles. In Mary's room; Peter and Stacey were playing a mouse game. Peter possessed Jeremiah and was animatedly chasing a stuffed mouse on a string being led by Stacey. I had to take a second look at Mary, she looked absolutely adorable. Her brown hair was in thick tight curls and she wore a puffy white dress with white nylons and shiny white shoes. The nylons were reinforced with socks that frilled at the ankles. She had a big plastic rose at the waistband.

"Do you like it?" Asked Peter the cat when he noticed my gaze.

"Did you do it?"

He made the cat look at me with a sarcastic smirk, "Well, who else?"

Stacey was making the stuffed mouse poke the side of his head while he was talking. Mary continued to giggle.

"Did she have breakfast? What time is it?" I asked.

"Honey, she's had breakfast, lunch and dinner. But since she didn't go to bed till almost four in the morning, her schedule is now off. It's seven thirty in the evening." Peter informed me.

"Oh." I rubbed my eyes. Silence wasn't expected for another couple of hours. They continued with their game while I went downstairs and onto the patio. The sunset made the cloud a pinky orange. Another day gone.

"Hey Gabby." It was Joseph. I closed my eyes at the sound of his voice. I seriously couldn't wait till he was gone after the wedding. I wasn't attracted to him, it was just this annoying electricity I felt on my skin every time he was around me. I turned to him.

"Uh, hi Joseph. How is Stan holding up?"

"He's good but I'm sure you can see for yourself." He nodded his head sideways towards the patio doors. I looked in that direction and listened for Stan's mind. He was practicing his vows. Well at least *he* wrote his. I glanced up at Mary's bedroom window then looked back at Joseph.

"How are *you* doing?" I asked, "A lot of shit to take in I assume."

His heart beat a little faster at the question. It made him nervous. I resisted the temptation to look in his head any further. I already had a feeling what was going on in there.

"I'll be alright." He shrugged, "I just can't believe all this shit is real. It's like, I knew something was up but to have everything confirmed is just a little disorienting."

"Yea it's a little fucked up." I agreed.

He smiled at me.

"What?" I was curious of his smile.

He put his hands in his pockets and looked down at his feet. He lifted his head slightly and gave me a pretty seductive smile. My stomach went tight. I had to correct my thinking for a second.

"I knew there was something special about you when I met you." He admitted.

I thought about that, "Are you sure you didn't think there was something dysfunctional about me? I'm sure I did a good impression of a 'just waking' coma patient." I stated.

He laughed, "Yea and I still gave you my number."

I smiled too. That he did. Then Stacey was at the patio doors.

"Gabby, can I show you the ring I got for Stan?"

She looked at Joseph and then at me.

"Sure let's see it." I said.

She walked out to us and pulled it out. It was white gold with a big black stone and little green emeralds in the shape of an 'S' in it. Joseph smirked. Stacey looked at him.

"What's wrong with it? I got it because it looks like a football players ring. He loves football."

I grinned with Joseph and looked at her, "It looks like he's going to play Quarter back for Slytherin."

Joseph couldn't hold in his laughter.

"Gabby! That's not funny!" She nearly wailed at my grin. "I put a lot of thought into this!"

I sighed. "I'm sorry Stacey, but do you want me to lie and then shrug when he looks at you funny? Or *if* he does, I mean."

Panic crossed her face. "What do I do?"

"Who is his favourite team?" Joseph asked.

"Patriotically? The B.C. Lions. Otherwise it's the New England Patriots hands down." Stacey said impatiently.

"Then just take him to the Lion's games all season and try maybe five games of the Patriots. I'm sure I could whip you up some tickets. Now for this ring.....why the green stones?"

"He's a Taurus, May 5th remember? His gemstone is emerald."

I looked at her, we both knew every zodiac had numerous stones. But she looked at me desperately anyways.

"And it's his favourite colour."

"Ah."

That's one ugly ring. Joseph thought. I smacked him on the arm. He looked surprised for a second then pointed to the ring.

"Just take out the 'S' and make the stone an emerald." He suggested.

It wasn't a bad idea.

"Okay let's see how it looks." Stacey allowed.

She put the ring in her palm and I stared at it. It turned to sand and turned into the ring Joseph suggested. The stone was a bit smaller but it was now an emerald. He was right, it did look better.

"Yea that looks way better. Besides, aren't wedding rings supposed to be simple?"

Besides the engagement ring, the rings Peter and I have are just golden bands. I saw in Stacey's head that she agreed about the simplicity but her face was still pouting.

"What's up Stace?"

"It doesn't feel like it's from me now."

I looked at Joseph and he shrugged. I changed the ring back to the way it was which made her feel better. She hugged me.

"Okay, let's get you into a dress." She looked at Joseph, "Peter is going to do your and Stan's tux's. He's downstairs with Stan and Mary right now so you'd better get down there."

Joseph left with one long glance at me as he walked by to get inside. Then with a long sigh I allowed Stacey to drag me upstairs.

Ugh! I thought when she pulled out the million clippings of Maid of Honour dresses she had for me. I didn't try on a bunch, I simply eyed the dresses. I narrowed it down to three choices in about twelve minutes. Two red and one violet.

"No, not purple. I change my mind on that colour, it's Valentine's Day so I only want white and red. Oh and by the way, I want white and red rose petals everywhere when we go to set up after Silence arrives." Her voice and tone switched to snooty in two point two seconds. Bridezilla moment anyone?

We were going to the Wolf's opening in the woods across the water.

"I could just get the Wolves to do it." I said lazily.

"Can you do that? Where are they going to get the roses?"

I'll make the petals fly there."

I walked to the window and my eyes went white. I searched for Matthew's mind.

Well hello my queen, he thought surprised.

Matthew, I'm sending decorations your way, see if Joan will be willing to put a little finesse on the wedding area please? I'll do the rest when I get there if it's an issue. I looked for some ideas within Stacey's mind and projected them to him so he could inform Joan.

Yes my queen, we will do what we can. He thought back.

For some reason that irked me.

No, just do what you're told you fucking mutt! But I kept that to myself. I looked at the trees and two giant ones burst into white and red rose petals. They swirled towards the Wolves. Next I turned another two into thousands of fireflies. They too sped towards the Wolves. Finally I turned my attention to the vines growing on the trees to my right. They disconnected and went down the same path.

Okay that should be good enough for now. I thought to myself. I walked back to Stacey and tried on the first dress. The material was too shiny. I thought the shine was just from the paper it was printed on but apparently not. It looked like I was wearing red plastic. Stacey stifled a laugh. Disgusted, I changed into the second dress. This one was much better, it was simple and flowed nicely. There was no pattern and it was strapless. Kind of. There were straps but they hugged around the arm as an accessory rather than a necessity to keep the dress up. They were about two inches thick.

"I love it!" Stacey exclaimed.

I twirled for her amusement and she squealed. I sanded back to the clothes I was wearing. Silence arrived just on time; I could smell him coming up the stairs. He knocked before opening the door enough to poke his head through.

"Ladies, if you would accompany me to the patio please, I have an announcement before you leave across the waters."

We followed him downstairs where everyone was waiting. Peter was on the couch with Mary on his lap while Stan and Joseph were standing at the fireplace.

"Why aren't you dressed yet?" Stacey almost shrieked at Stan.

Bridezilla moment strikes again.

"Stacey settle down, Peter can zap on clothes in a second too you know."

She calmed down. Silence cleared his throat politely and everyone looked at him.

"This is an important night. Tonight we bind two souls together. May their love and happiness influence everyone around them. Ladies, a tent has been made for you to change and gentlemen, you will stay here until Gabriel gives the signal."

Signal? What signal?

He smiled, "Anything to tell us you are ready to start."

"Oh Okay...... Like what?" I asked looking at everyone in turn.

Stacey smiled at me. *Oh! Shooting stars!* She thought.

I raised an eyebrow quizzically.

Dude I don't know if I can do that......

I thought about it for a second as she pouted at me.

I'll try, I thought to her. She beamed. I projected the idea to Silence but told him to look for fireworks if the first idea didn't work.

"Very well." He said aloud.

"Okay let's go Gabby." Stacey urged.

I turned to Mary, "Come on honey bee."

Mary jumped off Peter making her thick curls bounce. She ran into my arms and I grabbed Stacey's hand. We exploded into sand and arrived right in front of the white tent. Joan came out to greet us with a smile on her face.

"My queen, I must show you what I've done with the decorations you've sent."

Joan, like all the Wolves, *loved* weddings. It was one of their most sacred ceremonies; the event was the most crucial time for their everlasting relationship. Unfortunately, Joan didn't have any siblings. Which I thought was odd for a Werewolf but then I saw it was because of her father's death when she was only a year old. Her mother never remarried, and eventually from a lonely heart died herself, when Joan was only twelve years old. She didn't have very much experience with setting up weddings. She's only witnessed a handful through her thousands of years, mine included. She was a lone wolf for a very long time. If she were to be exiled, it would be hard but not completely punishing.

She was ecstatic when she heard I had requested her help. I hoped one day she could have her own wedding. We walked around to the other side of the tent and my jaw dropped. One side had chairs and the other side had cedar piles for the Wolves. They would be in their Wolf form. The fireflies littered the sky just fifteen feet above the ceremony and surrounded the area like a wall of stars. Red and white rose petals were strategically scattered down the aisle and the makeshift altar. It looked kind of like a stage, painted white and two steps high. It had red petals all over the place. I raised my hand and adjusted the fireflies light, making them glow more of a white then yellow. Now they really looked like stars. Perfect.

I looked at the 'stage' and saw that the vines I sent were made into an arbour, with a very Celtic looking twist in the way they weaved around each other.

"Oh wow Joan, it's beautiful." Stacey whispered. Stacey hugged Joan appreciatively. Joan looked at me.

"Bang on, I barely had to do a thing. You did an amazing job." I said with a thumbs up.

We went into the tent and got our dresses on. Mary sat on a chair and watched. I had my hair straightened while Stacey had hers in waves. I didn't want to go too dramatic with the makeup, but I ended up going with the smoked eye look. Stacey made me give her at least six different looks before she finally made up her damn mind. She looked like a beautiful porcelain doll.

"Okay can you try the signal?" she asked me.

Fuck. I forgot the damn signal. I hesitated. Man, I just got my dress on. This means I'll have to go into my warrior form. But her beautiful big green eyes twisted my arm.

"I'll *try*. If not, you're just going to have to settle for fireworks."

Mary jumped down from the chair.

"What are you going to do mommy?" She asked curiously.

"I'm going to see if I can make the stars fly honey bee."

We went outside and I transformed. I looked at the stars in the sky; actually, I think shooting stars were just comets or asteroids or whatever that just got too close to the atmosphere when passing by, so I didn't really concentrate on the actual stars. It was an assumption but I guess we'll see if I'm wrong or not. I tried to suck in all my energy to my core to make it more concentrated and potent, then I shot it to the sky in a blue transparent cloud. The sky looked electrified with my energy, making the stars look brighter. Then to my amazement, hundreds of shooting stars sparked across the sky.

Hoy shit! It fucking worked!

"Okay back in the tent. The groom can't see you till you walk down the aisle." Joan said to Stacey.

We hurried back into the tent just in time. Peter sanded the guys to the 'alter'. I changed back into my human form with my maid of honour dress.

"Wow this looks great." I heard Stan say.

"Everyone, it is time." Silence announced to the Vampires and Werewolves.

Apparently there was a little Vampire band. They played some music I've never heard before, on instruments I've never seen before. From their heads, the instruments were nowhere near our century. Peter stood at the 'altar' with Stan and Joseph. Joan went first, she was also wearing a red dress that was strapless and simple. She held a bouquet of red roses and handed one to me before she left the tent. I was next soon, I crouch down to Mary.

"Count to ten then follow." I whispered. I handed her a basket of rose petals. "Throw these as you go okay?"

"Okay mommy." She whispered back.

I kissed her on the forehead and left the tent. Peter's eyes lit up when he saw me. I tried to control my face when he sent me very tempting images.

Not now! I thought to him.

Well obviously I meant later. He smiled.

I rolled my eyes as I got to my spot. Then Mary came out and I looked at Peter. He was picturing the day he would give her away at her own wedding. This thought brought a pain to my chest. I was overwhelmed with grief.

Nothing is going to happen, she's going be fine. I told myself. I tried to breathe but my chest still hurt. We were going to beat this vision like we did with Matthew. I was trying to convince myself that we would win but something told me it was too late. This is ridiculous.

Mary took her place at my side and I placed my hand on her soft hair. I looked at Peter, I think he noticed my anxiety but by then the music changed. It wasn't 'here comes the bride', it was a serene sound that felt like it was lifting my soul. It was music from centuries ago, the kind the Vampires played for their own weddings.

I no longer felt the grief. I felt hope and faith in everyone and everything, especially myself. Stacey stepped out and I swear I heard Stan swallow. Stacey practically glowed in the night light. The fireflies were definitely a nice touch to the effect.

"Holy fuck." Stan whispered. Peter smirked as he glanced down at his feet. Peter heard everything Stan was thinking. Yea, that's the reaction I was going for. I projected it to Stacey and she blushed. From the look on his face and the voice in his head, Stacey was going to have the night of her life.

If she wasn't already pregnant, she would definitely be by morning. I made a mental note to put a barrier around the guest room so I don't have to hear it. Stacey got to the 'altar' and took Stan's hand. Silence cleared his throat and started the ceremony.

* * *

I cleared the chairs and cedar piles and stretched the stage into a dance floor. I kept the fireflies as a wall around it but made one side open for people to enter or exit. The Vampire band played for a while but Stacey got restless with it.

"Gabby can you do something about the music? It's beautiful and all but I need to jam out."

I nodded and flicked my wrist, muting the instruments. The Vampires looked confused.

"I'm sorry, but we need a more modern sound right now." I said to them. They muttered and left the area. It was kind of rude of me but they didn't verbally complain, and for some reason I didn't care. I flicked my wrist again and a giant stereo appeared. Speakers surrounded to dance floor.

The music started and Stacey and I took over the dance floor and lip synced till our hearts content. We got pretty animated but we didn't care when we heard the laughter or saw the shocked faces at some of the lyrics. We danced, perfectly reacting and gesturing to the lyrics and the beat like we practiced it. We just knew the songs really well. When we were all jammed out it was time for some slow songs. I didn't notice at first, but then the first couple lines of the first verse hit me.

This was the song Peter and I danced to at the ball before he kissed me. When I made this realization I looked instinctively at the stereo. Peter was standing there with a smile on his face.

You fucking cornball. I grinned. He reached his hand out to me. I looked around and saw Stacey sitting with Stan and Joseph. Joseph was looking at me. I looked backed at Peter and walked over to him. I grabbed his hand and he pulled me into his arms. I stared into his eyes.

"I'll never let you go." He whispered. It was part of his wedding vow.

I took note of that right away but my heart sank nonetheless.

"What's wrong?" He asked.

"I don't know. I just think it would actually kill me if I never saw you again."

He furrowed his eyebrows, "Why would you think that?"

I shook my head, "I'm just being paranoid. It's like a fairy tale, I have my prince and I'm wondering 'what's the catch?'"

"Should I be super clingy, annoyingly jealous, and egotistical to balance everything out?" he smirked.

"No, no, small doses are okay." I joked. Actually, I would be thrilled with that. In a really sick co-dependant sort of way.

He kissed me without parting his lips. Just the pressure of our lips fully connected made my heart gush with emotion. I lived and breathed for him. In this tiny moment I felt powerful in his arms.

And yet something told me it was going to end.

CHAPTER TWENTY

Mary fell asleep in my arms as we said our goodbyes to the Vampires and Werewolves. So instead of sand travelling, we just flew.

"What about us?" Stan asked as Peter and I started to float.

"Just think happy thoughts." I said sarcastically.

"Gabby!" Stacey half scolded.

I laughed and Peter flicked his wrist this time. Stan, Stacey and Joseph started to float.

"Use your minds to guide you." Peter told them.

Stan and Stacey held hands as Joseph did back flips. I had Mary in my arms so Peter wrapped his arm around my shoulder. The five of us flew to the house just as the sun was rising. We landed on the patio and I went upstairs to put Mary to bed. Stacey and Stan went to the guest room while Joseph and Peter were outside when I made it to the hallway stairs. Mary's window was open when I tucked her in. I went to close it but I heard Peter beckon to Joseph before Joseph could go inside. I silently listened.

"Joseph," Peter started, "What is your last name?"

That was an odd question. It was silent for a moment.

"I don't really have one." Was the response. What?

"Well, tell me about yourself. We never really got to talk at an adult level."

"Uh, well, my mother didn't know who my father was and we were poor. She never applied for my birth certificate and even though my birth was on record at the hospital, there was never an actual name to put on file. When I was six months old, the ministry took me from her. My mom worked the streets and left me with random neighbours. One of them called her in. I was eventually adopted when I was eleven. The ministry gave me the name, Joseph Smith. But I didn't want that name."

I heard him sigh before he continued, "The family that adopted me was nice at first and I ended up as Joseph Peddamin. Later, they regretted the adoption when they realized the costs. I didn't make it to high school. My adopted father started drinking and beating his wife while I started doing drugs and stealing cars. I went to a Juvenile detention centre at fourteen, they disowned me and I was a street kid, in and out of that place till I was nineteen. I went to provincial for burglary, got eighteen months and that was twelve years ago. I live in New West now with odds jobs here and there."

I felt so sad for him but Peter gave a frustrated sigh.

"You know you can't lie to me right?" Peter said impatiently.

"What have I lied about?"

"You're not working any jobs, you're a petty drug dealer who owes a lot of money. That's why you jumped on Stan's idea of coming here for a while."

What the fuck? And here I thought it was because of me.....

"Well if you can read my mind then you know damn well that was practically a side thought to the *real* reason." Joseph said daringly.

Ah, there it is, yea it was me.

"Tread carefully Joseph. I've been extra tolerant with you." Peter warned.

"Yea? And why is that? Tell me Peter, what's this Obedient shit Matthew was talking about? Why did he look shocked when he smelled me and why did you butt in to distract him? Am I one of them? Is that it?"

Wow. Joseph was pretty receptive. Fuck this was really annoying. I bolted demon fast to the patio door before Peter could speak.

"What's going on out here?" I asked. Both men looked at me.

"Nothing. I'm going to bed; I'll leave as soon as I wake up." Joseph said moodily. He was pissed. As he turned, Peter looked a little smug. Joseph walked past me to the basement. When he was out of sight I looked at Peter.

"What are you doing?" I asked. He looked at me innocently.

"What do you mean?"

"You know exactly what I mean! You almost told him about the Obedients! I could see it in your head!" I pretty much hissed at him.

"So what? Maybe he *should* know."

What?

"Are you insane?! Then he'll want to know how he gets his powers. Do you *want* me to sleep with him?" My anger was almost at the tipping point. I wanted to tear up, was I not important to him anymore?

"No, of course not." Peter stepped back.

"Then what the fuck are you on? You're freaking me out." I was going to go ape shit in three point three seconds.

"Listen Gabby, I'm sorry, I didn't think that through."

Obviously!

Frustrated, I stormed back to my room. Yes I said *my* room because I planned on locking the door, put up a barrier and make the fucker sleep on the God damn couch! I slammed the door and flicked my wrist to lock it. I sanded off my clothes and got into bed with my black lace booty short underwear and a black lace bra. I got comfortable and stuck my ass out. I knew that this would be the position he should find me in to make him ponder. But he wasn't getting any.

I'll just tease the fuck out of him. I flicked my hand at the window and gusts of a floral aroma filled the room. It was all part of my master plan.

He knocked on the door, "Gabby?"

I ignored him.

"Come on Gabby, unlock the door."

I continued to ignore him. I knew he was going to do it, that's why I manipulated the scent in the room and positioned myself temptingly. He sanded under the door and materialized. He smelled the air then noticed me.

"Psychological warfare?" He asked.

"Is it working?" I peaked at him curiously. He had his head cocked to the side and he was smiling at me.

Oh fuck you!

I nearly melted at the sight of him. Not only was it the way he smiled and angled his face just right but he sanded on a black wife beater, which was tight fitting, and black boxer shorts. I don't know why, but that look on him made me forget what I was mad about. For a second.

Mother fucker!

I whipped my face back to staring at the wall and made the sheets cover me. It wasn't fair; he knew exactly what to do to make me want him. I wanted to punch him in the face and fuck the shit out of him at the same time. He lay down beside me.

"You fucking reversed me." I said angrily.

He laughed, "I what?" In his head he totally thought something else. He wasn't in on my irritated loop. I 'thoughtfully' let him in on the secret and he laughed again.

"Interesting." He said as he leaned over. Doing psychological warfare on a psychologist is a futile effort. He pulled the sheet off my shoulder and kissed my neck. He slipped himself under the sheet and traced my side with his fingertips, going around my hip and then rested his hand on my thigh. He pressed his body up against mine and, oh man, I felt his soldier standing at attention against my ass.

"When did you take off your boxers?"

"I didn't."

"What? Let me see." It felt really defined. *Completely* distracted now, I flipped around and grabbed for him. I didn't believe him.

"Oh." I said surprised. My muscles between my legs pulsed.

"You know, while your hand is down there......" he trailed off. I smiled and kissed him. Sticking my hand in his boxers, I started stroking and squeezing him in all the right places.

* * *

The smell popped my eyes open. By the time I bolted out of bed it was gone.

"What is it?" Peter mumbled.

"I smelled sulphur." I whispered.

Peter sanded right into Mary's room without a second thought. I followed at human pace. She was sound asleep in her bed. Not even a trace of sulphur was in the air.

"Are you sure you smelled it? Peter whispered to me as we made our way back to our room. It had only been two hours and the sun was out. I actually didn't know all the rules about demons and the sunlight. I only knew Vampires and Werewolves couldn't go out during the day. I think my father said something about some demons being able to go out in the day but he didn't really elaborate.

"I don't know, maybe it was a dream." I whispered back.

I wasn't really sure about that though. I went to the bathroom to wash my face. My hands were trembling. I closed the door and sat down on the floor in front of the tub. All the dread and grief I had been bottling up, broke out and I silently cried and tried not to rip my hair out. I couldn't help but hear a little voice telling me we were going to lose. Mary was going to die and I was never going to see Peter again. I had left the tap running.

I don't know why I had no confidence, like she was already gone. But it was eating me alive. A sob escaped my lips and I sniffed. A moment later Peter knocked on the door. Fuck, I didn't want him to hear me. I didn't want him to know I was breaking apart because something was telling me we were going to fail.

"Are you okay in there?"

I tried to repress it but I was sure he already felt my anguish.

"Y-yea, I'm okay." I sniffed.

"Gabby, I know your lying. What's up? Can I come in?"

No, fuck off and let me wallow in my cowardly delusions in peace! But I kept that thought to myself. I just didn't want to explain why I was crying. I sighed and wiped my face.

"I guess so." I mumbled.

The look on his face when he saw me was slightly alarmed. He has seen me 'cry' but not 'freak out' like I was a moment ago. I saw in his mind my face was blotchy like I got slapped around and my eyes were all puffy and bloodshot. He pretty much ran to me, went on his knees, and pulled me close to him.

"Hey, it's going to be okay. It's going to be okay." He whispered in my ear. I held onto him. It made me want to freak out more. I didn't know how I was going to lose him but I didn't think about that now I was in his arms. I let him carry me to the bed; I wanted to be in his arms forever.

* * *

Joseph left without saying goodbye to anyone. Stan was a little ticked about it, Mary and Peter seemed happy enough, Stacey didn't care, and for me? Well, with him gone I felt lighter. The electricity was gone and I didn't notice how bad it was before but I also felt less stressed. But only a little. Everyone was up before me again. I was sleeping so much lately. Stacey, Mary and Stan were eating Chinese food. Peter actually ordered take out. I could smell it in our room. Ugh! I waved a hand and the bedroom door closed loudly and the window burst open. That shit fucking stunk! I guess the door closing caught their attention because I heard Peter say to Mary,

"I guess your mother's up. I'll be right back honey bee."

I didn't want to go anywhere or do anything. I was having a moment where I thought the world could go fuck itself.

Peter was now in the room with me, "I think you're depressed."

Oh yea? What was your first clue? I thought to him.

He walked around the bed and crouched in front of me. I opened my eyes and looked at him. He petted the side of my head then tucked some hair behind my ear.

"What's going on in there Gabby?"

I looked away from him, I couldn't tell him.

"It's not healthy to internalize." He tried to poke around in my head but I blocked him. He sighed.

"Just give me a bit Peter." I said to him.

"How long?" he rested his hand on my cheek.

"I don't know. A couple days?" I said it like a question; I had no idea how long this would last.

"Okay, we'll see how you feel in a couple of days." Then his eyes went to the window. "Silence is here with Luke. Don't worry, I'll handle this. You rest up."

He kissed me then left, closing the door behind him. I turned over trying to get comfortable but it wasn't working. I flipped onto my back. I couldn't help but hear downstairs.

"We have urgent news." Luke said.

"What is it?" Stacey asked.

"Fafnir has already consumed a psychic so we must be careful. Depending on what gifts the psychic has, which I'm sure have proven to be quite useful, we should be on our guard till we know who he has consumed." Luke silently explained that his government made secret recordings of psychic bloodlines, bloodlines that carried high potencies in powers. Some developed over the decades, so not all were on the list but at the moment the government were hunting down the ones on record just in case. Most bloodlines were chosen to work alongside the Vampires and Werewolves.

"What is the difference between a psychic and a witch?" Stan asked. Silence answered him.

"That depends on what your definition of 'witch' is. For most they are one and the same. For some, they are completely different. A human in touch with their gifts who have practiced and redefined their gifts. This is a psychic, with gifts of extraordinary strength, telepathy, seeing the future fates, telekinesis. The word Witch was at first used by the Christians with hatred toward any belief that was not their own but usually the people of the old ways, where everything is energy, all is life within male and female origins, ancestors are respected alive and dead. The word witch was used out of spite and now, finally, out of pride. The Wicca belief is a consort of ceremony and spirituality with no relation to the catholic or Christian beliefs yet continuously stereotyped to 'devil' worship. That is not to say there isn't dangerous moves to be avoided. Dealing with any energy, whether you call it God or Satan, The All, or Hades, or demons or Monsunes, deities, the good and bad are not the practice but those who practice it."

All I heard was silence, like no noise for a minute before the breathing Silence continued. "A psychic is blessed with an actual sixth sense and a brain slightly more evolved. To be realistic, all children are born that way but society and life itself is fickle and the ability fades or if evolved at birth, gets stronger while unintentionally practiced. Some become aware of their gifts and practice, becoming even more evolved and some even live longer. The Oracle was, minus the five we thought she had lived, was a hundred and twenty."

Holy shit, that's probably the most Silence has ever talked in over a thousand years. I felt giddy to hear such a blue moon event.

"Oh." Was all Stan could say.

"Do you know where he is?" Peter asked.

"No, is your wife ready to train tonight?" Luke asked.

"Um," Peter started, but before he could say anymore I had bolted out of bed, sanded on some clothes and was at his side.

"Let's go." I said. Mary looked up with her mouth full. A noodle was hanging from her lips. Peter put his hands on my shoulders and faced me.

"Are you sure?" he asked quietly. I nodded but avoided eye contact.

"Yea, I can do this." Finally I looked at him. But he still looked worried.

"Okay."

"Daddy, can we fly again before bed?" Mary asked.

Peter turned to her, "Of course honey bee."

Stan smiled and ruffled Mary's hair. I turned to the Vampires. They bowed to Peter. The three of us went onto the patio and I sanded us to the clearing.

*　　*　　*

We arrived to snarling and snapping.

"What is that?" From their heads I knew what it was but I couldn't believe my eyes.

"That, my queen, is a Chimaera. A European creature. We brought him here to test your communication skills." Matthew said as he walked over to us. I looked wide eyed with my eyebrows all the way up at the creature. It had the head and body of a lion, a goat head and neck in the middle of its back, and a damn serpent for a tail. The fucker was breathing fire to boot.

"Um." I didn't know what to say.

The creature, um, Chimaera, was pretty big and looked kind of pissed. The guard had out their special blades and was trying to keep the Chimaera in one spot that was fenced. The Chimaera pawed at the air in front of it and roared.

"How did you get it here?" I looked at Luke then to Silence.

"They had my help."

The voice was raspy, in a very sexy way and he had an accent that just made it irresistible to want to hear more.

What the fuck? Why am I thinking like that?

I turned around and nearly fainted. It was my third Obedient! From my vision in the Valley. Shit! He had the herbal scent but he wasn't earthy or salty smelling. He had that sweet smell like Joseph and James but the herbal, sweet, and whatever the third smell was combined, was very intoxicating. I pinned it down, it was like a fresh rain smell. It was weird but it kind of made the sweet scent smell like marshmallows.

"Gabriel, this is Adam. He's a high priest from Europe. He is also a very powerful psychic who can move objects with is mind." Luke said.

Yea.... I can do that too.... Big... whoop..... But now I get how the Chimaera got here. I was only partially listening, and giving my secret sarcasm a half assed effort because I was slowly getting lost in Adam's blue eyes. I didn't even look at the Vampire as he spoke. Adam was the one to lead the army of angels and he was a high priest, go figure.

"Are you okay?" Adam asked. I looked down. It didn't matter because I wasn't going to use the Obedients, I had Peter. But I was overwhelmed with grief as soon as that thought entered my head. Don't fall apart in front of everyone Gabby. Pull it together. My eyes went piercing blue and my clothes changes as my wings sprouted out of my back. I looked right at Adam as I stood straight with my face revealing no emotions.

"I'm just fine." I told Adam in a cool voice. My sound and tone came out a little more seductive than I wanted it to. I didn't want to seduce at all. Oops. Adam swallowed, Luke caught that and coughed.

"Well, let's meet the Chimaera." Luke offered smirking from the one side of his mouth.

"Right." Adam turned and rushed off towards the creature.

Nether Vampire or Werewolf had experience with the past Angel Obedients before their awakenings, so they had no idea and I certainly wasn't going to tell them. Adam has been working with them for over twenty five years. He knew everything about the Witchdemon that they knew. He was almost as old as Peter. He was so in touch with his gifts. I looked a little more in his head as we followed him towards the Chimaera. He was exposed at the early age of one, making his bottle come to him from across the room. Afraid of his gifts, his parents gave him up. It was the Oracle who encouraged him and raised him till he was twenty.

Oddly enough, he went to look for his parents but when he arrived at the house it was already burning to the ground. The Oracle told him to go to a church in Europe, not far from where he lived. It was hard to see exactly where, he seemed to be able to partially block himself from intruders. He was taught at this church how to excel his gifts. The church notified Luke and Matthew right away because they knew he would be very useful to them. As Silence mentioned, the strong psychics were given the privilege to fight alongside the Vampires and Werewolves.

Adam attended med school and got a PHD, in what is unclear, but he still continued to practice the church's values and morals. He loved to help people.

And holy fuck, he was still a virgin.

But he wasn't a stranger to the orgasm. His full name was Adam Spencer McCormick. And he was a cancer on the astrology circuit.

Why the hell do I care about that? (Because Virgo and Cancer are compatible?)

He stopped just behind the Guard. Joan turned around and bowed to me. Nicolas and Mark did the same. They moved out of my way and so did Adam. The Chimaera stopped snarling and looked at me too. I didn't have a clue what to do, so I thought to him.

Hi, I said.

The Chimaera just stared at me. My intuition clicked in. It was more set on spiritual energy and actions rather than any human communication, it didn't speak any human languages. So I projected my emotional energy. Caring and love flowed out of me and the Chimaera sat down. The goat head was calm and the lion licked his lips. I raised my hand and slowly stepped towards him. I was right in front of, wait a minute, *He* was a *She*. I was right in front of her when she went to all fours. I was nervous at first but she pushed her face into my hand and purred.

I smiled and scratched her behind the ear. I raised my other hand to stroke the nose of the goat. Both heads had their eyes closed. I felt her energy, it was beautiful. Her aura was orange and she smelled like fresh mown grass. She didn't know human languages but I'm sure she trusted me enough to learn. I took my hands away and projected everything I knew about the English language. Both heads blinked a couple times.

Do you understand me now? I asked. The Chimaera bowed her head. I took that as a 'yes'.

Can I name you? Again, she bowed her head. I thought about it for a second, *how about Sia?*

The Chimaera purred. Sia it is. I turned to my friends.

"A success I see?" Adam half asked. I nodded. Sia came and sat beside me while I petted her goat head.

"Yes, Sia and I are best friends now."

"Sia?" Adam looked puzzled.

"Yes, that's what I named her."

"Her?"

Come on really? I closed my eyes, impatiently let out a breath, and reopened them. Sia huffed and pawed the ground.

"Yes, *her*. You see, she's a little pissed because she's pregnant and you took her from her nest." Sia licked my face, her breath smelled really earthy. I hoped there wasn't a missing Werewolf somewhere......

"Well then, I'd better take her back." Adam said but Sia whined.

"Can she understand me?" he asked.

"She can now." I said, "I think it would be best if she stayed here." We all looked at Matthew.

"Alright," he shrugged, "But I don't really have a choice do I?" he looked at me and I shook my head. "What does she eat?" Matthew asked.

"Pretty much anything." Adam answered.

Sia let out a weird meow sound.

"Actually she prefers stag." I corrected. Sia head butted my shoulder.

"What about the goat? Or the serpent?" Adam challenged. He wasn't acting very priesty.

"They don't eat. The goat breathes the fire and the serpent bites and poisons. The lion eats enough for all three." The goat head nibbled at my hair and the serpent twisted around my hand as the lion continued to purr.

"I think she likes you." Luke observed.

"Yea, I think I'm going to keep her." I smiled.

* * *

For the next few nights I went to the clearing with Sia. It seemed the cure for my depression was some animal therapy. I could see in her head, the father of her soon to be cubs was a Celtic dragon. Adam stuck around too, and all too soon I started to feel the electricity on my skin whenever he was around. The sixth night of my animal therapy was ending and I was getting ready to go home when Adam approached me.

"Gabriel."

I was in my human form in the little hut I made for Sia. I was crouched down in front of her while she lay on the giant cedar pile that was her bed.

She loved it. Sia was purring with her eyes closed as I petted her head to say goodbye when he walked in. The electricity charged me and I think even Sia noticed it in me. I stood up and slowly faced him.

"Yes?"

He stuttered with his thoughts for a second. Shit, he was feeling the same thing I was only he thought it was just plain attraction and he was forbidding himself from saying anything. Then he shut off. He was able to shut himself off from me if he thought I might take a peak but he wasn't able to hold the block for long. He hadn't mastered that technique because he never had the need to. Not that I cared, I stopped looking. Too much info.

"Silence, Luke and Matthew agree that we should start training you in combat. They want me to help you."

Um alone? Just me and him? The thought made me a little nervous.

"How will you help me?"

"Basically, I'll be throwing objects at you with my mind." He smiled.

I raised an eyebrow, "Okay, when?"

"As soon as possible."

I thought about it, I looked away to the left a bit to pretend to think hard on it. It's okay, you'll be fine, just keep your shit to yourself and things won't get awkward.

"Alright, let me go home and get some rest, then I'll have to hunt. I'll see you around midnight." I decided.

"Alright then." He turned and left.

I walked out of Sia's hut and looked at the sunrise. I wandered how many days were left before I lost my happiness forever. I closed my eyes, sighed, and then sanded home.

CHAPTER TWENTY ONE

I was sooo hungry when I woke up. Peter hadn't eaten in a while either. He was so preoccupied with Mary at nights, he couldn't go hunt. She's been having a lot of nightmares lately and I was trying not to see it as an omen. But tonight, Stacey, Stan, and Silence were going to keep her entertained while Peter and I went hunting. I missed him a lot. For someone so worried about losing him, I was spending a lot of time away. And I was going to spend more by the looks of things if Mary's nightmares didn't quit. I had to train and there was a battle on the horizon.

It was eight o'clock in the evening when Peter and I left the house. We didn't sand travel this time. We simply flew above, hidden by the clouds. We weren't paying attention to where we were going either. Embraced and kissing like we were going to die the next day, you know, if that were even possible. I guess he missed me too. He stopped kissing me for a second to look me in the eyes.

"How do you feel?" he asked.

"Way better." I smiled.

"You haven't told me what you've been up to for the last week."

I projected Sia and Adam but left out the fact that Adam was the third Obedient. I don't know why but I really didn't want to deal with some jealousy bullshit. But on second thought, I actually, should tell him.

"Interesting." But he noticed I was hiding something because of my hesitation at the end of the projection, "What are you keeping from me Gabby?"

"Um, Adam's kind of the third Obedient from my vision in the Valley."

His body went rigid and made me panic a little.

"He has no idea and neither do Luke or Matthew. They never dealt with the Angel Obedient before and since his psychic abilities are so advanced, they never made the connection. Only you and I know." I blurted as fast as I could.

"But didn't you show Luke your vision?"

"No, that was my second vision I showed him, when I *created* the doorway"

Peter rolled his eyes, "Well I'm glad that's all cleared up."

Sarcasm was thick with this one.

"Oh, I smell dinner." I turned away from him and headed towards the ground.

"Well technically it's breakfast." He muttered but I ignored him.

I landed very gracefully and looked around. From the looks of it we were in White Rock, only in the 'goony' area. Like, butt fuck nowhere. From here, I knew the way to the U.S. border which was near the Native reserve. I'm not sure what the name was, beautiful area, not so beautiful houses. Fucking awesome parties though. I looked down the street and remembered I was at a party at some guy's shack a couple blocks away from here when I was like, fourteen. In reality it was an empty place he was just squatting in. I was just starting my three year love affair with crystal meth. Oh I used to see that one every once and a while afterwards but we drifted apart a couple years ago. I doubt if I'll even be able to feel anything if I smoked a fat bowl right now.

Ha. And I thought *those* days were crazy.

I had landed on a deserted street, for two blocks ahead, left, right and behind there was two houses. Both to my right. I was on Ninety Ninth. The other street sign had been ripped off. I continued past the 'ripped off' street down Ninety Ninth, closer to the two houses. Nothing but fenced field to my left. One of the houses to the right, a two storey, was boarded up and it stood in the middle of the field on my right. About twenty yards in. Almost an acre away on the same block, these were long fucking blocks, street sign to street sign made city blocks look small. An old couple lived there, I could actually see them in the living room window which wasn't covered fully, watching T.V. at this fine hour.

They owned the whole 25 or so acres of property and the boarded up house. They couldn't rent it anymore due to rumours of it being haunted. They had some looky loo's after that who pretended to have 'experiences' and pass out. There were a couple of unfortunate murders in that house but the spirits themselves were gone. Just a lot of hype and fake people.

The smell of dinner was a few more blocks away. I ran down the street I was on at demon speed then stopped at a corner where an old convenience store used to be. Oh shit, across the street was where that old shack used to be. Looked like a bunch of rubble now, I guess the landlord's finally rebuilding. The smell was coming from the side where the store used to be, so I headed down this mini street. The street looked like it fit only one car at a time. Like a little alley than a street because it was pretty much a dead end. I knew there was an old rancher who lived down at the end. That's where they were. I looked around me, where the fuck was Peter?

I'm up here, he thought to me. I looked up to see him flying towards our next meal. From the smell of it they were corrupted Vampires. There was something else. Peter smelled him too and soon he was out of sight. It was Otr we smelled. I ran to the horse ranch just as Peter was landing at the gate.

Repress your energy. I told him.

Fuck that, Peter thought back to me.

I rolled my eyes, *Fuck whatever then.*

I was mad for a second until he kissed my forehead. Yea he was right. We glowed red and quickly transformed into our demon selves. I could smell more than a hundred corrupted Vampires. Peter looked at me.

Let's go, we fight and feed till we find Otr. He's all yours honey. I'll take care of the rest of the corrupted while you're at it. I kissed him hard while I thought these words. I nearly forgot where I was and had to force myself to stop. We were both gasping as this is super sensitive in demon form.

There was a huge barn in the back that four dozen corrupted piled out of just as we passed the house. They ran at top speed. I jerked my arms and my blue blades popped out of the top of my wrists. Peter was on them, grabbing bodies and tearing out throats with his teeth, trying to get to the barn faster. I spun, sliced off limbs and making the blood pour out of the wounds to my mouth while I skewered and sliced some more.

Six corrupted jumped in the air and I beat my wings to fly up and meet them. My blades went back in, I spun with my wings out looking like a giant blade myself, I met them and they exploded. All their demon blood flowing into my mouth before I even landed. Their dust falling like glitter behind me. Peter stood there watching, all his opponents destroyed.

And they want you to practice combat skills. Peter's mind muttered. He was totally jealous of Adam but he knew better than to voice it. I knew he trusted me and Mary was a priority right now. We made it to the barn. I made blue flames consume one side of the barn. As soon as Peter saw Otr in his demon form, he bolted for him beating anyone in his way with his fists. I beat my wings and made the entire group of corrupted rise with me. This I knew put a smile on Peter's face as I saw Otr look absolutely like he shit himself.

I spun forward with my blades out. I beheaded a bunch in my path as I went from one side of the barn to the other. I stopped and jerked my arms again, making the blades disappear through my wrists. I stretched out an arm and twisted my hand up with my claws curled upwards. The corrupted screamed, their red eyes bleeding. I loved doing this technique. I loved making them suffer and I absolutely enjoyed consuming their blood.

I sent some Peter's way, *just swallow sweetheart.* I said with a small smirk.

Otr exhaled Hell fire at Peter. The blood went through his mouth as he breathed in. He glanced up at me and then exhaled his own Holy fire which Otr backed off from.

Isn't that my line? He thought back to me as he beat his wings forward to make another wave of Hell fire go astray. I didn't respond, I was watching them fight. Otr had wings instead of arms and talons instead of feet. He was covered in feathers that looked like they were matted with blood. He looked up at me and smiled, like his beaky mouth curved to smile. It looked cartoonish and creepy.

What the fuck?

Peter's left fist connected with his face and then the right connected as well. Without a second going by Peter rammed his horns into the demon's chest.

"Wait Peter." I landed beside him and Peter pulled out his horns. Otr was still smiling at me.

"Where is the soul catcher device?" I demanded.

Otr spit up some blood, it smelled wonderful.

"With my brother." He whispered. He showed all his sharp teeth as he laughed. I stepped back and Peter stepped in front of me to cover the ugly thing with Hoy flames. I was irritated that Otr didn't have the device or tell me where it was. We had no idea where fafnir was. I huffed and crossed my arms. Peter faced me and went back into his human form.

"We'll find it." He said to me.

"Yea." I closed my eyes and went into my human form as well.

"Let's go, I have to get back to Mary." He said.

He still wasn't happy about the Adam situation, but as I saw it, one of us had to stay with Mary at all times, even tonight was a risk but Stacey didn't see any battles in Stan's or Silence's future within the few hours we would be potentially gone. And while I train, Peter will acquire those skills anyways because we will mentally link up and he can practice while I'm at home to watch Mary. He was totally in my mind when I had these thoughts so I took it as him agreeing with me because when we sanded home, he didn't mention anything when I had to leave again.

I hugged and kissed Mary, gave a wave to Stacey and Stan, and when I stepped out onto the porch with Silence Peter grabbed me. He pulled my face to his and kissed me without parting his lips. I like this kind of kiss; it felt powerfully potent with emotions the way our lips were pressed together.

"I love you." I whispered to him when he let me go.

"I love you too." He stroked my cheek and I closed my eyes. My hand surrounded his and I brought it to my lips.

"I'll be back soon."

I turned and took Silence's hand. Peter waved just before I turned to sand.

*   *   *

So it started with Adam throwing trees at me, which I obliterated with my sword. Then boulders of many sizes, from all different angles came at me at the same time. My reflexes and speed were phenomenal. Adam was smiling at me with every victory I made. I was a natural.

"Very good, but you're holding your sword wrong." Adam came up to me and put one hand on my shoulder and lifted my arm with the other. He smelled really fucking good. I had to hold my breath.

"When you hold it, try and use its weight to your advantage. So you may smoothly adjust to where your targets are." He then let go of my shoulder and put it under my arm as the other tried to adjust my hold on my sword. When he touched my hand, a warm tingling sensation went up my arm. My heart started beating rapidly. We looked at each other for a second. I should have seen this cliché coming. I turned, quickly pulling out of his reach and saw Luke coming towards us. I felt so tense right now.

"I'd better go see Matthew." He said suddenly, he just wanted to escape as much as I did. I watched him go and when he got far enough, I exhaled in a 'whoosh'. Luke noticed my eyes and actions.

"Is there something going on?" He pointed to Adam, then to me. His thoughts had many implications but none were the one I was afraid of him knowing.

"No, why would you assume something like that?" I asked in an annoyed tone.

"I just notice things."

"Yea well, mind your own business." I said angrily. I turned and marched over to Sia's hut. It was as if she was waiting for me, she came out to greet me just as I neared the hut. I went over to her and hugged her tight. She purred and licked my face as I rubbed her goat's head.

"We brought her some food as soon as the sun went down, but she wouldn't eat."

His voice surprised me; I didn't realize he followed me. I turned to look Luke face to face.

"What do you mean?" I asked.

He motioned towards a pile of dead deer not too far from the edge of the trees. I looked at Sia then felt her stomach. She closed her eyes and made a whimpering sound. Luke stepped closer.

"She just doesn't feel well, her babies will be coming soon." I said as I looked at her eyes.

"I apologise if I was intruding. It's just that both of your hearts accelerate when you see each other."

I sighed and changed back into my human form. "Luke, he's the third Obedient."

Luke froze, "are you sure?"

"Yes, when I first went to the Valley, it showed me all three of them.

And recognise his scent from my soul's past. Peter knows but he trusts me. Don't tell the others please."

Luke thought about that, "So you know who the Werewolf Obedient is?"

"Yes, he's my fighting instructor back at the studio by my father's old church. But he's probably moved to a new job by now."

"I see."

"Why do you ask?" I wondered curiously.

"Although the Oracle was not herself, the demon was convincing because he had a lot of knowledge from the real Oracle's stolen memories. Didn't she say the Obedients will show up when they are needed?"

I knew where he was going with this but what he didn't know was that there was a lot more to it. He didn't know I was a train wreck with the possibility of losing Peter. And having to use the Obedients was for from my 'To Do' list, but fate had plans brewing.

Fuck I hated fate.

I looked away as my thoughts carried away to branches of horrible possibilities. My thoughts were too much and I felt like breaking down. Sia whined and nudged my face.

"Are you okay?" Luke put his hand on my shoulder. I looked at him as a tear escaped my eye. He looked into my eyes and then looked at Sia.

"Sia? You can understand me?" Sia bowed her head to him. "Can we use your home for a moment?" Sia bowed her head again. Luke grabbed my arm and led me inside. I looked back and saw Adam watching us. Luke stopped in the middle of the hut and turned me to face him.

"You need to tell us what's going on. Psychic energy can control emotions. It's harmful if you're not in control of your emotions. You can't be corrupted but if you're unstable, no one will follow you. We were unsure when the first Witchdemon was born. It was Gabriel the Archangel who came to us in the Valley and told Matthew and I the reason for such a being. But not everyone agrees and we may lose many to corruption if they see that you may lose. Either that or they are exiled for their petty rebelliousness. For a Werewolf, to be exiled is to be utterly alone which is an absolute horror. But for a Vampire, to be exiled is to be bound my diamond thread and left in the sun to burn."

This shocked me, "You agree to such punishment?"

"Only when it is deserved. If John was in my Court, he would have burned."

His stare was intense. I looked into his mind and saw that being exiled was exactly how his father died. His father was doing favours for the corrupted. The Court found out and his punishment was sudden. Did I mention the Vampires weren't very family oriented? Luke watched his father die without emotion and even watched as his mother bolted out to help his father but burned to dust herself before she even got half way.

Vampires cared for themselves, their mates, and the safety of humanity. Then maybe family stuff. Protecting offspring was necessary, but when punishment is required, bloodlines are forgotten completely. It was really dysfunctional thinking, to me anyways.

I sighed, I looked at him and then closed my eyes. I projected my dream, what happened in Mary's room, what I smelled when I woke up a week ago, my freak out in the bathroom five minutes after that, the feeling I get whenever I had Peter in my arms or thought about him, and finally, the little voice at the back of my head telling me we're doomed to never see each other again.

I also told him how Peter doesn't know about the little voice, not a literal one just my continuous doubts, or my complicated emotions. More tears fell from my eyes when I opened them. Luke looked at me with deep sympathy.

He pulled me into his arms and hugged me. I let more tears fall as he gently petted me on the head. I realize this makes everything I just said about Vampires....well I look like a liar, but right now I wasn't going to over analyze or complain. He's the only one that knows that wouldn't be horribly depressed by it. I was grateful. I just didn't want anyone else to know.

I pulled away a bit and looked at him. "Luke please don't-" I started.

"Shhh." Still with an arm around me he put a finger to his mouth and then with the same finger, pointed to the door of the hut. Adam was out there. I went back to the hug and he went back to petting my head.

I won't tell I promise, I won't even think about it. But you shouldn't keep these things from Peter. Luke thought to me.

Do you think I'm being Paranoid? I asked.

Not at all. Everyone has fears of losing the ones they love the most. It's worrying about the fears that make you blind to reality. Face the troubles as *they come not as they might be. Maybe you should go to the Valley and consult* *the spirits.* He suggested.

Hmmm, not a bad idea.

We broke off the hug and with a hand at my back he slowly guided me back out of the hut. Adam walked over to us and my stupid fucking heart sped up. I knew Luke heard it too. I glanced at him and there was a smirk on his face. I slapped him on the arm for it. He raised both hands and walked the other way to the trees on my right.

The Vampires had built their own property area with underground catacombs. Took them two weeks and it was almost a hundred acres of brick mazes. Vampire photographic memory helps and with the speed and strength they make very handy construction workers.

"Gabriel." Adam caught my attention with his voice. I looked at him, I didn't realize I was staring at the direction Luke left in while I was thinking. I didn't want him to leave me alone with Adam but he was already gone. Dammit space cadet Gabby.

"Are you and Luke.....?" he started but I cut him off A.S.A.P. I saw it all in his head and I was sooo irked.

"Are you retarded? We both have mate's we've pledged our souls to. Don't be ridiculous, what's wrong with you?"

Then I froze, he was jealous! They didn't even tell him I had a mate either, that I was actually married.

"You have a mate?" Adam asked.

"Yea and he's a Witchdemon too. Not an Obedient, his eyes are brown."

He looked like he was going to pass out, "How is that possible?"

"Because he is the reincarnation of Damien."

His eyes bugged out, "What? This is dangerous! He is the enemy!"

He had grabbed my shoulders and brought his face so close to mine I almost impulsively kissed him but caught myself. I brought my arms together, then my hands up between our faces and pushed them out, breaking off his grip so I could punch him in the gut. Lightly; I didn't want to break or bruise anything. He bent over with the wind knocked out of him.

"First of all, Peter and I are married. Luke and Matthew have agreed to respect him as their king so I suggest to take your opinion and shove it up your ass. I'm done with my combat training; I don't want to see you when I come back here. You should leave as soon as you can." I glared at his bent over body then walked away.

I was going towards Matthew's hut to tell him to make sure Adam left right away. But then Sia whined, like, really loud. I turned around and she fell sideways and landed hard.

"Sia!" I ran to her in a blink of an eye and touched her stomach. Everything forgotten, Adam was there and went to his knees beside me. He placed one hand on my shoulder and the other on Sia's stomach.

"It's her cubs, they want out." He whispered to me.

"Do something."

Sia cried out again. I petted her head and tried to calm her with some positive energy. "Shhh Sia, it's okay. It's just time to have the babies now."

Adam was at her rear. The serpent was hissing at him and the goat was crying out as well. Actually the goat was really annoying but I kept my eyes on Sia's eyes. She 'lion' meowed. Like a roar that sounded like 'meow'. I was reminded of a kid burping the alphabet. She reached her paw out to me. I grasped it in both hands and held it in my lap.

"Okay here we go, I see the head. Oh wow."

I looked and saw why he was so surprised. The 'cub' looked like a lion cub only it was black with little scales instead of fur, only they moved like fur as if each hair was super thick and hard. It had a black serpent for a tail and black dragon wings on it back. The little one had solid white eyes. It coughed out black smoke. Adam placed the cub at Sia's stomach so it, actually *he*, could drink his mother's milk.

The next cub was also a lion like cub but with white fur, really white fur not scales, with white dragon wings and a white serpent for a tail. This one, she, had solid black eyes. She also had puffs of smoke coming from her mouth, only white like fog. The last cub looked the most like its mother. Lion cub body with the tan fur, only a green serpent tail and yellow dragon wings. *His* eyes were beautiful. One was solid green while the other was solid blue. And yes some grey smoke spilled from his little nostrils.

Adam set the third cub with the others at Sia's stomach and I watched them with a smile on my face. They were so adorable.

"Good job Sia." I said to her and she purred. I stood up and went to Adam as he stood too.

"Thank you." I kissed him on the cheek then turned and walked away,
His heart and my heart were going like jack hammers.

"You still want me to leave?" he called out to me.

"Uh, yea. I think you're done here."

Without turning to look at him, I burst to sand and went home.

CHAPTER TWENTY TWO

Peter was thrilled when I told him why I looked so annoyed when I got home and he was even more ecstatic when I told him what I did about it. Basically I told him Adam pissed me off; I punched him in the gut and then told him to beat it. I was on the fence of taking Luke's advice and telling Peter all my fears and why I've been depressed lately. But I didn't want to plant a seed in his head and have him worry too. So I kept that all to myself for now.

The next day I told everyone about Sia and her babies. Stacey was fascinated and Mary wanted to see them. The five of us went to the clearing, rematerializing right outside the hut.

"Sia, I brought some friends who want to see you and the babies." I called.

Sia came out with her cubs behind her.

"Oh wow." Stan said with eyes wide.

"They are adorable!" Stacey said as she stepped towards them Sia felt the adoring energy from Stacey and allowed her near her cubs. The black one walked right up to Stacey and started licking her hand. The white one walked over and went on her hind legs, resting her front paws on Stacey's legs, wanting to be pet next. The tanned one stayed at the entrance of the hut with his mother.

"Very interesting creatures. What was Sia again?" Peter asked me.

"She is a Chimaera. She's from Europe."

"And the father?"

"A Celtic dragon."

I looked over at Sia as Peter walked in her direction with Mary. They got just five feet behind Stacey when Sia started growling. She rose to all fours and her hair stood up a bit. The goat made an angry 'baa' noise and the black and white cubs made hissing noises at Peter and Mary. Peter froze and tugged Mary behind him.

"Sia? What's wrong with you?" I let her feel my disapproval. She calmed down and whimpered. Her cubs ran back to her and they all went back inside the hut. That was really fucking weird. Either she's jittery of too many people around the babies or she feels Peter's soul as Damien.

"Mommy, what's wrong with the kitty?" Mary asked me.

"I don't know honey bee."

Peter looked at me and I mentally told him my theory. He nodded.

"Makes sense."

Mary was pouting.

"Awe it's okay sweetie." I said to her. I went to go pick her up but she clung to her father's leg. I stopped short, did she just glare at me? I blinked but her face was fine. She really wanted to see the 'kitty'.

"Why did she act like that?" Stacey asked as we walked back to us. I looked at Peter then to Stacey.

"Um, I think it's because Peter is Damien's reincarnation. She must sense something."

Like what, I had no idea. Peter's energy wasn't hostile so I didn't understand. And Mary was just a child. Stacey looked at Peter.

"Awe that sucks. I'm sorry Peter." She didn't want Peter to feel bad about it and neither did I.

Peter put up a hand, "It's okay, thanks anyways Stacey."

"Gabriel." A voice rasped. We all turned around and saw Adam.

"What are you still doing here?" I demanded. I walked right up to him and again punched him in the stomach. He only leaned forward a little then straightened up again. I swear I hit him harder than last time. Then I saw in his head that he used his ability to soften the blow. He smiled.

"Nice to see you too." He meant that more then he should. I could almost hear Peter grind his teeth together. Our hearts were beating a little more quickly again. I was aware of Peter, and realized he thought Adam's was from attraction and mine from anger, which it was but also involuntary soul crap.

"I told you to leave." I continued.

"I couldn't. Not right away anyways. Sia needed assistance getting better through the night and this morning. She has improved this afternoon wonderfully."

"Good, now you can get lost."

"I can't, I'm still needed here. So are you going to introduce me?"

He moved past me to Peter and Mary. "Hi, I'm Adam. High priest, doctor, and psychic." He put his hand out to Peter but Peter just stared at him.

"Psychic? What can you do?" Stan asked. Adam dropped his hand and turned to Stan.

"I can move objects with my mind." Adam said proudly.

Peter rolled his eyes. Stacey caught that. "That's not all that amazing. We've seen Gabby and Peter do that and more." She said a little snobby like.

Well, she's a keeper. Peter thought. Peter and Stan looked at each other with a short nod and Stan folded his arms across his chest. *Him too.*

It's a bonding experience.

Adam recollected himself, "Yes well, I'm sure they can. I take it you're Peter?" Adam said to my husband.

"Yes I am." Peter said with a very 'unhappy to talk to you' face. I impatiently walked up and made introductions to everyone.

"This is Stan, Stacey, my *husband* Peter, and our daughter Mary." I wanted to get them over with so he would fuck off. Instead he spun on me, nearly choking on his tongue.

"Daughter?" he looked like he was going to shit himself, I almost thought I heard his heart seize.

"She's my step daughter, fuck, relax stupid."

Adam let out a breath. "Oh, I see." He slowly broke from his complex.

Peter started laughing and so did Mary. Stacey was smiling but Stan looked confused.

"So you're a high priest? From where?" Stan asked.

"Europe." Adam answered.

"Where in Europe?" Stan wondered.

Why the fuck do you care? I rolled my eyes and left to Sia's hut before Adam could respond. I was annoyed.

"Oh! Let me come too!" Stacey ran after me. We linked arms and went to Sia's hut.

"Sia?" I called. She looked at me while her cubs fed. I went up to her, knelt down and held her face in my hands.

"What's up with you? Why did you act like that?" I whispered to her. Sia whined her 'sorry'. She had sensed danger. Yea it was probably because of Peter's soul and his graveyard soil scent. Stacey was still at the doorway; I turned and motioned for her to come closer. I stood up and moved over, closer to the cubs then sat down.

"Hi Sia." Stacey said to my Chimaera.

Stacey crept over and sat down where I was. Stacey scratched behind Sia's ears making her purr. The tanned cub stopped eating and looked at Stacey. He yelped all needy for her attention. Stacey laughed and scratched him behind the ear with her other hand. The cub turned his head to be scratched in other places and moved forward and bumped his head into her thigh, purring away.

"We should name them." Stacey suggested. She stopped scratching Sia and used both hands on the cub.

"Yea we should," I agreed, "What do you think Sia?"

Sia purred and bowed her head. The goat nodded. The other two cubs stopped feeding and looked up at us curiously. I picked up the black one and looked him in the eyes.

"I think this one should be named Anubis." I said as I put him beside me. He lay down and rested his chin on my leg. I looked at Sia and she bowed her head. Stacey clapped her hands and then pointed to the white cub.

"Okay her name should be......Snowball?"

I burst out laughing. Oh yea, the cool Anubis with his sister, fuckin *Snowball*. Sia actually huffed and the cub hissed.

"Uh, no dude." I said between giggles. Stacey was giggling too.

"Okay, okay. How about Celeste?"

We both looked at Sia. She bowed her approval and the goat 'baaa'ed.

Stacey picked up the last cub. He was so hyper; he wiggled and tried to lick her face. He reminded me of a dog.

"Now what do we call you?" She asked him.

"You know, the black one, Anubis, is one of the Gods associated with the underworld. Like he represents Hell." I started. Stacey knew where I was going.

"And Celeste is short for like, a celestial being, kind of representing Heaven." She finished.

"So let's name him something that represents earth." I suggested.

"That's a good idea. Hmmmm. What was the horned God's name?"

"Um, I think it was, um, Cernunnos. But they *eat* stag dude." I pointed out

Stacey laughed, "Yea true but who cares. It's a cool name and you're not going to find one that represents earth as well as that one."

We looked at Sia; she closed her eyes then opened them.

"Is that a yes?" I asked. She bowed her head.

"Well that settles that." Stacey brought Cernunnos to her face and he licked her from her lips to her forehead. I smiled. Then Stan was at the doorway, Stacey and I looked up at him.

"Uh, can I come in?" he asked.

"You have to ask Sia."

He looked confused but then he looked at the Chimaera. "Can I come in Sia? Please?"

All three of us looked at her. The goat nodded. Sia was falling asleep but the goat was wide awake.

"I think that's a yes." I said.

Stan walked over to us and sat down. Celeste trotted over to him and sniffed his hand. When she was satisfied, she crawled into his lap and started purring. The sun was going down; I could see the orange light from the window and doorway.

"Peter and Mary left." Stan announced.

I looked at him and he looked back at me seriously. I could see in his head that Peter was not very happy with Adam. Peter had walked up to Adam and told him to leave, that he was not wanted.

"Ugh!" Stan said, closing his eyes.

"What?" Stacey asked but Stan was looking at me.

"Why didn't you tell me you and Peter could read minds? You were just doing it right now weren't you? I could feel it. Like a weird pressure in my head. I didn't notice before but Joseph told me and now I notice all the time."

I sighed, "We had already told you so much and we didn't want you to feel paranoid or uncomfortable. Besides, we don't do it all the time, well, I don't anyways."

"Is that it?"

"Um, we can project stuff in your head, which I'm sure I've done forgetting I haven't told you though. It's easier than explaining it all if it's a long story."

"Ah. Well you might as well continue then." He said pointing at his head.

"Nah, I got the jist of it thanks."

All three cubs were falling asleep.

"Joseph also told me something else." Stan hinted.

"What's that?" I asked.

"He's in love with you Gabby."

"What? We barely know each other. We hardly talked when he stayed over and when we did it was seriously trivial. I don't understand."

"I know. I know. I tried telling him how serious you are about Peter but the guy can't help the way he feels."

Another thought passed through his head that irked me a bit.

"Give Joseph a chance? Are you nuts?" Okay I was more than irked.

Stan raised both hands, "Hey, hear me out. Peter's great, it's just lately he's been a bit off. Like every time he comes back from taking Mary flying, there's something off about him."

Alarm raced through me. Why would that bother me? But Stacey even nodded.

"Yea, he's like super quiet and then just stays in Mary's room till you come back. At first I thought he was just watching her fall asleep but..... the vibe is all wrong."

"Stacey, you're the one who said you couldn't see her future after the wedding. He's just being protective and he probably has some grim thought going on." I defended.

"Gabriel." Adam said, poking his head in the hut.

Oh for fuck sakes! What do you want? I blatantly ignored him. The sun had completely set. I didn't notice at first because with *my* eyes, everything was clear.

"You guys just sit and talk in the dark with me?" I smirked.

"I'm fine." Stacey shrugged.

"Could use some light in here, but we should go see what he wants." Stan said, the fucking kill joy.

"Gabriel." Adam repeated.

She couldn't see me but I could see her. There was annoyed looks on both our faces. She didn't like him because he was a high priest and she was a little prejudiced towards 'bible thumpers' and I was annoyed for the other reasons I already explained. My eyes went white and I made the three cubs float to their beds. The goat was asleep now too. All four serpents were still awake though. My eyes went back to normal. The three of us got up and walked to the doorway and past Adam, completely ignoring him.

"Gabriel, can I talk to you please?" He said a little impatiently. I tried poking in his head so I wouldn't have to hear his stupid fucking sexy accent and then just sand home, but the fucker blocked me from his head.

"We'll just go see if Matthew and Hannah are up." Stacey said as she pulled Stan along. I pinched between my eyes and sighed with frustration. The electricity was back and my heart was pounding, but I was pissed. My mood was swinging and I just wanted something to rip apart. I might have to go hunt or something.

"What do you want Adam?"

"Have you discovered who the Obedients are yet?"

Oh fuck right off! I just can't win. My heart beat faster.

"N-no." I lied; I couldn't even look at him. As mad as I was, I actually felt bad for lying to him. I could feel him assessing me.

"Are you sure?"

I couldn't do it. The urge to tell him the truth was too powerful. I could keep it a secret, but to be asked straight out like that? I couldn't hold it in and what irritated me more was I knew exactly why I had the urge to begin with.

"Listen Adam, I found all three. I saw them in my vision in the Valley and I've actually met them all as well."

"Who are they?"

"What does it matter? I'm not using them. I have Peter."

"Yes, I don't think that's going to last."

Now I gave him what I knew was a menacing look. That comment hit home and I wanted to carve up his face for it. My eyes went white again. He saw this and raised a hand.

"Calm down, I just mean that the Obedients don't normally show up if they are not needed. If you saw them in your vision that's different, but if you met them all then that means your relationship is not going to last or you and your husband are going to have to come to an understanding. Now please, who are they?"

Why do you want to know? But I didn't ask that like I should have, I just blurted the truth.

"My friend Joseph is the Vampire Obedient, my old fighting instructor, James, is the Werewolf Obedient, and I just met the Angel Obedient a little while ago."

"So Joseph, James, and?"

I didn't want to say it. I closed my eyes and felt them go brown.

"And?" he pressed.

I sighed then looked him dead in the eyes. "You."

It was like an echo. I saw his brain stutter, then I saw it click.

"What?" It came out barely above a whisper, but I knew it was shock that only allowed his voice to escape so much.

"Um, yea, it's you. You're the third Obedient. But I wouldn't bother fantasizing because I'm not using the Obedients."

He blinked a couple times, "This is bad."

"Well that's your opinion but-" he put his fingers to my lips.

"No listen, you should never tell a potential Obedient that he's an Obedient. They are only incorruptible *after* the awakening. Telling them what they are beforehand gives them a small space for greed to take over. They could love you but if there is any selfish thought, no matter how small for that power, they die anyways. Powerful soul or not."

Yea well I don't plan on using you anyways like I said so......why do I feel alarmed about that?

"Well good thing you're a high priest eh?"

Oh fuck off, did I really just do the Canadian thing?

"I'll keep this secret for now, does anyone else know?"

"Stacey knows about the other two, not you, but she will, and Peter and Luke know everything. Matthew only just discovered Joseph, and Stan knows nothing of the Obedients at all. Joseph knows the supernatural stuff but he only heard about the Obedients briefly, he doesn't know any more than that even though he has suspicions."

"Okay, try and keep it that way. What did Luke say to you the other night?"

Fuck you're nosy! I'm not telling you that. It requires too many explanations. I hesitated; I had to tell him something. Why? I have no fucking clue.

"He told me to consult the Valley."

Adam nodded, "That may be a good idea. You should do that right away."

Everything happens for a reason, the memory of my father's voice told me.

"I will, right now." I told him.

I walked away from him and instantly sanded to the field where I created a doorway. The field was covered with trees except for a small little clearing. It was a perfect circle. I didn't need my angel form to make the pentagram appear. It seemed to know I needed it and it appeared all by itself. The blue flamed star threw shadows amongst the trees. I stepped into the middle of it and laid down with my palms on the earth.

I opened my eyes to the white atmosphere and red sand. I sat up; there weren't even any bones in the sand. I furrowed my eyebrows.

Uh, I'm in the right place, right?

I stood and walked around. Nothing.

"Father?" I called out. Nothing.

"Thomas? Isis?" Again nothing.

I was confused. Then I heard a child crying. I turned around. It was a little girl sitting with her knees up and her arms wrapped around them, crying with her face hidden.

She had long curly brown hair. My heart thudded hard and slow. I felt a lump in my throat and my stomach was in knots.

"Hello?" I said to her, my voice shaking.

She looked at me and my world shattered into a million pieces.

NO.

I fell to my knees with my eyes overflowing with tears, my face expressionless.

"Mommy!" the little girl screamed. She ran into my arms and hugged me tight. My hands shook as they slowly embraced her.

NO! NO! NO! *NO!*

My lips trembled.

"M-Mary?" I whimpered. My face finally crumpled. But I still stared straight ahead, I didn't dare look down even at the top of her head.

"Oh mommy, I've been so alone. I tried calling you but you never found me." Mary said with her face hidden in my chest. I nearly choked. "I missed you mommy. When they took me and my first mommy, a monster scared me so bad I woke up here. My friend Thomas showed me how to find you but then a different monster locked me up and took Thomas away from me. I've been all alone." Mary cried.

My face slowly crumpling more and more through her explanation. My eyes still open, even though I felt like I was in so much pain. I put my hand on Mary's head and stroked her hair. Then an eerie calm look over me. My face expressionless once again.

The Mary we rescued was really Fafnir. It was all part of their plan. That's why Linda was already a demon, that's why 'Mary' hated Joseph, that's why Sia growled and sensed danger, that's why I've been hearing my daughter scream for me.

Then an even more horrible realization hit me.

Fafnir was faking nightmares to get Peter to fly with him at night. He has the soul catcher device and Peter has been acting funny afterwards. Otr's smile flashed in my mind. FUCK!

"Honey bee. I have to go. I have to save daddy."

"Can I come mommy?" she pleaded.

"Of course you can baby." My eyes went piercing blue and I took her hand. I busted a doorway through the dimension so she could come and go as she pleased and the other spirits could too.

*   *   *

I woke up and was in my warrior form. I saw a transparent image of Mary dancing to the trees.

"Be careful sweetheart."

I will mommy. Her voice echoed as she disappeared. I had to go back to the clearing and.....A howl broke through the night. The Wolves were in trouble. I was about to leave but then I smelled Silence, he was on his way to my house to get Peter.

Silence! I thought to him.

Yes? He thought back. I projected everything and told him to be careful.

I will find them and destroy the demon, he was outraged.

Don't do anything rash. I don't want you to die. I don't know if this other attack is part of their plan or not but just tell Peter as loud as you can in your mind. I'm sure if you help him he'll kill Fafnir. I told him.

And what are you going to do? He asked.

I have to help my friends.

Very well, I shall see you soon Gabriel. Then he took off.

I was torn between going to Peter and going to the Wolves. But Stacey and Stan were down there. I sanded down there as fast as I could. Everyone was in chaos. The rest of the infected demon clan that followed Judah, wanted revenge.

They all had red special blades forged in demon blood, the same kind Judah used to infect the humans. The Wolves were all in their Wolf forms drunk on demon blood. The blades didn't infect the uncorrupted but it was still very fatal to them. My Vampire friends had their white blades. So did the Guard. Just a slice and the demons were dust. But it was almost six hundred infected demons against only two hundred uncorrupted Vampires and Wolves. This was the rest of the original clan, while it was now under new management, this was only a quarter of the total. I scanned for Stacey and Stan

"Gabby!" Stacey called. She and Stan were in Sia's hut. I instantly put a barrier around the hut, making it so dust would be the infected demon's future if it got too close.

"Stay in there, the barrier will protect you." I shouted.

"Get Adam!" She screamed and pointed to the edge of the trees. Adam was slouched down at the foot of a pine tree. I grabbed him and rushed him to the hut.

His stomach was sliced open, deep. His blood slowly becoming infected.

CHAPTER TWENTY THREE

"Oh my God! Gabby do something!" Stacey shrieked as she saw the bloody mess of Adam's stomach. I laid him down in the middle of the hut. I had no idea what to do. Adam's eyes started to go black. I scanned my brain for three feverish seconds, and then it hit me.

"Stacey, Stan, get back." I said.

I was knelt beside his body, so I carefully climbed on top of him not putting my weight on him. I grabbed his face in my hands and looked him in the eyes.

"You're going to be okay." I whispered to him. He looked back at me in pain as the demon blood went through his veins, he was losing time. I closed my eyes and brought my lips to his. My wings extended back and I forced my pure energy in his body through my kiss. My heart didn't hammer, it almost sang. I sucked the demon blood out of him. When I ended the kiss we stared into each other's eyes for a second and then I got off of him and went to the doorway.

"Gabby that was amazing." Stacey cried. I looked back; Adam was all healed and staring up at me.

"All of you stay here." I said.

I flicked my wrists and my hands became balls of Holy Fire. I walked out into the fight. I had to get Peter. He had no idea it was Fafnir and not Mary. I doubted that Silence was able to get through to him if he was all tired and weird from flying with 'her'. Rage went through me. I pulled my energy to my core and brought my wings forward to cover me. I extended them back and raised my arms back as well. Suddenly I slammed my flaming hands together and my wings forward again. The effect was epic.

My energy exploded with the blue flames in a wave that succumbed every demon in the clearing to dust.

The uncorrupted stopped and looked at me. I need Luke and Matthew. As soon as I made eye contact with them they were at my side. Each of them took one of my hands and we sanded to the edge of my property. I walked forward, expecting them to follow but when I turned around Matthew and Luke were still at the edge.

"We can't move. The barrier around your house has been manipulated. Look." Luke put a hand forward and his two fingers turned to dust. He pulled it away and they grew' back. Intuition clicked. I didn't say a word. I repressed my energy and held my breath. I looked for Silence's mind. Nothing. Hopefully he noticed the barrier right away and is on his way back to the clearing. I nodded at them and waved them away.

Look for Silence. Luke nodded and they both left.

I walked forward and nearly stepped on Jeremiah, dead on the grass. I searched for Peter's mind. I saw him in a park with Mary, overwhelmed with joy and no stress. In his mind he was human. I almost believed the delusion myself except I could feel his energy in the house. Fafnir was using Mary psychic abilities from the piece of her soul he consumed to manipulate Peter's mind. Using the love for his daughter as a weakness.

I beat my wings and went up to Mary's window. I looked inside and saw Peter on the chair beside her bed. He was slumped over with his head bowed. I could see 'Mary' standing in front of him. I could see both their auras. 'Mary' had a pink aura surprisingly enough, but then it soon turned red as I watched. Then I noticed a small wooden object in her hand that started to glow. She pointed it at Peter.

Rage increased through my veins. With one thought the wall in front of me turned to sand. Energy flowed out of me to my hand creating my sword. 'Mary' turned just her head all the way around to face me. Her eyes were red and she smiled.

"You're too late, his soul is ours." It was her voice and a deeper voice talking at the same time. I went to swing my sword but a wave of invisible energy threw me out of the room through the opening I came from. I flapped my wings hard where I was still facing the opening but just a few feet away from the house. I didn't bother to hold my breath or repress my energy anymore. I screamed for Peter.

"Peter! Wake up!" But my yells fell on deaf ears. He was so happy in his delusion even my thoughts seemed to be bouncing back to me. Sulphur filled my nose, and again the voice filled my head.

"He doesn't want you. He never told you. You ruined his life."

And I believed it. But I still wasn't going to let them take his soul. The transparent cobra appeared in front of me and I swung my sword at him. He dodged left and tried to strike me with his invisible teeth which I'm sure would have made very real injuries.

"Get out of my way!" I screamed. I whipped my sword and it semi-detached into many pieces, stretching and wrapping around the snake. I pulled and the blue flames from the surface of the blades scorched the snake making it visible ion some black splotches, then the sword reassembled itself again. He spun with a hiss off black ashes and then exploded.

Cool. I thought while looking at the sword.

I flew back into the room and saw white mist leaving Peter's body and flow into the wooden object in Fafnir's hand.

NO!

I twirled the sword and as quickly as possible I shoved the sword through his Mary body from the back and out through the little chest. The white mist flowed back into Peter and he woke up. He saw my sword in Mary's body as I pulled it out.

"Mary?" he went on his knees in front of her with wide eyes.

"Peter it wasn't-" I started.

"Daddy?" Fafnir said in Mary's voice edging it with confusion and pain. Her body turned black and fell to pieces. In Peter's head I saw her eyes had conveniently been back to normal. Then I saw the anger. Peter's head snapped up at me. He was furious. I backed up as he advanced on me.

"You!" he shouted.

"Peter listen-" but he was far from rational. He just saw me kill his daughter. They have been doing this for a while; he thought he was helping her with her gifts. He grabbed me by the throat and busted into his demon form. He lifted me off the ground.

"You killed my little girl!" he bellowed.

His grip was so tight. I dropped my sword and tried to remove his hand. His hatred was impossible to avoid. The hurt made me useless, it made me helpless. He beat his wings and we sped out of the house with his hand still around my throat, busting through dozens of trees to the mountains with his anger. He slammed me against the base of the mountain.

Peter that wasn't Mary, it was Fafnir the whole time. I thought to him.

"Don't lie to me! You said everything was going to be okay! I trusted you!" a look of disgust crossed his face, "I love you......" He whispered, "But you killed her! You ruined my life!" He shouted at me, slamming my head against the stone with every word of the last sentence. My heart ripped in half.

Peter I'm not lying, I swear! I love you. I pleaded in my head to him.

His face smoothed over for a second, then with is hand still on my throat he brought his face close to mine.

"I.....hate.....you." He whispered with a snarl on his face.

So many things happened at once. My world crashed. My soul dimmed. My heart completely obliterated. My mind went blank and my emotions went numb. He was the enemy. I collected my energy and shot him backwards. My sword reappeared in my hand. He spun before he hit the trees and faced me as he stopped. I glared at him.

"Let's do this." I said as I twirled my sword.

I knew I wasn't really mad, that I wasn't prepared to look at him as my enemy. But I had to force myself not to let it show. To not let him know how much he hurt me. He charged at me with is horns. I swung my sword forward hitting him dead on. I almost lost my grip the impact was so hard. He flew back crashing through half a dozen trees. I flapped my wings and followed landing a few feet in front of him. The sword did a number on his energy.

"This whole time you've been flying with what you thought was your daughter, you've been daydreaming of the life you would have had without me? You regret being with me? You think I chose this? You told me you loved me, yet you won't even give a chance to what you saw wasn't real." I shouted at him.

He glared at me as he stood up. He heard nothing, this was no longer Peter. His anger blinded him to everything I just said.

This was Damien. My Peter was gone. I froze. I would never hear his laugh, I would never see him smile, and I would never feel his warmth against mine. This was the end. My happiness was gone. Flashes of our time together went through my head. The ball, laughing with Mary, every touch, every kiss.

I will never let you go, he had said to me.

His fist connected with my stomach. I slammed into the mountain. I slipped back into my human form. I was on my hands and knees when I looked up at him marching my way. And I.... was afraid. He was supposed to be my security. I used to feel safe in his arms but now I was afraid. My heart and soul were ripping piece by piece from every second that went by with that look of hatred on his lace. I was afraid that if I stayed any longer I would lose my humanity and no longer care for anyone or anything anymore.

He would crush me because I loved him so much. I stood up with tears welling up in my eyes. He bent his head and charged. He pierced his horns through my chest and pushed me all the way against the mountain. As soon as my back hit the stone, my eyes closed, my tears escaped, and I turned to sand.

*   *   *

I materialized back at the clearing. The first thing I did as I knelt there on my hands and knees, was put up a barrier on this whole side of the water. That way Peter could never enter. He could never see, smell, sense, hear, or feel any of us. My face was nearly touching the ground. It happened, my fears came true. My tears fell from my eyes and landed on the back of my hand. I opened my eyes and saw my tears were made of blood. My chest was sore and bleeding too. After the barrier was made it started to tingle. I knew that meant it was healing. But the blood continued to flow from my eyes and I still felt a pain in my chest that had nothing to do with my wounds.

This is it, this is where I die. I can't live.....without him. The sun would be up soon. I slammed the ground with my fists, I was so furious with the world, with myself. I lifted my head to the sky and cried out at the top of my lungs. More bloody tears flowed down my cheeks. Once more I slammed my fists into the earth and a huge wave of energy exploded from within me. I fell back and passed out.

*   *   *

I came to smelling a dank clay smell. There were a couple minds passing by in the hallway. I was in the catacombs. I opened my eyes. My face had been wiped down and my clothes were changed. I was surrounded my brick walls. I was in a room with a bed so stiff it was actually a relief to sit up from it. My whole body was sore. I looked down at my chest, there were two pink scars. One right above my heart. It was so unfortunate that I couldn't die. What was the point of living anymore?

A knock sounded at my door. It was Silence.

"Come in." I said, my voice sounding hoarse. He opened the door. "Holy shit, I thought you were dead Silence."

"No, the barrier wouldn't allow me through so I turned around, but by the time I got back you had already left with Luke and Matthew. Adam ran to meet me and told me everything about your discovery of the Obedients."

I thought priests were supposed to be the masters of confidentiality? That little fuck.

"Is there something else?" I asked. I sensed hesitation.

"What happened Gabriel?"

"Are you going to tell everyone else?"

He thought about it, "Come with me, maybe you should tell everyone yourself. Your friends are here as well."

I thought of Stacey and Stan, thank God.

"How long have I been out?'

"Five days."

I stood and he led me through the maze of the catacombs. Finally we entered a giant room with extremely high ceilings. Matthew and his Guard were on one end while Luke and his Court were on the other. Two men with their backs to me were talking to Stan and Stacey and Adam in the middle. Everyone looked at me as I entered. The two men turned around. What the fuck?

It was Joseph and James. Both men smiled at me. Silence and Adam found them and kidnapped them. Silence explained everything except the Obedients part to James. Stacey witnessed that herself. Joseph already kind of knew about them but wasn't given any further information, especially the fact that he was one. That again was monitored by Stacey. And Stan was finally told about the Obedients but only because Joseph kind of knew but he wasn't given any more details than Joseph. Luke and Matthew stepped forward and dropped to one knee.

Matthew stood. "Are you alright my queen?" He asked as Luke stood.

You know I'm depressed when I can't get properly annoyed with Matthew about the 'queen' shit.

I sighed, "No, I am not. I must inform you all what has happened."

I projected every detail of my vision in the Valley to the events at my house and the tragedy at the mountains. Adam was barely surprised. Stan, Stacey and Joseph looked shocked. Stacey had tears fall down her cheeks when she thought of Mary. The Guard looked sympathetic and the Court had frozen faces because this confirmed their mistrust from the beginning. James, although warned, looked kind of freaked out.

Luke and Matthew had grim looks on their faces; they had grown to really like Peter.

"What will you do?" Luke asked nervously.

"He has gone to Egypt." Silence interrupted from behind me. Everyone except James and Joseph knew what that meant. By 'he', Silence meant Peter. He was consumed by his hatred for me. He was no longer Peter, he was Damien now, my enemy.

I have no choice but to use the Obedients. I thought to Luke, Matthew and Silence. *But keep that between us.* I added.

"Why am I here?" James spoke up. Silence had a quick answer.

"We told you about the danger and what Gabriel is. We also told you of your psychic aura and scent did we not? Well, the two of you are associated with Gabriel and may be at risk. If a demon smells you are a psychic, horrible things may happen. As you just saw, it has many consequences, be grateful she even remembered your scent and felt the need to mention your name for safety at all. Adam is a psychic, it may be wise for the two of you to get acquainted with him to discover and practice your skills while you are here. Please be rest assured it is for your safety, and the fact that you are friends she doesn't want to see harmed.

Wow, that was pretty slick there bud. I thought to Silence. He smirked a little.

Luke and Matthew looked at me.

Are you sure? Luke asked.

I have no choice. I felt defeated.

* * *

"Mommy, why can't daddy see me?" Mary asked. I was in my angel form. In this form, Isis gave me the skill to ask the spirits for guidance. I wonder what she would say if she knew I was doing it for this reason.

"I don't know honey bee." I said. I was walking outside on the grass in the clearing. I felt secure here.

"Yes you do. I thought you gave him that skill too."

She knew I gave her father powers, she just didn't know *how*.

"I thought I did too but I don't think your daddy will be using his angel form for a while sweetie."

"I miss him." Mary pouted.

"There is nothing we can do right now except be patient. All you can do is guide him in the right direction."

"I will mommy, I promise. One day he'll forgive you. I love you mommy." She stopped in front of me and I crouched down to her height.

"I love you too honey bee. The sun is coming up."

"Okay mommy, I'll go watch over daddy with Thomas. Same time later?" She asked.

"You bet." I smiled.

"Bye mommy."

"Never say 'goodbye'. Say 'see you later'"

Mary giggled. "Okay, see you later mommy."

She turned and disappeared as the sun rose. I turned back to my human form still looking in the direction she left.

"See you later." I whispered.

Printed in the United States
by Baker & Taylor Publisher Services